Advance praise for *Forbidden Magic* by Cheyenne McCray

"*Forbidden Magic* is escapism in its truest form . . . I forgot about the laundry pile! The characters? Unforgettable. The chemistry? Scorching! You'll read it again and again. A yummy hot fudge sundae of a book!"
—MaryJanice Davidson, *New York Times* bestselling author

"Cheyenne McCray has written a sexy adventure spiced with adventurous sex."
—Charlaine Harris, *New York Times* bestselling author

"McCray does a remarkable job of blending the familiar and the fantastical, creating a rich paranormal world with sexy and engaging characters."
—Kelley Armstrong, *New York Times* bestselling author

"Erotic with a great big capital E. Cheyenne McCray is my new favorite author!"
—Bertrice Small, *New York Times* bestselling author

"*Forbidden Magic* is a fabulous faery tale. The writing is sharp; the story hot!"
—Virginia Henley, *New York Times* bestselling author

"Cheyenne McCray has crafted a novel that takes the imagination on an exciting flight. Full of fantasy, with a touch of darkness, a great read for anyone who loves to get lost in a book that stretches the boundaries!"
—Heather Graham, *New York Times* bestselling author

"Not for the faint of heart! *Forbidden Magic* is *Charmed* meets Kim Harrison's witch series but with a heavy dose of erotica on top!"
—Lyndsay Sands, *New York Times* bestselling author

More...

Forbidden Magic

Cheyenne McCray

St. Martin's Paperbacks

FORBIDDEN MAGIC

Copyright © 2005 by Cheyenne McCray.

ISBN: 0-312-93761-X
EAN: 9780312-93761-4

Printed in the United States of America

St. Martin's Paperbacks edition / December 2005

St. Martin's Paperbacks are published by St. Martin's Press, 175 Fifth Avenue, New York, NY 10010.

10 9 8 7 6 5 4 3 2 1

To my mom and dad, Karen and Robert Tanner,
who taught me that I could do anything I wanted to
do, be anything I wanted to be. From the time I was a
little girl they never doubted that one day I would
realize my dream and become an author.
I love you, Mop and Pop!

Acknowledgments

A resounding thank you to my editor, Monique Patterson, for believing in me. She said she was going to push, and damned if she didn't mean it! Without Monique, this book wouldn't be what it is today.

So much appreciation goes to Susan Vaught, who has critiqued *Forbidden Magic* countless times and is my writing hero. Without her, my rhyme would have no reason.

To my other wonderful critique partners, whom I couldn't do without: Sheri Gilbert, Mackenzie McKade, and Patrice Michelle—you gals are the greatest.

Much love goes to my husband, Frank, and my sons, Tony, Kyle, and Matthew, who put up with my obsessive writing habits and allow me to disappear to write in coffee shops and my favorite bookstore cafés.

To my agent, Erin Murphy, who handles all the boring stuff so I can concentrate on my writing, and is one fun lady.

A special thank you to the wonderful lady who reminded me to "enjoy the ride."

October 23

1

San Francisco

Silver Ashcroft slipped through night and shadows, heart
pounding and rage simmering. Although she belonged to a
D'Anu Coven that practiced white witchcraft, there was no
doubt in her mind this situation required a good dose of gray
magic.

Behind her, Paranormal Special Forces Captain Jake
Macgregor walked as soundlessly as she did despite the fact
he was tall, big, and muscular, and had to weigh a good two-
twenty. "Are you sure, Silver?" the handsome dark-haired
man asked through the transmitter attached to her ear.

She paused only long enough to toss him a glare over her
shoulder. "Have I ever been wrong?"

Jake answered with a wink and she shook her head as she
reached the fire escape. It was one of the older boarding-
houses on the southern side of San Francisco, and it showed
its age with its cracked and peeling paint, rusted drainpipes,
and weed-choked yard.

Without waiting for Jake, Silver grabbed a rail. The paint-
chipped metal felt rough beneath her palms and she caught
the smell of rust. She swung up and onto the fire escape and
landed soundlessly on the mesh floor.

Below her Jake swore under his breath, but she heard it
over the communication device. He hated to have her
involved in the actual bust, but when she led them to illegal

paranormal activities like ritual sacrifice and the use of magic to destroy property or steal expensive items, she insisted on taking part. She often made the take-down easier, but knew the officer still didn't like her putting herself in danger.

Smells of garbage, dirt, and weeds met her nose as she grasped the metal bars that would take her to the next story. She'd have to be careful the creaking fire escape didn't catch the attention of the occupants in the third-story apartment.

When she was at the second story, she whispered into the transmitter, "Make sure your team is ready."

In the next moment she ran her hand down in the air before her face, drawing a glamour around herself and disappearing from human sight.

Jake murmured to his team into the communicator on his jacket as Silver continued her climb. Chill air penetrated her black gloves, jeans, and jacket, and her nose was so cold it was nearly numb. She heard the captain swing up and onto the fire escape to begin his quiet climb. He would stay one floor below her, knowing she needed her space to perform her magic.

PSF team members eased from the shadows and waited on the ground, their guns trained on the third-story windows. More officers blocked all escape routes and some had already slipped into the boardinghouse to await Jake's orders.

When Silver finally crept onto the third-floor fire escape, she crouched near the dingy window closest to her. She peered through a pair of frayed white curtains parted just enough for her to see into the room. With her glamour she had no fear of being seen, but she always took care just in case she ran into *something* that could actually see an invisible witch.

Her gaze took in the sparsely furnished room. She caught the odor of cigarettes, and that musty smell of old buildings, along with a more bitter odor—calamus root and dragon's blood. Countless black candles flickered for attention, giving the room enough light to see by.

As sharp and hot as a desert wind, heat flooded her at the

sight of the inverted pentagram burned into the frayed carpet, a lidless eye at its center. It was identical to the others they'd found near dead witches.

For a moment she didn't see anyone through the window, but then a form in a black robe appeared, entering the candlelit room from another part of the house. The hood dropped back away from the woman's face. With her long blond hair and classic looks, she was beautiful by human society's standards.

Silver would never have taken her for a Balorite warlock, but she knew she needed to shed her stereotypes of warlocks. These Balorites were a whole new breed. Unfortunately, practicing evil didn't make them *look* evil. In fact, rather the opposite, as if those initiates with physical flaws were culled.

From what Silver had scried using her pewter cauldron, she had learned that Balorites definitely used blood magic—the spilling of blood to draw on energies and beings far outside the warlock's own ability—for personal gain and power. Also for the purpose of hurting other living things. Rumor had it they intended to rule the underground magic world and ultimately take political power for themselves.

And like members of the D'Anu, by day many of the Balorites already served in high positions in the government, and in major corporations. Positions of power.

But by night, many of the Balorite Clan—or their minions—wreaked havoc that the D'Anu worked to overcome with white magic.

Except for me. Gray magic was what Silver practiced, unbeknownst to her Coven.

She attempted to shake off the feeling of evil from being in the mere vicinity of obvious preparations for a Balorite ritual. But she could feel it creeping down her spine, making her squirm in revulsion.

"Are you all right?" Jake's voice crackled in her ear from the transmitter.

Even though she knew he couldn't see her because of the cloak of magic she wore, she nodded and responded with a

"Shhh," as she moved to the next window. She squinted, trying to peer through another set of curtains, but they were shut tight. With her gloved hands, she attempted to lift the window only to find it locked.

Biting her lower lip in concentration, Silver flicked one finger in the air, sending her magic to do her bidding. In the next second she heard the rusty scrape of metal against wood as the latch unfastened.

She held her breath, hoping the warlock hadn't heard.

After pausing two heartbeats, Silver gripped the bottom of the window and her muscles tightened as she slowly pushed it up. Wood scratched wood like fingernails across a chalkboard, as she eased the window high enough that even a grown man could crawl through. It took a moment for her eyes to adjust to the darkness when she parted the stained green curtains, but then her heart thumped in her throat.

It was the same scene she'd witnessed with her scrying cauldron earlier that evening. The missing child was curled up in a ball in an exhausted sleep, her cheeks grubby and tearstained, her hands bound in front of her with cloth strips biting into her small wrists.

Silver's blood boiled even hotter. This girl had been kidnapped to be used in unspeakable rites, harmed in ways that made Silver ill to think about.

Blood magic. The blackest of all black magic.

Remaining in a crouch, Silver moved back to the first window and saw that the woman had been joined by two men, both wearing black robes identical to the one the woman wore. One man was slightly turned, so that she could make out his aristocratic profile. The second man had pierced ears, shaggy brown hair, and a day's growth of stubble. He was speaking to the other Balorite warlocks. Silver caught the words "Darkwolf," "initiates," "ritual," and "soon."

Silver tamped down fury that threatened to overcome her, that threatened to make these warlocks *pay* in a way that would make them wish they'd never been born to this world. But that would be black magic, and she walked the fine line of gray and white. Never black.

If she'd been Janis Arrowsmith or any older member of the D'Anu Coven, they would simply have let the PSF officers take over once they directed the cops to the house where the child was held. Rhiannon, Mackenzie, and Sydney often helped Jake, too, but as far as she knew, they used only white witchcraft.

Not Silver. She would ensure these warlocks wouldn't escape the justice due them.

The barest of thumps on the fire escape startled Silver so badly she nearly cried out. At the same time she cut her gaze toward the sound, she flipped out two short, thin, and extremely sharp stiletto daggers sheathed inside her boots.

A man was mere inches from her, and from her crouched position she had to look up—way, way up—to fully see him. His massive arms were folded across his powerful chest, his stance wide, shoulder-length ebony hair whipping in the breeze. He wore all black, a snug sleeveless shirt and tight leather pants with a glimmering sword sheathed to one side of his lean hips, a dagger at his other. A fierce expression crossed his rough features, and his jaw tightened as if with anger.

He was one of the most gorgeous men she'd ever seen.

A man who made her heart pound, and fire burn in her blood.

A man who shouldn't have been able to get past Jake.

Silver clenched her jaw and gripped her knives tighter, but the man held his fingers to his lips in a "shush" motion. *"Quiet,"* came a voice with a strong Irish brogue in her mind. *"I will help you get the child to safety before you attempt to finish your assignment."*

Silver was speechless. He'd seen through her glamour *and* he had spoken in her mind.

Before she could react, he leaned in through the now open window, his longer body and sheer strength giving him an advantage she didn't have. In mere seconds he reappeared with the sleeping child in his large embrace.

He held her tenderly, as if she were a precious treasure and might break if he wasn't careful. He stroked a strand of the girl's matted brown curls from her face. *"A leanbh,"* he murmured aloud, his amber eyes focused on the girl, a look of compassion on his strong features. "You are safe now."

He looked to Silver and his features hardened, and again he spoke in her mind. *"The warlocks. Stop them."*

Silver's gaze shot to the room where the three black magicians were placing flickering black candles around the inverted pentagram.

She glanced back to the man and the child—

They were gone.

A chill gripped Silver's chest and she cursed herself. Where had the man taken the girl? And how had he gotten past her?

A few heartbeats later Jake spoke through her transmitter. "One of my men has the child. I don't know how, but she's safe."

Relief coursed through Silver and her muscles relaxed. Somehow the man had gotten the child to the officers.

But how?

She shook the question off. Time to take care of business.

She flipped her blades back into her boot sheaths. When they were safely tucked away, she raised her hands and projected gray tendrils of fog through the window. The fog streaming from her fingers slowly crept along the floor, growing thicker and thicker, until it was swirling around all three Balorite warlocks like dark chains of mist.

The fog caught the attention of one of the males. "What the fuck?" he said at the same time he dropped to his knees from the power of Silver's magic.

It was too late for the man. It was too late for all of them. With fierce concentration, Silver wrapped the fog around the three warlocks, forcing the other two to kneel. Their eyes became vacant, unseeing, as her power over them expanded. At the same time her anger grew and she tightened the fog around the three, causing them to gasp, choke, and sputter. A sense of satisfaction flowed through Silver that shouldn't have been there. She shouldn't feel pleasure at causing any living creature pain.

An icy feeling gripped Silver, quick and sudden, like cold fingers closing around her heart. Grabbing her, yanking her toward the dark. Her vision blurred and she clenched her teeth to maintain her control over the Balorites.

A man—no, a warlock—appeared in her mind, blocking out everything around her. She no longer saw the Balorites, no longer saw the window, or anything else. Only the warlock.

He was stunningly handsome, dark-haired with high cheekbones, a cleft in his chin, and a sensual look in his dark eyes. *"Darkwolf,"* someone whispered in her mind. *"Darkwolf."* A face to a name she'd heard so many times but had never been able to scry.

The Balorite high priest motioned to her, drawing on her gray magic, calling to her to join him. The call was sensuous, seductive.

And powerful. So very, very powerful. She could feel the need for that power growing within her. Could feel herself sliding closer to it.

Dark, the dark. So alluring. So masterful.

The warlock's mouth curved into a carnal smile and Silver shivered.

Her gaze dropped from Darkwolf's face to his chest. A black stone eye dangled from a chain around his neck, against his bare skin.

Something about the eye vibrated to her. Called to her like Darkwolf had.

Then it began glowing, a vicious horrible red.

The eye looked directly at Silver, seeing straight through her, straight into her soul.

Terror ripped through her and the real world crashed down. She reeled, barely maintaining control of her witchcraft. She yanked herself away from the call of the dark and almost collapsed on the fire escape.

Oh, goddess! What in the Ancestors' names just happened?

Her breathing came hard and heavy, her body weak with fatigue. It took all she had to maintain her hold on the warlocks with more force than was necessary, just long

enough to project thoughts to the bastards—gray magic
needed to get them to obey her.

"You will not attempt to escape," she ordered the warlocks with her magic. *"You will tell the Paranormal Special
Forces everything you know about the dead witches and the
kidnapping."* Everything.

The moment she finished her spell, the fog stopped flowing from Silver's fingers. Her glamour failed. She collapsed
onto the fire escape, her back to the wall and her breathing
heavy, her hands braced to either side of her on the metal
grill. Knots twisted in her belly and perspiration coated her
skin.

The glowing eye. Goddess, the eye!

She couldn't get it out of her mind.

Lately, every time she used gray magic, the call to the
dark had grown stronger and stronger. But this was the first
time she had seen Darkwolf. This was the first time she'd felt
herself slipping over the fine edge between white and black.

How much longer could she fight it off?

Jake was at her side before she knew it. "Dammit, Silver."
He squeezed her knee with his large hand, his gaze raking
over her, taking in how exhausted she was. "You've over-
done it again. You should let me handle things."

"Sure—shoot and ask questions later," Silver said between breaths. "Just get them. We need to find out how to
locate their stronghold. We need to stop all these murders."

The PSF captain spoke into the transmitter on his vest,
and within seconds she heard the front door crash open and
the shouts of officers as they trained their weapons on the
warlocks and began searching the small apartment.

Silver had started working with the PSF about a year ago
when her sister Copper vanished after performing a moon
ritual alone. The night before she disappeared, Copper had
one of her dream visions. The vision had shown her that she
must "draw down the moon." Copper had been evasive and
had insisted on performing the ritual herself. Silver had ar-
gued against it, but had lost the battle.

When Copper hadn't returned home by dawn, Silver had

gone in search of her sister at their sacred stretch of beach. All she had found were Copper's tools of the craft . . . along with a lidless eye perfectly outlined in the sand.

Not long before her disappearance, San Francisco's police force had finally come to terms with the fact that some crimes needed a special touch, a special sort of investigation. Crimes related to paranormal practices were on the rise, and Copper's disappearance confirmed that beyond all doubt. The police department set up a Paranormal Special Forces Unit, secret to all but those involved.

Silver's chest squeezed at the thought of her missing sister, and she sank farther against the rusted railing of the fire escape.

No trace of Copper anywhere. Barely a hint of her energy left in the universe. Silver didn't think her sister was dead, but she was so afraid something bad had claimed her, like what had been happening to the murdered witches. Silver had tried and tried to scry to find out where her sister had disappeared to, or if something worse had happened, but not even the slightest clue had come to her.

Now she was driven to help save other witches before they disappeared or were murdered. It frustrated her to no end that she'd only been able to lead the officers to cold crime scenes—until tonight.

Thank the goddess they had saved that child. There would be no killing tonight, at least by those three warlocks.

And that was the crux of it, really.

Silver also helped the PSF because she was against killing of any kind. When things were going down on a paranormal crime scene, she wanted to make sure the suspects were under control. She didn't want the perps to attack and force the PSF officers to fight back. So whenever she could, she used gray magic to control those committing the crimes.

Even if she did tweak it just a bit to make a few suffer— but only the ones who had hurt other people.

Silver had learned gray magic from Mrs. Illes and an ancient Grimoire handed down through time from gray witch to gray witch. A Grimoire given to her by Mrs. Illes. Gray magic was anything that helped, but could risk disrupting the natural order and might cause indirect harm to a living creature or subvert a creature's natural will. Gray witchcraft could call on minor energies or good to neutrally aligned beings outside the witch's control—a definite no-no by D'Anu standards.

The risk of using gray magic—if a witch's own wishes, angers, wants, needs, or emotions flowed into it, it could become about personal gain and power instead of the general good. Touching gray, a witch could *sense* the immeasurable and powerful flow and pull of dark magic.

Almost tap it. Just another inch.

Silver's belly clenched and she gripped the fire escape railing tighter.

Gray magic could draw her so close to the dark. Just like when Darkwolf had called to her.

After Jake climbed down the fire escape, she waited a few long moments for her strength to return. Her arms ached, her head throbbed, and she felt as if she were going to throw up. When it came to using gray magic, there was always a price to pay.

But how high would that price climb?

From the shadows across the street, Hawk watched the rest of the events unfold. The special unit managed to not attract attention from neighboring homes. He had to admire them. They were stealthy, quick, and quiet.

For humans.

Hawk ground his teeth at the thought of the little girl he'd held so briefly in his arms. If it had been his daughter Shayla, he would have ripped apart the warlocks responsible. Humans and witches had softer ways of dealing with fiends.

Unfortunately.

Pushing aside his anger, he focused on the witch named Silver while she climbed down the fire escape. She was lithe and slender, her movements fluid and graceful. After the Great Guardian had sent him through the veil, Hawk had followed Silver from her residence to where she led the law enforcement officers to the girl and the warlocks.

While he was watching, the intense urge to assist the witch and the child had come to him, and he'd been compelled to aid her. When Silver had drawn the daggers, she did it with such speed and agility that he had nearly been taken off guard, and his admiration for her had grown.

The witch was beautiful. He remembered every detail— her silvery-blond hair peeking from beneath her black cap, her delicate features, small nose, and her stormy gray eyes. Anger at the warlocks had emanated from her in waves. From where he watched it was easy to see the fury still raging within her.

Her powerful gray magic, it hugged her like a lover. Gray magic that had sent Hawk to this very witch. The Great Guardian of the Elves had Seen that Silver was the one.

When Silver reached the bottom of the fire escape, she swung off the edge and landed on her feet in a crouch, one hand on the ground. From beneath her jacket sleeve he saw a silver snake bracelet curled from her hand up her wrist, its eyes glowing in the night like amber flame. A silver pentagram flashed at the hollow of the witch's slender throat, its amber center matching the snake's eyes.

He shuddered at the thought of snakes. He hated the slimy little bastards.

Silver strode toward the house with the officer she had been working with, then vanished through the doorway and into the dark building.

Impatiently Hawk waited for the witch to reappear as it drew closer and closer to the time he would have to return to Otherworld.

Silver marched toward the decrepit house after she'd had a chance to recover from using her gray magic, and once she had shaken off the vision of Darkwolf and the eye—as best she could.

She was determined to be in on the questioning of the warlocks. This was the first time they'd actually made it to a scene where there were no dead witches lying beside an inverted pentagram at a cold crime scene. Silver wondered what use her scrying was if she couldn't reach the witches in time to help them.

Jake strode a little ahead of her, his long legs eating up twice the distance and making her have to work to keep up with him. They had known each other for just over a year now, since the time they had met at the PSF headquarters. Once they had even come close to becoming lovers—but not that close. A couple of months after they had met, they had gone on two dates, and both had been disasters. Humorous in hindsight, but disasters nonetheless.

Wooden stairs creaked beneath her boots as she moved smoothly up the stairs to the porch. She shook her head at the memory of the first date, when Jake took her for sushi and she had had a violent allergic reaction to the whitefish. All those red spots—and his suit jacket never recovered from her, ah, ridding herself of the toxin. And then there was the second date, when Jake's broken ankle, thirty stings, and her black eye made it clear they were not meant for each other. She *did* tell him not to try to climb that trellis to get her a rose. He just wouldn't believe her when she told him about the hornet's nest.

When they could laugh about it they decided it best they remain friends and work together to solve paranormal crimes throughout the city. She thought of the lug more as a big brother now, and he was as overprotective as one.

While they worked their way up the stairs to the third story, Silver glanced at Jake. "There was a man on the balcony with me. How did he get past you?"

Jake halted on the wooden staircase and caught her by the arm. "What man?"

She frowned at him. "The one who took the girl to one of your team members."

"No one got by me, Silver." He shook his head and the lines at the corners of his mouth deepened as he returned her frown. "Jameson is the one who ended up with the girl. He thought McNulty handed him the child, but she doesn't know anything about it."

"Well, damn." Silver moved up the stairs, mulling over the strange man and his appearing/disappearing act. No, he wasn't a man. He was definitely something *other*.

But what?

When they entered the room where the warlocks were being held, someone turned on the lights, making it so bright that Silver had to blink to regain her vision. As soon as her eyes adjusted, Silver narrowed her gaze at the warlocks and had the intense desire to tighten the fog binding them. Their wrists were cuffed and each kneeled placidly on the carpeted floor near the pentagram. PSF officers had high-powered rifles trained on each of the captives. The room was silent save for the sounds of cloth brushing cloth as the officers shifted to make room for Jake and Silver. Each officer was dressed like a SWAT team member, only no identification marked their clothing. The PSF was a highly secretive force that left no clues behind.

Remnants of the gray fog still swirled around the warlocks. For a second, Silver's vision of the handsome warlock and the red eye flashed before her and air felt trapped in her lungs. With a shudder, she shook off the images and tried to breathe.

She raised her chin and strode toward the Balorites, her booted heels thumping on the thinly carpeted floor.

"Why did you kidnap the girl?" Silver said to the blond woman, who looked almost angelic. The warlock had smooth, unblemished skin and clear green eyes that looked so innocent.

A slight smile flickered across her face. "We needed her blood for the ceremony," the warlock said calmly in her trance-induced state, as if it were nothing to sacrifice a child.

The mere thought sent flames throughout Silver's body. She clenched her fists. "Why?"

"Darkwolf was supposed to bring new initiates." The woman stared vacantly ahead. "We need blood for the conversion."

At the sound of Darkwolf's name, Silver felt as if she'd been slapped.

Her vision . . .

The eye . . .

She blinked, shoving the images away, and focused on the woman. "Why are witches and warlocks turning up dead?"

The Balorite female gave a slight shrug with one shoulder. "If their magic isn't strong enough during the conversion ceremony, they die."

"Only the strongest witches," one of the male warlocks added as he cut his blue gaze to Silver, "can be turned to serve Balor."

With one hand clasping the pentagram at her throat for comfort, Silver jogged down the wooden steps inside the boardinghouse beside Jake.

By the time they'd finished grilling the warlocks for information, what little they had learned was that Darkwolf had been performing the ceremonies in different places throughout the city to avoid being caught. He had an agenda, but the warlocks couldn't tell her exactly what that was. All they knew was that the powerful high priest was searching for practicing witches and warlocks with strong powers. In addition to the others in his Clan, he'd only found one or two more who hadn't died, while at least a dozen others had passed away during the conversion ceremony. Those who resisted were most at risk of dying.

None of the dead witches were D'Anu. Until tonight, Silver had believed that Darkwolf was unaware of the descendants of the Ancient Druids, the most powerful of witches in the world. Yet after her experience on the fire escape, Silver had a feeling Darkwolf now knew who *she* was, and that thought alone caused the hair to rise along her arms.

They had also learned from the captured warlocks that there was a Balorite Clan meeting hall. However, only a few key warlocks knew where it was located, and those clan members led the lesser warlock initiates in cars and to the hall blindfolded. Unfortunately, the three they had captured this night were among the lesser warlocks.

Silver's and Jake's boots thumped on the wooden porch and she turned to him when they stopped. "I'll see you tomorrow night. We're going to find these bastards," she said with grim determination.

Jake's look pierced her, as if he could see how upset she was. "Are you all right? This one shook you up a bit more than usual."

She brushed him off with a little wave of her hand. "I'm fine."

"Let me walk you to your car." His mouth tightened into a grim line. "What about the man you saw on the fire escape?"

"You know I can take care of myself." Silver really hated when men went chauvinistic on her. "I'll pull a glamour," she said, even though she knew the being who'd rescued the girl had seen straight through her last one.

Jake paused, then gave a single nod. "Tomorrow night."

She didn't bother to answer. Her mind still churned over what had happened, and her emotions were too raw. She hurried down the porch steps and strode away from him. At the same time she drew her hand down in the air in front of her, effectively vanishing from his sight and anyone else's. She pulled off her black cap and let her long silver-blond hair tumble around her shoulders to the middle of her back and stuffed the cap into her jacket pocket.

Silver shivered. Despite the glamour, she felt as if she were being watched. *Perhaps by the being who rescued the girl?*

Shaking off the feeling, she walked around the corner, away from everything that was happening and into the darkness.

This time the night didn't feel like a friend. It raked at her like demon claws and she shuddered. The hair on her nape prickled and Silver almost stopped mid-stride.

Blood rushing through her veins a little faster, she reached the alleyway, bent and flipped her stilettos out of her boots. The knives gleamed in the pale glow of a nearby streetlight.

Her arms were grabbed from behind so fast it had to be something inhuman.

Her heart slammed in her chest.

Why hadn't she seen him? Before she could blink the person—the being—had pinned her wrists at her back, holding them fast in one hand. Her daggers slipped from her fingers and clattered to the ground.

A large palm clamped over her mouth before she could scream.

A masculine scent immediately invaded Silver's senses, along with the smell of leather. Terror ripped through her like scissors cutting her flesh. With her wrists bound she had no power. Not even an incantation or a mind spell would work without the use of her hands.

She kicked backward with one boot and connected with something solid. For a second she was gratified when she heard a male grunt of pain. The next thing she knew, she was being dragged into the dark alleyway, deeper and deeper. Anger pushed away fear. Adrenaline rushed through her, replacing the exhaustion she suffered after using gray magic. But she still couldn't hold on to her glamour and it slipped away. She kicked and struggled and wished her hands were free so that she could blast the bastard with a ball of spellfire.

She bit a finger on the hand clamped over her mouth hard enough to draw blood. The man swore in what sounded like Gaelic, of all things.

"Stop fighting me, witch of the D'Anu," a rough male voice with a strong Irish brogue said when they were deep into the darkness.

The same voice as the man on the fire escape who'd spoken in her head.

Silver went still. And this man—or whatever the creature was—knew she was one of the thirteen secret D'Anu witches in all of San Francisco.

Not good. Not good at all.

First she'd sensed Darkwolf's discovery of her, and now this.

"You have little time before your world changes." The

man's brogue was deep and sensual, and Silver shivered despite herself. "Your Coven could be lost forever."

She tensed, wild thoughts racing through her mind. Was he threatening her? Or was he warning her? Her stomach pitched at the thought of anything happening to even one member of her Coven.

"I will release you if you promise to listen instead of fighting me," he said close to her ear, and she shivered again. "Then you may go."

Without hesitating, Silver gave a sharp nod and was rewarded with freedom. Quickly waving her hand with an illumination spell, she lit the alleyway with a soft blue glow. At the same time she whirled—and came to a complete halt, heart beating so hard her chest ached.

It was indeed the same gorgeous man who had been on the fire escape with her.

But this time he had wings.

Huge ebony-feathered wings.

"Tuatha D'Danann," Silver whispered. She had no doubt the sexy winged man before her was one of an ancient race of Fae beings long absent from the mundane plane of existence. "You don't belong here. You belong in Otherworld."

The man gave a single flap of his massive wings. "I have come to warn you."

Silver shook her head. "No. The D'Danann are neutrally aligned, like the Elves. They don't warn. They don't take sides."

The corner of his mouth curved slightly. "You know our history."

She almost rolled her eyes. The D'Anu were all at least partial descendants of the Ancient Druids. How could they not know of the D'Danann?

Silver gathered herself and raised her chin. Her hands twitched at her sides, ready to perform spellwork if necessary—although who knew if anything she did could faze a D'Danann? Damn, but she wished she had her knives. She would never kill with them, but they had served her well in many other ways.

"What do you want?" she asked.

He took a step closer and it took all her control not to back up. She could best the strongest of men in a battle using her magic and her athletic abilities, and her daggers were often a big help. But this man wasn't human. If he really was D'Danann . . .

Goddess help me.

Silver stared in amazement as she heard the pop of bone while his massive wings folded away and *vanished* right through his sleeveless shirt. By the time the man stood within a hairsbreadth of her, she could barely breathe. His masculine scent of forest and mountain breezes enveloped her, and she grew almost heady from it.

She swallowed, trying to maintain her bravado. "What's your name?"

"Hawk." He reached out and stroked her cheek with the back of his hand. His caress felt so warm and electric that awareness traveled unbidden from her scalp to her toes. "And you are Silver."

Of course he would know. He was D'Danann, one of the strongest beings in Otherworld. But what did he want with her?

She straightened her jacket, cleared her throat, trying to ignore this strange magnetic hold he had on her. "What did you come to warn me about?"

"The Great Guardian of the Elves has Seen the Balorite Clan delving into magic beyond their control," he said, drawing his hand from her cheek, and suddenly she felt lonely, bereft of his touch.

Silver narrowed her gaze. "But Elves have no interest in human affairs."

"The Elves have something at stake in this matter," Hawk said. "I do not know what it is, but it is important you learn what I have come to warn you about."

Her thoughts went back to what he had said earlier. "What is it that the Balorites are attempting?"

The D'Danann warrior crossed his arms over his massive chest. "Darkwolf is being influenced by Balor, the God of

Death. Soon, the Balorites will summon our old enemies, the former sea gods."

"The Fomorii?" Her eyes went wide at the mention of the beasts of Ireland, dark gods of old who had been banished by the D'Danann to Underworld.

Balor had led the Fomorii in the battle to take over Ireland. After the Sun God, Lugh, had defeated Balor in combat by striking out his single eye with a golden slingshot, Balor had vanished. The D'Danann proceeded to defeat the Fomorii. God status had been stripped from the Fomorii and they had subsequently been turned into demons for their crimes. The fiends were to roam beneath the world's oceans and lakes forevermore, paying for their many evils.

Silver's skin chilled. "The Balorites are calling the demons here, to this city? That—that's impossible."

Hawk shook his head, his long ebony hair brushing his shoulders. "You had best use your abilities, Seer, to convince your Coven to act against them."

"Goddess help me." Silver moved her hand to her forehead as the enormity of what he was saying sank in. Her gaze shot up to meet his eyes—eyes that were as amber as the stones on the jewelry she wore. "The D'Danann, will they come to our aid?"

He paused for a moment. "The Chieftains will not evaluate the situation unless the D'Danann are called upon. Summoned. You must try."

"Why did you come to me?" Silver studied his amber eyes. "Why not to our high priestess?"

"Because the Great Guardian believes only you will listen," he said quietly. "Only you allow your conscience to rule, to lean to the gray like the Elves. Convince your Coven."

"The D'Anu belief is strong—passed down through the centuries." Silver pushed her hand from her face in a distracted movement. "Summoning beings from Otherworld could prove to be our ruin. It is forbidden. We can't."

"You must." Hawk reached out and gripped her upper arms, his gaze intense. "The old beliefs must be suspended, or your kind will perish."

"They'll never buy it." Silver noticed how firm yet gentle his grip was, and she had the strangest feeling, like she could melt into his embrace. She cleared her throat. "The D'Anu are so blessed dogmatic when it comes to the Coven's doctrines."

"You must," he repeated, lightly squeezing her arms.

Silver bit her lower lip before saying, "If I'm going to try, I have to have some kind of proof."

"Use your Seer's powers." Hawk trailed his hands down her jacket sleeves, and a shiver traced her spine just before he released her. "Find a way to convince them."

"Why don't you come with me?" If a giant Fae couldn't convince them, who could?

"I was able to cross worlds to warn you only because the Great Guardian opened a temporary window. It is time for me to leave now." His expression had turned from one of concern to something she couldn't read. "I will not be able to return in time to help you unless you perform a summoning." With that he stepped back. His wings unfurled and slowly opened and closed. "Go before it is too late."

Hawk gave her a slight bow, then looked over his shoulder. To Silver's amazement, the apparition of a tall, beautiful woman stood behind him, motioning for him to come to her. She had long glorious hair and ethereal features that all but glowed in the night.

One of the Elves. She had to be.

With one last look at Silver, Hawk turned and walked toward the woman. While Silver watched, his body dissolved into so many sparkles.

In a mere blink he was gone.

2

Otherworld

The unfamiliar sensation of crossing through the veil sizzled through Hawk's body as he arrived back in Otherworld and faced the Great Guardian. He had to steady himself to maintain his footing. It was daylight here, but the sun was mild in the middle of the forest. A breeze buffeted his body and he yearned to take to the skies now, to feel the wind beneath his wings.

He had returned to the exact location he had left from, at the center of an ancient transference point. Elvin runes had long ago been carved around the circular platform made of a stone like gray marble, only far stronger, far more enduring.

Normally veils could only be crossed by the Elves during special times through the year, such as the solstice or equinox. But they could also travel through doorways—over ancient bridges, or beneath great mounds of earth—none of which led to Silver's San Francisco.

However, the Great Guardian had made this trip possible with the use of the transference stone which he now stood upon. Only a being with Elvin blood and very strong magic could use the stone to guide another to Otherworlds. It was not frequently used as the Elves preferred to use existing doorways.

Taking Fae across had never been done. Until today.

Summonings were the only alternative to crossing through the veils—unless one was at least part Elvin. Hawk was not.

The Guardian waited patiently for him to fully materialize. As always, she wore a look of serenity on her beautiful features. She stood a few steps away, near a narrow footbridge spanning a small stream. The sound of running water trickling over stones and the breeze through the ancient trees was almost haunting.

When he was fully standing on his feet, he drew his sword, knelt, and laid the weapon at her feet. Like all D'Danann weapons, it was made of the strongest and finest of metals, with no trace of iron—iron that could be deadly to Fae and Elves alike.

The Guardian pressed her fingertips to the top of his head. "Rise, Hawk of the D'Danann."

He left the sword at her feet and moved several paces away, to look upon her grace and beauty.

The Elvin woman was nearly as tall as he was. Her hair was so blond it was almost white, and it hung straight and smooth, all the way to her feet. Her pointed ears peeked through strands of her hair and her skin was smooth, perfect. She appeared young, but the wisdom in her blue eyes spoke of knowledge that most likely went back to the dawn of time.

Hawk gave her a respectful bow. "I have done as you bade, Guardian."

She approached, her steps so fluid it was as if she floated to him, over his sword. When she reached him she rested her slender fingers on his hand. Her scent of leaves and earth surrounded him. "You have served the greater good." The warmth and power flowing through her voice and touch was calming.

He glanced toward the forest, in the direction of the Chieftains' large gathering chamber. It was beyond his sight, but tension corded his muscles again at the fact he had gone without their knowledge. To take such an action was a punishable offense, but Hawk had tremendous faith in and felt such reverence for the Great Guardian.

And after meeting the witch Silver, his heart told him the Guardian was again correct. The D'Danann must help the witches defeat the Fomorii.

But will the witches be strong enough to fight as well?

"The D'Anu are witches of the highest order," the Guardian said, obviously reading his thoughts. "Direct descendants of the Ancient Druids, they are a race of beings unto their own, perhaps more compatible with beings from Otherworld than typical Earthbound humans. The D'Anu are not human. If one mates with a human, her child will be either human or D'Anu."

Hawk turned his gaze back to the ethereal beauty of the Guardian. "I fear the Chieftains will not find it in their hearts to intervene."

The Guardian simply smiled. "The first time the witch named Silver performs her summoning ceremony, you alone must go. The second time, other Enforcers will cross over."

He couldn't help the doubt in his soul. His people were neutrally aligned. They did not interfere unless they believed what was occurring was against the natural order. "What if the Chieftains disagree?"

"I have Seen." She didn't so much as raise her brow. "The battle will commence."

Hawk absently scrubbed his hand over his stubbled jaw. "Will you go to the Chieftains to convince them?"

"You know I cannot." A flicker of something passed across her features and was gone almost instantly. Annoyance perhaps? Sadness? "The Fae and Elves . . . it will be long before one will accept the other again. Anger and distrust runs deep and has for countless centuries."

Hawk gave a slow nod. "I trust your wisdom, Guardian."

For one moment he saw Davina's smile in the Guardian's eyes and it made his heart ache. His dead wife had been part Elvin and part Fae, making her not wholly accepted by the D'Danann. And for that he had never forgiven his own people. Because of Davina, Hawk had formed ties with the Elves that the D'Danann hierarchy barely tolerated.

Davina's mother had been Elvin, her father D'Danann—
they had met in the woods when her father was hunting and
her mother was walking through the forest searching for
herbs. They had fallen in love, and despite the wishes of each
race, and the fact that their races had never intermarried,
they had handfasted and had conceived a daughter—Davina.
She had grown up among the D'Danann, but only Hawk saw
true to her heart and had loved her with all of his own.

It was for his own daughter Shayla's sake he insisted on
not severing the connection, as well as his own respect for
the race of beings. The rivalry between Elves and Fae was
unwarranted in Hawk's eyes, but centuries of animosity
were difficult to overcome at best, impossible at worst.

Hawk took a deep breath. He had complete confidence in
the Guardian. "I will do as you command."

"It is not my command." The Guardian folded her hands
together. "It is as I have Seen."

Without another word, she turned and slowly walked over
the small footbridge. Halfway across, she vanished into the
Elvin Otherworld.

After retrieving and sheathing his sword, Hawk flew back
to his village riding on the wind above the forest, breathing in
the clean scents of pine and juniper that he preferred over the
polluted air of the place he had visited. After their defeat by
the Milesians, the D'Danann were sent to live in Otherworld,
no longer Irish gods, but Fae living in their own sidhe.

Countless races of Fae existed in Otherworld, but the
D'Danann was the only warrior race among the Fae. While
the Sprites, Faeries, Dryads, Pixies, Leprechauns, and other
Fae beings were generally slight of build, small, and secretive, the D'Danann were large, powerful, and dominating.
They had retained their god forms and their superior fighting
ability once they left Ireland, but had been gifted by the goddess Dana with wings, the ability to cloak themselves, and
near immortality.

For a moment Hawk soared above his village, watching
the bustling activities as his people went about their daily
business.

There were hundreds of D'Danann living in the area surrounding the Otherworld village, a great many of them warriors. However, only a handful were members of the Enforcers sent to Otherworlds, as Hawk was.

The D'Danann hierarchy consisted of lords and ladies of the court, along with the King and Queen of the warrior Fae. However, all followed the counsel of the Chieftains.

Hawk grimaced. Usually.

Life went on for the D'Danann much as it had for time on end. Below him the cobblestone street wound through the crowded village where smoke floated from chimneys carrying the scents of roasted fowl and baked bread.

Wooden carts rolled over the cobblestones, wheels squeaking and rattling. Horses' hooves rang against stone as they pulled carts filled with hay for animals or vegetables to market. Shops crowded against one another in the close-knit village that was kept sparkling clean by its inhabitants. Unlike the world he had visited this night, there was no garbage littering the streets or walkways, no stench of waste.

A flash of anger sparked within Hawk as he flew past the grand Council Chambers and into the village. His frown deepened as his thoughts turned to the Chieftains. Of late they had become more and more conservative, refusing to involve themselves in wars they believed to be part of the natural order of things.

He gritted his teeth. But the Fomorii . . . the Chieftains would have to realize it was unnatural to allow the demons to escape from Underworld.

He touched down on the multihued cobblestones and folded his wings away as he approached the toymaker's shop. He wanted to take home a surprise for his daughter.

Before he could enter the shop, a large palm slapped his back, and Hawk turned to find Garrett behind him, his closest friend and ally.

The two men grabbed one another's forearms at the elbow in a firm handshake, the D'Danann greeting that came from centuries ago when they lived among the Celts.

They released one another and Garrett hitched his shoulder up against the doorway to the toymaker's shop. Like Hawk he wore all black leather as befitted a D'Danann Enforcer. His blond hair ruffled in the slight breeze and he wore the same carefree grin as he usually did. "Greetings, brother." Garrett's warm brown eyes appraised Hawk. "I have not seen you in the village or the training yards of late."

Hawk returned his friend's smile, but his mind was too busy with thoughts of what was sure to be the coming war with the Fomorii. He gave a slight shrug. "I have been occupied."

Garrett jerked his head toward the alehouse. "By the look on your face, methinks you could use a bottle of ale . . . or many."

Hawk gave a single nod. Perhaps he could stop and clear his head—and share his news with his closest friend.

After Hawk purchased a miniature poppet with dark feathered wings and long black hair like his daughter, he carried the cloth bag with him into the darkened alehouse where he met up with Garrett at a table in the corner. He set the bag on the rectangular table and climbed over the bench to sit before his friend. The alehouse smelled of roasted pork, turkey, and fresh baked bread. Hawk's stomach rumbled.

Garrett had already ordered ale for each of them, along with slices of pulled pork and bread on a metal trencher placed before each of their seats. Hawk picked up the heavy metal mug and took a deep swallow, enjoying the thick malt, honey, and hops taste. When he set the mug down, he slammed it harder than he intended and ale sloshed onto the wood.

After taking a large bite of his pork, Garrett simply looked at Hawk as he chewed. They had been friends for so many centuries that no doubt he could read and interpret Hawk's every movement, his every expression.

"Remember when we were mere boys?" Hawk said with a half-smile as he picked up a chunk of pork with his fingers and placed it on a thick slice of bread. "We used to play with wooden swords, imagining ourselves to be D'Danann Enforcers."

"Aye." Garrett let out a soft chuckle while he sopped his bread in the pork juice. "And you and Keir tried to best each other even in those days."

At the sound of his rival's name, Hawk scowled. Keir and Hawk had always tried to surpass the other's skill level. Theirs was a competition born during their childhood, and carried on as adults.

"He was as much of an ass then as he has been for all the centuries since," Hawk growled. "I think the only reason he formally opposed my bonding to Davina was that he wanted her for himself, half-blood or no."

"He only wanted her because you wanted her. It hurt him that your father always favored you, even though he was your father's bastard, and you a child of your father's true union." Garrett shook his head in amusement and then his expression sobered. "Never mind these old battles. Tell me what is on your mind that bothers you so."

Hawk let out a long sigh. They had now been of the D'Danann Enforcers for centuries, battling in Otherworlds to save various races *if* the Chieftains responded to the summoning of a particular people. It had been some time since the Chieftains had approved any fighting of that sort.

Hawk gripped the handle of his ale mug, his knuckles whitening from the force he exerted. "We will be going to war against the Fomorii."

Garrett's brows shot up and he dropped his piece of bread into his trencher. "I know you cannot be serious."

"The Great Guardian of the Elves has Seen it," Hawk continued before Garrett could interrupt again. "We will be summoned. And if the Guardian is correct, the Chieftains will approve."

Garrett picked up his bread, soaked from juices in his trencher. "You know the Chieftains do not approve of you speaking to the Elves."

Hawk gave a low rumble. "It is not for them to decide my associations."

His friend merely shrugged.

While they ate and drank their ale, Hawk explained what the Guardian had shared with him, and his own crossing from Otherworld to warn the D'Anu witch.

When Hawk paused to take a swig of his ale, Garrett said, "It is difficult to believe that the demons could be freed after all this time. It has been centuries since our battle with them."

Hawk slammed his mug on the table again, almost onto the bag holding his daughter's poppet. "Somehow Balor, the God of Death, has found a way to convince human warlocks to summon his people."

Garrett's expression of disbelief intensified. "If the Guardian is correct, and enough Fomorii escape Underworld, it will not be a war easily won."

Hawk sucked his breath through his teeth. "No, it will not."

After finishing one mug of ale, along with all of his bread and pork, Hawk grabbed the bag with the doll and left Garrett at the alehouse.

Hawk spread his wings and flew through the forest for a while, dodging trees and bushes, passing by the many creatures of the forest—deer, rabbits, foxes, and other animals. Otherworld was so different from the modern Earth version. Here the forest was sparkling and clean. Greens were more vivid, blues deeper, reds brighter, and yellows more vibrant. Sunshine glittered through frilled tree leaves, and other leaves shaped in perfect circles. Sounds echoed in the forest, of birds, the howl of a lone wolf, and wind chimes hanging from the many homes in the trees overhead.

When he had given himself a good workout and cleared his head, he flew to his own home. As soon as he landed on both booted feet and folded away his wings, he heard the flapping of much smaller wings. "Daddy!" sang a small voice from nearby.

Warmth rushed through Hawk when he heard Shayla's voice. The music of his daughter calling to him was the most beautiful sound he'd ever heard.

Shayla flew to him, her gleaming blue-black feathers fluttering at her back as she landed. He crouched and held open his arms. His little girl ran up to him and threw herself into his embrace. Gods, she smelled so good. Of wind and wildflowers and the sweetest nectar.

She folded her wings away as she hugged him just as tightly. She drew back and kissed him on the nose. "Breena said it would be a looooong time until you came back. But you didn't stay away so very much this time. I'm so happy you're home." Shayla wrapped her little arms around his neck and buried her face against his chest. "I love you, Daddy."

"And I love you, *a leanbh,*" he murmured as he squeezed his precious girl. Hawk brought his daughter up with him when he stood and she squealed with laughter as he tossed her up and then hugged her in one arm.

He handed her the cloth bag and she cried out in delight as she withdrew the tiny poppet and caressed her hair and wings. "She's beautiful." She looked up at Hawk. "I love her."

Hawk pinched Shayla's pert little nose. "And I love you."

Shayla laughed and didn't stop talking as he carried her toward their enormous tree home. He met his daughter's vibrant blue, almond-shaped eyes and they both smiled. A replica of her mother, Shayla was absolutely beautiful with her long blue-black hair, oval face, and twin dimples and the slight point of her ears. She was a mere six years old, and wore bright yellow blousy pants and a yellow top with puffy sleeves.

Hawk stopped in front of the tree and put his hand to the rough bark. A portion of it shimmered, then vanished, revealing a small chamber carved into the wood. He carried Shayla into the tree that smelled of cinnamon and cedar. The wood was intricately carved and polished on the inside.

The transport carried them up into their home. The D'Danann had no need for transport, but most trees had them for wingless guests—a condition of the Dryads, who ruled the trees. When the door opened, Hawk stepped into the great room. Outside the floor-to-ceiling windows of the crescent-shaped room, tree branches waved and leaves danced in a strong breeze. They were too far up to see the forest floor from where he stood. Other homes perched high above the ground in neighboring trees. Catwalks rounded each tree house and bridged one home to another. It was a delicate maze of artistry that blended into the ancient forest.

The scent of cedar and cinnamon was even more prevalent inside his home. Talented craftsmen had carved intricate designs into the walls, some showing D'Danann in flight and some in battle. The wood was well polished, a deep mahogany shade. Curved doorways led to other rooms, and the ceiling arched high above their heads.

The floor was a massive slice of the tree that showed hundreds if not a thousand rings radiating from the center. One could only see perhaps a fraction of the rings, and the rest were in the other rooms. Because they were Fae, they lived in harmony with nature, and always the craftsmen asked permission of and bartered with the Dryads before creating a new home.

Shayla had continued chattering like a happy little bird. When she squirmed out of Hawk's embrace, she darted through a doorway, calling, "Breena!" to their housekeeper and Shayla's caregiver. "Daddy's home!"

Hawk took in a deep breath as a feeling of loneliness clamped around his heart. This was the place they had moved to after Davina had died.

His smile slipped away. He hadn't been able to bear living in the home he and his wife had shared together once she had been killed by the snake—or what he had believed to be a snake.

Her death had been his fault.

And he would never forgive himself.

3

Underworld

Junga paced the length of the cavern, her thick blue hide shimmering in the green glow of the chamber's lichen. Water steadily dripped in one corner, with an increasingly annoying *plop . . . plop,* and the whole place stank of decay and ancient dirt. Far, far above was the underside of the ocean, an underside she was sick of seeing. The Fomorii should be in the sea, not beneath it.

The demon's knuckles dragged the floor and she gnashed her needlelike teeth. To get out of this Balor-forsaken place was all she cared about anymore. Centuries of existing in the pits of the world while feeding on grubs and rodents extinct from mankind was making her ill.

She missed everything about their lives before being banished to the depths of Underworld by the Tuatha D'Danann, the Elves, and the goddess Dana. Fomorii were *meant* to conquer other races, *meant* to rule. Once they had traveled easily between Otherworld and Earth, and overpowered race after race.

Junga sat back on her haunches as she remembered her favorite part. Sex as Shanai, human, or other races. With a mere touch they could shift into another being, killing that being instantly and taking over his or her body and mind until the Fomorii chose another body to consume. They could change forms at will, but only into the most recent host body, or into their normal demon forms. The only beings they hadn't been able to overcome were the Fae, including the D'Danann, Elves, and Mystwalkers.

She scowled at the other demons roaming the cavern. She had tired of sex with her own kind and she craved more, needed more—variety. Her people were beautiful, of course, all in different shapes, sizes, forms, and colors. Some had several eyes, others took after the god Balor and only had one. A few demons had as many as nine limbs, and some merely had three. There were hundreds of her kind, all different, all unique.

They survived with other races banished to Underworld, but Junga considered those beasts—especially the Basilisks—evil. Junga and her legionmates were not evil. They simply lived life as they were meant to.

Some of her people had regular lovers while a very few had chosen lifemates, and yet others fucked a different demon at every opportunity. Occasionally an infant was conceived, but in this damnable place it was a rare occurrence. The Fomorii needed freedom to expand, freedom to grow their race.

When it came to sex, the sensations with other Fomorii were not as pleasurable, nor as intense as with other races. Junga's usual lovers over the course of countless centuries no longer held appeal. Neither Za's brilliant green skin and slender multilegged body, nor Bane's hulking red form and his two penises attracted her. Nothing was enough anymore.

But soon they might have the opportunity to leave. And to conquer once again.

And the Basilisks would aid them.

Basilisks were beasts of the night. They often took the form of a common, though poisonous, snake, but when attacking their prey or enemy, they grew to their full and formidable height, twice that of a mere human, and as thick as three men. Their scales were like armor, and they had few weaknesses. They looked like a giant snake, but with a fan of skin and bone crowning the back of their heads. And their fangs—the poison injected into their victims was so deadly that even the Fae were susceptible to it. Only the Fomorii had resistance to the venom.

The Basilisks had been caught up in the same spell that banished the Fomorii to Underworld. For centuries the two races had fought one another, but had eventually come to a truce—with the promise that the Fomorii would find a way out of Underworld and a way to seek revenge against the D'Danann.

Revenge against the D'Danann. Yes, they would have that.

"Junga!" came the queen's snarl.

Junga whirled toward Queen Kanji and lowered her head in a submissive posture even though she wanted to claw out the queen's heart and feed her to the rest of the demons. From the top of her eyes she saw the white-skinned queen limping toward her, claws digging into rocks and dirt.

If not for her father, Kae, Junga would not be groveling in front of this white bitch. Her father had served Balor as his right hand, positioned to become King of the Fomorii once they defeated the Tuatha D'Danann.

But no. Kae had let down his guard. Had allowed the Sun God, Lugh, to put out Balor's great eye. If not for her father's stupidity, for letting the bloodline down when he underestimated the D'Danann all those centuries ago, Junga would be queen and ruler over all Fomorii.

Instead she'd had to fight and scrabble to reach her position of legion leader, despite being next in line if the queen died. And to do it, Junga had never let a male or female dominate her, save for the queen.

When she reached Junga, the queen growled, "The Old One has been spoken to by Balor. The human Balorites have begun the summoning." Junga raised her head as the queen continued, "Take your best warriors and two Basilisks to the Temple of Balor and prepare."

"Yes, my Queen," Junga said, trying to keep excitement from her voice. A new species to dominate, to possess, to dine upon—the children of Earth, who populated the world after all gods and goddesses had left to Otherworld or Underworld.

This was Junga's opportunity to prove to all the Fomorii that *she* should rule, not this bitch. Junga would take control and slowly her people would overrun the world from which they were wrongfully banished.

"We haven't much time." The queen came so close to Junga their snouts nearly touched. "The Old One has been informed by Balor that the D'Danann warned one of the D'Anu—a gray witch named Silver Ashcroft."

Junga gave a low growl. "How dare the bastards interfere? What of their creed of neutral alliance?"

The queen snorted. "One rogue D'Danann is not likely to convince an entire legion of his people. They will realize it is the Fomorii's day to rule again."

"And if they don't," Junga said, her skin heated with fury, "this time we will win the war."

"We have something that will ensure our victory." Kanji's voice was almost a seductive purr and Junga couldn't help but be intrigued. Her mind filled with visions of two ways to slay the arrogant D'Danann—tearing out their rotten hearts and slicing off their useless heads. The bastards were near to invulnerable otherwise.

Yesssss.

Blood.

Blood and triumph.

"How will we defeat them once and for all?" Junga's fangs gnashed in blind excitement. "Tell me, my Queen."

Kanji quivered in apparent delight, then flared her talons and stared at the tips. "Magic." Her snarl was one of bloodlust and vengeance. "Not enough for all of your best warriors—but half, at least. And even a few Fomorii with this enhancement . . . the Old One has Seen our coming glory."

Kanji rose and her claws clicked against stone as she came close enough to Junga that their noses nearly touched. "You dare not fail to set up a suitable residence and summon *me* within one Earth week's time." The queen's glare would have slain a lesser demon. "Or I will ensure you are eliminated when I do arrive."

"Of course, my queen." Junga seethed as she waited for the bitch to depart.

Kanji gave an intimidating growl. "Hurry to the temple where you will be readied for the Balorite summoning."

Junga bowed her head and shoulders. "Yes, my queen."

Once the queen had returned to her lair, Junga moved. With more hope than she'd had in centuries, she loped toward the Temple of Balor.

October 24

4

San Francisco

Far below the busy streets of modern San Francisco, silence reigned in the ancient stone chamber. To Silver, the absence of sound felt like a physical weight. How could the twelve other D'Anu Coven members be so eerily quiet?

The night after meeting Hawk of the D'Danann, she stood ready to convince her Coven the Fomorii had come. She had scried it with her cauldron, and now she would provide the evidence to her brothers and sisters in magic. She had spoken nothing of it until the vision had finally come to her, knowing the Elders would not listen to her without proof.

They might not listen to her *with* proof.

Even now, the D'Anu Coven ringed her like a grim jury. Twelve other witches, male and female, all descendants of the Ancient Druids, passed judgment. Some with disbelieving eyes, with frowns, with the slightest shake of the head. Others with curiosity.

Silver felt the tension in her jaw, in her neck, in the agony of her doubled fists as she fought to support the weight of her pewter cauldron. Her posture was rigid. Her silvery-white hair hung limp and straight in the damp underground air. Her silver and amber pentagram was warm against her throat, and the silver snake curling around her wrist seemed to tighten with warning.

Warning of what?

She had never felt so insignificant, so foolish—and so incredibly desperate. The Coven had to believe her. If they didn't, if they ignored the warning she brought them, she couldn't imagine what would happen next.

Not for the first time, Silver wished she could have belonged to one of the other twelve groups scattered across the United States. Maybe they would be more accepting, more progressive. Thirteen American D'Anu Covens, each with thirteen witches, gifted with the Druid legacy, powerful magic of older days and older ways—and she had to be stuck in the most traditional of all.

Considering San Francisco was such a liberal city, she'd thought the Coven would be much more open to progress, changing with the times rather than sticking strictly to old traditions.

Runes glittered in the low light of torches and candles, shining from chunks of granite comprising the walls. The *Ogham*. The Language of the Trees. Just the sight of the symbols urged wisdom, kindness, the keeping of tradition.

What traditions would be kept this night?

Silver shivered. The scent of juniper incense rose around her, filling her senses, making her dizzy on top of being so nervous she had to work to keep her teeth from chattering. The cauldron felt as if it were filled with lead instead of purified water.

Even the pentagram in the dirt beneath Silver's bare feet seemed to evaluate her, scrutinize her as brutally as the high priestess seated in her ceremonial dais at the head of her twelve D'Anu charges.

Behind the ring of thirteen stood apprentices who would fill an open position in the Coven should one arise. Each one had to serve as an apprentice for twenty years and a day. Silver was the youngest of the Coven, having been part of the D'Anu for only three years after her required two decades as an apprentice. She had been granted Mrs. Illes's position when the ancient witch had passed to Summerland in Otherworld.

The three years Silver had been part of the thirteen Coven members were three years that hadn't been so smooth. Every stumble, every mishap had been held against her. If they discovered she practiced gray witchcraft, she would be banished.

Janis Arrowsmith, the high priestess, was one of the oldest witches in the country, far more than a hundred years old, yet she looked no more than sixty at best. D'Anu witches tended to age well, and Janis was no exception. Her dark gray hair was pulled back so tightly that it stretched the skin beside her cold gray eyes. The *Ogham* was embroidered in gold along the sleeves and hem of her forest-green robe that shimmered in the candlelight.

The high priestess leveled her aged, frosty gaze on Silver yet again. "I'll ask you just once more, and this time, please try to make sense. Why have you called this emergency meeting?"

Silver gripped the handles of the pewter cauldron tighter in her aching hands and kept her voice calm even though her heart seemed to race against time itself. "I believe this matter is urgent. If we don't deal with the threat immediately, it may be too late."

In purple robes was Mary, a tall, stolid witch whose dark brown hair flipped up at the ends. She had a sharp nose and her thin lips were twisted into perpetual disapproval. The witch glared at Silver. She fancied herself to be one of the most powerful of the D'Anu, and for some odd reason had always seemed to resent Silver. It could have been due to the fact that Silver had predicted Mary's dog familiar would be hit by a bus. Silver had only been trying to forewarn the witch, but she hadn't listened.

Tonight Mary's huff of disbelief was loud enough for all to hear. "I can't believe you would have anything of value to bring to the Coven—especially on an urgent basis."

Ignoring Mary, Silver took a deep breath and forced herself to step forward, farther away from the ring of Coven members. The D'Anu dressed in a variety of colorful ceremonial robes, much like those the Ancient Druids themselves had worn. Only Silver wore white satin that rippled in the flickering light like liquid mother-of-pearl.

Her thoughts continually strayed to Hawk's warning, the warning that had prompted her to scry with her cauldron all day. Until she had *Seen* the warning that had shown her what she would try to convey to the Coven this same night.

Silver came to a halt just feet from the dais where Janis Arrowsmith sat waiting—less than patient, judging by her drawn, frustrated expression.

Ignoring the decided chill in the elder witch's eyes, Silver at last set the cauldron on the floor. The priestess raised an eyebrow and Mary snickered. The other witches murmured softly or remained quiet. Silver felt their eyes on her, though, boring into her, judging her.

Not waiting for approval she knew would never come, Silver slowly began her chant.

> *"Ancestors, hear us and light our way.*
> *Show us the truth we must see today.*
> *By the power of water, wind, and tree,*
> *Warn us, save us. So mote it be."*

For a moment the silence returned, filling the basement like an insidious spell. Silver heard nothing but the faint rustle of robes, and even fainter, a scrabbling that seemed to come from far below the D'Anu Coven hall.

From the cauldron, nothing.

Not even a ripple.

Silver caught Mary's expression of satisfaction from the corner of her eye. Her own hopes began to fail as the water in the cauldron remained motionless.

Then, as if to chastise her for her lack of faith, a wisp of white fog rose from the cauldron. Silver's nose caught the unmistakable hint of meadowsweet.

Soft murmurs penetrated the quiet as the fog grew thicker, rose higher.

At least the Coven was taking notice.

Silver released a breath of relief, yet fear of the unknown, of what would be revealed, shook her confidence. She backed up into the circle of witches until her hands clasped Rhiannon's on one side and Mackenzie's on the other so that all hands were joined as the witches circled the cauldron.

Rhiannon was Silver's best friend, one of her only true companions and supporters, and she enjoyed the company of Mackenzie and Sydney as well. Silver's other two friends, Eric and Cassia, were still in training and both usually stood to the side of the ring with the rest of the apprentices. Tonight Eric was at home sick.

Silver had the abilities to scry and to heal, but her local Elders still considered her powers juvenile at best. She rarely performed under the watchful eyes of her entire Coven, and they truly didn't know how much her powers had grown. She kept part of herself restrained—as if the other Coven members would *know*. She certainly couldn't allow them to have any idea she practiced gray magic.

Fog began to coalesce above the cauldron, turning an eerie shade of green as it grew within the circle of witches until it became like a round viewscreen. Images appeared, and gasps escaped the lips of some of the members of the D'Anu Coven.

"The Balorites," Mackenzie whispered. "They *are* growing in number."

Sydney shushed her while the rest of the witches remained transfixed on the scene before them. Silver's heart pounded harder, faster, as she watched the scene unfold, the same one she had seen earlier.

Three-dimensional images of the Balorite Clan crystallized.

Full-color visions of ritual murder.

"Goddess," someone whispered.

"Blood magic," another witch said through clenched teeth.

"That eye . . ."

So, they did see.

Silver allowed herself a tiny measure of relief.

Her Coven at least realized that the Balorites had crossed into new and more terrible crimes. Because of the God of Death. Because of Darkwolf.

Silver started at the thought of the alluring warlock. She made herself stare at the vision to remind herself why Darkwolf was a monster, why she couldn't allow herself to think of him in positive terms.

In the image, the Balorites wore black robes with a large red eye embroidered on the back. They stood in a circle with their hands locked together. Thirteen warlocks. Their lips moved as if in a chant, but the words could not be heard. At the center of the Balorite circle was an inverted pentagram burned into the wooden floor. In the middle of the pentagram was a body slashed to ribbons. Blood flowed over a single eye carved into the floor next to the corpse. Silver could barely gaze at the corpse, and she almost couldn't watch the horrid, lidless abomination on the floor as it moved slowly, back and forth, back and forth, blinking in the crimson fluid.

The warlocks lifted their joined hands and a hooded priest raised a black pitcher as he slowly walked the expanse of the circle. When he began to pour, more blood spilled from the pitcher and splattered on the wooden floor. Silver's gut churned.

So much blood.

It was a massive ritual, a true overreach of human witching ability.

A dark summoning.

Sara, one of the apprentices, gave a soft moan.

The men's and women's mouths moved faster and faster. Then, as one, the warlocks released hands and stepped back. The hooded figure continued to pour blood on the eye and the corpse. The fluid crept into the engraved outline of the inverted pentagram, almost obscuring the lidless eye at its center. Blood flowed from one groove and into the next until every channel was filled. When the pitcher emptied, she saw the high priest's face and she swore he looked directly at her.

Darkwolf.

Silver swallowed.

Once more, she remembered the strength of Darkwolf's call when she had used her gray magic against his warlocks—the sensuality in his dark eyes and wickedly handsome face. Her heart clenched, feeling again that tremendous pull that she had to mentally fight to break away from. It was as if he were in this room right now, coming to her, wanting to be with her.

She closed her eyes for a moment, then they snapped back open when she heard a scrambling sound again, louder this time. Was it the vision or reality?

The priest in the vision gave a knowing smile and stepped away from the bloodied inverted pentagram. He handed the pitcher to one of the warlocks and it vanished behind a black cloak. Darkwolf lifted his hands and his mouth moved in a chant. The warlocks all raised their hands.

Even though she'd witnessed this when she used the cauldron earlier, she still jumped when the wooden floor at the center of the bloodied eye exploded upward in the middle of the warlocks. Shards of wood flew through the air, along with concrete and dirt and the corpse. Silver flinched, almost expected to feel something strike her. Some Balorite warlocks were flung to the floor of their chamber while others scrambled away. Only Darkwolf stood calmly to the side as if only an observer, but the eye hanging from his throat glowed an incredibly bright red.

The D'Anu witches watching the images cried out in shock and stepped farther from the cauldron as demons flooded out of the hole. Horrible beings with tough-looking hides, bulging eyes, and odd-sized limbs. They were all sizes and shapes and colors, with horrible maws lined with gnashing teeth. Following them were two enormous, snakelike creatures—Basilisks!

Silver wanted to turn away from what she knew was going to happen next, but she forced herself to watch. Several of the creatures attacked the warlocks, ripping out their throats and dining on their flesh. Silver could almost hear the screams as blood spattered the warlocks' meeting hall.

One large malformed blue creature pushed its way through the hole in the floor, knuckles dragging against wood and concrete. From its horrible mouth came something that must have been a command, since the demons immediately stopped attacking the Balorites. The apparent leader of the creatures pointed to the remaining terrified warlocks, who were herded into a small group with their hands pinned behind their backs by Fomorii demons.

Arms swinging like an ape and walking on its knuckles, the blue demon reached one of the dead warlocks and touched the body.

The demon slowly began to shape-shift into the dead warlock.

Within seconds, the demon *became* the dead person. The gaping hole at the throat closed as if it had never been. Every scratch vanished. Only blood remained on the clothing. The man the demon had overtaken threw back his black hood and gave a calculating smile that froze Silver to her marrow.

The fog of the vision dispersed in a rush, images fading at once, until the D'Anu witches were staring at one another with horror in their eyes.

"Fomorii." Sandy, a redheaded apprentice behind the ring of D'Anu witches, said with fear in her voice, "They summoned the ancient sea gods from the Underworld—demons."

"What would possess anyone to do something so insane?" Rhiannon's auburn hair gleamed in the flickering torchlight and her green eyes sparked with fire. Silver's friend glowered at the cauldron and clenched her fists, her multicolored robes flowing around her like a rainbow against dark sky.

"This will upset the balance." Mackenzie, a petite blond, blue-eyed witch, hugged herself. Her royal-blue robes swished with her movements. "We'll be revealed to society— overrun, overwhelmed! The power we draw from keeping our secrets will be lost forever."

"This is a vision of what has happened—or what could happen?" the high priestess asked, once more turning her gaze on Silver. This time, the woman's eyes were wide instead of scornful. Most of her ceremonial stiffness had been swept away by the horror of what she had been shown. "Tell me, Silver. Have we time to prevent this?"

"This is a vision of what *has* happened." Silver held the high priestess's gaze. "I am certain of it."

She swallowed hard and looked from one member of the Coven to the other before saying, "Evil is already among us, flooding into the nonmagical world even as we discuss the problem. We must take action now to save the city and ourselves from these demons."

"We'll begin banishing and protection spells immediately, and we must divine where they will strike next and attempt to block the beasts with spellshields," Janis said with a nod of agreement. "May the goddess and the Ancestors bless our efforts."

Silver released Rhiannon's and Mackenzie's hands and stepped forward. "That's not enough. Didn't you see those things? Those were the Fomorii!" Silver gazed around the circle of Coven members, looking at them one by one. "We don't have any choice. We've got to summon the Tuatha D'Danann from Otherworld. They are the only beings who have ever defeated the Fomorii."

Coven members gasped while others shook their heads. Mary sneered again, and Silver wanted to slap her. But it was the high priestess who commanded her attention.

Janis took a deep cleansing breath, her shoulders rising and falling with the movement. "Absolutely not, Silver. That would be gray magic, and we practice only white."

The white. Druid magic. Several of the D'Anu could make plants grow immediately from seeds, fast enough that an enemy could be bound in an instant. They could "talk through the trees" using old oaks. Another talent was affecting tides and weather within the natural balance. Many had had the ability to deep-heal wounded animals and worked to keep species from becoming extinct, and most could heal minor wounds in human and witch alike.

The white was anything that helped without disturbing the natural order, without causing direct or indirect harm to any living creature, or calling on energies outside the witch's own abilities. Calling upon any beings from any Otherworld was considered dangerous for that very reason.

Gray often came from the fury and power of storms and other natural things, like tidal waves, hurricanes, tsunamis, earthquakes, and volcanoes. Calling on a hurricane had been Silver's worst mistake—she'd been dead to the world for a week. One time her sister had asked for help from an elemental and ended upside down in a tree, hanging by her ankle.

Yes, calling on any beings from Otherworld could be very dangerous.

But this time they had no choice.

Silver thought she heard the scrabbling noise again as she clenched her fists at her sides. "The Fomorii *ate* those witches. They made the Balorites' magic look like children's parlor spells. Simple white witchcraft banishing and protections won't save us or San Francisco." She pushed her long silvery-blond hair from her face in a frustrated movement. "We need the D'Danann."

"We do not." John Steed's deep baritone filled the room as his bushy brows narrowed. The D'Anu witch's bearded face was set in a frown and his brown eyes were intense, penetrating. "The D'Danann are neutrally aligned beings." He pushed away his earth-brown hood, revealing his dark hair interspersed with gray. "They will only serve a cause if they believe it will restore the natural order of things."

Silver opened her mouth to argue, to tell him about Hawk, but John cut her off with a dismissive wave. "The D'Danann could just as well believe it's the Fomorii's time to rule Earth." His bearded scowl burned her insides. "For that matter, the Tuatha D'Danann could choose to align with the Fomorii. What would we do then, Silver?"

"John is correct." The high priestess's lips thinned. "Bringing the D'Danann could allow even *more* dangerous beings and spirits into our world.

"We'll do everything we can," Janis continued, as if speaking to a wayward child. "But we'll do it our way, within the tradition of the D'Anu."

"It is our tradition—our *duty*—to fight against evil wherever it manifests." Silver's voice rose. "We can't just sit by and pretend the Fomorii haven't come, or that they'll go away by themselves."

"*Silence.*" Janis's ice-blue eyes held finality. "We will *not* summon the D'Danann."

"We have to!" Silver wanted to kick over her cauldron, but she managed to restrain herself.

Janis stood. On her dais, her natural height and power seemed magnified. "Are you challenging my authority?"

Silver's mouth went dry. Her temper, her knowledge of right and wrong, made her want to scream "yes, yes, yes!"

But her better sense held her in check.

For hundreds of years, the thirteen American D'Anu Covens had functioned without rift or fissure, keeping their secrets. They used white witchcraft in battling black magic behind the scenes, under the surface, in forgotten places outside the awareness of the modern world. If even one of the D'Anu Covens lost its full strength, the balance of good versus evil—the fate of the world itself—might tip in favor of chaos and darkness. Silver didn't want to be the one to bring about that disaster.

Yet, disaster seemed already at hand. With the Fomorii on land, taking human form—hadn't the balance already been destroyed?

"I believe the D'Danann are our only hope," Silver managed to say to Janis. "Ours, this city's—maybe even all the D'Anu. All the world." Again she started to try to tell the Coven about Hawk, but stopped when she saw the high priestess's expression.

Janis's flashing eyes narrowed to slits. "Don't think about

acting on your own, Silver. I promise you, if you attempt a summoning without my blessing, without the strength of your Coven, I'll banish you."

Anger burned through Silver like wildfire. "You would fracture us now, when we most need to pull together—because you disagree with me? Because you *think* I might do something you don't like?"

The older woman didn't answer. She only glared, as did many of the rest of the Coven.

Anger doubled on anger, heating Silver past her tolerance point.

"So be it." She turned and pushed her way through the witches, blinded with fury and not caring about anything but what she knew had to be done.

Behind her she heard Rhiannon speaking with the high priestess, asking her to consider Silver's plan.

To one side of Silver strode Cassia, one of the apprentice witches who worked in the Coven's metaphysical store that Silver managed. When she was across the large room, near the stairs leading from the meeting hall, Silver stopped and looked to the young witch. Cassia had curly blond hair, and pleasant features that were twisted into a worried frown.

"Don't follow me," Silver started to tell Cassia. "Where I'm going, what I'm going to do—your apprenticeship will be disavowed and you'll be banished with me."

The scrabbling sound coming from below was so loud now that Coven members were looking at one another in confusion. Janis stood ramrod straight and plunged her hand into her pocket.

Hair prickled at Silver's nape and she raised her hands.

The floor exploded upward like a dark fountain.

Dirt and rock pummeled the basement, and silt rained down on Silver and the other Coven members. A chunk of rock slammed into Silver's thigh and fire flamed through her leg. Across the room where the other witches stood, a hole widened in the dirt floor—directly where the pentagram had been.

And from that hole poured twisted, mangled Fomorii along with a putrid rotten-fish stench.

Screams filled the room as the former sea gods lunged outward, grabbing, grinding their horrid teeth.

The demons didn't eat the witches, or kill them. No. They were herding them. Grasping their hands behind them before they could use their magic to defend themselves. Taking advantage of those caught off guard and driving them into a circle.

They were so fast!

Janis yanked her hand from her pocket and dropped a large seed to the chamber's dirt floor. A vine instantly sprung up through the earth, its base becoming thicker, its tendrils lengthening. It wound its way through the chamber like a living rope and wrapped around the first Fomorii it came to, a hulking yellow beast, rendering the demon helpless. Janis raised her hands, putting more of her tremendous power into the vine's growth, whipping a curling tendril around another beast. Before she had a chance to further enhance the tree, grow it to bind more Fomorii, a slender green demon with tremendous strength slammed into the witch's side, knocking her to the dirt floor.

Rhiannon flung out a gold rope of power from her hand, binding the arms of a blue wart-infested Fomorii. Rhiannon's auburn hair was wild around her smudged face, her robes covered with dirt. She shot out another stream of energy, backing against the wall so that no demon could come up from behind. Yet the moment she turned her head to bind a Fomorii pinning Iris's hands behind her back, another multilimbed demon attacked her from the side, diving in like a baseball player sliding into third base, grabbing Rhiannon's ankles, and driving her to her knees.

Fury burned through Silver, hot and molten. She gathered a blue spellfire ball in her hands. Her hair crackled around her shoulders and her skin tingled with power like thousands of tiny pinpricks. With all her might she flung the ball straight at a Fomorii coming for her and Cassia.

The spellfire slammed into the great red demon and drove it across the room and against the far wall so hard its head hit with a crack loud enough to be heard in the melee. The beast squealed and landed on all fours, blood pouring from its head. It staggered, but regained its footing.

From her side vision she caught Janis's expression of obvious shock at Silver's use of gray magic and extreme force.

Silver faltered only a moment before she formed another ball of spellfire and slammed a different red beast to the dirt floor. It shrieked as the blue fire surrounded it, and Silver caught the unmistakable odor of burned flesh mixing with the rotten-fish stench. The power flowing through her was tremendous and filled her with a sense of dark satisfaction. Her hair rose about her shoulders and her body vibrated with her witchcraft. Just another blast and she could do away with the beast.

The image of Darkwolf wavered in her mind. The eye hanging from the chain about his neck glowed. *"Kill it."* His sensuous voice filled her mind. *"Destroy the creature."*

Yes, she had to. Had to do away with the demons capturing the other witches.

"Kill it."

More heat, more power flowed from her, and then her own voice rang through her head.

No killing. Doesn't matter what the creature is, no killing. Contain the beast.

She mentally shook herself. The image of Darkwolf vanished. Sweat poured down her face in rivulets from the force it took to yank herself back from the edge of the dark.

Instead of harming the monster further, she bound the Fomorii in a blue rope of power and started to go for another.

In her furious state Silver realized two things. Every one of the witches but her and Cassia had been captured and were bound.

The rest of the demons were rushing the two of them.

With a quick movement, Silver waved her hand and formed a protection bubble around Cassia and herself before the demons reached them. The snarling Fomorii bounced against it, clawed at the magical surface and gnashed their horrid teeth. The demons' rotten-fish stench penetrated the bubble.

The next second she felt Cassia's power join her own, strengthening the protection.

Silver's heart climbed to her throat as a mammoth blue Fomorii shoved its way through the others and approached the bubble. It was the same demon that had taken over the man's body in her vision, Silver was sure of it. The creature bared its wicked needle-sharp teeth and its bulging blue eyes studied Silver as if it knew who she was.

Silver glanced to Cassia. There was only one thing they could do now.

She grabbed the witch's hand and shouted, "Run!"

The pair of them pounded up the stone stairsteps. Silver could feel the demons launching themselves against the protection bubble. Could almost feel the heat of their rancid breath down her neck. Their growls were loud and hideous, the scrabble of their footsteps against stone raking her senses.

Cassia stumbled on a step and Silver almost stumbled, too. Instead she clenched Cassia's hand tighter in hers and kept them moving forward until they reached the top landing.

Silver grabbed the door handle and they flung themselves into the foyer beside the stairwell. Silver tripped over a rug and dropped to her knees. It took all her power to maintain the bubble as she scrambled to her feet. Her palm was slippery with sweat and she almost lost hold of Cassia's hand.

The demons continued to slam into the bubble, the pain of each blow like a bruise to Silver's flesh. She barely had the presence of mind to grab her car keys from the desk beside the stairwell before they wrenched open the back door of Janis's house and hurled themselves into the night.

The demons followed them into the near darkness, their growls and snarls sounding like a pack of vicious dogs.

She hesitated only a moment before running to her little VW Bug. The demons hounded her, never letting up. Silver yanked Cassia around to the driver's side door, knowing that separating their hands or their magic would be a really, really bad idea.

The witch panted beside Silver and every now and then gave a soft cry when a demon slammed into their protection.

When they reached the car, Silver shoved with her magic and broadened the bubble to encompass the entire car. She yanked the door open and had Cassia crawl across the driver's side to the passenger side while still holding on to her hand. Cassia tangled her robe around the gearshift and Silver heard cloth tear as she pushed the witch over so that she could climb inside, too. She slammed the door shut behind her.

"I'm going to have to release you when I put the keys in the ignition." Silver's heart raced so fast she could barely speak. "Can you still help me hold the shield in place?"

Cassia's quick nod was all that Silver needed. They released hands and for a second Silver felt the protection waver, but then it grew stronger. Demons crashed against it, trying to get to her, get to the car. Three of them had followed, hideous and malformed and so very deadly.

Silver crammed the keys into the ignition, stomped on the clutch, and pressed on the gas pedal as she started the car and slammed the gearshift into reverse. In the next moment she released the clutch and jammed the gas pedal to the floor. Thank the goddess they had gotten there early enough to have been parked by the back door and late enough that they were at the foot of the driveway behind Rhiannon's car.

Demons flew away from the Bug as she backed out of Janis's driveway. The Fomorii weren't giving up, though. They bounded after her until she entered the main street. Her tires squealed and she smelled burned rubber through the ventilation as she whipped the car backward and barely avoided hitting a parked car.

She shoved the gearshift into first and the car bolted forward, sending the demons flying away from the protection shield once again.

Silver tore down the street and didn't think to breathe until the demons were no longer in sight in her rearview mirror.

5

The brisk San Francisco breeze chilled Silver's naked flesh through the opening of her robe. Her hair was still damp from sweat and she still trembled from the fight with the demons. The use of gray magic had sapped much of her strength and she'd had to let herself recover, at least a bit, before she could do this.

It all came down to this moment. She would do what she had to do. To save the city and the D'Anu Coven from the evil that now preyed upon them. The evil that had taken her Sisters and Brothers less than two hours ago.

From where she stood on the beach, distant lights glittered along the Golden Gate Bridge. She was hidden in a small cove surrounded by solid rock that could not be seen from the road and could only be accessed by a narrow footpath. It was a place of power, of great magic, that had been known only to—and protected with spells by—D'Anu witches for generations. Here she usually felt safe and secure, and able to perform her necessary rituals.

Would she ever feel safe again?

She pushed away the hood of her white robe and allowed the open garment to slip over her shoulders, down her graceful arms, so that she was completely skyclad. The satin landed in a soft pool that glowed on the pale sand in the light of the waxing moon. The robe landed beside her familiar, Polaris. The python hissed and raised his head.

The air smelled of brine and fish, mixing with the almond scent of her body oil, and the sandalwood incense burning on the altar at her feet. Waves slapped against the shore, the constant rumble of the ocean throbbing in time with the throbbing of her heart.

Fear tasted bitter on her tongue, but she knew she had no choice. She had to perform the ritual. For the future of the planet. If dark triumphed, if those demons won out, the world as Silver knew it—as everyone knew it—would end. Not fast. No. Not merciful, either. A long, cruel, and bloody massacre.

It was up to Silver to save the D'Anu witches, her city, and maybe much, much more.

Rhiannon. Mackenzie. Dear goddess, would Silver's precious friends live after what they'd been through? *Will I be able to save them?*

Yes! I will not allow doubt to cloud my thoughts.

Thank the Ancestors she had been able to protect Cassia, and that Eric had been at his home, ill. She had forced Cassia to remain behind at the Coven's well-warded shop, instructing her to further ward the floor in addition to the wardings protecting the rest of the store and apartments above it. The D'Anu had never expected something to come up from the ground. Silver knew better now.

Her reasons for leaving the apprentice were twofold. They needed the extra warding done and in no way was the young witch ready to perform the powerful ceremony Silver was attempting this night.

This would be the greatest risk Silver had ever taken. She would draw down the strength of the moon . . . and she would attempt to summon the Tuatha D'Danann.

Would Hawk be one of those who answered her call?

She shook off the thought. She had to concentrate. "Ancestors, help me now," she whispered.

Polaris curled around her feet, and she felt the strength of his support and an inkling of his magic. At least the familiar agreed with her.

"Get busy, Silver." She tried to relax and set aside the constant thoughts of the attack. It wouldn't do to be tense during the ceremony. "Stop thinking about what can't be changed," she said as she stepped away from Polaris. "Think only about what you can do now."

Drawing her athame from her box of ceremonial supplies, she gripped the worn ebony handle. The double-edged dagger had been passed down from generation to generation in her family's long line of witches, and contained strong magic.

She laid the athame upon an engraved pentacle on the wooden altar, alongside other tools of her Craft—a flickering white candle, smoking sandalwood incense, a silver chalice of purified water, and a plate of salt. Sand shifted beneath her knees as she knelt before the altar and held her hands, palms down, over the dagger. Polaris was now curled up beside the altar, watching her, his tongue flicking out as if telling her to proceed.

Silver's voice rose above the crashing waves as she chanted.

> *"Athame, athame, steel for me,*
> *In the name of the Ancestors, I consecrate thee.*
> *Athame, athame, gray as the sea,*
> *In the name of the Ancestors, I consecrate thee.*
> *Athame, athame, true and free.*
> *I consecrate thee, so mote it be."*

Silver projected protective energy from her body into the tool as she chanted, then picked it up. She trickled salt over the instrument for the Element of Earth, then passed the blade through incense smoke for Air, through candle flame for Fire, and finally sprinkled the athame with fluid from the chalice for Water.

When she finished, she eased upright, sand moving and whispering against her bare feet. With her right arm straight out in front of her, the athame pointing east, she slowly turned clockwise while she chanted, "Earth, Water, Fire, and Air, I cast this circle true and fair."

At the same time she spoke, a magical circle cut the sand, following her movements, surrounding her and her familiar. Wind buffeted her naked body, but not a grain of sand trickled into the circle she drew from the air. The white candle and incense on her small wooden altar continued to burn, barely flickering in the rising breeze.

A silver crown was perched upon her hair, the upturned crescent moon positioned at the center of her forehead. Her silver and amber pentagram swung above her bare breasts and began to heat. The silver snake that curled around her wrist grew as warm as the pentagram while she closed the circle. The snake was her totem, and her familiar a python. Both added strength to her magic.

With a wave of her hand, candles flickered to life where she had placed them at the cardinal points . . . green at the north, for the Element of Earth; blue to the west, for Water; yellow at the east, for Air; and red to the south, for Fire.

Throughout the time she spoke the ritual words, made the ritual movements, and consecrated her space, Silver fought the feeling that she needed to hurry or all would be lost. She couldn't rush it. If she didn't perform the ritual properly, all *would* be lost, of that she was certain.

When she finished her preparations, Silver set the athame on the altar and stood at the center of the circle. She already felt the power of the waxing moon overhead, and the power of the moon ritual. She tipped her head back, closed her eyes, and raised her arms to either side of her, palms up, her feet firmly planted in the coarse sand.

The crescent moon graced her supple flesh with its white glow. She could see it in her mind's eye, traveling over her skin, caressing her in unabashedly sensual ways. She felt the power and strength of the Ancestors streaming from the moon, down from the night sky, and through every pore in her body.

A strong tingling sensation started at her belly and worked down to her mons, her legs, her toes. At the same time a tickling feeling moved up to her chest, her nipples, her arms, her fingers, her face . . . until her long silver-blond hair rose at her scalp, stirred about her shoulders, and brushed the small of her bare back. The spirit of the Ancestors, the great Druids, filled her, the energy vibrating through Silver's entire being until she joined with them and they became as one.

When her body trembled with the force of the joining, Silver uttered a small prayer. "I am thankful for your graciousness. For the life you have given us. For the Elements of Earth, Air, Water, and Fire. I ask of you now to allow me to call upon the Element of Fire that will invoke the Tuatha D'Danann to save all your children."

She waited for a moment and the tingling in her body grew stronger. She felt a gentle push at her mind and knew the Ancestors were gauging her intentions.

A caress, as warm and light as a summer breeze, slid over Silver's skin and radiant warmth filled her. She smiled. The Ancestors had blessed her. Had anointed her with their power.

"Thank you," Silver said in a voice as clear as the night.

She felt Polaris curl about her feet, channeling his magic through her. She kept her eyes closed and started the summoning. She imagined a tiny spark as small as that of a match, even smelled the hint of sulfur. The flame in her mind flickered, growing stronger until it was the size of candlelight. The odor of burning tallow filled her senses.

Pushing harder with her magic, she caused the flame in her mind's eye to sprout to the size of a blazing campfire, and she smelled hickory smoke. With another nudge, it roared into a bonfire. Wood crackled and the fire hissed and spit like snakes. The smell of burning wood—this time a wild blend of pine, oak, and ash—was strong in the night air.

Forcefully, Silver pushed and shoved with her magic until the bonfire in her mind erupted from the ground. The earth shook and cracked. A cone pushed through the fissure, expanding, thrusting upward, rising until it became a volcano spewing forth lava. Smoke ringed the crater, sparks rained on blackened rock, and lava oozed from its cavernous mouth.

The image burned so brightly in Silver's mind that sweat coated her once cool skin and her body blazed with fire. The heat of the volcano burned through her and she could almost smell the sulfur, could almost feel ash coat her skin, and an occasional spark pock her naked flesh. Even her bare feet practically ached with cuts from the ancient lava rock she stood upon.

In the fierceness of her vision, Silver called upon the D'Danann.

"Winds from the South, call those who would heed." Her voice rose as she spoke above the booming volcano. "Bring warriors to save many souls in need. This day I cry for all those now lost. This day I cry for the coming cost."

She took a deep breath before she cast the spell that would bring her people's saviors . . . or their doom, if she invoked beings who were neutrally aligned, who believed the destruction of her city was the natural order of things.

With all her heart she knew the D'Danann were truly the only beings who could help the witches.

If they chose to do so.

"Fire, burn bright, to bring the Tuatha D'Danann," she said in her most powerful voice, and she felt her familiar's magic enhance her own. "Guardians of good, from far away. I call on the D'Danann for balance and light. I call to the D'Danann, come now to fight!"

Silver's entire body shook with the force of the volcano's eruption, and lava shot into the murky sky clouded by volcanic ash.

The heat of the volcano eased as her vision turned to that of a forest, green and lush.

Silver saw men and women standing in a circle on a mossy carpet of grass—men and women with wings! Huge wings of multihued feathers. Some white, some black, some blue, among other colors. Large, powerfully built men and women with finely crafted and muscled bodies.

At the center of the circle stood a single man.

Hawk.

Tall, proud, with long ebony hair, and broad shoulders,

leading to a muscular chest, tapered hips, and powerful thighs. He wore only black from head to toe, just as she remembered. He spread his wings, dark against the green of the forest. And his eyes . . . a warm amber that heated her through, reminding her of that first meeting.

She shivered.

The D'Danann heard my call. They will come now.

The vision of the forest faded, and in its place returned the volcano. Its heat was so intense she felt nearly afire with it. Polaris hissed and she knew he felt it, too.

She forced the image of the volcano back, back . . . In her mind the volcano melted into itself, disappearing into the fissure in the ground until the fire was as big as a burning building. It decreased gradually to the size of a bonfire. Sweat coated her naked skin and trickled between her breasts. In her mind she gathered the bonfire into a smaller space, containing it in a rock-surrounded campfire, then made it smaller yet, until it was but candle flame. She mentally extinguished the flame until a thin trail of smoke was all that remained. All pain she had felt from the vision vanished.

Her eyes still closed tight, Silver let out a soft sigh, then caught her breath.

The ground rumbled and bucked beneath her feet. The ocean roared with the power of a tempest. Sparks burst behind Silver's eyelids and turned to flame. A cold blast of air slammed into her body. The Ancestors were surely ordering the Elements of Earth, Water, Fire, and Air to answer her call.

Thunder crackled in the sky, in a city where there were rarely, if ever, thunderstorms.

Then all went quiet.

Heart pounding and limbs trembling, Silver opened her eyes.

The beach was empty.

A sigh of disappointment eased through her. The only movement was the fog creeping in from the ocean along with the endless pulse of the water as each wave rolled up along the shore, retreated, then pushed its way up the sand again and again. Where she hadn't felt the chill of the night because of her magic, it now wrapped around her, causing her to shiver, and goose bumps to rise along her skin. The remnants of burning candle wax mixed with the sandalwood incense and the strong salt and fish smell of the ocean.

There was no sign of anything else.

How could that be? The D'Danann heard her. Hawk had heard her. She was sure of it.

Maybe we aren't worthy. Maybe they chose to leave us to our fate.

Heart heavy, she slowly closed the circle, extinguished the candles and incense, and started to gather her ritual supplies and put them back into the wooden trunk. What would she do, what could she do now, alone? She had to contact Jake and the PSF, of course, but could they actually do anything to help? Would their guns be able to fight off demons?

Somehow she didn't think so.

Silver took off her crescent crown and tossed it into the box. In a bout of frustration she whirled and kicked the sand, scattering it across her altar and over the white candle.

Polaris hissed and turned his head toward the sky.

Silver's hair rose along her arms. She heard the whump of wings. Large wings. Louder. And louder yet.

A shadow marking the moon jerked her attention to the dark sky. Through the night she saw an even darker object approaching, closer and closer. She stepped back, heart beating so hard her chest ached. When it came closer still, she froze, unable to move.

A tall winged being came to an easy landing on the sand, his boots sinking into the soft sand as he touched down. Wind from the push of his wings slid over her body in one small gust.

Hawk. Hawk alone.

He flapped once more, revealing an impressive wingspan. The metal of his sword glinted in the moonlight. He was exactly how she remembered him, the cut of his jaw, the powerful physique, the long dark hair reaching his shoulders. He stood just feet away and she could easily see his eyes were just as intense and a deep clear amber as she remembered.

"Hawk." Silver swallowed and brought her attention back to the reason he was here. "Where is everyone else? Where are the other D'Danann?"

Hawk couldn't take his gaze from the beautiful woman posed before him. Her lithe body was gods-created perfection, every naked curve meant to be caressed by a man's hands. Her nipples peaked from the ocean breeze, her long hair floating about her shoulders like pale silk tumbling nearly to her hips. Moonlight graced her skin and gently touched upon the seafoam curls between her thighs.

The silver snake wound around her wrist, its amber eyes glowing like twin candle flames. He raised his gaze and Silver's eyes locked with his.

A low rumble of desire rose within Hawk's chest, and his cock hardened.

Her chest rose and fell with the heaviness of her breathing and his gaze fixed on her nipples before returning to her face.

Slightly dazed, he could only stare at the one who had summoned him, trying to manage the feelings of lust raging through his body.

And then he saw the snake.

His heart began to pound like hammer against steel.

All the old memories, the old fears and anger burned within him.

The large beast rose up from beside Silver, its tongue flicking and its intense black eyes focused on Hawk.

His fear and fury heated him through as he drew his sword, his eyes never wavering from the slithering beast.

"What are you doing?" Silver asked, her voice barely penetrating the anger that had overcome him at the sight of the snake.

"Step away, Silver." He moved forward, his gaze fixed on the huge beast as he raised his weapon. He would slice the snake's head off. One clean blow.

From the corner of his eye he saw Silver's gaze flick to the snake and back to him as he stealthily approached. "No," she said firmly as she stepped in front of the creature. "This is my familiar, Polaris. Don't you dare try to hurt him."

Hawk was a mere foot from Silver now. The snake curled around her legs and began winding its way up her naked body until she held it in one hand and petted its head casually with her other. "Now put your weapon away."

Heart still pounding, mouth still dry, Hawk met Silver's gaze. "You have a snake. As a familiar."

She cocked her head, her silvery hair floating around her shoulders in the breeze. "You have a problem with that?"

Gathering his warrior's mien, Hawk sheathed his sword and hardened his expression. "I merely thought it might attack you."

Starting with its tail, Silver unwound the eight-foot snake from her body and deposited the beast on the sand. Hawk could swear the snake was laughing as it flicked out its tongue and studied him with those fathomless black eyes. "Polaris isn't dangerous, unlike other pythons his size, and won't grow any bigger," Silver continued. "He's well over a hundred years old from what I know of him, and he has strong magic."

Hawk just watched the snake.

"They usually don't get that old, but like I said, he's a familiar." Silver bent over and Hawk's attention was drawn to her breasts as she scooped up her white satin robe, then straightened and began shrugging into it.

Every movement she made was sensual. His gaze traveled from her breasts to her slim waist, over the curve of her buttocks, down her elegant legs, and all the way to her delicate ankles. Gods, the woman was beautiful.

But she had a snake. A damn snake.

When she had cinched the robe at her waist, hiding her body from his view, she gave him an amused look, but then her expression changed to one of concern. "Where are the rest of your people?"

Hawk found his voice again. "I came alone."

"A-alone?" Silver couldn't believe what he'd just said. "How can just one D'Danann fight so many Fomorii?"

"How many?"

"At least a dozen, I think. I don't really know. They have at least two Basilisks, as well." Silver pushed her hair out of her face and she couldn't help the tremble in her voice. "The Fomorii took my Coven tonight. Everyone but me and two apprentices."

"Basilisks?" The word came out of his mouth like the vilest of oaths. Anger, loathing, and something more was on his strong features. "Godsdamn." Hawk's jaw tightened and his eyes were like amber flame. "I had hoped with the strength of your Coven we might end this war before it starts."

Silver shivered at the mention of war. It brought to her images of death, destruction.

Darkwolf.

"We have no choice now," she said. "We need the D'Danann."

"The Chieftains have not made their determination yet." Hawk scowled. "I came at the bidding of the Great Guardian, against the wishes of the Chieftains."

Hope sank within Silver's belly like a rock tossed into a pool. "If they don't come soon, I'm afraid of what might happen. I don't know why they took the D'Anu witches." She paused. "Unless they mean to keep us from fighting them."

"Or force you to aid their cause," Hawk said, his face a mask of seriousness.

It was Silver's turn to frown. "The D'Anu would never help such evil. They wouldn't even help me summon the D'Danann when I asked them to."

Hawk simply watched her. "I must search for their lair at once. Will you be all right to return to your home alone?"

"Of course." Silver tossed her hair over her shoulder. "I can take care of myself."

He gave her a respectful bow from his shoulders. "Then I will see you when I have finished scouting."

Before Silver could say a word, he spread his beautiful wings, flapped them hard enough that sand swirled around her feet, and began his ascent into the sky.

And then he simply vanished, the night cloaking him as if he'd never been there.

Silver stood for precious seconds, her heart pounding in her throat as she stared at where Hawk had been. A mixture of emotions whirled through her like foam on the waves swirling against the shore and back again.

Hawk had come, but no others had.

And then she frowned. How would he know where to find her again?

October 25

6

Junga paused and smirked at her host body's reflection in the window of the hotel's lobby. Elizabeth Black the woman had been called, before Junga had bitten her pale throat and sucked down her sweet, rich blood. Then one touch was all it had taken to *become* Elizabeth, and to banish the wounds Junga had inflicted upon the dead woman's shell.

Darkwolf had led the Fomorii in the mid of night to this very hotel where he had helped Junga locate the owner. From Elizabeth's memory imprints, Junga learned that the hotel owner had spurned Darkwolf's advances, no doubt causing him to seek revenge in this way. She was also rich and not without power, which would be useful to them.

In favor of the more powerful host, Junga had ditched the warlock shell she had possessed after the Fomorii had spewed into the Balorite chamber. After they found her in her office, Junga had taken over Elizabeth's body before the bitch knew what was happening to her. It had taken mere seconds.

Ignoring the buzz of the hotel and its patrons and employees behind her, Junga let her smile widen, almost let her fangs slip from their sheaths. Centuries of exile hadn't lessened the Fomorii power at all.

Merciless conquest. The Fomorii way.

Before being exiled to Underworld, Fomorii lived their

lives as sea gods in absolute freedom, with absolute abandon. They were more intelligent, stronger than any known beings, predestined to be the dominant species. Other races were simply food, meant to be conquered, enslaved, and eaten.

No mercy. Never mercy.

"All hail Balor," Junga said to herself.

Too bad the Fomorii couldn't maintain the warlocks' and witches' witchcraft by taking over their bodies. That was the one thing the demons had never been able to do—keep the host body's powers. Junga had tried to summon the black magic when she had become the dead warlock. But of course, no witchcraft remained in the host body.

However, she rather liked this Elizabeth, although the human shell was extremely fragile. The intelligence imprints within her tiny brain enabled Junga to easily meld within the society the Fomorii had entered. Elizabeth had been self-assured, confident, rich, and considered beautiful by human standards. She had been known as a bitch, a ballbuster, a woman with brass ovaries. And she had reveled in it. The perfect host body for Junga.

Fortunately the bitch's family was back in New York City, so she didn't have to deal with them. Not that Elizabeth had cared to have any relations with them.

Junga smiled. *How convenient.*

She continued to study her reflection in the hotel's thick glass window. The host body she now owned was tall, slender, and "chic" according to Elizabeth's mind imprints. Her long, glossy black hair hung loosely around her shoulders and she had what was considered by humans to be a "sophisticated" look—an oval face, collagen-filled lips, blue eyes, and a small plastic-surgeon-perfected nose.

Humans were indeed a strange but intriguing race. In physical appearance they now looked so different—and certainly much cleaner—than she remembered of them in the days when the Fomorii ruled the seas and sought to conquer Ireland. At that time all humans had looked the same to her. Now she could see the differences, and found herself marveling at all the changes in this world from the last time they were here.

She held out her new hand and studied the long, bloodred nails. Useless things. Nothing like Fomorii claws. Especially now that they were tipped in iron to give them an edge over the D'Danann. This soft human skin made Fomorii vulnerable to attack, but as long as they didn't attract attention in their human forms, they would slowly be able to take over the city.

With the D'Anu witches' powers to exploit—once the witches were brought into line and realized they had no other options—it wouldn't be long until all her people would be able to make the journey from exile into this plane of existence.

According to Darkwolf, they simply needed enough witches who would cooperate by Samhain—the time when the veil between worlds was at its thinnest—and San Francisco would belong to the Fomorii. Then they would expand their rule across other states, taking over governments, extending their power. Bedamned those who imprisoned them in the first place. The Tuatha D'Danann.

Bedamned her father who had led them to that fate. If only he had been strong enough to protect Balor, they could have won the battle.

"Junga." Bane called to her from across the lobby of Elizabeth's small, privately owned hotel that Junga and her warriors had taken over.

Bane's voice sounded strange uttered from the unfamiliar human body, yet there was a recognizable rumble to it. As one of her legion mates, she had used him to pleasure her, along with his warrior duties. She was looking forward to the time she would take him in this form and enjoy human sex.

"Elizabeth," she growled when he came closer. "You must call me by that name when among humans."

Bane gave a slight bow at the shoulders. "Yes, *ceannaire*." The Fomorii word translated to "leader" in the language called English. Bane's human body was tall, and he had oak-brown hair with hazel eyes. He wore the same impeccable black suit and red tie the hotel manager had been wearing when Bane had overcome him.

"We have begun interrogating this night's catch of D'Anu witches." Bane kept his voice low this time so that no hotel guest might hear him if one passed by. "The Balorite warlock priest believes many of the witches have great potential. Providing we can get them to cooperate."

Junga listened to her host body's instincts and raised her hand to touch Bane's face. Her snarl turned into a sensual smile. She trailed the pads of her fingers over his stubble, enjoying the unfamiliar sensation. Leaning closer, she raised her face to his, licked his lips, then brushed her mouth across his. "Your taste pleases me," she murmured.

Strange vibrations rippled throughout Junga's body. From her nipples to her belly, to what Elizabeth had called a *pussy*. The wildness of the feelings and the host's instincts prompted Junga to bite Bane's lower lip, then thrust her tongue into his mouth.

Erotic words came to Junga's mind. She liked the sound of the human words for the sexual act and organs. Fuck, cock, pussy.

Bane emitted a low groan and smashed his mouth tight to hers. Junga wanted more, wanted all of him. She had the violent desire to claw off the fragile clothing they both wore, climb on top of him, and slide his erect cock inside her. She wanted him to do with her what he would. To take her any way he wanted to.

This was unlike anything she remembered experiencing before. She felt as if she were flying, her body and her thoughts spinning—

With a cry of frustration, Junga ripped herself from Bane's kiss and shoved him back. By Balor's name, she would *not* lose control of herself.

Nevertheless, her breath came hard and fast and she felt an aching wetness between her thighs. Images of Bane fucking her in human form raged in her mind.

She would take him, but it would be under her terms. When she was completely in charge.

By Balor, she hoped no one had noticed her kissing Elizabeth's employee. She clenched her fists so hard the red nails dug into the soft flesh of her palms. How could she have lost control like that? "I want to see the witches and their apprentices."

Bane appeared somewhat dazed and confused, and there was still a large bulge in his trousers. When she gave a low growl, he quickly regained his composure, his features becoming impassive, the bulge vanishing.

With a stiff bow of his head, he gestured toward a hallway near the elevator bank. "This way, *ceannaire*."

She raised her chin and strode past him to the hallway leading to the sectioned-off small ballroom where the witches had been retained.

A few of her legion mates were already installing themselves temporarily in a few of the warlocks' lives—only those warlocks they had murdered before Junga had stopped them from killing more. They needed the rest of these creatures to perform another summoning, but were short of the number needed to reach thirteen.

She growled again. Her patience easily wore thin and she hated this farce. But what must be done must be done, until they were in charge of this Earth, this world that was rightly theirs.

A laugh rose up within Junga and spilled from her human lips. No more exile for her people. The D'Danann would be in for a wicked surprise very, very soon. The weak, treacherous gnats thought they had defeated the Fomorii and imprisoned them beneath the seas forever—but her proud race was not so easily put down.

She would deal with the D'Danann later.

She moved down a hallway, reached the closed ballroom door, opened it, and quickly shut it behind her so that none of the hotel guests would have the opportunity to see the witches inside if a guest were to pass by.

She stepped onto the floor. Folding her arms under her breasts, she almost laughed as she surveyed the captured witches. They stood behind Darkwolf's shield of magic that restrained them. The shield glimmered in soft waves of purple, its dark magic slowly breaking them down. Initially they had tried to use their magic against the shield, but after numerous attempts, they had finally given up.

Pathetic beings, this lot. They tended to huddle in packs, consoling one another, meditating, praying to their goddess. As if that would do the miserable creatures any good. Once they were converted to warlocks, they would serve the Fomorii.

By the almighty Balor, Darkwolf would surely find some way to convince these D'Anu witches to cooperate.

Her gaze rested on Darkwolf as the imposing warlock strode toward her. Something about him appealed to her human body, and she felt her nipples rise and her panties become damp. He had a wicked, carnal look to his dark eyes that made her want to take him down to the floor and slide him inside her. A feeling that was much stronger than the one she had experienced with Bane.

When the high priest reached her, his eyes held hers for a moment and she couldn't help a small shiver. She dropped her gaze to the black stone eye on the chain at Darkwolf's throat, and this time her skin chilled.

Balor's eye. The eye he had lost when Lugh shot it out.

She wanted to touch it, but did not dare.

Junga wet her lips with the tip of her tongue and her gaze returned to the warlock's. From the Old One she had learned how Darkwolf had come by Balor's eye. When he was on a trip to Ireland, the eye had washed upon the shore at Darkwolf's feet. Immediately the eye had opened, and the high priest had heard the voice of Balor in his mind, ordering him to do as he bid. The god now channeled himself through Darkwolf.

And soon, the great god would come to rule once again with the help of the Fomorii.

A knowing smile creased Darkwolf's sensual lips and

Junga almost shivered again. She looked down on the warlock and feared him at the same time, and that bothered her deeply.

Balor's eye. It must be the eye.

"We need the thirteenth D'Anu witch." Darkwolf's powerful voice reverberated through her. "She is known as Silver Ashcroft."

"Why?" Junga swept her hand out to encompass the witches in the room. "Convince these pitiful ones to do your bidding."

Darkwolf smiled. "Oh, they will do my bidding. But these D'Anu—unlike other witches their magic is far too strong to force them into serving Balor. They must *choose* to do so. My magic will see to that, but it will take some time. Silver Ashcroft will be much more . . . susceptible to my persuasion. And together she and I will be able to quickly convert these white witches."

"Why do you think this Silver will be different from the rest of her Coven?"

"She has strong gray magic and Balor believes she can easily be swayed to the black. He has felt her slipping. I have felt her slipping." His dark gaze flickered to the other witches in the room before returning to stare down at Junga. "Just a little push, and it's possible the gray witch can be turned."

Junga studied him for a long moment before giving a slow nod. "Then we shall get this witch named Silver."

7

The four hours of sleep Silver had managed to get last night were four hours too few. After the ordeal with the demons and with summoning Hawk, her body was griping at her for not giving it enough rest.

But she had to do this. And she had to do it now.

It was early morning, barely after six o'clock, and Silver was standing in the driveway behind Janis's home, staring at the back door which was open by several inches. When she'd driven up she had seen the other Coven members' vehicles were gone. Every one of them.

Where had all their cars gone?

Had it all been a nightmare?

If only she were so lucky.

One thing she knew was that the ever fastidious Janis Arrowsmith never left her back door open for any reason. Yet now it stood ajar.

Silver pushed a wayward strand of hair from her face and tucked it behind her ear as she took a deep breath. The rest of her long hair was held back in a Celtic-knot clasp to keep it out of her face. She had dressed for the occasion, wearing snug black jeans, a black shirt, and low-heeled boots with her stilettos ready in their specially made sheaths inside the boots. Whatever was called for, she was prepared.

Her gaze narrowed on the open doorway. Could any of the demons still be within Janis's home? Silver thought for a moment that maybe she should have called Jake. If that Hawk guy had hung around, he no doubt could have been of some use.

"Knock it off, Silver." She clenched and unclenched her hands. She was ready, her magic was ready. "You have to find it." She desperately needed her scrying cauldron to attempt to see where the demons had taken her Coven, or what had been done with them.

She thought about pulling a glamour, but that tended to work against humans, not the inhuman. Besides, she needed her strength—just in case.

Silver walked away from her yellow VW Bug. Her steps carried her closer to the house and she didn't pause until she reached the open door. Her heart beat faster as she placed her palm against the wood and pushed.

The hinges whined as the door slowly swung open, revealing Janis's rear foyer. The ornate table stood untouched beside the thick wooden door that would open to reveal stairs leading down into the Coven's chambers.

Her breath caught at the sight of claw marks etched into the foyer's tile and the thick smudges of dirt on the usually pristine white. The stench of rotten fish hung heavy on the air, lingering like the smell of mayonnaise left in the jar too long.

Her boots squeaked on the tile as she walked in and she stopped short.

A gust of wind whistled through cracks or windows. The door slammed shut behind her.

Silver's pounding heart leaped straight to her throat and her hands were at her boots. In a quick movement both of her daggers were in her hands. Ready.

She waited a full minute and heard nothing but more wind whistling through cracks and an occasional gust rattling the door slightly against the jamb.

Silence. She'd never been in Janis's home when it had been so eerily quiet.

Coming up from her crouch, Silver walked around the table and approached the door leading to the ancient chamber below. It was closed tight. Damn.

After shifting one of her daggers to her other hand, Silver turned the old brass knob, which gave a rusted sound with her movement, and the wood of the door scrubbed against the tile. She flinched and then again when the hinges gave a high-pitched squeal.

It was dark, completely dark. And if anything was there, it had to have heard all the noise she'd just made.

She waved her hand for an illumination spell. Immediately a blue glow spilled down the rock steps, but she still couldn't see into the chamber.

The pounding of her heart reached her ears and sweat beaded her upper lip. She took a careful step and managed to not make a sound. She chanced a glance down and in the blue glow saw more claw marks etched into the stone. The memory of those demons chasing her and Cassia out of the house came back even stronger than before.

The stench of their breath, their horrible roars, the sound of their claws scrabbling against stone.

Clenching her daggers, Silver took a deep breath, then step by step slowly made her way down. When she could see the chamber in the blue glow of her magic, her stomach turned.

The sacred meeting hall was virtually destroyed. A large hole desecrated the floor, the pentagram that had once graced the earth gone. Debris was scattered from one end of the chamber to the other. The high priestess's dais was flipped over, the candles and incense burners toppled onto their sides, along with ceremonial tools—two chalices, a wand, an athame, a ritual sword, and the altar, along with other items. Only the *Ogham* on the far wall remained unmarred, but it did not glitter like it normally did.

Everything looked so eerie in the blue glow of her magic. The plant Janis had magically grown from seeds remained in the room, its leaves and tendrils completely still. Part of the plant had been chopped or clawed away, no doubt where it had been wrapped around the two demons. The magical ropes Silver and Rhiannon had used to bind the other demons had vanished the moment each of them had lost their focus. Unlike Janis's plant magic, the fire magic would dissipate when no longer tended. Even Silver's gray fog wouldn't last long without her attention.

Every step Silver took brought her closer and closer to the destruction. Fear turned to anger. Anger at the Balorites for calling upon the Fomorii in the first place, and anger at the demons for what they had done.

When she reached the floor, a clump of dirt crunched beneath her boot and she paused.

Silence. A silence so deep she heard ringing in her ears.

But no movement, and no movement was good.

Silver carefully swept her gaze around the chamber. *Where is that blessed cauldron?* It had been near the dais when she had set it down to show the Coven the vision of the Balorites and Fomorii.

She worked her way to the side of the room where the dais had been, stepping over the enormous vine and over items scattered on the floor. It wasn't until she reached the far wall that she finally saw it, half buried beneath a pile of rubble. She slipped one dagger back into her boot, but held on to the other as she made her way to the cauldron, which glowed faintly in the blue light of her magic.

When she finally grasped the metal and lifted it, thick mud rolled from its insides and spilled onto the ground at her feet. With a feeling of relief, Silver clutched the cauldron in one hand, her dagger in the other, and started to make her way back across the room when she heard a tiny scrabbling sound.

A chill rolled down her back and she swallowed.

The scrabbling sound again. But not coming from the hole in the center of the floor. No, it was coming from behind her.

Silver set down the cauldron and turned toward the noise, the dagger raised in one hand, magic sizzling from the fingers of her other.

Nothing.

But then came the scrabbling sound again, louder this time, yet small.

She glanced down at her feet. Janis's familiar peeked its little head out from between a clump of dirt and rocks.

Silver almost laughed. "Mortimer." She shook her head at the black and white mouse as she bent down and offered him her palm. "You scared the crap out of me."

The familiar scampered onto her palm and raised himself on his hind legs, nose wiggling and whiskers twitching. With surprise, she felt his ancient magic flow through her, as if the mouse were her own familiar. He made small chittering noises and grew agitated, as if he were trying to tell her something.

Silver frowned, but before she knew what he was doing, Mortimer scampered up her arm, over her snake bracelet, and to her shoulder where he chittered, becoming more and more frantic.

Hair prickled at Silver's nape and the reek of rotten fish hit her like a slap.

She whirled just in time to see a great yellow demon launching itself from the hole, claws extended to grab her.

Pure instinct took over. Silver slashed at it with her dagger. The blade sliced through the tough hide along its arm at the same time she hurled a spellfire ball at the beast.

Blood spurted from its arm. The demon shrieked as it swung its claws out at her. But the blast from the spellfire knocked it off balance and Silver ducked beneath its grasp.

In a practiced movement she turned sideways, brought her foot up, and rammed her boot against the demon's chest. It stumbled backward but its claws clamped onto Silver's pant leg, pulling her feet out from under her.

She cried out when her head struck a rock and light sparked behind her eyes. Mortimer squealed and fell off her shoulder.

With a roar that shook the chamber, the demon rose up, its grotesque teeth bared, its three eyes focused on her, its yellow hide tinged with blue from the magic illuminating the room.

Just as it lunged for her, Silver flung spellfire at it with all her might, directing her gray witchcraft into that flaming blue ball. It slammed into the demon and coated its body like living fire. The beast shrieked as it toppled over, but still scrambled back to its feet.

Even as she watched, the demon's wounds began to heal.

She felt Mortimer scamper onto her shoulder and up to the crook of her neck as she got to her knees. Silver's breathing came in harsh gasps and sweat coated her skin. She formed another spellfire as the demon charged her and slung it as hard as she could.

The blazing ball struck the beast broadside, knocking it off its feet. It landed on a pile of rubble.

Silver kept her hand held out, pushing, pushing, pushing against the Fomorii. She wanted to cause it pain, wanted to hurt it for what it and its kind had done to her Coven and her friends. The desire to kill it was so strong she could taste it.

One push. It was only a demon. A hideous, murdering beast that belonged back in the Underworld. She could kill it, send it to whatever hell Fomorii went to when they died.

"Yes . . ." a seductive voice said in her mind. *"Kill it, Silver. It's only a demon."*

Of course. It wouldn't be black magic to kill such a horrible being. She would be serving the good. Yes, the good.

Something nipped her ear so hard that her concentration and connection with the dark was shattered. "Ow!" She slapped her hand to her ear and almost flattened the mouse.

Mortimer. The familiar had called her back from . . . from what?

Her own dark urges?

Something shadowy . . . trying to possess her?

Silver shook her head and felt blood trickling down her neck.

This time when the demon charged, Silver felt the familiar's magic join her own as ropes of blue power shot from her fingertips. The ropes wrapped around the demon, binding it tight from shoulders to horrid clawed feet.

She was very tempted to bind the beast so tight it couldn't breathe, but she heard the note of warning when Mortimer gave his low chitter.

So like Janis to have a familiar that wouldn't allow Silver to use any gray magic.

"Let's get out of here before any more of the bastards come," Silver said more to herself than to the mouse.

Keeping her focus on the magical ropes, Silver scooped up the cauldron with her free hand, her other still clenched around her bloodied stiletto. Mortimer's tiny claws dug into her shirt as he clung to her.

Silver stumbled over rocks and debris as she made her way to the stone steps. The demon writhed and shrieked loud enough to cause her to wince. Its three eyes glared at her with hatred.

She felt the tiny familiar's power enhance her own, keeping the demon bound while she jogged up the steps as fast as she could. When she reached the top of the stairs she extinguished her magical light and slammed the thick wooden door.

She yanked open the back entrance of Janis's home and tore out of the house and to her car as fast as she could.

As soon as she parked the VW behind Moon Song, the Coven's metaphysical store and café, Silver hurried to unlock the back door. She felt the tremendous power of the building's wardings and it gave her some measure of relief as she pushed her way inside and slammed the door behind her.

It was still early in the morning, but Cassia was pulling something from the oven, obviously baking for that day's café crowd. The kitchen smelled of pumpkin spice and freshly baked blueberry muffins.

For an instant Silver thought that odd, that Cassia was baking as if it were a day like any other, but then realized it was probably the apprentice's way of coping with everything that had happened. She tended to be a disaster at most things, but cooking and baking was one craft at which she excelled.

Cassia turned from the stove and stared at Silver. Cassia was a curly-headed blonde with almost translucent skin, a pert nose, and blue eyes that were an uncommon shade of turquoise. She generally dressed in flowing skirts and loose blouses, and today was no exception. She wore a light turquoise skirt and blouse that made her eyes even more startling, more unearthly than normal.

"What in the goddess's name happened to you?" Cassia set down the hot pad she'd been holding. "What were you doing out of the shop?"

Silver was too exhausted to talk about it—her adrenaline rush was fading and weakness from using her gray magic was kicking in. Instead of explaining, she held up the muddy cauldron. "I got it."

Cassia's jaw dropped. *"You went back?"*

"I found Mortimer." Silver reached up with her free hand and let Janis's familiar scamper onto her palm. "Well, he sort of found me. Maybe you'd better keep him with you in case Polaris forgets the familiars-don't-eat-familiars rule."

"Better keep him from Spirit, too," Cassia said, referring to Rhiannon's familiar, a large cocoa-colored cat. Cassia wrinkled her nose as she approached and let Mortimer daintily step from Silver's hand onto her own. "Smells like you've both been doused in fish oil. And your ear is bleeding."

Silver was already turning for the stairs leading up to the apartments. "I'll be upstairs until opening time."

"So we're keeping the store open? I was getting ready just in case."

Silver paused in mid-step and looked back at Cassia. "We need to keep money coming in for the Coven, and it's probably best we keep up some semblance of normalcy."

Cassia nodded, an odd look passing over her face. Not for the first time Silver had the feeling that there was more to Cassia than met the eye. And once again, she couldn't help feeling how much Cassia reminded her of her sister Copper. Not in looks, but in something else. Something almost indiscernible.

Silver turned away from the apprentice and hurried up the stairs, the muddy cauldron clutched tight in her hand. She had mentioned to the Elders that she'd thought there was something different about Cassia, but she'd always been told that she was imagining things. Cassia had an impeccable background and even came from the same Coven as Silver's father.

Perhaps that was what bothered her.

After a long, hot shower, Silver felt more refreshed. She dressed as she normally would for the day when she worked in the shop and café. She felt sexy and confident in a short skirt, silk blouse, and three-inch heels. Her long silvery-blond hair hung loose around her shoulders, and as always she wore the snake bracelet that curled around her wrist and the pentagram at her throat.

Her bedroom was one of her favorite places to retreat. The furniture was natural oak, and the carpet and bedding was a rich cream. Colorful impressionistic paintings graced the walls, and rose throw rugs dotted the floor. Stained-glass lamps perched on nightstands on either side of the bed, and she always loved how their colors scattered across the white bedding.

She strode across her carpeted bedroom and onto the hardwood floor of her living room that served as her study and her dining area, as well. Her small living room was decorated in soothing shades of blue and off-white, vases of brilliant flowers scattered about to add splashes of color.

She took the cauldron to the sink in her postage-stamp-sized kitchen, and ran tap water over the pewter, cleansing mud from inside and out. Her earlobe still ached a bit, but she healed quickly and the herbal cream she'd put on it would help. She wasn't sure if she should be thankful to the mouse or not.

A chill washed over Silver and her eyes lost focus as the scene played out before her once again. What had she been thinking? What if she hadn't stopped and had actually *killed*?

And Darkwolf. It had definitely been his voice that she

had heard. He was playing with her. Using her gray magic and urging her to the dark.

Water spilled over the side of the sink and Silver cursed as some splashed on her skirt. She quickly turned off the faucet and shifted the cauldron so that she could lift out the drain plug and let some of the soapy water out.

After she finished cleaning the cauldron and thoroughly dried it, she placed it on the small dining table in the little nook in front of one of the bay windows. To her great relief, Polaris was curled up on one of the chairs.

"There you are." Silver headed back to the kitchen. "I need you to help me with the vision."

Her heels clicked across the wooden floor as she lugged a large bottle of consecrated water to the table. She tipped it into the cauldron, pouring the water until it was almost full. When she finished, she set the bottle on the floor, took a deep breath and stared at the cauldron. Polaris raised his snaky head, too, and focused on it.

What now? What would it show her?

Silver bit her lower lip, almost afraid of what she would see. She took another deep breath. Pushed her hair behind her ear. Wiped her sweating palms on her skirt.

Polaris's tongue flicked out and she felt the strength of his magic join with hers.

Now or never. She opened her mouth. Cleared her throat, and then began.

> *"Ancestors, hear us and light our way.*
> *Show us the truth we must see today.*
> *By the power of water, wind, and tree,*
> *Warn us, save us. So mote it be."*

Silver held her breath after she said the chant, and it wasn't until she saw the first tendril of fog that she let it out again in a long, slow exhale. Her heart pounded as she watched the fog rise and figures began to form and coalesce.

She forced herself to calm down and relax, unfocusing her eyes and letting the world slip away.

Images appeared, one slow wave after another. A large, dim room with a chandelier at the center of the ceiling. Silver frowned. A ballroom? With demons standing guard before a pair of wooden doors.

Her Seer's sight roamed the room and her heart banged against her breastbone when she saw D'Anu Coven members behind some kind of magical force field that shimmered beneath the ballroom lights. Some witches paced while others slept, and a couple simply stared into the darkness with glazed eyes. She saw Janis, John, Iris, Mary, Sandy, Mackenzie, Sydney, and the others, including the apprentices. And there—Rhiannon!

The images vanished, leaving only a thin trail of fog.

"No!" Silver's eyes grew wide with panic. "You didn't tell me where they are!"

Polaris hissed.

From the cauldron, nothing.

"Please, please, please!" She grasped the handles and urged her magic to join with the water, to coax from it another vision that would tell her where the witches were being held as prisoners.

Nothing.

Silver waited a full five minutes, pleading with the Ancestors to show her more, but it was no use.

Frustrated, she whirled away from the table and headed toward her computer station. Her heels rang loud and sharp against the wood flooring, every step a staccato echoing her anger. She flopped onto the computer chair and immediately brought up the American D'Anu Covens' secret Web site. It also had an e-mail system, a special means of communication that had been developed by one of the members who was a software engineer.

She entered the system and searched the roster for each of the telephone numbers of the high priestesses and priests of the twelve other Covens spread across the country. She'd never had need of calling them before, and she didn't have the slightest idea what to expect. They would be willing to send help, wouldn't they? Surely they would.

The twelfth was her father's Coven and she was too chicken to contact him yet. She'd save him for last. When he found out she had summoned the D'Danann . . . she didn't even want to think what his response would be.

Silver picked up the cellular phone from beside the computer and punched in the first number.

8

The shop's plate-glass window felt cool against Silver's palm, contrasting with the burn and frustration in her body. Her breath misted the pane while she stared out into the early evening fog. It was the same afternoon that she had scried the scene of her Coven members being held prisoner.

Of those D'Anu priestesses and priests she'd been able to contact by phone, the reception had been awkward, chilly even. Especially when she mentioned the Tuatha D'Danann. However, each one had promised to convene an emergency Coven meeting to discuss the matter and whether or not they would be willing to send aid.

Those she hadn't reached, she'd left messages for, and hoped they'd get back to her soon.

The only Coven she hadn't called *yet* was the Salem Coven—her father's. She knew she needed to contact him, and that he would find out sooner or later. She just didn't have the guts to tell him what she wanted to do—and what she had done—yet. She was also afraid he would insist on coming to San Francisco, and for selfish reasons she didn't want him or her mother anywhere near the danger.

But the other Covens . . . *they should send help!*

Silver had also called Jake, and he'd promised to stop by this evening. They'd been through a lot together, but he was never going to believe this. He had to—she needed as much help as she could get.

Unable to sit idly by and wait, Silver had tried scrying with her cauldron again, but it had shown her nothing.

Nothing.

Goddess bless! Her heart felt wrenched in two. She didn't know what to do to help her people now.

"But I *will* find a way," she muttered, fogging the window even more. "Even if I have to perform the summoning ceremony a thousand times."

Only she was afraid each time she performed the ritual, it would make her weaker, even more unable to protect herself or her people. Mrs. Illes had taught Silver gray magic before the ancient witch passed on to Summerland. *"Gray magic,"* Mrs. Illes's voice whispered through Silver's mind, *"there is always a price to pay."*

But the price was necessary.

While she stared out into the growing darkness, she let her fingers trail through the mist on the pane. The fog was denser than normal, somehow more eerie. She could barely make out the cracked sidewalk or even the pock-marked and scarred asphalt street. The outside cold seeped inside the building and into Silver's bones. What if the Fomorii were out there now, ready to take her, Eric, and Cassia?

She shuddered and turned away from the window to the Coven's shop, which usually gave her some amount of comfort. Moon Song was the name of the Pagan metaphysical store and tea shop she managed. Normally it filled her with a sense of serenity to look at the crystals, candles, incense, chalices, and blank journals for new Pagans to fill in to make their own Book of Shadows. Moon Song was piled high with innocent items, beautiful trinkets to encourage faith, joy, and bliss—not the powerful tools of the D'Anu. It was like a respite from the dark, twisted evils she saw in the night, a break from the sobering responsibilities of D'Anu heritage. Silver loved seeing New Age Pagans and Wiccans step onto the path of self-discovery, loved knowing the universe would have more positive energy.

In happier times, she could focus on the old phrase, "Every little bit helps."

But all the little bits in the world seemed insignificant now. The shop didn't soothe her. Maybe never again.

Outside the store she heard the familiar clang of a trolley. A foghorn sounded in the distance, drowning the trolley's last happy chime with a low, mournful note. The wail gave her a shiver. She had lived in San Francisco for many years and she was used to listening to foghorns, but this one sounded flat. Ominous.

Angry tears burned at the back of her eyes. Sure, the news channels would report record numbers of people missing over two nights' time—between the Balorites and the D'Anu—but would they ever discover, even believe, how it had happened?

Not that there was anything that anyone could do about it. Except for the D'Anu witches—with the aid of the D'Danann, if they agreed to help.

If I can get any of them, witch or Fae, to listen.

Behind her, light chatter rose from the few patrons in the tea shop. Moon Song was known for its pastries, especially Cassia's scones, and the variety of herbal teas and flavored coffees they served.

But right now Silver wanted complete silence. She pinched the bridge of her nose with her cold, cold fingers. *Plan. I have to come up with a plan.*

Silver swallowed hard as she remembered the winged man from last night. *Hawk.*

Where had the D'Danann gone? Would he return to help her?

I'm so confused. Ancestors, help me, please!

"I'm finished with the repelling potion," Cassia said from behind her.

Silver started, dropped her hand to her side, and turned to the apprentice. Judging by the woman's pale features, she was still shell-shocked from the happenings of last night.

"You used every ingredient from my Book of Shadows?" Silver asked.

The blond novice witch gave a quick nod, her earrings and bracelets flashing with her movements. "It's ready for the ritual."

"Let's finish, then." Silver tried to keep doubt from her voice. Out of every apprentice she'd ever known, Cassia was—well, she was a disaster. Most of the time. Silver did have to give her credit, though. The young witch was an excellent cook.

Heels clicking against the wooden floor, Silver slipped her hands into the pockets of her short skirt as she followed Cassia. She dodged display stands of herbal oils and balms and slipped between the two tables where patrons were enjoying Moon Song's popular edible delights.

Cassia's blue broomstick skirt swished as she bumped into the back of one elderly woman, causing her to drop her pumpkin spice scone onto her plate. "I'm so sorry." Cassia whirled to apologize only to hit the edge of another table with her hip. Ginseng and peppermint tea sloshed from porcelain cups onto their saucers in front of the two women at the table. "Oh, dear," the young witch said to the two women. "May I get you more tea?"

The women simply smiled and declined. Silver took a deep breath of relief as she and Cassia made it to the café counter without further incident. "I'll join you in a sec," Silver said, and Cassia nodded as she slipped into the kitchen.

After a customer paid for a slice of caramel-covered cheesecake, a biscotti, and a large café mocha to go, Silver caught Eric's attention with a wave of her hand, summoning him from where he was shelving new books on herbs, Faeries, and Pagan rituals. He was one of her most valued employees and a powerful witch in his own right. He had nearly completed his twenty years of apprenticeship and would soon be ready to fill a position in the Coven that might open.

Providing there was a Coven left.

He slid in one more book, then sauntered to the café's counter. Eric wore jeans and a GRATEFUL DEAD T-shirt, had short black hair, a broad build, and a swagger that went along with his pretty-boy good looks. But today the thirty-three-year-old man lacked his usual charismatic smile. His expression was tight and his eyes held anger, anger that Silver also felt. Thank the Ancestors he had not been at the meeting hall when the Fomorii had taken the rest of the Coven.

The thought that he could have been taken chilled Silver, but she steadied herself by bracing her hands on the countertop. "Mind closing up shop while I help Cassia with a repelling potion?" she asked, low enough that no one else would hear.

Eric was handsome and always had females fawning over him. But with his expression today, he'd probably scare the hell out of them instead. He attempted a wry smile. "Cassia's making it, eh?" he said.

Silver's mouth twitched despite herself. "She's trying."

"Just watch that she doesn't drop the whole damn cauldron on the kitchen floor." Eric shook his head. "Or we might all be warded from the kitchen," he said, even though he knew that anyone Silver allowed into her circle of protection wouldn't be warded or repelled from her shop.

She raked her hand through her hair. "Are you sure you won't stay in one of the apartments here?"

Eric gave her an almost irritated look. "I live next door, for the goddess's sake. I'll be fine."

Silver bit the inside of her cheek. She truly didn't want any of them to be separated. "Head on home, then, when our guests are gone. But *be careful.*"

"I'll be sure to lock and ward the doors once these people leave. Looks like they're about done," he said, and headed to the front door to flip the OPEN sign to CLOSED.

Silver strode into the small but neatly organized kitchen, where Cassia had gone ahead of her. It always smelled of herbs and spices, freshly baked bread, and whatever delicacies Cassia was cooking. Unfortunately, the witch always managed to break a stoneware bowl or two. Silver had gone to purchasing copper and cast-iron cookware and bakeware since taking Cassia under her wing less than a year ago.

It would be another thirteen years before Cassia could serve as one of the thirteen in the Coven should an opening arise. During her apprenticeship, the witch had to serve a year and a day, sometimes longer, with each member of the Coven. She would serve remaining years with the high priestess until she was an Adept. Silver had serious doubts about the young witch, but only fate knew what would become of her. One never knew.

"I did everything exactly as outlined in the book," Cassia said as she stood at the stove.

Silver nodded, but the scent of the brew told her at once that two key ingredients were missing. How Cassia could bake incredible pastries yet leave spell ingredients out of a potion was beyond Silver's comprehension.

She went to the bookstand where Silver's precious family Book of Shadows was opened to a repelling spell. Cassia ran her finger down the list of ingredients. "I put in the pinch of sandalwood, a dash of rosemary, two tablespoons of dragon's blood, one cup of pennyroyal, and two cups of nettles."

Silver sniffed. The sandalwood, rosemary, and nettles smelled just right. The dragon's blood and pennyroyal were a little off, but close enough. Silver fingered the ancient parchment page of the book. The page was beautifully decorated with dried herbs and flower petals pressed around the antiquated script, just like all the other pages in the book.

Silver carefully turned the page and pointed to the top two ingredients as she glanced at the witch. "Did you remember the thistle and bergamot oil?"

Cassia's cheeks blushed bright pink. "I didn't think to turn the page. Damn—er, bless the moon."

Silver barely kept her focus on Cassia as the apprentice put in several drops of the oil and a thistle plant. Her mind kept returning to last night, and to her memory of Hawk. Why had she been chosen for the warning?

And why had she been the only one able to escape the Fomorii?

Her gut clenched at the thought of Rhiannon being taken along with other Coven members. If only her fiery friend was here, she'd have somebody to talk to, somebody to plan with—fresh ideas. Maybe a more level head than her own.

Goddess. Is Rhiannon still alive? Are any of those from my Coven still whole? Mackenzie, Sydney, all of them, gone. And a year ago Copper. Goddess, this is too much loss.

Her attention snapped back to the apprentice who now stirred the concoction that boiled in several cups of consecrated water. When Cassia finished, Silver took a deep breath of the brew. "Perfect," she said, and Cassia smiled.

"Stir the brew exactly three times clockwise, three times counterclockwise, and three times clockwise again," Silver instructed Cassia.

While the apprentice did as Silver bade, she chanted.

> *"Ward this shop and all who keep it.*
> *Turn back outsiders who would do harm.*
> *Reverse all sent spells, ill-will, and charms.*
> *Keep us free and clear and fit.*
> *In the name of the goddess we make this plea.*
> *Ward this shop. So mote it be."*

"That should do it." Silver glanced at Cassia. "For good measure pour the liquid from the brew into these vials." She gestured toward a collection of blue, green, and brown bottles in a glass-fronted cabinet. "Pour a vial along the front and back thresholds, and along every windowsill." As an afterthought she added, "It wouldn't hurt to mop the floor with it. Last thing we want is something to get through our other floor wardings and come up from below."

The witch gave a quick nod, then bit her lower lip. Silver could see fear in the apprentice's eyes.

"Will this keep those—those demons out?" Cassia glanced at Silver. "The traditional warding spells and blessings didn't keep the D'Anu safe last night."

"The D'Anu never expected anything to come from the ground." Silver gave her a hug and patted her back. Cassia smelled of the cinnamon and other spices she'd used to make pumpkin cheesecake earlier. "Between the potion, the spell-casting, and every other repelling charm in this shop," Silver said, "I think we'll be safe here. We have far more warding than the Coven had, and the potion will simply make it stronger."

Warding bells tinkled in the shop and Silver heard the side door slam. Something in her gut told her that she'd better double-check to make sure the door was locked. Eric was usually very careful, but still . . .

She turned to head through the kitchen doors to attend to it. She heard a crash and a low curse behind her, but simply sighed and left Cassia to whatever destruction she would cause in Silver's absence.

She paused just before pushing the door open and stepping over the kitchen threshold. Cold fingers of instinct dug at the back of her neck.

Something . . . off.

Something . . . wrong.

The shop was noticeably silent, but it was more than that. A presence. Something that didn't belong.

Evil? Her heartbeat doubled. *But why don't I detect it?*

She stepped from the kitchen to behind the café counter, and the door swung closed behind her. Her fingers twitched and sparked.

Her shop was eerily empty and the lighting seemed dimmer than normal. Apparently the last of their customers had left, along with Eric.

Only those within her circle of protection could cross her warding spells—unless their magic was far stronger than hers. The thought made her stomach clench and she wished the repelling potion had already been distributed to enhance her own magic.

Warding bells on the side door tinkled again. Air breezed through the shop. Her heart slammed in her chest.

She wasn't alone.

9

"You let her escape?" Junga growled at Hur as she dug her nails into her human palms. "I send you to fetch a single witch and you could not perform such a simple task?"

He glanced at the other employees currently checking guests into the Marquis Hotel. One of the women looked at them, but quickly turned back to hand a guest his key card.

Junga lowered her voice but didn't keep the scowl from her face. "The next time I send you after her, you had better not fail me." She clasped her fingers around his wrist and allowed her magically enhanced Fomorii claws to lengthen just enough to pierce his soft skin. "Darkwolf wants her."

He winced but held still. "I understand, *ceannaire*."

Still seething, Junga retracted her claws and strode toward the ballroom. When she walked into the room, one look took in the witches kept behind Darkwolf's powerful shield of magic. The warlocks were not contained, but they were not allowed to leave the ballroom, except for the high priest. Junga wished they had all thirteen warlocks instead of having dined upon the unfortunate few.

Darkwolf and Bane were talking just feet away from the shielded witches. "I can get none of the witches to cooperate," Bane said through clenched human teeth as she approached.

"What about that one?" Junga indicated a strong-looking female witch clothed in an iridescent robe that shimmered beneath the lights. She had a proud tilt to her head and an expression of fury on her face. In her multicolored apparel, and with her fierce look, she stood out among the other somewhat blander candidates.

Bane gave a stiff nod of his human head. "I will retrieve the prisoner and bring her to you."

Junga simply focused on the witch who refused to lower her gaze or turn away. This one was full of spirit—spirit that Junga had every intention of turning to her own advantage. Rage, willfulness, pride—all of those qualities made a witch vulnerable, with the right shaping.

When he reached the force field, Bane looked to Darkwolf. The warlock held up his hands and his dark eyebrows narrowed in concentration. Purple light spilled from his palms as he projected his energy through the shield. Thick purple ropes lashed around the witch, binding her hands to her sides so that she could not use her magic. Fortunately, these witches had to use their hands and were not capable of mind incantations.

The high priest used a pushing motion with his hand and the shield bowed inward until it passed around the witch and refastened behind her so that she stood alone. Her eyes were angry, defiant, as Bane grasped her upper arm. He dragged her so that she stumbled across the ballroom floor until she stood mere inches from Junga. Bane took the witch's shoulders in a firm grip, forcing her to stay in place.

The interesting captive said nothing, simply stared at Junga. With a cold smile, Junga reached out and caught the witch by her chin. Again she followed Elizabeth's instincts. She brought her mouth to the witch's and slowly licked her lips. The witch jerked her head back, but Junga tightened her grip, and Bane didn't let her shoulders go. Junga bit the witch's lip and she cried out in surprise, allowing Junga to force her tongue inside the woman's mouth. Apparently Elizabeth had delighted in the pleasures of females as well as males. Junga enjoyed breaking through the haughty witch's reserve with the intimate, unwelcome kiss.

Junga raised her head and lightly stroked her fingers over the witch's cheek. The woman had a look of revulsion upon her face. "I believe I heard one of the others call you Rhiannon, yes?" Junga trailed her hand down the woman's throat until her fingers grasped the witch's neck. "Of course it is so. I have a perfect memory. You are Silver's friend."

Rhiannon continued to glower at Junga, her green eyes flashing with fire, but kept her silence.

The Fomorii's smile grew colder. "Tell me how to draw out this witch. Tell me where to find Silver."

The woman finally spoke, slowly and deliberately, as if addressing a simpleton. "May the Ancestors banish you back to Underworld."

Junga reacted immediately, as Elizabeth would have. She drew her hand back and slapped Rhiannon so hard the witch's head snapped to the side. A white handprint remained and quickly turned to red. It would no doubt become a healthy bruise. Rhiannon slowly turned back to face Junga, her features almost expressionless, as if the slap had meant nothing.

A low, fierce growl rose in the Fomorii legion leader and her own instincts took over. Her fingers elongated into claws. The new magic from Queen Kanji's smith flashed at the tips. Her teeth lengthened long enough to pierce her tongue. The taste of blood flooded her mouth and she had the intense desire to eat this bitch, to devour her while she still lived.

She slashed her claws across the other side of Rhiannon's face, slicing four perfect lines through the thin flesh of the witch's cheek. This time Rhiannon shouted her surprise and pain, then bit her lip as if to hold back any more cries. Blood welled in the cuts and dripped down the witch's face. And the cuts—they seemed to burn into the witch's face. Perhaps witches were vulnerable to iron, as well?

With all her strength, Junga regained control of herself before she destroyed the witch. Her claws slowly retracted back into her human fingers, and her teeth returned to their human size.

She curled her lips as a thought occurred to her. She leaned forward and lapped at Rhiannon's cheek, the taste of the witch's hot blood pleasant on her tongue. She licked the witch's lips next, spreading the red fluid across her mouth. Junga drew back. Irritation flashed through her when Rhiannon didn't so much as flinch. But it pleased Junga to see blood flowing freely down the witch's cheek, to her neck, to splatter onto her colorful robe.

"You will be of great use to me." Junga gave her a wicked smile. "I know exactly how you will assist me in capturing the witch."

Not even a flicker of concern passed over Rhiannon's features and Junga wanted to lash out at her again. Perhaps this time opening her throat. Instead, Junga gestured toward Bane to return Rhiannon to the magical holding cell, Darkwolf assisting with his magic. Rhiannon's bonds were released and Junga smiled when she saw the witch rub the blood from her mouth and cheek with her sleeve.

The next few moments went quickly as a red-scaled shape-shifting Basilisk and a Fomorii warrior were stationed at the doors and lights dimmed for the night. Still furious, Junga caught the attention of the Balorite high priest, who was speaking with Za in one corner of the room. She slowly perused the warlock whose Balorite name was Darkwolf.

She motioned for the warlock and Bane to accompany her into the quiet hotel lobby. "Follow me," she ordered the two males. She had to work off her anger and frustration so she could think clearly. She knew exactly how to do it. She'd wanted this for so long. *Needed* it.

Bane was still in human form as she had not instructed him to return to his natural state. Not one of her legion mates would do anything without her instruction.

Darkwolf kept his expression blank, yet she swore she saw a knowing glitter in his eyes.

The heels of her bloodred stilettos clicked across the marble floor of the hotel lobby toward the bank of elevators as they threaded their way through several of the hotel guests. The heels matched the tailored suit Elizabeth had been wearing when Junga had taken over the woman's body, mind, and soul. Bane still wore the expensive suit of his host. The warlock had donned his usual black robe.

Junga led the males into the elevator and up to Elizabeth's penthouse on the top floor. She keyed in the entry code, then strode into the sumptuous suite with its thick white carpet, black furnishings, and freeform works of art. She sank into the exquisite leather of one of the black couches and crossed her elegant legs. The short skirt of her suit slid up her thighs in an enticing manner. Every instinct ingrained in Elizabeth's body and mind came automatically and naturally to Junga.

Elizabeth's essence even relished Junga's rage, and her blood pounded all the harder because of the sensations associated with the emotion. Heat. Strength. Violent urges not unlike bloodlust. Junga knew she had to relieve the fury, and she knew how she planned to calm the raging beast within her.

"Strip," she ordered the two males.

Without question, Bane removed his clothing, from his suit jacket and shirt, to his shoes, socks, belt, trousers, and boxers. Junga's host body reacted immediately to the sight of him. Elizabeth had considered him a perfect male specimen. Junga's breasts ached, her nipples tightened, and her pussy was drenched with juices.

She turned to the warlock. His arms crossed his chest, a dominating glint in his eyes. "Remove *your* clothing," he demanded in a tone that shocked Junga. She'd never been spoken to that way—ever. But somehow it turned her on. Made her pussy spasm.

She hesitated, but then drew on her authority. "Watch yourself, warlock. Because I am in the mood to play, I will allow this game to continue. But do not overstep your boundaries."

He slowly approached her, like a wolf pacing its prey, his dark eyes glittering.

Junga shivered with lust. What harm could it do? If the man annoyed her too much, she would eat him, useful or not. Eye or no eye.

"Now," he commanded, and his dark power emanated off him in waves.

Her heart pounded as she slipped off the red heels and stood. She was shorter and smaller than the males. Her fingers trembled as she unbuttoned, then slid off the tailored suit jacket to reveal her satin bra. Vaguely she was aware of Bane, and a part of her wondered what he would think of her allowing herself to be dominated. But all thought fled her mind as desire rushed through her at the hungry look in Darkwolf's gaze.

"Hurry," he demanded, and she rushed to unfasten her skirt and let it drop to the carpet. The warlock's eyes burned through her as she removed the bra and shimmied out of the garters and the tiny scrap of panties.

When she was naked, she enjoyed the rush of cool air over her body, the silken feel of it on her human skin, and her long black tresses caressing her shoulders and back.

The warlock gave a soft murmur of approval. He slowly walked around her and she shivered from the heat of his gaze.

These human bodies might be pathetic in many ways, but the sensual feelings she experienced were so much stronger now than when they were in Fomorii form. It had been centuries since they had been exiled to Underworld. Centuries since she had taken over other beings. She truly hadn't realized just how much she had missed sex in another creature's body.

The heat of her anger returned, and she needed immediate fulfillment. Without ceremony, she shoved the Balorite warlock backward. Darkwolf looked enraged, but Junga didn't care. He winked out of her consciousness like a distant star.

"On your back," she ordered Bane. When he obeyed her, she straddled him and sank down to her knees. She wrapped her fingers around his cock and he sucked in his breath. She enjoyed the feel of the soft skin covering the hard shaft. So different from a Fomorii's.

From somewhere in a distant universe, she heard Dark-wolf growl, "Fine, if that's the way you want it . . ."

Junga dismissed him from her mind again. All that mattered was Bane and his cock, and getting the damned thing inside her before she burst from fury and frustration. With hurried, commanding movements, she guided his cock into her pussy, and couldn't help the purr of pleasure that rumbled in her chest as his thick girth widened her, filled her.

Yes. This was it. Just what she wanted. Definitely what she needed.

Bane groaned in obvious pleasure and he grasped her by the waist. She bent down and kissed his mouth, her nipples brushing his chest as she rocked her hips. "Yes," she hissed. The sensations were incredible.

Rough hands grabbed at her shoulders, pushed her forward. "What?" The word came out in a gasp as Junga felt Dark-wolf's cock press against her anus. The pressure was elec-tric, making her clench on Bane's throbbing erection.

"What are you doing? I haven't given you permission to touch me!"

Darkwolf slapped her ass and she cried out in both sur-prise and pleasure. The warlock shoved his erection into her tight hole and she nearly screamed as he took her. Appar-ently, this was something Elizabeth had enjoyed before and Junga felt little pain at the intrusion. Mostly pleasure as his long, thick cock forced its way into her ass.

Pleasure, and rage, and a small, growing distress that this situation had somehow left her control.

Junga began rocking back and forth, feeling the fullness of both cocks nearly to her belly. "Fuck me," she gasped, and both males responded with eagerness.

Ah, yes. This was how she could regain control. Males were males in any species, led by the drive to breed and be pleasured.

"Fuck me, now. Harder! Work for it, both of you."

"I'm going to fuck you so hard, you'll see stars," Dark-wolf said in a voice so deep it could have been a demon's. She shuddered but rocked faster against him.

"That's it," she purred until she could no longer speak as the two males drove into her. Bane grasped her hips as he thrust up and Darkwolf held her waist as he knelt behind and plunged in and out of her.

No matter how she tried, she couldn't hold back moans of pleasure as the warlock and the Fomorii fucked her so completely. She rode them hard, demanding, pushing back, pouring her energy into the motions and sensations until any last thread of anger faded as she gave herself up to the experience.

"Do not climax until I give you leave," Darkwolf ordered Junga, and she was too overwhelmed, too filled with lust, to be angry at his command. "This is going to hurt so good." He slapped her ass between thrusts, forcing her to cry out.

Bane and Darkwolf slammed into her so powerfully she cried out again at the pain and the pleasure of it. Her orgasm rose closer and closer, alien in its intensity. When she felt herself reach the peak she said, "I'm going to come!"

Darkwolf slapped her ass again. "Not yet."

Mini-shudders took over Junga at the feeling of being fucked by two males at one time. Even the sensation of being slightly over the edge . . .

They fucked her until she trembled so badly she knew she couldn't hold back any longer. At that moment Darkwolf shouted, "Come, now!"

Everything was so wild, so strong, that she saw sparks in her head, just like the warlock had promised. She felt the throb of the cocks filling her, felt their fluid shooting into her pussy and her ass.

A very female human sensation overtook her, as if she were bonded with these two males. What did they think of her? What did they think of her body?

Horror at the weakness of her thoughts caused her world to darken and she tumbled closer to the abyss. She collapsed against Bane's chest, clinging to the last shreds of consciousness until she could do nothing but let it slip away.

10

Silver's jaw tightened. Before she could demand that the being show itself, a man stepped from around a shadowed corner of the shop.

The D'Danann.

Or was it?

Silver narrowed her eyes. She splayed her fingers on the
polished wood countertop, prepared to use her gray witchcraft to do whatever was necessary to protect herself and
Cassia, no matter the cost.

He moved toward her slowly, his stride lithe and smooth.
When soft lighting touched his features she saw that yes, it
was Hawk of the D'Danann, but without his wings. The
man's eyes were warm amber, and his expression concerned.
A measure of relief eased through her.

This man—this being—was in full control of himself, it
was obvious. His shoulders were broad, his chest muscular,
his stride confident. He wore a sleeveless leather shirt with
the ties hanging loosely at the neck. His arms bulged with
power and his boot steps sounded loud and purposeful
against the shop's wooden flooring. He wore all black
leather, and a sword and dagger sheathed his sides. His
ebony hair brushed his shoulders, and stubble darkened his
rough features.

And those golden-amber eyes. They focused on her,

mesmerizing her, trapping her. Instinctively she realized this was a man who knew no fear. She didn't understand it, but her heart told her he was proud, arrogant, perhaps reckless . . . but honest and loyal.

"Hawk." She tried a smile. "You returned."

He gave a deep nod. "As I assured you I would." The heavily accented words rolled over his tongue, sounding almost Gaelic, which would make sense considering the D'Danann had driven the Fomorii from Ireland.

"I don't suppose any more of you just happened to show up." Silver pushed the heavy fall of silver-blond hair from her face in frustration. "These demons are running loose in the city, and I have no help."

He stepped forward and rested his hand on one of hers and an electric feeling tingled through her body that had nothing to do with fear, just like that touch in the alleyway that had sent her senses reeling. "I am here," he said.

"I can't believe there's only one of you." Just the contact of his palm against her hand was enough to unnerve her, so she moved her hand from beneath his. "How can just one of you help save us?"

"There are others. We are Enforcers, an elite group of D'Danann warriors," Hawk said quietly. "More will come. It is what we do."

"But your race is neutrally aligned." Silver braced her hands on the countertop again, only to have Hawk capture one beneath his palm a second time, as if he needed the contact. "How do we even know your Chieftains will choose to serve our side?"

"We will learn their decision if—*when*—you perform another summoning." Hawk squeezed her hand tightly. "But I believe the D'Danann will come to the aid of the D'Anu. After all, we are all the children of the goddess."

She pulled her hand from beneath his again and rubbed her palm along the silver snake bracelet, seeking some kind of comfort. The snake's tail rested on the back of her hand while its body and head crawled up her wrist. As she rubbed the snake, its amber eyes glowed.

A tickling feeling prickled at the back of Silver's neck.

Her heart pounded like ritual drums. A wave of cold swept over her body. She raised her hands.

Hinges creaked on the back door and warding bells jangled.

From her side vision, she saw Hawk draw his sword from its sheath, the scrape of metal against leather loud in the stillness of the shop. His features tightened into a grim line. "What is it?" he asked in a low tone.

A shadow flickered across the opposite wall. Hair on Silver's nape rose and her fingertips sparked.

A tiny, dark figure darted around a rack of robes—

Silver's fingertips sizzled brighter until she saw the little furry figure.

Spirit. Rhiannon's mischievous cat.

By the Ancestors!

Silver relaxed with relief, but was tempted to blast the familiar just for scaring the spells out of her.

She wanted to blast Hawk, too, when the corner of his mouth twitched into a grin.

"Stupid cat." She wheeled on her heel and marched from the café's counter to the closed door and flung it open. She strode inside the kitchen, leaving the cat and the man behind her.

Cassia was withdrawing a pan from the oven. The warm smell of fresh-baked chocolate chip cookies enveloped Silver. Her stomach growled, which only heightened her irritability at being scared spell-less by Rhiannon's devil of a familiar.

At the thought of Rhiannon, Silver's gut twisted, and her anger multiplied. She would give anything to have her friend here. She would gladly trade places with Rhiannon so her friend would be safe and sound.

"Did you distribute the potion at all the windows and doors?" Silver asked Cassia, knowing that had been impossible considering the apprentice hadn't been out of the kitchen.

Cassia frowned as she placed the pan of cookies on a cooling rack. She flushed, her cheeks a glowing red. "I don't know what I was thinking."

Trying to hold her temper, Silver placed one hand on her hip and made a sweeping gesture with her other arm. "What could be more pressing than protecting—"

Hawk bumped Silver's shoulder as he strode past her. Cassia's jaw dropped.

"Mind if I have one?" he asked, reaching for one of the saucer-sized cookies. The heat of the pan or the cookie didn't seem to bother him as he scooped one up.

Silver's irritation over the warding failure eased when she saw the witch's distress. She moved to Cassia's side and put an arm around her shoulders. "This is Hawk of the D'Danann." She glanced up at the man. "Hawk, this is Cassia."

Cassia's eyes grew wide. "You truly summoned them?"

Hawk held the gooey cookie in his big hand and glanced hungrily at it.

Silver waved her fingers. "Go ahead."

The D'Danann sighed in obvious bliss as he took a bite. "These were not around the last time I was on Earth."

Silver couldn't help a little smile at the boyish look on his face. For such a big, strong warrior, part of him was like a little kid.

"Spirit?" Cassia glanced down at the cat who must have followed Hawk. The cat hissed. Arched its back. Scampered up the stairs to the rear of the kitchen. Silver frowned as the cocoa-colored cat disappeared from sight.

Mortimer peeked out of Cassia's pocket and this time Silver laughed. Looked like the little familiar could more than take care of himself.

Silver turned back to Hawk. He had one hip against the counter with a half-eaten cookie in his big hand—his third already—a smudge of chocolate on his lower lip. Silver had the sudden desire to lick the chocolate off, and she had to mentally shake the thought away. Hawk stuffed the rest of the chocolate chip cookie into his mouth, looking utterly blissful as he devoured it.

"How did you get in?" she asked.

Hawk shrugged one large shoulder. "The back door was unlocked. I locked the door behind me to ensure we wouldn't be disturbed." He frowned. "I don't understand how that cat entered with the door secured."

"Spirit has his ways. He's like a ghost." Silver brushed that question aside, more concerned that Eric had left the door unlocked. How could he do that when he knew they were in danger? They all needed to rise above carelessness and normal mistakes.

Hawk was now licking chocolate from his fingers. Silver blinked. All six of the giant cookies were gone.

Great. She had one hulking bird man with a thing for chocolate chip cookies, and he was her only hope for battling the Fomorii.

Silver barely heard Cassia chattering about something. The smudge of chocolate was still on Hawk's lower lip. She found herself moving toward him as if bespelled. She brought her fingers to his mouth and rubbed the chocolate away. His lips were firm, yet soft, and a thrill shot from her breasts to her belly.

Hawk's eyes darkened to a deep shade of amber. Hunger flared in his gaze, and certainly not for more cookies.

When she realized what she was doing, her cheeks heated and she took a step back. "You had some chocolate . . ."

Something about him called out to her. Intense. Fiery. Magical.

She took a deep breath. *I'm losing my mind. Yup. Definitely losing it.*

He gave her a slow, sensual grin.

Before Silver could bind his lips shut with a simple little spell she'd practiced, the door to the kitchen opened.

Hawk whirled, drawing his sword in the same motion. Silver's hands automatically raised and her fingertips sparked.

But the moment she saw it was Jake Macgregor, her muscles went limp with relief and her fingertips no longer sizzled. Blessed goddess, hadn't they locked that door, too? Were they all losing their minds?

In the next moment, Jake had drawn his gun and had it trained on Hawk. "Put down your weapon," Jake ordered. "Silver, step away from him."

"Hold on." Silver pushed her way past Hawk and stood between the two men, in the line of fire, facing Jake. "It's all right. He's a—a friend."

"Who in the name of the gods is this bastard?" Hawk growled behind her.

Silver marched up to Jake and brought his gun arm down with a tug of her hands on his wrist. "He's here to help me, okay?"

Still eyeing Hawk with suspicion, Jake lowered his gun and holstered it.

Silver whirled on Hawk. "Put that thing away."

Hawk's glare never wavered from Jake, but he sheathed his sword.

"Men." Silver moved around Jake and shut the kitchen door behind him and this time made sure it was locked before coming around to look from the face of one man to the other. "Jake, this is Hawk. Hawk, this is Jake." She gestured to Cassia who stood behind Hawk. "You both know Cassia."

"I'm so glad to see you." Silver turned to Jake, meeting his blue eyes. He was in full PSF gear, the heavy vest, black pants stuffed into black boots, and cap making him look as sexy as usual. "Thanks for coming."

Jake frowned. "On the phone you sounded like something serious was going down." He folded his arms across his chest and studied Silver. "You'd better explain."

"I'll just go ward the doors and windows now," Cassia said as she snatched up several bottles of warding potion. She dropped one that clattered on the tiled floor and quickly picked it up before escaping into the shop.

While Hawk and Jake continually traded suspicious glances, Silver did her best to explain about the Fomorii and what had happened to the witches and warlocks. It wasn't easy telling him the whole frightening story, and her gut twisted when she told Jake about her Coven members being rounded up by the demons.

When she got to the part about her returning to Janis's home this morning, alone, to retrieve her cauldron and meeting up with the demon, both men cursed. They each grumbled about her going off on dangerous errands by herself. She ignored them and continued speaking.

"We've been through a lot, Silver," Jake said when she finished her story. "But this is hard to swallow."

"You have to believe me." She laid her hand on his arm and searched his blue eyes. "The Fomorii can shift into anyone. They could take over the body of a businessman, a military official, or a cop for that matter. You just don't know."

"Believe it," came Cassia's voice as she entered the kitchen again. "We lost everyone but the two of us and Eric."

"It does not matter if you believe." Hawk's brogue was low, controlled, powerful as he spoke, and Silver shivered despite herself. "We do not need your assistance, human."

Jake focused on Hawk. "What do you have to do with all of this?"

"All right." Silver put her hand to her forehead. "Show him, Hawk."

Hawk's amber eyes flashed with anger as he met Silver's, but she didn't flinch. "Show him that you are D'Danann."

The cop's hand moved toward his gun as a scowling Hawk pushed his chair back and stood at the center of the kitchen. Silver had to squeeze Jake's arm to make him relax. "Hawk is one of the D'Danann warriors I told you about. He's from Otherworld."

Hawk's arms crossed his chest while he stared at Jake. That sound of popping bone jarred Silver's teeth as Hawk's ebony-feathered wings slowly unfolded through his shirt, to their beautiful and full appearance.

"Holy shit." Jake's jaw dropped. "How the hell did he do that?"

"He can fly for you, if you need more proof," Silver said.

Hawk turned his glare on her. "I will not." With a mere thought, he folded his wings away, causing them to disappear again. "This *human* either believes or does not. It matters not to me."

Jake scowled and got to his feet so that he was facing Hawk, but he glanced to Silver, his words obviously intended for her. "Where and when do we start?"

"Soon. I'm not sure *where* to start just yet." Silver stood, moved near Jake, and reached up to kiss his cheek. "I appreciate your help."

When Silver kissed Jake, Hawk wanted to kill the bastard and have done with it. Such incredible jealousy blazed through him that he almost couldn't see straight.

At the same time he wondered why he should care. But for some foolish reason he did. He'd had one mate, and he would never love another. So why this jealousy?

"There are so few of us," Silver was saying. "I don't know if guns have any effect on them, but if you need to—"

"When are we moving out?" Jake said, ignoring Hawk.

Silver rubbed her temples with her fingers. "Goddess. I don't even know where they are." Her gaze shot to Hawk's. "Do you?"

"No. I was unable to locate them last night." He was furious the damnable beasts had evaded him. "They must be cloaked by dark magic."

"Great." She looked back to Jake. "I'll try scrying with my cauldron again. I'll get in contact with you when we're ready. Okay?"

A muscle in his cheek twitched. "You call me the minute you set out after these bastards. Got it?"

Cassia piped up from where she was pouring warding potion along a windowsill. "I'll make sure."

Silver squeezed Jake's arm once more, and Hawk wanted to kill him all over again. "I promise," she said with a half-smile.

She let Jake's arm slip away as he moved toward the door. Jake nodded to Silver before he unlocked the door, opened it, and walked out, shutting it with a solid thunk behind him.

Silver braced her hands on her hips and stared at the closed door. "Jake is one of the best."

"A human will only hinder us." Hawk's expression was one of irritation. "They have no magic, no powers."

Cassia moved to another kitchen window and poured warding potion along the sill. "We can use all the help we can get."

Hawk and Silver faced off with each other for a solid minute while Cassia locked the back door and warded the threshold with potion.

At that moment, the way he was looking at her made her nipples tighten beneath her silky blouse and that place between her thighs tingled. Damn, but he was sexy.

The telephone rang, jarring Silver, bringing her back to reality.

"I'll get it." Cassia dodged around Silver and Hawk, grabbed the phone, and punched "on" before Silver had a chance to fully shake herself from Hawk's mental hold.

That was it—he was using some kind of power to enchant her. To make her want him so badly the world seemed to slip away. It wasn't that he was devastatingly handsome. No. It was something more.

Everything came crashing back to reality as Cassia said, "Silver. It's your father."

Talk about a dousing of cold water. Nothing could cure a good case of lust faster than being told her father was on the line.

Her eyes snapped from Hawk to Cassia. She took a deep breath, threw her shoulders back, and made it across the tiled floor to where Cassia held the portable phone.

Silver took the handset from the apprentice. She clenched the phone so tightly she thought the plastic would crack in her hand. She covered the mouthpiece so her father wouldn't hear. "Don't forget the extra warding with the potion at all the windows and doors upstairs. Oh, and remember to mop the store's and the kitchen's floors with it."

Cassia nodded. "Right away."

Silver gave Hawk a fierce look. "You . . . don't go away. We need to talk."

Without another backward glance, Silver brought the phone to her ear and began walking up the stairs to her apartment.

As Silver left the kitchen, Hawk watched her gracefully mount the stairs. While he studied her, he focused on the way she looked right now. She was simply exquisite. Her long silvery-blond hair drifted over her shoulders and down her back, and he could imagine how it would feel caressing his chest. The tilt of her eyes and the elegant shape of her face reminded him of the Mystwalker women in Otherworld. Her scent lingered, of lilies and a moonlit night.

Silver's silk blouse pulled against her breasts as she brought the phone to her ear. Her skirt was so short he was tempted to tilt his head just right to see what she wore under it, like a besotted young warrior might. Her shoes clicked on the stairs, the high heels making her legs look even longer and sexier.

She murmured a low, "Hi, Father."

Immediately, garbled noise of what sounded like a tirade spewed from the phone. Silver sighed, then disappeared from Hawk's view as she climbed higher.

He clenched his fists at the thought of anyone speaking to Silver in such a manner, but he knew he had no right to interfere. His job was to fight and protect peoples in need.

So long as it was the natural order of things.

With the exception of Davina, such feelings of fierce protection and possession over a woman from any of the Otherworlds had never before happened to him. Yet he had the overpowering desire to keep Silver safe.

Hawk folded his arms across his chest and turned his focus on Cassia, who busied herself by putting a double warding on the threshold and the windows. She had blond curls and eyes of such an intense turquoise shade they seemed almost Otherworldly. And she had an air of innocence that he didn't quite believe. His senses told him she was . . . different. That she was cloaking who or what she really was.

Intuition told him all was not as it seemed.

But if *he* could not determine what she was, then she must be someone—or something—very powerful.

"You're not who Silver thinks you are," he said, watching Cassia closely.

She jerked her attention from her task to Hawk. She gave him a puzzled yet calm look. "Excuse me?"

He waited a few moments to answer, hoping her anxiety would rise. "I'm not sure what you are," he said, "but you're not what you pretend to be. You are something *other.*"

Cassia didn't even look flustered. "I'm a D'Anu apprentice."

"You're more than that," Hawk said quietly. "*What* are you?"

When her blue-green eyes met his, they were wary, perhaps holding a hint of anger in them. "I'm Silver's apprentice. And I'm her friend." She frowned as she brushed her hands on her blue apron. "I don't need to explain myself to you."

He strode toward her so that they were standing but a few inches apart. Being much taller than her, he had to look down to meet her gaze. "If you are a threat to Silver, I will know."

She studied him, no fear in her eyes, only a self-assurance he hadn't seen there before. "Regardless of what you think I am, be assured I would never harm her."

A mouse peeked its head from Cassia's pocket and chittered at Hawk, as if reprimanding him.

Hawk glanced at the mouse, then back to Cassia's face. His gaze held hers a few seconds, and then with a final flash in her eyes, the witch turned away.

Thoughtfully, he watched her for one more long moment. He sensed no animosity, no danger from her. She might bear looking out for, but he sensed nothing beyond the fact that she was *other.* "Thank you for the cookies," he said, before leaving the kitchen to walk back into the shop.

His boots thudded on the wood flooring as he entered the darkened, cluttered store. A variety of smells assailed him. Some familiar, some not. Most came easily to his mind, like this place's language did. Scents of vanilla, sandalwood incense, herbs, juniper, and countless more smells filled the room.

He strode around the perimeter of the shop, as best he could while dodging hanging wind chimes and glittering crystals. He rounded shelves containing books, candles, bottles of potions, and packages of herbs, passed an elegant display case with a variety of jewelry, mostly silver, including multiple pentagrams. Even in Otherworld, the pentagram was a powerful totem.

Who is Cassia? he asked himself as he pushed aside colorful robes hanging on a rack to where the back door was almost hidden. He would tell Silver of his feelings when he had the opportunity.

He tried the knob to the back door and found it locked, but bells jangled above it when he gave it a hard tug. *How did the cat called Spirit enter the shop?*

He rounded the room again and paused to look out one of the front windows. His expanding knowledge of this place through assimilation, and his studies in Otherworld, told him that the metal contraptions occasionally moving up and down the steep hill were cars—a method of transportation.

Hawk snorted. Give him his wings and a good, strong wind over these pollution-causing vehicles.

Before he had arrived at Silver's business and place of residence, he had spent some time investigating the city. The smells, the taste of the air were alien to him. As were the machines called airplanes that flew overhead, the buildings known as skyscrapers, and countless other unfamiliar things. Earth had been nothing like this when he had fought the Fomorii in Ireland all those centuries ago.

While he stared out the window, Hawk's thoughts turned again to Silver. He could clearly picture her as he had seen her on the beach last night. Moonlight caressing every inch of her bare skin. The beauty and grace in her stance, in her poise. The rise of her nipples, the soft seafoam curls between her thighs.

His cock stiffened at once. Gods, how he wanted to touch Silver, to feel her, to be deep inside her. More had called to him than her summoning spell. It had been her spirit, her keen desire to protect her people. Everything about her drew him, almost too much. He could easily lose himself to her, and that was something he couldn't allow to happen.

Guilt at the mere thought assailed him. He would never love or care for another as he had loved Davina.

Never.

11

While she headed up the stairs toward her apartment, Silver bit her tongue hard enough to taste blood. Her father's rants often had that effect. She loved the man deeply, but when he was on a roll, he wouldn't let her get a word in edgewise. Her head pounded with the sound of his voice. What she would give for a good headache tonic right now. Victor Ashcroft's dominating personality had helped drive her away from home to join the San Francisco D'Anu Coven all those years ago.

Victor Ashcroft's deep baritone thundered with reprimand. Silver fought a sense of shrinking to the size of a young clumsy witch who hadn't mastered a single spell.

Ridiculous.

She was an Adept of one of the most powerful D'Anu Covens.

Before the Fomorii had taken every witch in her Coven.

A dull ache settled in Silver's stomach as she pressed the phone to her ear. Still listening to her father yammer, she slipped into her apartment and stepped onto the hardwood flooring. She kicked off her heels and moved to a plush blue and white throw rug that felt soft and comforting beneath her bare feet.

"The entire Coven." Victor's voice chased away any semblance of comfort. Her father always managed to make her feel like she was being yelled at even though he hadn't yet raised his voice. "Gone. All but you and two apprentices!"

"They took us by surprise—" she started.

"Don't presume to think I don't know about your using dark spells, young lady." She could picture his heavy body tense with anger, his face red and his jowls shaking with the force of it. "I saw in my scrying cauldron that you attempted to invoke beings you had no earthly right to call upon. What did I teach you, Silver? No dark magic under any circumstances. We didn't use it to find your sister, and we won't use it now. *No dark magic!*"

Oh. That's why he's so mad. Of course, he thinks gray witchcraft is nearly as bad as black magic.

She straightened her spine. "I did *not* use dark or black magic. Nor will I ever." Even though he wasn't in the room with her, she raised her chin. Clenched one fist at her side. And didn't tell him about the hundred or so times she had used a gray spell to try to locate Copper—with no success. "I am a gray witch, Father. Not a white witch, not a black witch, but gray."

This time his voice blazed as he spoke in a slow, measured tone. "By the Ancestors, I will disinherit you if you dare say that again."

"I am a gray witch," Silver said forcefully. "Copper was—*is*—a gray witch. We believe in fighting back to protect the innocent and those we love. If that means using magic that leans to gray, we will."

"That's it, young witch." His voice went impossibly lower, yet still had the power to intimidate. Still had the power to make her tremble. "You are no longer—"

His words were suddenly cut off as Moondust Ashcroft came on the line. "Silver, dear," she said in her ethereal tone. Silver could picture her mother in a flowing white dress, her platinum-gray hair spilling over her shoulders in a shimmering waterfall. Her gray eyes filled with concern.

In the background, Silver heard her father bellow, "Gray witch, my Grimoire! That's no doubt what brought Copper to her fate. I'll not lose another child to this madness!"

"Hi, Mother." Despite the horrors of the past two days, Silver felt a wash of peace as her attention turned toward her mother. Moondust had that effect on most people, Victor being the exception. But Moondust was the only person who could contradict him, calm him even, take control of a situation without appearing to do so.

"What's this about being a gray witch?" Concern laced Moondust's voice. "You know the line between gray and black is so fine . . ."

"Yes, Mother." Silver kept her tone even. "But I believe that evil allowed to exist could harm us all. What I'm doing is fighting evil, and I believe that's a witch's duty. Protecting the innocent. Balancing the scales of magic. We can't pretend this is all going to go away if we ignore it."

Moondust sighed. "My little witch—"

"I'm a full-grown Adept." Silver pushed her hair over her shoulder as she clenched the phone tighter to her ear with her other hand. "I know what I'm doing."

Silver imagined the determined look on her mother's Elvin features as she said, "I think it best if we come for a visit."

Fear tightened Silver's gut. "No! Stay in Massachusetts. It's too dangerous here now."

Moondust's voice was soft, musical, but Silver knew all too well that her mother would never waver once she made a decision. "When we're packed and find a house sitter, we'll head out on the earliest flight we can catch."

"You can bet your Book of Shadows we'll be out there!" her father roared in the background. "Straighten her out!"

No doubt if witches could really fly brooms like in folk tales, or appear and disappear at will, her father would already be standing next to her. Yes, she *needed* strong witches like her father beside her, but she didn't want her parents anywhere near the Fomorii.

"It's not safe." Urgency and heightened fear rushed Silver. "Let me handle this."

"See you soon, love," Moondust said in her peaceful tone. "Blessed be."

The line clicked. All Silver heard was the hum of the dial tone. A sick feeling filled her belly. Her parents would be here—in danger.

She punched the off button and barely restrained herself from throwing the phone to the far wall. Instead she flung out her arm. Pent-up magic burst from her fingertips, sending her couch pillows flying and tumbling across the room.

One pillow shot past her and took out a vase on an end table, with a smash of glass as it shattered across her hardwood floor. Another pillow slammed into the wall, knocking down an oil painting of the Golden Gate Bridge. The frame broke with a loud crack as it landed. The third pillow gave a soft thud as it hit something directly behind her.

Silver whirled. She stumbled backward as she found herself face-to-face with Hawk. How the warrior had come to be in her apartment so silently, she had no idea. He had one of her sapphire-blue pillows clutched in his big fist and an expression of concern on his handsome features.

Immediately she caught the scent of him. Wild, untamed, and utterly masculine. A thrill rippled through her. The attraction she felt every time he was near was madness.

"What are you doing in my apartment?" She snatched the pillow from him and held it to her chest, doing her best to ignore the immediate effect he had on her. Why did her body tingle from head to toe, just from his mere presence? By all the magic in the city, things were too critical now to be thinking of anything but saving her people.

Besides, she didn't even know this man, this D'Danann.

"We need to talk," he said with an apologetic shrug. "Your door was open."

Silver tossed the pillow back onto the couch and set the phone on her coffee table with a loud thunk. Frustrated, she turned to look at the glass scattered on her floor. Normally she didn't use her magic so casually, but she was in no mood to mess with it in the human way. She snapped her fingers. The glass scooted across the floor into a pile, until her magic retrieved every piece.

She ignored Hawk while she slipped into her closet-sized kitchen, grabbed the garbage can from beneath the sink, and returned to the living room. With another snap of her fingers, glass shards rose into the air and spilled into the can in a glittering waterfall.

Silver returned the can to the kitchen, and after picking up the broken picture frame and putting it aside, she came back to where Hawk stood. He was so large that he dwarfed his surroundings. His arrogant expression and regal bearing dominated the very air between them. The broadness of his shoulders, the way he carried himself—this was a man who commanded attention, who always got what he wanted.

And he was damn sexy.

Silver flicked her fingers at the front door, and it shut with a loud thump. She stuffed her hands into the pockets of her skirt, plopped down on the cream-colored couch, and sat on the edge of the soft cushions. Immediately she jumped up and began to pace. "We're wasting time. Goddess, what is happening? We have to do *something*."

Hawk sat on the couch, on the edge, facing her, his sword scabbard lightly scraping the floor. He looked so out of place on the delicate furniture. His black leather clothing was a sharp contrast against the white of the couch, as were his dark looks.

Out of nowhere came a thought that caused her whole body to flare with heat. What would her pale skin look like against his tanned flesh?

Silver brought her thoughts to an abrupt halt, mentally shaking herself. But then her eyes locked with his for one long moment. A connection sizzled as if one of her spellfire balls had grown between them, drawing instead of repelling.

Hawk could barely take a breath as his eyes held Silver's. But then a movement caught his attention and he tore his gaze from hers. In a flash his dagger was in his hand and poised to strike an enormous snake. It was slinking up the back of the couch behind his shoulders, its tongue flicking out and its wicked eyes focused on Hawk.

His shoulders remained tense even as he realized it was Silver's godsdamn familiar. He *hated* snakes.

Silver moved toward the couch. Gently stroking the snake's scales, she glanced at Hawk and he could have sworn a smile teased the corner of her mouth. "Don't you remember Polaris?"

Hawk slowly lowered his dagger, keeping his eyes on the snake. Adrenaline still rushed through his system as he shoved the weapon back into its sheath. The python flicked his tongue at Hawk who just grunted. The damnable thing had to be eight feet long at least, and as thick as an apple. A very large apple. Out of every creature in this world, the witch had to have a snake.

Silver perched on the edge of the couch again, opposite Hawk. Polaris eased along her shoulders and partially into her lap so that she was stroking his head. "You're the expert on the Fomorii. Tell me what we need to do to send them back where they came from, and we'll do it," she said with a combination of conviction and uncertainty in her voice.

Hawk tried not to look at the snake and studied Silver for a long moment. The proud tilt of her chin, the determination in her gray eyes. Gods, she was beautiful. It took effort to focus on her words. Although the snake made that task a bit easier.

"We need more of my people." He clenched his hands in frustration that other warriors hadn't joined him when he'd been summoned. "Only the D'Danann can slay the demons."

"No killing." Silver shook her head. "They must have weaknesses that can aid us in returning them to Underworld. They can shape-shift into human form, so they have to have some human weaknesses while they're changed, right?"

"That will be to our advantage." He moved his hand to rest on the hilt of his sword.

Silver leaned forward, and Hawk's gaze dropped to the opening of her blouse. The silky material gaped, exposing the curve of her breasts, and he almost groaned.

"How do we know who they are?" she asked while he struggled to focus on the conversation and not the way her nipples rose beneath the silk of her blouse. "They can look like any human," she continued. "For all we know, a Fomorii could now be the governor of California." She frowned. "Which would explain a lot."

"I can sense them—normally." He raked his hand through his hair in frustration. "I believe the warlocks' dark power is shielding them from me somehow."

Silver's pretty mouth twisted with concern. "What if they summon more Fomorii?"

"Because the membrane is so thick between Underworld and Otherworlds, it is likely to be difficult for them to bring over more of their kind." Hawk tapped his thigh with his fingers. "Until the veils are at their thinnest . . ."

Silver's eyes widened. "Samhain. That's when it's easiest to cross worlds."

He gave a slow nod.

"Crap." She rubbed one bare foot over the other. "Tell me more. Maybe something you tell me will help me scry in my cauldron."

"They tend to work in legions. Each legion with a leader," he said. "And likely they found a location to use as a lair and will stay close to it until they summon more of their kind. Not to mention they smell of rotten fish." He frowned. "Except when in forms other than Fomorii. It makes it very difficult to detect them when they are not in their demon bodies, even without the help of dark magic."

She slipped Polaris from her shoulders and draped him along the back of the couch as she eased to her feet. "I need to relax so I can think better. I'm going to make a cup of tea. Would you like anything?"

He followed her lead and stood. "Do you have any more cookies?"

Silver rolled her eyes. Hawk wasn't certain, but he thought he caught the slightest hint of indulgence in her expression. Perhaps a bit of . . . affection? Interest?

Her bare feet padded across the wooden floor until she reached the kitchen's linoleum flooring. "I'll fix dinner and we'll talk about what we need to do next."

With one fleeting glance at Polaris, Hawk took off his weapon belt and draped it over the arm of a chair before following her to the tiny kitchen.

Silver couldn't escape her overawareness of Hawk. When he reached the kitchen he hitched his shoulder against the doorway, dominating the space, his arms folded across his broad chest. Hawk's mere presence unnerved Silver, making her body feel jittery and shivery all at once.

"What would you like to drink?" She peeked into her refrigerator. "I have water and beer."

"Ale would do," he said.

She grabbed a bottle from the fridge, popped it open with a bottle opener, and handed it to him. While he took a swig of beer, then made a face and mumbled about strange brewing practices, she put a small copper kettle of water on the stove and turned on the burner. It made a snapping, then a whooshing sound as it came on, followed by the scent of natural gas and flame.

"What is Cassia?" Hawk asked, startling Silver with the bluntness of his question, as well as his surprising intuition.

"An apprentice witch." She studied Hawk for a moment, then quietly added, "But . . . to be honest, I don't know if she's exactly who or what she claims to be."

His amber eyes expressed his displeasure with her answer. "Why do you allow her to remain if she has not been honest with you?"

She sighed and opened a cabinet to withdraw her favorite teacup and saucer, the one with colorful sprigs of wildflowers gracing the white porcelain. She reached for a handmade teabag with cinnamon sticks and other spices and placed it in her teacup. "I've gone to the high priestess about my feelings, but Janis will hear nothing of it. I'm certain she must know that Cassia is . . ."

"Something *other*," Hawk finished for her.

"I guess so." Silver frowned. For a moment she was silent and heard only the tick of her kitchen clock and the soft hum of the teakettle as the water closed in on its boiling point. "But what exactly she may be," she finally said, "I don't know."

The kettle began to whistle and she turned back to the stove and switched off the flame. "However, I don't think Father would have allowed her near me if he was concerned. She came from the Massachusetts Coven, where my father is high priest."

Hawk still didn't look satisfied when she glanced at him, but as far as she was concerned, there was nothing left to say about the apprentice witch. If she was a witch. Silver would never totally let down her guard, and for now that would have to be enough.

Silver tipped the kettle and poured the heated water over the bag in her teacup. The scent of cinnamon filled the air. While the tea steeped, Silver switched on the oven and set the temperature.

Hawk studied her every movement as she focused on throwing together dinner, his amber eyes dark and sensual. A slight shiver raced through her at the way he was watching her.

From what she remembered from her studies, the Tuatha D'Danann were notorious for their hunger. Part of the legend of the D'Danann was that they even had a cauldron in Otherworld that provided a never-ending supply of food.

Hawk's stomach growled and she managed a smile. "Hold on. I'll have something ready in no time." Silver turned away from him, opened the fridge, and began retrieving the vegetables, homemade sauce, tofu, goat's milk cheese, and handmade pasta she needed to make her favorite meal— organic vegetable lasagna. She gathered the ingredients and placed them on the counter.

While she focused on making dinner, she found herself wanting to know more about him. "Do you have any family?"

When she glanced at him she saw sadness sweep across his face. "My wife Davina is dead." But then the sadness was replaced with a gentle smile. "I do have a beautiful daughter."

Silver's heart ached for his loss as she wrapped her hand around the wooden handle of a vegetable knife, preparing to chop up vegetables for the lasagna. "What happened to your wife?"

Hawk hesitated. Cleared his throat. "I saw a venomous snake near our home, the home we lived in before she died. I could have killed it with my dagger, but I feared it, and believed that my aim wouldn't be true." He rubbed his eyes as if trying to relieve an ache there. "I went into our quarters to retrieve my sword. When I returned, my mate lay upon the ground. A Basilisk's fangs had pierced her chest. Poison flowed from her body and I was helpless to save her." His jaw was tense and his eyes filled with anger. "The Basilisk was nowhere to be found. If only I had not left, if I had killed the snake before it took its true form. I would have gladly died in her place."

"I know what it's like to lose somebody very close." Silver swallowed and put her hand on Hawk's. "I'm sorry."

"I do not deserve your sympathy." He pulled away from her. "I should have slain the filthy serpent with my dagger the instant I saw it."

For a long moment silence filled the kitchen. Silver didn't know what to say. Finally a question spilled from her lips that she'd had no intention of asking. "Why do you fear snakes?"

Hawk ran his palm down his face and for a moment he looked tired. So, so tired. "Keir." His jaw clenched. "When I was a child, my fosterling brother always played tricks on me. He was jealous because he was the bastard son of my father and did not know his mother, whereas I was born of my father's true union.

"One day he made a pit and filled it with countless snakes he had captured in the woods." Now the look in Hawk's eyes changed to fury. "I was so young, so small. Keir shoved me into the pit. It wasn't very deep, so he knew I wouldn't be hurt . . . But the snakes. They crawled all over me. Inside my tunic, over my head, into my boots. I did not know they were not venomous, and I was beyond terrified.

"My father came to my aid and punished Keir. For weeks upon weeks I had nightmares of snakes crawling over me, eating me, killing everyone I knew. I should have outgrown the fear, but I never did." His voice was rough and filled with both anger and remorse.

Silver set aside the knife she had been using to cut vegetables as he spoke. She went to him and reached up to cup his cheeks in her hands. He felt warm and real, his stubble rough beneath her palms. His eyes were tortured as his gaze locked with hers. "I'm so sorry, Hawk." She slipped her arms around his neck and placed her cheek against his chest and hugged him, giving him what support and comfort she could.

He was tense beneath her arms, but then relaxed and hugged her back for a few long moments. When they finally parted, she brushed a lock of his long dark hair from his face. "Nothing I say can make you feel better, but I hope one day you will realize it wasn't your fault Davina died."

He gripped her shoulders and set her apart from him, his features hardening back to a stoic mask. "That I shall never believe."

Silver sighed and turned back to preparing dinner. "You must miss your daughter when you're away from your home."

"Aye." He sighed. "If not for my duties as a warrior—duties I chose—I would be home with her now."

She finished slicing eggplant on a wooden cutting board. She grabbed a zucchini and chopped the vegetable as she spoke. "What's your daughter's name?"

Silver glanced at Hawk and saw a smile of pride cross his handsome features. "Shayla. She is beautiful. Strong-willed, and perhaps impetuous, like her father." His smile melted into a frown and a sigh. "I miss her and never leave her for long. She is still so young, even by Earth's standards."

Silver nodded and grabbed a yellow crookneck squash and began to chop it up for the vegetable lasagna. "Of course. Shayla needs you."

Knowing that Hawk was a father, a loving one, she saw

him in a whole new light. He had seemed dangerous and exciting, as well as protective, caring, and kind, even if on the arrogant and dominating side.

Now she tried to picture him holding a beautiful child with dark hair and amber eyes like his own. Kissing the little girl's forehead, hugging her tight, and tucking her into bed.

The thought warmed her heart. What would it be like to have a child? Being so busy with the shop and the D'Anu Coven kept her from thinking about things like having a family, with young witches of her own. She'd had occasional relationships with men, but had parted with each man on friendly terms. Her spirit had always been free and she'd never found a man she wanted to bond with.

After she finished chopping all the vegetables, Silver took another sip of tea to calm herself. She then withdrew a pan from a cabinet and began layering the sauce, pasta, tofu, vegetables, and cheese. When she was finished she slipped the pan into the oven. Hot air rolled over her through the open door before she closed it.

Silver stepped back. "It shouldn't take too long until it's done."

"What, you can't magically bake it?" Hawk said with a smile, and his stomach rumbled loud enough for her to hear again.

Silver withdrew a bag of frozen homemade breadsticks from the small combination freezer/refrigerator. "I could use spellfire, but I'm not sure you'd be up to charred lasagna."

"Right now I could eat anything." He shifted against the doorframe as she arranged half a dozen breadsticks on a baking sheet, then set it aside.

Silver paused on her way to the fridge, and his gaze caught hers. The sudden energy between them was so palpable hair prickled on her arms and at her nape. She forced herself to turn away, to tear her gaze from his. She opened the fridge and withdrew a bunch of romaine lettuce, a tomato, and carrots and took them to the counter.

"Tell me about your family," Hawk said.

Was his voice husky, or was she imagining what she wanted to hear?

Silver paused in mid-motion, then tore pieces of the romaine and tossed them into the bowl. "My mother and father live in Salem, Massachusetts." Tension gripped her body at her next thought. "But they'll be coming soon, after they find a house sitter and catch a flight here." She glanced at Hawk. "I really don't want them anywhere near the Fomorii, but what can I do?"

He shifted. "What are they like?" he asked.

She gave a small shrug. "Mother is beautiful and the calm at the center of the storm." Her mouth quirked as she glanced at Hawk. "My father *is* the storm."

"And siblings?"

Silver finished slicing the tomatoes and tossed them onto the lettuce, then withdrew a grater from another cabinet for the carrots. "One."

When she didn't say anything further, he said, "And . . ."

"She's missing." She swallowed the last of her tea, then finished grating the carrots and added them to the bowl of salad. Without looking at Hawk, she started to clean the counter, wash the dirty utensils and put them away. "About a year ago Copper vanished after she'd left to perform a ritual. One day she was here, living with me and helping me with the store, and the next she was just gone."

"There were no clues?" Hawk's voice lowered, concern in his tone.

"One." Silver concentrated on washing her hands and drying them on a towel hanging on a hook on the cabinet beside the sink. "An outline of Balor's eye had been drawn in the sand. The Balorites must have had a hand in her disappearance."

Memories of her sister washed over Silver as she braced her hands on the porcelain sink and stared at the ring of rust around the drain. "She was so full of life. There was a sparkle to her. The mischievous gleam in her green eyes, the soft glow of her copper hair. And her clumsiness. She would look so beautiful and elegant, and then trip over her own feet. But she laughed. She always laughed."

Hawk came up so quietly behind Silver that his touch startled her when he rubbed his palms along her upper arms and then began to massage her shoulders, her neck, her upper back. His fingers were so strong, so sure. The scent of the lasagna drifted through the kitchen and she heard his stomach rumble again.

The room became quiet, a comfortable silence that lasted while his touch relaxed her, calmed her. She leaned into his grip, welcomed the strength of his hands. Until that moment she hadn't realized just how much she needed this.

When she finally turned to face him, he braced his hands on the sink to either side of her, caging her with his arms. "You are so very beautiful," he murmured in that incredibly sexy Irish brogue that sent waves of desire through her. He studied her with those amber eyes that seemed to see straight into her heart and soul. The heat of his body warmed hers, even though he was inches from her. His scent was intoxicating, filling her in a way she'd never been filled before. She felt comforted by his presence, yet completely aware of him as a man. A man who attracted her like no other man had ever done.

The strong smell of lasagna caught her attention. She had no idea how much time had passed. She ducked beneath one of his arms and grabbed a pair of blue and white potholders dangling on a hook by the stove. "This kitchen is so tiny. You'll have to step back so I can open the oven door."

Hawk moved back to the doorway, and she brought the bubbling pan of lasagna out of the oven and set it on a hot pad. While it cooled a bit, she slipped a pan of breadsticks into the oven to brown. The entire time the bread was in the oven, he kept looking at the lasagna and his stomach rumbled like a lion. She was tempted to grin. She enjoyed making him wait. He looked like such a little boy.

She swallowed the rest of her tea and then decided to add crumbled goat's milk cheese to the salad. After the

breadsticks were browned, Hawk helped her by carrying the
pan of lasagna to the dining area, along with the salad and a
bowl filled with the cloth-covered bread.

The table was in a tiny nook situated in one of the bay
windows that looked out onto the steep hill below, where
she had a view of other businesses, apartments, and the
Transamerica building. She brought another bottle of beer
for Hawk from the fridge, and made herself a cup of hot citrus tea, with a sweet orange scent to it.

While they ate, Silver watched Hawk. He devoured the
meal like a man who hadn't eaten in days. She only played
with the food on her plate, her mind returning to what had
happened to her Coven, trying to figure out what she
needed to do. She set her fork on her plate and rubbed her
arms, attempting to control that antsy feeling that she was
going to crawl out of her skin if she didn't do something
now. But right now she had no place to start. How could
she make plans when she didn't even know where her
Coven had been taken?

Hawk ate everything except what was on her plate. He
wolfed down almost the entire pan of lasagna, five breadsticks, and the rest of the salad.

After he was done, he wiped his mouth with one of the
blue cotton napkins and gave her a boyish look. "Have any
more of those cookies?"

Silver laughed and moved into the kitchen. "I think I can
whip some up for you."

Again he watched as he followed her. He obviously felt
comfortable in her home by the casual way he reclined
against her counter. After she gathered all the ingredients,
she began measuring them into a bowl. She had a feeling
she'd never have enough chocolate chip cookies for this man.

In a large handmade pottery bowl, she combined butter,
brown and white sugars, vanilla, and eggs. Separately she
sifted together salt, baking soda, flour, then tossed the dry
mixture into the pottery bowl. Everything she used was organic and of the finest quality, just as the shop's café did.
She chose a wooden spoon out of a fat jar of utensils, stuck

it into the bowl, tossed in the chocolate chips and started stirring.

While she blended the ingredients, she glanced at Hawk. "Now, why don't you fill me in on more about the Fomorii and the D'Danann?"

Hawk frowned as if trying to determine exactly what to tell her. "We are the people of the goddess Dana. We were the last generation of gods to rule Ireland before the Milesius invasion. We left to be in our own sidhe, a subterranean court in an Otherworld." His features softened. "It is a world of beauty"—he paused—"and dangers."

"I read as much in the ancient scrolls." Silver gave a slow nod. "But what about the Fomorii?"

"At the second battle of Magh Tuireadh we defeated the Fomorii with our superior abilities and with four great talismans," Hawk said. "As you witnessed, no doubt, the Fomorii are violent and misshapen demons. Evil beings led by the most evil of all—Balor." Hawk looked troubled at that. "If the Fomorii summon Balor, things will not bode well for your battle."

A lump formed in her throat at the thought. "Bastards."

"The goddess Dana sent the Fomorii to Otherworld after we defeated them." Hawk's mouth thinned into a grim line. "They preyed upon any races they could capture. The beasts can take over any body they wish to by simply touching their prey. When they move on to another host, they leave behind nothing but an empty shell."

While Hawk talked, Silver stopped stirring the dough. She began scooping out golf-ball-sized amounts of the dough onto a cookie sheet until a dozen large cookies were arranged on the pan.

"The D'Danann lived in another part of Otherworld, so we were not troubled by the Fomorii," Hawk said. "The D'Danann Enforcers were called upon by the Shanai who begged for our assistance. Our elders agreed. We answered their call and again battled the Fomorii. At first we had much difficulty defeating them, as they had developed great fighting skills in Otherworld."

Hawk gestured as he spoke, and Silver found herself fascinated by his strong hands and his long fingers as he told the story.

"Then the tide of battle turned," he continued, "when the Elves and Fae suspended our differences long enough to work together to defeat the Fomorii. We rounded up every one of the demons we could find. We sent them to exile in Underworld."

Silver slid the large pan of cookies into the oven, shut the door, and set the timer. "How did you do that?"

Hawk eyed the oven hungrily. "The Druids now reside in Otherworld, along with other powerful sorcerers and shamans and guardians. With their aid, the Fomorii were sent to roam the depths of the earth, beneath the oceans and lakes. The climate is sufficient to support life, and they have plenty of nutritious slugs and other below-ground creatures to eat. It isn't luxurious, but more than the beasts deserve. Otherwise they would have been sentenced to death."

Silver pushed her hair out of her face as it occurred to her that these D'Danann stood for what she didn't believe in. No matter how evil they were, did the beings the D'Danann fought deserve death? Banishment, yes. Death, no.

"It wasn't until now that some of the Fomorii escaped exile." Hawk glanced at the remaining chocolate chip cookie dough in the bowl. "May I?"

Silver raised an eyebrow and handed him the bowl. Hawk used the wooden spoon to scoop out some of the cookie dough and took a big bite. He closed his eyes for a moment and he gave an orgasmic groan of pleasure. He opened his eyes and dug into the dough. With a smile she just shook her head and watched him devour it.

"Since the D'Danann are neutrally aligned, they may not help us like they helped the Shanai," Silver said quietly, keeping her gaze focused on Hawk.

He sighed and put the spoon back into the bowl. "This is true. If the Elders believe it is time for the Fomorii's rule again, then they will do nothing."

Silver bit the inside of her cheek, hard, before she responded. "And you?"

His eyes met hers. "I want to send the bastards back where they belong. Back to Underworld."

She felt as if some of the load had been lifted from her shoulders. If Hawk agreed to help, wouldn't other D'Danann?

By the time Hawk polished off the cookie dough and all the baked cookies, it was late. Silver had cleaned the kitchen and washed the rest of the dishes, and found herself dragging. It had been a long couple of days and she was beyond exhausted. She needed to be fresh and energized tomorrow if she was going to find her Coven. She had no doubt in her mind that she would.

She was still in the cramped kitchen, with Hawk blocking the doorway, when she was ready to drop. Silver held her hand over her mouth, trying to suppress a yawn. "I don't suppose you have anywhere to stay." She gave him a teasing glance. "Or roost."

Hawk stared at her with those hot amber eyes and she froze. For what seemed like time on end their gazes remained locked.

Magical feelings sparkled throughout her body and suddenly she wasn't so tired any longer. Lust built within until it burned through her, hot and fiery. A need so deep she couldn't deny it any longer.

And she had no doubt he was imagining the same thing she was—

The two of them. In her bed. Naked. Now.

Silver mentally shook herself. What was she thinking? One day of getting to know Hawk and she wanted to have wild and crazy sex with the man? Repeatedly.

Yes!

No.

She took a deep, centering breath and moved toward him. "Excuse me," she said as she tried to squeeze by, tried to escape the confines of the kitchen and the power of his presence. She needed to—had to—do *something*.

Instead of letting her pass, Hawk caught her by her shoul-

ders and pinned his amber eyes on hers. He lowered his
head, and his mouth was so close she only had to move a bit
and their lips would meet. His masculine scent of leather
and forest breezes enveloped her and she tasted his warm
breath as it danced upon her lips.

How she wanted to kiss him.

No. This is crazy.

Who cares?

"Thank you, Silver," he murmured.

"For what?" Her own voice was barely a whisper.

"This," he said, and brought his lips to hers.

12

Hawk gently brushed his lips back and forth over Silver's in a soft, sensual movement that caused her to shiver from head to toe.

She closed her eyes and her sigh became a low moan. He moved his mouth more firmly against hers, and gripped her shoulders tighter. She flicked her tongue over his lips and tasted chocolate chip cookies along with the malt flavor of beer.

It seemed natural to be kissing him. She brought her hands to his chest and felt the play of muscles beneath her fingertips while he moved his hands from her shoulders to the curve of her waist. He eased his palms down to her hips, and moved slowly back up again as if he owned her body.

Silver leaned more fully against Hawk, feeling as if she were sinking into him, becoming part of him. The roughness of his leather clothing branded her through the thin silk of her blouse, and his erect cock pressed hard against the soft skirt at her belly. She grew damp between her thighs with the power of her need for him.

Hawk had to restrain himself from taking Silver down to the floor of her kitchen, hitching up her tiny skirt, and driving into her. By the gods, he needed her, needed to be inside of her.

He had to have Silver. It was all he could think about. His body cried to be with her, demanded it of him.

No, he couldn't. He couldn't take this woman he would never see again once the battle of the Fomorii was over.

Still he couldn't help it as his mouth moved over hers. Lightly he bit her lower lip and she moaned again. Her weight was fully against him and she slipped her fingers into his hair when she wrapped her arms around his neck. With a groan, he thrust his tongue into her mouth. A sweet gasp, then she followed his lead, their tongues meeting. The lightness of citrus tea blended with her sweet feminine flavor. Gods, would he ever get enough of her?

Wilder and wilder their kiss grew, until Hawk thought he was going to lose control. He wanted to rip her clothes from her body and drive his cock deep inside her wetness. Wanted to feel all of her, inside and out. He slid his hands down to her waist again, but this time he grasped her ass, raised her off her feet, and started carrying her toward the couch.

She didn't protest, didn't stop kissing him. Rather, she was like liquid fire in his arms, burning hot against him, her hands moving, exploring. She tore her lips from his and spoke while she sprinkled kisses down the line of his jaw. "My bedroom. Through the blue door."

There was only one door besides the one leading out of the apartment. Hawk reached it in mere strides and flung it open. Her bed crouched at the center of the room, waiting for them.

"Turn on the light," she said in a breathless voice, pointing to a stained-glass lamp. "Pull the chain." Still holding her, he leaned over and yanked the chain on the lamp. Immediately, colorful shades of light sparkled across the white bed covering. He sat on the bed and rolled onto his back so that Silver was on top of him. In a fast movement he flipped her beneath him.

They rolled back and forth, kissing, touching, the fire between them growing hotter and hotter. Soon he didn't know which way was up or down. Felt her softness below him, above him, found himself between her legs, and her thighs wrapped around his hips. He'd never felt anything in his life like this. It was beyond comprehension. As if she had bewitched him completely.

When he was on his back again, Silver placed her hands on his chest. She pushed herself up so that she was staring down at him, her lips parted and swollen, and the luscious curve of her breasts exposed where her top button had come undone. Her skirt had hitched up around her pale thighs. He ran his hands from her knees to her hips and back again, enjoying their softness beneath his callused palms.

He remembered so clearly how she had looked last night beneath the moonlight. She had taken his breath away. Her naked breasts kissed by the silvery light, every perfect curve and swell of her body silhouetted. Even more so now he craved the taste of her skin, the feel of his naked body sliding against hers.

While she looked down at him, her breathing came in soft gasps. Her nipples were hard against the silk of her blouse, and the scent of her desire filled his senses. He swore he saw the hint of a sparkling blue aura around her.

"I want you so badly." Her gray eyes were dark and intent.

He reached up to slip his hand into her silken hair and cupped the back of her head. "What are you doing to me?"

Silver believed in fate, believed in destiny, but this—this was crazy. She wasn't the kind of woman to have sex with a man she'd just met. She had to get to know him first, make sure they connected on a cosmic, spiritual level.

Although, for some reason she felt that deep connection with Hawk.

It was crazy. Crazy, crazy, crazy.

But she didn't care.

She dove for his mouth again, needing to taste his heady male flavor. Her bare folds pressed against the bulge in his pants and her breasts ached for his hands and his mouth. She never wore underwear—all it would take was a simple tug of her blouse over her head, her skirt over her hips, and her body would be free to experience every part of him.

Hawk's hands roamed her body, the heat of his palms stoking the magical fire burning within her. He slipped his hands up to her silk-covered breasts and cupped them, massaging them until she was nearly out of her mind with the desire for his touch on her bare flesh. When he tugged her blouse out of her skirt, she gave both a moan and a sigh of satisfaction as he slid it over her head and her breasts were finally freed to his fiery gaze.

Silver rose up just enough that her breasts were over his mouth. He grasped them both and flicked his tongue from one nipple to the other. She trembled from the incredible pleasure. His mouth was hot and the way he scraped his teeth over her nipples caused her to suck in her breath.

"I want you naked." She rocked her hips against his, feeling the incredible bulge through his pants. "I want to know what it feels like when your skin slides against mine."

Hawk groaned.

She rose up, and with a little maneuvering, she slipped out of her skirt and flung it behind her. Feeling gloriously free and sensual, she moved her bare hips harder against him. She moaned with satisfaction at the feel of the hardness of his cock through the leather of his pants, sliding up and down her slit with her movements. The scrape of leather felt wildly erotic between her thighs. She knew she could climax so easily. It wouldn't take much more.

Her world suddenly spun as Hawk flipped her onto her back and she now looked up at him. "I've got to taste you, woman." His voice was a guttural growl that sent thrills throughout her. "Your scent is driving me mad."

She shivered at the mere thought of his mouth between her thighs. He kissed her hard, then slowly moved his lips along the line of her jaw to the curve of her neck. Rumblings rose up from his chest as he licked and lightly nipped her skin.

Her moans grew more intense. She gripped his long dark hair in her hands, and squirmed beneath him. "Lower. I want your mouth on me."

A low chuckle rose up from him as he laved his tongue over one of her nipples. "My mouth *is* on you."

Wrapping her hands tighter in his hair, she tried to force him lower, down where she wanted his mouth. "You know what I mean."

"Tell me." He kissed a lazy trail between her breasts toward her navel. "Exactly what you want."

She'd never said aloud the more erotic words. They seemed forbidden somehow, and that made her more excited. Squirming beneath him, she murmured, "Lick my pussy, Hawk."

"Hmmmm?" He dipped his tongue into her navel and she cried out. It felt like her belly button was connected to her clit, and she throbbed with the sensation. "I didn't quite hear you, *a thaisce,* my treasure," he said in that Irish brogue that made her want to climax from the sound of it.

"My pussy," she said louder this time. "Lick my pussy. *Please.*"

He traced a path with his tongue through the curls of her mons. Silver didn't let go of his hair and guided him to her folds. He grasped her thighs with his large hands and pressed her legs farther apart so that she was wide open for him.

Hawk audibly inhaled, his eyes closed, and he appeared to be experiencing true ecstasy. "Your scent . . . incredible . . . intoxicating."

She shivered at the intimacy of the act and his words. She was almost out of her mind with the need for his tongue on her. "Hawk. Now."

His amber eyes focusing on her, he used his fingers to pull her slit open so that her folds were completely bared to his view. "Mmmmm. You are so beautiful." His rough stubble scraped the inside of her thighs when he lowered his mouth to her pussy, ever so slowly, until she was ready to scream.

He pressed his mouth to her folds.

Silver couldn't help the cry that spilled from her lips, couldn't help arching up and pressing herself tighter to his face. He licked her from her channel to her clit in one long swipe and she cried out again. His tongue was magic, pleasuring her to the point she was completely mindless. She was barely aware of releasing his hair and grasping the bed-covers in her hands, clenching her fists until they ached.

Her moans and cries grew louder the closer she came to climax. The feel of his stubble scraping the inside of her thighs and the folds of her pussy, the roughness of his tongue against her clit drove her wild. When he thrust two fingers into her channel, she exploded.

Swift and sudden, she cried out as her climax burst through her, suffusing her, surrounding her with brilliant white light that she swore lit up every corner of her bed-room. Sparkles exploded around her. She felt the touch of the Ancestors in her spirit, the call of all the Elements from every direction. Sweet, sweet music that she'd never heard before played through her mind.

The orgasm continued to rock her body until she couldn't take any more. As limp as a lightly stuffed poppet, she collapsed against the bed, her breathing heavy and a light sheen of perspiration covering her skin. She felt boneless, yet somehow complete. And even more full of desire than before—her breasts heavy, her nipples taut, her clit throb-bing. She'd never felt so out of control in her life.

Hawk smiled at the look of sweet ecstasy on Silver's face, and his cock tightened at the thought of fucking her. But no—he would not take advantage of her after all she'd been through. When the time was right, and when he knew she was ready, he'd take her then.

"Mmmmm . . ." Silver murmured.

She tried to face Hawk as he moved up to lie beside her, but he merely turned her onto her side, and spooned her body next to his. He nearly groaned aloud at the feel of her ass through the leather barrier covering his cock. Just the thought of sliding inside her was enough to make him harder than ever.

"Aren't you going to take me now?" she said in a soft, husky voice. "When I wish it, my magic protects me. From everything. It's a shield inside. That way I can feel you, every bit of you."

This time Hawk did groan aloud. He pressed a kiss to her nape. "Rest, *a thaisce*."

"No—you—" she started, but Hawk brought her body tighter to his.

"Rest," he repeated.

Silver sighed. "Only a little while . . ."

When her breathing became deep and even, Hawk eased off Silver's bed. She shivered, as if missing his warmth. He drew the bedcover over her, and disappointment eased through him as it hid her lovely body from his view. But her features were relaxed. Likely she hadn't slept well, if at all, since the Fomorii attack. She had probably passed out from need of rest.

After he gave one last longing look at Silver, he flipped off the light switch on the stained-glass lamp, enveloping the room in darkness. He slipped from the bedroom into the small living room. He started toward the armchair to retrieve his dagger and sword. He stopped mid-step. Polaris's thick, long body was wrapped around Hawk's sword belt and the sheathed weapons. The snake's head was up, his wicked eyes focused on Hawk. Polaris's tongue flicked out.

Again irrational fear squeezed Hawk's insides, as if the python were wrapped around his gut.

Polaris curled his body tighter around the weapons, taunting Hawk, as if sensing his aversion to snakes.

The python's eyes became tiny slits as he rose up several feet and hissed.

Hawk approached the python. He never went anywhere without his weapons, and he was not going to start now. Yet he halted when he was feet away.

He shook his head and gave a self-deprecating grin. He had battled beasts, demons, and other creatures from Netherworld and Otherworlds, and he was afraid of this earthbound snake?

Ridiculous. Time to end this now.

Polaris raised his head and hissed as Hawk approached. He snatched at the belt and the python squeezed tighter. The snake lowered his head, unhinging his jaws, widening his mouth.

With a powerful tug, Hawk jerked the weapon belt from Polaris's grip, backed up, out of the snake's reach. The python hissed and Hawk could swear he laughed, pleased that he had rattled him. Polaris slid over the side of the chair, like silent death, and lithely moved across the floor to Silver's bedroom and through the still open door.

Hawk tensed, his first reaction to keep the snake away from Silver, but he was certain the witch was in no danger from her own familiar.

He, on the other hand, didn't think he could sleep well without the bedroom door locked and Polaris on the opposite side of it.

While keeping a wary eye on the doorway Polaris had disappeared through, Hawk strapped on the belt with the sheathed sword and dagger. The apartment still smelled of chocolate chip cookies and the lasagna Silver had made for dinner. The scents mingled with Silver's exotic perfume that clung to everything in the room.

For a moment his thoughts turned to Shayla. Would she like chocolate chip cookies? He was certain she would. At the thought of his daughter, Hawk had to smile. His heart ached with missing her. Perhaps he enjoyed chocolate chip cookies so much because they were similar to a treat his daughter was fond of, *seacláide*.

He could picture her the last time he had given her *seacláide*, how her mouth and hands had been sticky with the chocolate. She had giggled, her vibrant blue eyes smiling as she sucked each of her fingers. She had been sitting on a chair at the table, her little feet swinging and kicking in the air since her legs were too short to reach the floor. The mischievous expression on her face had reminded him so much of Davina at that moment that his heart had ached.

Guilt suddenly hung heavy in Hawk's belly. He had pleasured Silver, had wanted to be inside her, had felt more than a passing desire to experience sex with her. How could he feel this way after Davina only being gone these two years?

After he relieved himself in the minuscule bathroom, he headed out the apartment's front door. He was confident all was well warded, and he would be able to slip in and out of the rooms with ease. He had no doubt the wardings would keep the Fomorii out, as the only magic the demons had was their ability to take over another being's body and shape-shift. He hated to leave Silver and Cassia at all, but it was time to hunt Fomorii.

When he was in the hallway, he stopped at the door to Cassia's room and put his palm upon the cool wood. What was she? A threat to Silver?

From somewhere down the hall, Spirit the cat gave a loud, "Meow."

If Hawk didn't know better, he would have thought the cat had just given him a vote of agreement. At least one familiar appeared to be on his side.

The wooden stairs squeaked beneath Hawk's weight as he strode down, and he hoped Silver and Cassia wouldn't wake from the noise he was making.

He went through the kitchen to the darkened shop, where he worked his way through the maze of cauldrons, incense, candles, wands, and crystals. Wind chimes stirred and gave soft tinkles as he passed by. The computer screen at the front counter spilled its eerie blue glow over the jewelry counter.

He stopped at the jewelry display case and studied the pentagrams. One in particular called to him, one that could easily be a match to Silver's. It was a silver pentagram with an amber center, only the pentagram was larger than hers. He moved behind the counter and removed the pentagram from the display case. It warmed his hand, the amber glowing in the dimness of the shop. Its power flowed through his body and he knew it was meant for him. He slipped the heavy chain over his neck. He would find a way to repay Silver later.

When he reached the front door, he caught the scent of
the warding potion Cassia had put at the doors and windows,
and had used to mop the floor. Warding bells tinkled when
he opened the door, the only sound on the otherwise silent
street. He twisted the simple locking mechanism on the
doorknob so that it would lock behind him. Quietly he closed
the door, entering the dark street illuminated by an occasional streetlight.

Making sure the fairly dark street was clear, Hawk
cloaked himself and unfurled his wings. With a push of his
mighty wings, Hawk launched himself into the air, rising
higher and higher until he was above the tallest of buildings.
He circled the city, for a moment simply enjoying the freedom of flying, the freedom from the bonds of Earth. When
he had stretched his wings, he coasted lower in the night sky
to begin his search for the Fomorii.

The city was relatively small, surrounded on three sides by
bodies of water. San Francisco was a crowded maze of streets
and hills, brimming with traffic and noise. Sounds of humans
talking, dogs barking, cars honking, the roar of buses, and
the grinding of truck gears met his sensitive hearing. This
changed world constantly amazed him.

Through smells of ocean air, smog, smoke, urine, garbage,
perfume, and countless other odors, he searched for the
unique rotten-fish stench of the Fomorii. His keen senses
sifted out and rejected scent after scent.

Anger burned his chest and he pumped his powerful
wings harder. He would find the damned Fomorii. But how
could he catch their scent since the Fomorii would know
enough to keep hidden, and likely would not keep their demon form?

Memories of his time with Silver continuously warmed
him in the cool night air. There was just something about her
that attracted him more than he wanted to admit. He could
hear her sweet voice in his mind, smell her delicious scent,
taste her on his tongue.

It took much effort to draw himself from the memory of
pleasuring her and to focus on his task. Demon hunting.

He searched and searched until he shouted his fury at his inability to find the damned Fomorii.

It had passed the mid of night when he headed back to Silver's shop, beyond frustrated that he had found no sign of the beasts.

October 26

13

Silver woke with a start, bolting upright in bed, her eyes wide. She knew. Was certain how she could find her Coven. The Fomorii had practically left a trail of breadcrumbs when they'd tunneled into Janis's home.

Early morning sunlight peeked through the curtains, its brightness such a contrast to the darkness of her task. Her gaze darted to the clock, the illuminated green numbers showing that she had slept well over six hours. She felt refreshed and energized, and ready to take on those damned demons.

She scrambled out of bed, almost stumbling in the twisted sheets. The state of the bed pulled her up short, brought reality back home too, too hard.

Heat flushed her cheeks at the thought of what she'd done with a near stranger, but the slight feeling of embarrassment was quickly replaced by pleasure. By the goddess, that had been the best orgasm of her life.

But she needed to forget about last night for now. She needed to tell him what she had realized.

Her head whipped to look at the bed and she saw that it was empty. Hawk was gone.

With a mix of frustration and calmness, she stared at the rumpled coverings. What she had shared with Hawk—it had been nothing short of magical. But why he hadn't sought pleasure himself intrigued her. He had given, yet had asked nothing in return.

And now he was just . . . gone.

She shook her head. She didn't have time for this. She didn't have time for anything. For now, she just had to go.

After Silver took a quick shower, she dressed for the hunt, all in black. She tugged on her jeans, a turtleneck shirt, boots, jacket, and then tucked her daggers into the boot sheaths. She fastened her hair on top of her head with a Celtic-knot pin and made sure her cap and gloves were stuffed into her pocket, then headed out of her bedroom.

First things first. She'd scry with her cauldron to see if she could learn anything new before she called Jake for backup. She hoped Hawk was still around somewhere because she was ready and determined to get going. His help would be invaluable.

But damned if she needed him. With or without the Otherworld warrior, she would take care of business.

When she reached her kitchen, she pulled the pewter cauldron from her cabinet of ceremonial tools, then set it out on the table. She dragged out the large bottle of consecrated water from the kitchen, then lifted it high enough to pour into the cauldron. The water made a chugging noise and rose up almost to the rim of the cauldron before she set the jug down on the floor beside her.

She felt the strength of her familiar's presence even before Polaris hissed and slithered onto a chair, then the table, to curl around the cauldron. His magic joined hers as she stared at the shimmering surface that rippled slightly with the python's movements.

Allowing herself to relax, Silver unfocused her eyes.

Within moments, steam curled from the edges of the cauldron and began to take shape. She raised her head and watched a hallway form within the magical fog. In the vision she could see herself walking down the hallway, straight past a pair of elevator banks.

Silver frowned. A hallway? Elevators?

She felt Polaris's magical push at her mind, as if criticizing her doubt.

The hallway was inside a building, perhaps leading away from a back entrance. Maybe one of the countless towering buildings on Market Street. Her heart started to beat faster, then faster still. All of her senses prickled.

This was just a hallway, a normal hallway in a normal building, but something was very wrong here.

Wary, breathing a little too quickly, Silver forced herself to walk along the corridor. She slipped through a door, into a huge storeroom filled with banquet tables, chairs, and risers. That sense of wrongness grew.

Darkness was afoot in this place. She could feel it seeping across the floor, chilling the air. Danger here. No question.

Carefully, Silver inched across the concrete floor to another door, braced for psychic combat, and shoved it open.

This time she was in a small ballroom. The room was empty and seemed somehow different from the one she had seen in her other vision. It took her a moment to realize the ballroom simply mirrored the other one. In a ghostly haze, she moved across the floor to a sectioned wall. Each section was hinged, as if the wall could fold like an accordion.

She put her hand on the wall.

Her stomach roiled.

Yes. Yes! This was it. Where she needed to be. Where she had to go. She wanted to cast all her spells at once, draw her weapons, charge in and—

A sudden noise jerked her attention away from the wall.

She whirled around—and straight out of the vision. In seconds, her mind was back in her own kitchen. The door to the apartment was flung open and Hawk shut it behind him with a loud thud.

Silver's gaze shot back to the cauldron. The fog vanished. The water went still. *"No!"* She grabbed the pewter edges and shook the cauldron. Water sloshed over the edge and Polaris hissed as it splashed onto his scaly head.

How was she able to break through so much this time? Was her gray magic growing stronger?

She stomped her booted foot on the wooden floor and glared at Hawk. "I was almost there!" she said. "Next time, come in a little quieter, all right?"

"What did you see?" He strode across the small apartment, quickly closing in.

For a moment she almost couldn't breathe as he came within inches of her. He was so gorgeous, and just last night those firm lips had—

Silver shook her head to rattle the image out.

He cocked a brow. "Nothing?"

She shook her head again. "I mean yes, I did see something. But right now it's not going to do us any good. First we have to find the demons."

"I could not locate the bastards last night." The tenseness of his jaw and the whiteness of his knuckles as he clenched his fists told her how frustrated he was. "The magic that cloaks them—Balor himself must be lending his powers."

Silver took a deep breath. "I think I know how to, um, sneak in, right through Balor's magic."

Hawk's eyes riveted on hers. "Speak."

"When the Fomorii attacked, they came up from the ground." Silver rubbed one hand over her snake bracelet. "I'll bet we can track them through the same way they came in."

Hawk's expression didn't change. "To battle that many demons, we need reinforcements."

"That's why I'm calling Jake." Silver walked across the floor to her computer desk as she spoke. "He and his team are professionals and they're trained to deal with the paranormal."

She heard the scowl in his voice when he said, "They are human. To battle Fomorii is beyond their limited abilities."

Irritation flashed through Silver. "Like I said. They're professionals. And unless you happen to have a small army in reserve, they're all we've got."

In her haste to grab the cordless phone, she knocked a picture frame from her desk. Before it tumbled to the floor, Hawk caught it with ease and grace. She grasped her hand around the phone and paused as he studied the picture.

With her free hand, Silver took the framed photograph

from him. Copper's mischievous grin and Silver's own smile told of happier times. The picture had been taken two years ago, but Silver felt much older now, that time had been passing by too quickly.

"That's my sister beside me," she said as she set it back on the computer desk.

"She is nearly as beautiful as you are," Hawk said quietly.

Silver bit her lip at the way he had used the present tense, as if believing that Copper were alive, just as much as Silver did.

After punching in Jake's cell phone number, she raised the handset to her ear.

"Macgregor," he said on the first ring.

Silver told him her plan. "How soon can you gather your team?"

"I'll pick you up in five minutes. My team can meet us at the location in fifteen."

"Good." Silver gave him the directions and punched the off button. She glanced up at Hawk. "Let's go."

When they reached the downstairs kitchen, smells of cinnamon rolls and coffee rose up to meet them.

"Back for more?" Cassia asked Hawk as she pulled a tray of the huge rolls from the oven. "Six weren't enough?"

Silver almost laughed at the boyish look on Hawk's face as he shook his head.

She told Cassia where they were going and the witch frowned. "I should be going with you." Mortimer peeked out from the pocket of her apron and twitched his nose in obvious agreement.

"Someone has to man the shop. I need both you and Eric to handle things." Silver turned her back on Cassia and slipped through the kitchen door, the warding bells barely tinkling as Hawk followed her. With a turn of her fingers she locked the door, then closed it behind her. They strode side by side to the front of the store.

Jake was already there waiting for her, his black motorcycle at the curb with two helmets resting on the seat. He had a dark expression that matched his black T-shirt and snug black jeans. She smelled the heat of the bike's exhaust, and it seemed something more was carried on the wind. Something that didn't belong.

"You know how to get to them?" Jake asked in his deep tone.

"Have I ever been wrong?" she said automatically, and Jake winked.

Their light banter eased a little of her nervousness, but did nothing to cool the anger boiling within her anew at the thought of the Fomorii taking her Coven, and no doubt murdering humans.

Jake flipped down the visor on his helmet and swung his leg over the motorcycle so that he was straddling it. He looked like the real bad boy he was, all in black from shielded helmet to black boots.

When Silver climbed onto the back of the motorcycle behind Jake, she caught Hawk's glare. He didn't seem too happy to have her riding on the bike with Jake. Why the heck was he acting so jealous or protective? Just because of one night of, er, pleasure?

The motorcycle roared through the morning as they headed toward Janis's house, with Hawk flying overhead, somewhere. The moment before he had taken to the sky, he had vanished, cloaked in his own magic.

While Jake guided the bike up and down the steep San Francisco streets, cool air slipped in through the tiniest openings of her jacket, and she shivered. Adrenaline rushed through her body as her mind raced through the options of what they could do to rescue the Coven members. By the Ancestors, she was determined they *would* rescue her people.

In no time they reached Janis's home and Jake parked at the curb. His team hadn't arrived yet and the street was eerily quiet once the purr of the motorcycle faded to silence. Silver eased her helmet off, some of her hair slipping from the Celtic-knot pinning it back.

Hawk suddenly appeared, his wings giving a few powerful flaps before he touched down on the concrete driveway.

Jake's jaw dropped. "Holy shit, he really can fly." Hawk

had cloaked himself before taking to the sky at the shop, so Silver wasn't surprised at Jake's reaction.

She slid off the motorcycle, left her helmet on the seat, and strode toward the back door of Janis's home, her heart pounding. What if there was another demon lying in wait? Maybe more? Would her magic be enough to fend them off, or would Hawk's fighting abilities be enough to destroy them? Would Jake's and his team members' firepower have any effect on the Fomorii?

Before she reached the house, Hawk grabbed her upper arm. "Wait," he commanded, and she frowned at him. One thing she *hated* was to be told what to do.

She started to respond when the PSF team's black vehicle pulled up to the sidewalk and Paranormal Special Forces agents spilled from its confines. The vehicle was the same type as often used by SWAT cops, like a huge UPS truck, but with no markings whatsoever—just pure black.

Hawk released her and she snatched her black cap from her pocket and tucked her hair beneath it, trying to get all the strands under it. PSF officers slipped silently from the vehicle and within moments were surrounding her, Hawk, and Jake. Each man and woman had a hardened expression. A couple of the men and one woman had a cocky look to their eyes, and Silver only hoped she wouldn't regret involving humans who might not be able to fight such powerful demons.

Jake briefed them on the plan. If all went well, and no demons were lying in wait, they would work their way through the tunnel left by the Fomorii—if it hadn't caved in and if it was stable. They hoped the tunnel would lead them to the demons' hideout where they would attempt to rescue trapped Coven members.

Silver insisted on leading the way into Janis's home, and Hawk insisted on remaining glued to her side. The knob squeaked as she turned it, and again the door creaked when she pushed it open.

Silence reigned as she paused at the threshold. The house smelled stale and still reeked of rotten fish. She almost choked on it when she took a deep breath to shore up her courage.

She moved silently across the scratched and muddied floor to the door leading to the D'Anu chamber that was sprawled wide open. Before she started down the steps, she eased one dagger out of her boot, and waved her hand to form an illumination spell.

The blue light preceded her down the scarred stone steps and to the destroyed chamber. She felt the presence of Hawk, Jake, and the PSF squad behind her. Jake had instructed two of the team members to guard the entrance to the home, and two would remain at the entrance to the hole, providing they could climb down into it.

Silver clenched the hilt of the dagger as she climbed over the rubble and reached the gaping maw of the hole left by the Fomorii. Jake and Hawk were to either side of her now, Hawk with his own dagger drawn, and Jake with his gun. She let the blue light of her magic spill into the opening and it illuminated a crude tunnel leading so far down she couldn't see how deep it went. The smell rising up from the hole was beyond the malodor of the Fomorii. It stunk like a—like a sewer.

She crouched long enough to pick up a small rock and dropped it into the hole. She held her breath as she waited—and heard it splash within a couple of seconds.

Silver turned to Jake. "Sewer?"

He nodded.

This time she didn't take a deep breath—the stink was too much. Instead she straightened her shoulders, ready to climb down into that hole, when Hawk pushed his way past her and sheathed his dagger. He braced his hands to either side of the opening. His biceps bulged as he lowered his large body into the hole.

Hawk's gut tightened as he climbed down the crudely dug tunnel illuminated by Silver's magic. Sharp rocks bit into his callused palms but he felt no pain as he found handholds and footholds in the dirt and rock. The stink rising from below was near to overwhelming, but he continued down, testing each foothold before putting his weight onto it.

As he lowered himself, he heard the steady drip of water, and the flow of the sewer just feet beneath him. His senses constantly sifted through every sound while seeking signs of the Fomorii.

His boot slipped when he found no purchase, only emptiness. He gritted his teeth as he slid down the tunnel, more rocks scraping his palms and dirt lodging beneath his fingernails. Torn metal cut into his hands and then he dropped.

He landed in a crouch, his boots splashing in the sewer's filth, but he maintained his balance, managing not to fall into the foul water. A pile of rocks and mud were just beneath the hole, where the Fomorii had obviously left the remains of their digging.

Hawk rose up the best he could, the metal tunnel not quite high enough, forcing him to hunch over to keep from banging his head. Once he was certain there were no Fomorii in the vicinity, he mind-spoke to Silver. *"It is safe. Be careful as you climb. I will catch you if you fall."*

He felt Silver's surprise at his speaking in her mind, and then her assent. Within moments, the blue glow grew brighter as she climbed down toward the sewer, and he could see her lithe form as she found footholds and handholds in the dirt and stone. When she reached the bottom of the hole, she swung down with her normal grace, landed with a thunk of her boots on the metal, then proceeded to lose her balance and almost fall into the sewer water.

Hawk's head banged against the top of the tunnel, but he managed to hook one arm around her waist and pull her to him. He felt her warmth against his body, the roughness of her breathing. She tilted her face up. "Nice catch," she said, and he smiled.

One after another, Jake and other members of the PSF team climbed down into the tunnel. A couple slipped and landed in the sewage, but quickly got to their feet as if nothing had happened. Professionals they were, Hawk had to admit to himself.

Jake's quick assessment was the same as Hawk's. He pointed in one direction. "The sewage drain has deep scratches heading that way."

Silver nodded and reached up to tuck errant locks of her hair back under her cap. Her silver snake bracelet glowed in her magical blue light, the serpent almost seeming to crawl up her wrist with her every movement.

They walked through the sewage drain, hunched over, as they searched for some kind of clue to the whereabouts of the demons. Their boots sloshed in the muck and the stench clung to their clothing. Even with the stink, Hawk could still smell traces of Fomorii. They passed manholes but ignored them as there was no indication the demons had used them as exits.

It wasn't long before they found an opening torn through the metal drain and a hole dug up into what appeared to be a room. A pile of rocks and mud were beneath the hole, much like the one where they had begun. Hawk insisted on climbing up alone, and found himself in what appeared to be a ceremonial chamber. He smelled remnants of Fomorii stench, but it was not fresh. Using mind-speak, he shared with Silver what he saw, and then eased back down into the sewage drain.

"That has to be where the Balorites hold their Clan meetings," Silver said when he reached her and he saw her shiver. "No doubt that's where they've been holding most of their blood rituals."

"Too bad we don't have time to scope it out," Jake grumbled. "I'd like to nail those bastards."

"You might just get the chance, if they're in league with the Fomorii," Silver said.

Hawk turned to follow the sewage drain and nearly slid down it when it sharply turned downward. Bracing their hands at the top of the drain, they amazingly enough managed to make it down the steep incline without landing in a pile at the bottom.

They hadn't gone much farther when they reached another hole with a bigger pile of rocks and dirt beneath it. The

Fomorii stench was much stronger and Hawk gritted his teeth. His senses told him the demons were close. Very close.

This time muted sunlight peeked through the hole. Hawk worked his way up the rough tunnel, his hands and feet braced on the walls in what footholds and handholds he could find, his dagger between his teeth.

When he reached the opening, he raised himself up and out onto a patch of dirt beside an enormous building. Silver was right behind him, and he grabbed her hand to help pull her up onto the ground.

"Their lair," Hawk said. "Magic may be shrouding the Fomorii, but this close I can sense the demons."

She shielded her hand with her eyes and looked up at the building. "It's a hotel. We'd better stay out of sight."

Jake and the rest of the PSF team made it out of the hole. The lot of them smelled so bad from the sewer that Hawk wasn't sure they would be able to search the building without being instantly detected.

"We must get inside," he said.

Silver frowned. "We can't just walk in there like this." She looked up and up and up. It must be one of the older hotels as it didn't tower as high as the more modern ones.

Hawk folded his arms across his chest. "I can gain access from the roof."

Silver bit her lower lip. "There has to be an easier way. A window, *something*."

Jake gestured to a second-story balcony at the back of the building. "If we can get there, I can break open the window."

"I can take care of the locks," Silver said. "Just let me get up there."

She didn't wait for the men. She climbed onto a low wall that shielded the hotel's generators. Thank the Ancestors for the dreary and overcast day. Hopefully no one would notice a bunch of people in black climbing up into a hotel. *That* would certainly go over well.

Jake followed, and without her asking him to, he took her by the waist and boosted her higher so that she was sitting on his shoulders. Now the balcony was almost within her grasp. Just as she went to push herself to stand on his shoulders, Hawk soared up, grasped her beneath her arms and carried her onto the balcony. The brief sensation of flying was exhilarating. She found herself breathing a little harder when they landed.

"Help Jake and the others," she said, pointing down to the cops who appeared to be looking for another means of getting up to the balcony.

Hawk grimaced, then flapped his wings and leaned over the edge of the balcony, just hanging by the toes of his boots. He reached for Jake, and the cop clasped arms with him. Hawk gave a mighty pump of his wings that almost knocked Silver back against the balcony window. His jaw tensed and his muscles bulged as he drew Jake up high enough that the cop could grab the top railing of the balcony, and swing himself up the rest of the way.

"Thanks," Jake said.

Hawk just grunted and folded away his wings so that they had completely vanished beneath his shirt. "I do not sense any Fomorii in this room."

Silver turned her concentration from the overdose of testosterone behind her, to the lock on the balcony door.

She searched for the lock with her powers and found them at once. There were two locks. A bolt and a pin. Easy enough. She raised one hand up, focusing on the pin lock, and heard a light scraping sound, then a chain's jingle as it fell away. With a twist of her fingers in the air, the bolt scraped clear. Silver reached up and tugged the sliding glass door open. They were in.

But the room wasn't empty.

14

A man and a woman were completely naked on the bed in the center of the hotel room. The woman was on her hands and knees facing Silver, and she moaned as the man drove into her from behind.

Silver raised her hands and said, "Oops."

The man rolled off the woman and onto his feet. "What the hell?"

The woman gave a furious scream, snatched the remote control off the nightstand, and threw it at Silver with the accuracy of a World Series pitcher. Silver barely dodged it and flung ropes of fog from her fingers just as the man strode toward her.

Magical fog whipped around the couple as Silver forced the man and woman to become completely motionless.

The man's hands dropped to his sides. The woman's expression went blank and her eyes glassy.

"Well, shit." Jake came up to one side of Silver and scratched the back of his neck. "Can you do something to— er, make them forget us, Silver?"

"That's what I'm doing." She tightened the fog and with her thoughts she ordered the man and woman to return to their bed and sleep.

The gray magic it took to force her will on someone else was intoxicating this time instead of exhausting. The mix of raw sexual energy, pheromones, and anger in the room—the gray magic fed off the combination, working a little too well, a little too fast. Drawing a little too deep on Silver, penetrating her just as the man had been penetrating the woman. Rough, hard, primal. Power. Ah, goddess. It felt so incredibly powerful to force this couple to bend to her orders.

For a moment, she held them still. Then she moved the man like a puppet. Back. Back. To the bed. On the bed. If she wanted to, she could send them back to fucking and leave them at it as the whole group trooped through the room.

Some dark part of her warmed to the thought while another part of her mind yelled for her to back away. Screamed about the edge, the brink, about points of no return.

A black wolf raced through her mind, its tongue lolling out, and it almost seemed to be laughing.

Around its neck was the red eye.

The vision nearly broke Silver's concentration. She narrowed her eyes on the couple and managed to get the man and woman into bed with their covers up to their chins, and fast asleep.

When she finished and her gray fog slowly vanished, Silver's shoulders trembled. What in the name of the goddess was happening to her? Why would she feel such pleasure in manipulating this pair of humans?

To Silver's surprise she felt a pair of strong hands rubbing her neck as if she were a boxer preparing for another round. *"Are you all right, a thaisce?"* Hawk asked in her thoughts.

She gave a sharp nod and ducked out of his grasp. Dragging her thoughts from the strange feelings of power, she turned to face him, Jake, and the other four armed PSF team members who had followed them. Jameson, McNulty, Sanders, and Chin were their names, all of whom Silver trusted implicitly. The other two PSF officers had remained below, just as two had remained at the entrance to the tunnel back at Janis's home.

"Let's make it quick." Silver switched on a dim bedside

light. The room they had entered was stuffy and also had that old-hotel smell to it. "We need to find out more about this place."

Jake moved up beside Silver. "You said you saw a small ballroom in your vision?"

Silver nodded. "To one side was a cloth-paneled wall with hinges, like it could fold away."

"Sometimes they separate a large ballroom into smaller ones by removable panels." Jake's expression was thoughtful. "If that's the case, then we could enter by a side room and get in that way."

"Hold on." Silver went to the desk in the room and started riffling through the room service menu and sightseeing pamphlets, until she found a brochure for the hotel. She scanned photographs of the hotel's amenities and within moments found a picture of the Grand Ballroom. "I think you're right. This looks identical to the one I saw in my scrying cauldron, only double the size."

After glancing through the brochure, Silver looked to Jake. "I'll go first so that you all don't scare the crap out of someone with your guns. I can do a quick memory spell on anyone we meet." She almost laughed as she added, "Likely they would be driven away just by the smell of the sewer on us."

Silver swallowed as they made their way past the bed with the sleeping couple and exited out the hotel room door. One reason she insisted on helping the cops and using her magic to keep the criminals from fighting back was that she was against any form of killing. But the feeling that these demons deserved death was so strong she could taste it.

And it scared her.

Weapons drawn—or in Silver's case, fingers ready—the seven of them crept down the hallway toward the stairwell, their shoes silent on the carpet. It was as red as blood. The way to the stairwell was short, and thank the goddess they did not run into anyone on the way.

When they reached the stairwell, Jake entered first,

followed by Silver and then Hawk. She knew the men were being protective of her and she tried not to let it piss her off. She could more than take care of herself.

On the first floor they eased out of the door from the stairwell. It creaked the moment they opened it and all froze. When there was nothing but silence, they slipped into the illuminated area of the elevator banks.

Silver's heart beat faster when she heard noise coming from the lobby. Her stomach clenched as she recognized the hallway she had walked down in her vision—straight past the elevators.

"I know where to go." She nodded down the hallway toward the noise. "In my vision the back way to the ballrooms wasn't far from here."

Heart pounding in her throat, Silver moved stealthily along the corridor. As soon as she recognized the door from her vision, she moved through it and into a huge storeroom. Definitely déjà vu time. She felt the presence of Hawk and the PSF team behind her as she glanced around the room filled with banquet tables, chairs, and risers.

The sense of wrongness she had felt in her vision swept over her in a powerful wave, much stronger this time.

Yes. Darkness. Definitely, black magic was close.

Carefully, Silver moved through the storeroom to another door, placed her hand against the cool metal, and held her breath. She felt the presence of Hawk, Jake, and the other men and woman behind her, but heard not a sound.

She pushed open the door and slowly exhaled when she saw the small ballroom, identical to the one in her vision. Again this one was empty, and mirrored the one the scrying cauldron had shown her.

Tension strained every muscle in her body as she crept over the floor to the sectioned wall. It was, again, just like her vision. Each section was hinged, as if the wall could fold away.

She found her hand trembling as she placed it against the wall.

Black magic slammed into her, so intense it nearly drove her to her knees. She gasped for air and tried to calm the sudden queasiness in her belly. With shaking hands, she reached down and drew her daggers from her boots.

The presence of black magic was so thick Silver's stomach roiled. She rose up, weapons in hand, then moved silently along the wall until she came to the end where there was a gap between the partition and the wall.

She peeked through the gap and caught her breath.

The witches—they were behind some kind of purple force field. Some braced their backs against the wall, others sat with their arms around their knees, and one of the witches was pacing.

Rhiannon! She's alive! Sharp relief rolled through Silver, followed by fear for her friend, along with anger so intense her vision blurred.

Standing guard at the door were two of the biggest, ugliest creatures Silver had ever seen. Their rotten-fish stench clogged her nose. The demons watched the room and the witches diligently but occasionally turned to one another to talk in a garbled language.

Silver turned back to the two men behind her. "This is it." She took a deep breath and tried to clear her thoughts. "I'm going to have to take out the two guards with my witchcraft, or we'll never get in."

Jake gave a quick nod and Hawk frowned.

She ignored them both and focused on her gray magic. With a small push of her mind, gray fog streamed from her fingertips through the crack in the wall between rooms. The fog slowly made its way along the floor, creeping toward the two demons.

The Fomorii didn't notice the fog as it wrapped around their ankles, and worked its way farther up their bodies. Sweat broke out on Silver's forehead and a droplet rolled between her breasts. She could feel herself weakening from the spell.

"Sleep," she instructed the demons. *"Sleep."*

For a few dreadful moments, nothing happened. If the damned things had been human, they would have fallen unconscious—maybe permanently—from the force she was using. But these were demons. Former sea gods.

Had she been crazy to think her magic would work against such alien monsters? Demons that had once been gods?

Shaking from a mix of nerves and strain, Silver poured even more energy into the sleeping spell. Binding, taking freedom, using gray magic to force her will on other beings. Distasteful. Exhausting.

Necessary.

More. I need more.

Damn it. What if she killed them?

Let them die.

Silver's lips pulled back in a wolfish snarl. Her power seemed to double, triple, filling her with such energy that her hair practically lifted from her shoulders and crackled with electricity as if joined with another, far darker magic.

She was using the gray for good, wasn't she? She could use the extra power, just a little.

Sleep. Sleep. Sleep . . . she repeated over and over in her mind. A burst of magic rushed through her fog ropes, straight to the demons.

In response, the monsters blinked their eyes. They seemed to lose a little color, even look a little sick. A black substance trickled out of one's snout. The other rubbed its throat and seemed to be gasping for air.

Silver didn't break off her attack.

"Sleep or die, you fucking monsters from hell. Your call."

The bleeding demon swayed a bit. Then the gasping demon staggered. Both were obviously in pain. They even looked afraid.

Silver felt her smile widen.

For one awful second she thought they were going to fall to the floor in two giant thuds that would alert every other Fomorii in the place. But each simply slid down the door panel and collapsed into deep trances.

A few of the witches murmured in confusion. The rest remained studiously silent, and someone even shushed the whisperers.

Silver waited one breath for the usual exhaustion that would make her momentarily weak.

Nothing. If anything, she felt energized. On fire with power.

One of the men brushed against her back. *Hawk.* Without looking, she could tell by the scent of him, the smells of wind and forest. The irrational urge to bite him nearly overpowered her.

She might have done it, too, but Jake paused to give her arm a squeeze.

When Silver looked down at his fingers, the wild energy waned enough for her to think—at least a little.

Jake winked, moved by her and began to pry open the door. It gave a small groaning noise and they all jumped. Silver's heart pounded faster.

Everything was quiet.

As soon as Jake opened that section of the wall, things were going to happen fast. But how were they going to get twelve witches and the apprentices out safely?

Silver took a deep breath and anger and adrenaline took over again. She *would* get them out.

When Jake had wedged open a space wide enough for two large men to fit through, Hawk slipped into the ballroom, followed by Silver, Jake, and the rest of the PSF team.

Witches started murmuring again, calling to Silver in low voices with pleas for help.

"Oh, my goddess," Janis Arrowsmith whispered. "How did you get in here?"

Silver didn't bother to answer. Her gaze rested on Rhiannon and Mackenzie, who were contained just feet away.

"Silver. Jake." Rhiannon came up to the barrier and placed her palms flat against it. An expression of relief crossed her friend's features, followed by concern. "You've got to get out of here before the demons wake."

Hawk was already beside both Fomorii. With a quick slice of his sword, he beheaded one sleeping demon, then the other. Without a sound, both of the demon bodies wavered, then collapsed to silt on the floor, as if they were nothing but mounds of soil.

Witches gasped.

Silver's gut reaction was extreme pleasure that the demons had been destroyed, followed by a sick feeling because she had been the one to make them easy targets. Still, she couldn't help feeling that justice had been delivered with their deaths.

Gray leads to black . . .

She moved up to the shimmering purple force field surrounding the witches. Goddess, the power radiating from it was incredible, beyond anything she'd experienced before.

"Okay," Rhiannon said as Silver moved closer to her. "So no worries about those demons. But you've got to leave before the others come. This force field is impossible to break down. We've all tried."

"Bet no one has tried using gray magic," Silver murmured without thinking, and Janis's gaze shot to her.

"We won't be a part of this." Janis narrowed her eyes. "Don't use our captivity as an excuse to violate everything the D'Anu stand for."

Where is that wild energy I felt? I should have bitten her, damn it.

Silver sheathed her daggers in her boots and focused on the shimmering purple wall. Her stilettos would do her no good here.

"Hurry," Jake said. He and the other PSF cops had their high-powered guns trained on the ballroom doors, and Hawk was beside her with his sword.

Silver called up a spellfire ball in her hands. "Move," she ordered the witches.

Janis was already at the far side of the magical prison, and other witches pushed against her.

The spellfire Silver gathered together was a brilliant blue. As she put all her anger into her magic, the ball grew brighter and brighter yet—and then became tinged with the slight hue of lavender, as if her witchcraft were mixing with someone else's.

Someone with magic that exceeded her own.

All Silver cared about was the immense feeling of power flowing through her body. Power so intense, so far beyond what she'd experienced before, that she almost laughed with the headiness of it.

She reared back and flung the fireball at the force field and her blood rushed in her ears as she watched the purple shimmer weaken while her blue spellfire rolled over it.

"Don't do this," Janis shouted. "Can't you see it's getting away from you? Where will it end, Silver? Stop!"

I'm saving your asses, Silver thought as she gathered another ball in her hands. This one was even bigger, stronger, and this time she did laugh.

Just as she reared back to fling the ball, she felt a presence touch her mind. Something dark—someone dark. The image that flashed in her mind was the darkly sensual and exciting Darkwolf.

Exciting? No. Was she losing it?

But her teeth were clenched. She was thinking about biting again. Biting hard.

"Use your anger," the voice said. *"Let it grow. It's delicious, yes? Would you like to feel how exciting* real *power can be?"*

She shook her head and focused her attention back on the wall. The anger within her was so great she couldn't have drawn back if she'd wanted to. She poured that anger, that rage at what the Fomorii had done, into her magic. She didn't even realize the spellfire in her hands had turned a deep shade of purple until she'd flung it against the barrier.

This time sparks flew and crackled in the air. The wall exploded outward and Silver felt the rush of black magic flow over her from the destroyed force field. She stumbled back into a strong pair of arms that she recognized instantly as Hawk's. Her stomach roiled from the presence of black witchcraft, so badly she almost threw up.

She jerked herself from Hawk's hold and ran toward the witches. Rhiannon met Silver halfway and gripped her in a tight hug. Through the haze of the wild power within her, Silver recognized the slashes and bruises across Rhiannon's face, and her anger rose all over again.

"Let's get out of here." Rhiannon tugged on Silver's

hand. The PSF team was backing up toward them, guns still trained on the ballroom doors.

The doors smashed open.

Five men ran into the room and slammed the doors behind them.

In an instant four of them shifted into demons.

The fifth into a Basilisk!

Witches screamed. Stumbled.

"Pick them off," Jake shouted to his team.

Hawk readied his sword and charged one of the demons.

Swearing loud enough to drown out the hiss of the Basilisk, demon-grunts, and shouting, Silver gathered spellfire in her hands. Her witchcraft raged within her, so great her body was afire with it. She flung the ball at the closest Fomorii. The blast slammed the demon against the far wall.

At the same time, expert PSF marksmen shot at the demons, the silencers on their guns muffling the sounds.

To Silver's horror, the demon bodies and the Basilisk absorbed each shot, the scales and skin mending as if the hole had never existed. The bullets merely slowed the demons up a bit, and angered them more.

"Outta here!" Jake shouted. "Save who you can and get out!"

A demon pounced on one of the PSF officers. Sanders went down. Witches screamed as the cursed monster ripped out the PSF cop's throat. The spellfire Silver flung at the beast was so strong it sent the murdering Fomorii sliding across the floor and into the wall with a crash of wood and particle board.

Hawk battled a demon, both his fists around the hilt of his sword as he swung. He severed one of the beast's limbs and black blood spurted.

Jake was shouting at the witches to get the hell out, get out, get out, but their way was blocked by one of the demons. Silver used her gray magic again to knock back the Fomorii, giving them room to escape.

The Basilisk sank its fangs into Jameson's body and

shook the man who shouted from what must have been excruciating pain.

Taking everything in within seconds, Silver saw at least three witches being herded out of the room. She was sweating so much that her skin was hot and flushed, her hair damp beneath her cap and her clothes sticking to her body.

"Flee," Hawk ordered Silver as the demon he was battling lunged at him.

"Not without—" Silver started when the room went silent and all the demons bounded away from Silver and Hawk.

A man walked into the room, his presence so powerful that Silver was stunned by it.

Darkwolf.

Nothing Silver had ever visualized had prepared her for the magnetism, the seduction of his smile. The pull of his black magic. Everything around her ceased to exist. It was only Darkwolf and her. Alone.

Mesmerized, Silver could only stare at him. Her body refused to work and she couldn't even raise her hands to form a spellfire.

"I've been waiting for you to come to me, Silver Ashcroft," Darkwolf said in a voice so sensual it caused her to shiver. "Your powers far exceed those of your Coven members. Your magic is already blending with the dark. I need you and you need me."

No, she tried to say, but nothing came out. Her tongue was so thick she couldn't even speak. She tried to shake her head but it was too heavy to move.

He moved closer to her, his black robe flowing around him. The stone eye on the chain around his neck swayed as he slowly closed the distance between them. "One more step, Silver, and you will have all of what Balor has to offer you. Witchcraft beyond your dreams."

His eyes . . . those incredible black eyes. They held her. They made her want to move to him, to be surrounded by his embrace.

His very presence was so . . . erotic. Like he was sliding his hands over her body, drawing her closer to him.

The dark. It was power.

Yes. Witchcraft she could use for good. Witchcraft that would allow her the abilities to help anyone in need. Yes, that was it.

Her gaze dropped to the stone eye at his throat.

The eye opened.

Bright red light seared her vision.

Fear and anger broke the hold Darkwolf had on her. Suddenly she realized the fighting had not stopped, that the battle had continued, she had simply been enthralled by the man approaching her.

He looked annoyed, obviously realizing he no longer had control of her mind. Before she even had time to think about it, she raised her hand and flung a spellfire ball at him.

It simply shimmered around a magical shield he threw up around himself. "Yes. That's it, Silver," the warlock said. "Again."

"Silver!" Hawk's shout brought her back to reality just as she started to fling more spellfire at Darkwolf.

Hawk grabbed her hand and jerked her through the gap in the partition. With swift recognition, she realized everything that had just occurred had happened in mere moments even though it seemed like it had been hours.

She heard Darkwolf's cry of rage. Felt him try to jerk her back toward him.

Goddess help her, but part of her wanted to go.

No!

On the other side of the partition, she grabbed Mackenzie's and Rhiannon's hands and surrounded the three of them with a spellshield. She practically dragged them through the opening to the other ballroom. The two witches seemed to gather themselves, their bodies probably flooded with the same kind of adrenaline rush pumping through Silver.

Behind her came the screams of witches, Hawk's battle cries, and the muffled sound of Jake's and the other PSF officers' guns firing. She tossed a look over her shoulder and saw Jake and Hawk had Sandy and Iris behind them as they followed her.

Furious that two of Jake's officers had died, and that some of her Coven was being left behind—*again*—Silver took the only logical action. She shoved Rhiannon and Mackenzie ahead of her, running for the service door that led them back in the direction they had come from. It was a wonder Silver's friends didn't trip over their robes.

Janis. John. Sydney. Left behind.

What if they just vanish without a trace like my sister? What if we can't even find their bodies?

Jake, Hawk, the others—dear goddess, please let both of them out of this hellpit alive.

For now, she had to save the souls she could save.

When she got the women into the service room, she paused to hold the door open for the two witches and the others running toward her.

"Get out of here, damn it!" Jake shouted as he glanced at Silver before putting a bullet through the head of a charging Fomorii, stalling the beast for just a brief moment.

Using her magic to keep the door open, Silver ushered the two women through the next door. Hawk, Iris, and Jake made it into the room. Sandy was nowhere to be seen.

Silver slammed the door shut behind them and locked it with a flick of her fingers. "This way," she shouted, as she worked her way through the next door and into the hallway with Rhiannon and Mackenzie. She could hear and feel the others behind her.

Silver expected to hear Fomorii shrieks and roars as she and her companions rushed past the bank of elevators and through the stairwell door. But for some reason there was only silence. Perhaps to avoid being seen or heard by the hotel's patrons?

But no. She heard additional pounding footsteps. The creatures must have turned back into their human forms.

The rescued witches stumbled on the concrete steps in the stairwell. Mackenzie and Rhiannon righted themselves and kept on moving, but Hawk threw Iris over his shoulder and carried her up the flight of stairs. Every time they went through any kind of doorway, Silver used her magic to lock the door behind them, stalling the demon-humans long enough to aid their escape.

When they reached the second floor, they ran down the hallway to the room they'd come in through. Before Silver could use her magic to unlock it, Hawk set Iris down and rammed the door with his shoulder. Wood shattered and metal tore away with a grinding crunch.

They all stumbled into the room.

"Did we lose them?" Silver's voice came out in a pant.

Iris leaned over and threw up on the carpeted floor. Mackenzie looked shell-shocked, but Rhiannon, always practical and headstrong, said, "Forget the demons. Let's just get the hell out."

Silver glanced at the bed and saw that the man and woman she'd bound with her magic were still sleeping.

Hawk and Jake went through the open doors to the balcony.

"Clear," they both said at once, then glared at each other for a fraction of a second.

Hawk sheathed his sword, reached for Rhiannon, and took her onto the balcony. His wings unfurled. Iris was wiping vomit from her mouth onto her sleeve but jerked her head up and gave a sharp cry of surprise while Mackenzie gasped.

"Tuatha D'Danann." Iris's features twisted with horror. "By the goddess. You called them. You went against the Coven and summoned the D'Danann into this world."

"Oh, shut up, Iris," Rhiannon snapped back. "Silver just saved your life."

Iris leaned over and threw up again.

The woman is so damn stupid, Silver thought, wanting to shake Iris while at the same time feeling bad for her as she puked her guts up.

"Hold on tight," Hawk said as he grabbed Rhiannon and flew off the balcony with her. Silver watched him take the witch straight to the ground and set her on her feet. Then he was soaring back for the window at the same time Jake was swinging down to the low wall. The remaining PSF officers and Silver were covering their backs.

Hawk grabbed Iris who started to scream, and he clamped his hand over her mouth. "Quiet, witch," was all he said before taking off and flying back down to the street where Rhiannon and Jake were now waiting. Jake had his arms outstretched, gun out, searching the area for any sign of the demons. The two PSF officers they had left behind when they had entered the hotel were backing him up, watching for signs of the beasts.

Just as Hawk made it back to the balcony to grab Mackenzie, Silver swung off and jumped to the low wall, landing in a crouch, and bracing herself with one hand. She leaped off the wall, grabbed Rhiannon's and Iris's hands, and ran like she had never run before. Behind her she heard the other three PSF officers jump down from the balcony.

Rhiannon's and Iris's robes made it harder for them to run, but run they did. Silver's heart thundered with anger and fear. What if they were caught? What if they didn't make it away from the demons? They didn't hear or see the Fomorii, but what if they had another way of reaching them?

Behind her came the pound of Hawk's, Jake's, and the other cops' boots, and the patter of Mackenzie's slippers.

In the distance she heard nothing. Nothing at all.

Silver paused and let the men catch up. One PSF officer held a hand over his bloodied upper arm that had been raked by claws. Another was limping, blood trickling through shreds in her pants. Each of the escaped witches were banged up and bruised and each looked horrorstruck. Only Hawk and Jake seemed to have come out of the fight unscathed.

Silver had to get them somewhere quick to heal them all. It was probably too risky for them to run all the way back to her shop.

Jake pointed up the hill with his gun. "Follow me."

15

Pacing back and forth in her human form, before her remaining warriors and Darkwolf, Junga gave a low growl. She had failed. They had set this trap, let it be sprung—and she and her warriors had failed. Damn it all to the lowest hells!

But why only one of the bastards?

Why not a legion?

Junga had thought that if the D'Danann came, it would be in force. She had planned to be waiting—her, and all the warriors carrying a surprise for the gnats of Otherworld. It had never occurred to her that only *one* D'Danann might be with the witches and humans. Now they had lost the powerful witch Rhiannon, along with two others. Had also failed to catch the thirteenth witch, Silver Ashcroft, the one Darkwolf wanted so badly.

The prior evening Darkwolf had used his seductive skills and thus far had only been able to bring one of the witches to the dark. The rest must be ready in time to perform the summoning on Samhain when the veil between worlds was a wisp of nothing. Only during Samhain and a handful of other times could they bring *all* of her people.

Junga's dark gaze pierced Bane, along with the few surviving members of the team who had lost the witches. All were in human form.

Her muscles tensed to the point she thought her tendons might snap with a single lunge at the throat of one of her warriors. All it would take was a quick shift to Fomorii, and she could easily destroy whoever she chose.

The Fomorii waited for Junga to continue. She noticed everything. The nervous twitch of their eyes, the deference in their postures, the fear in their gazes.

Except Bane. His eyes told her he knew her weakness, how she enjoyed being dominated sexually. She read the knowledge in his expression and it infuriated her. Frightened her.

Excited her.

She didn't dare look at Darkwolf at that moment, lest he see straight to her soul.

The thought only made her angrier as she continued pacing, her heels silent against the floor. By Balor's name, she hadn't been able to forget her night with Bane and Darkwolf. How they had both fucked her, dominated her.

And how much she had enjoyed it.

After she had passed out, she had woken in their arms. They stroked her, brought her human body back to life with such excitement she had lost herself. Had lost her mind. Bane had grabbed her by her long black hair, forced her to her human knees to suck his long, thick cock, and she had tasted her own juices. Darkwolf had taken her from behind once more, bringing her to orgasm again and again while Bane's fluid had spilled into her mouth.

She had been crazy with lust, wanting more, letting them take what they wanted from her. She hadn't resisted. Rather, she had begged for more.

Begged.

She growled low in her throat.

That complete loss of control, that desire for their dominance, how it infuriated her now. And scared her in ways she had never known.

Junga was not weak like her father. She was not!

Yet she wanted them again. Wanted more.

She was legion leader, a fearless warrior who dominated

those beneath her. She could not possibly have these desires to be taken again and again as a human. To be forced into sexual acts by dominant males.

It is Elizabeth's essence. That must be it. At my first opportunity, I need another more suitable host. Perhaps one without a pussy. Maybe I need a cock.

After that night with Darkwolf and Bane, she had avoided being alone with them. Her needs were too raw, her mind too confused.

She had never known confusion or self-doubt. Had never known anything but power and confidence.

Junga snarled. "I should rip your throats out for your failure."

Several demons stopped twitching, and genuine fear appeared in the eyes of every Fomorii.

Again, all but Bane. Somehow he knew she wanted him, and the warlock.

She should kill the pair before this obsession, this madness, consumed her.

But first she had to have Bane and Darkwolf once more.

A shiver rippled beneath her skin, and she only hoped it would be interpreted as anger.

Her black eyes riveted on Darkwolf. "We are running out of time. Convince these witches. Find a way."

"I told you before to leave it to me, but you failed to listen." The warlock smiled, but it was calculating, cruel. "Some are weakening and soon they will come to me. Come to the dark."

Junga shot back, "But you failed in retrieving the prize so dear to you when she was practically in your hands."

Darkwolf's eyes narrowed and she felt his power emanating from him in wave after wave.

She broke eye contact.

If she didn't get the witches to summon another contingent of Fomorii, the Old One, and Queen Kanji soon, Junga would likely be ripped to shreds by the queen's guard when they were finally summoned.

"Return to your posts," Junga said as she dismissed the warriors.

She fixed her gaze on Za and Bane, her highest commanders. "You two. Stay."

Junga kept her look fierce, predatory. She moved toward them as if stalking them like prey. "Take your best warriors, in human form, to search for the witches."

Bane and Za bowed. "Yes, *ceannaire*," they both said, and departed after she gave a nod of dismissal.

"Do what you will with the witches," Junga said to Darkwolf, and turned her gaze from him before she could see his answering expression.

Junga padded silently across the floor, ignoring Darkwolf. She had enjoyed being human far too much. When she had preyed upon various races in Otherworld, she had never found such extreme pleasure in possessing their bodies. Not Fae, not Shanai, nor other beings. But these humans, pitifully weak as they might be, intrigued her. Their constant desire for sex and the sensitivity of their bodies were enough to make her want to fuck all day long.

What frightened her, though, was the complexity of human emotions. Humans were weaker, inferior. Their emotions ruled them. She couldn't allow that to happen to her.

Was it affecting her people, too?

Junga turned her thoughts to their approaching task, once all Fomorii had been summoned on Samhain. Eventually the Fomorii would control San Francisco's government, then slowly spread throughout this interesting world as their numbers multiplied.

She licked her lips. A ready food supply of unwary victims. A species caught unaware. It was the way of the Fomorii. The reason they existed—to conquer lesser forms of life.

It would indeed be enjoyable.

16

Hawk continually kept watch to ensure they were not being followed by the Fomorii. His gut burned at the fact they had only been able to rescue three witches. They should have rescued them all.

Jake led the four witches, his team, and Hawk around the corner and a few houses down. "The police chief lives here," Jake explained when he stood on the top step and rang the doorbell.

Before he even stopped speaking, the door was yanked open and a tall, imposing man stood before them, dressed in full police uniform, including his gun holster.

He seemed to be searching for something to say as he stared at the group before he finally gestured for them to come in. "Captain. Welcome."

Hair rose at the back of Hawk's neck. All of his senses told him something was very wrong. "Back away, Jake," Hawk said as he drew his sword.

The witches looked confused, but Silver caught his gaze and nodded.

"What the hell are you talking about?" Jake glared at Hawk, then faced the police chief—

Who now had his gun trained on Jake.

"Come inside, all of you," the man said in a growl, "or this one dies."

"Fomorii," Hawk said to Jake. "Your police chief is already dead."

"Get them out of here!" Jake reacted so swiftly Silver barely saw him move. He shoved the demon inside the home despite the gun.

A shot rang in the night air. Jake staggered back. Stumbled down the steps onto the sidewalk. His head slammed onto the concrete.

One of the women screamed. The Fomorii, in human form, came back to the doorway, gun still in hand. Silver created a spellfire between her hands, flung it at the demon at the same time she dropped into a crouch. Another shot rang out and she felt the vibrations of the bullet as it went over her head.

The distraction gave Hawk enough time to get close to the Fomorii. He swung his sword in a lightning-fast motion and sliced the demon's head from his shoulders.

The body dropped. Slowly it began to shift into the hideous orange demon it had been. In moments it had crumbled into a pile of black silt.

Hawk's gaze shot to Jake. Iris and Mackenzie were on their knees beside him. Rhiannon's chin-length auburn hair fell forward into her face as she knelt to help Jake. She tied strips of cloth torn from her robe around Jake's bicep. Blood seeped through the cloth, but the more strips she put on it, the more the bleeding lessened.

"The bullet went right through the fleshy part of his arm," Rhiannon said as she glanced at Hawk. "What's actually worse is he hit his head on the concrete. Hard. No doubt he has a concussion."

Silver slowly ran her hands along Jake's body and small blue circles and sparkles of light ebbed from her, as if straight from her soul. Hawk could only stand helplessly by. He kept his sword unsheathed as he watched, prepared for any Fomorii that might have followed them. The remaining PSF officers surrounded them, stances wide and guns ready despite their injuries.

Guns that were useless against the Fomorii.

Silver gritted her teeth as her energy ebbed and flowed through Jake's body. Healing was white magic but such deep healing stole strength from her.

But it was her fault so many were injured. Her fault two of the PSF officers had been murdered. If she hadn't allowed herself to be enthralled by Darkwolf, she would have better protected them and would have gotten more witches to safety.

Silver pushed more of her healing energy into Jake. He groaned. Squinted. Opened his eyes. "Must have been one hell of a party," he said, his speech slurred.

Drained, but determined to make right what was her fault, she went to the other witches who were healing the two injured PSF officers. "You're injured," she told Rhiannon and Mackenzie. "Let me."

The witches tried to argue, but Silver pushed them aside. Again she used her healing magic to stop the flow of blood, to help alleviate some of the pain. They would need more attention as soon as they got back to safety, but this would do for now.

Hawk knelt beside Silver in time to catch her as she slumped back after healing the last officer. "I'm okay," she said, drawing in a ragged breath. "Just need a second."

"We'll help Silver," Rhiannon said as Mackenzie moved closer. "You get Jake."

When Jake could stand, Hawk helped him walk, Jake's good arm over Hawk's shoulder. Rhiannon and Mackenzie assisted Silver even though she tried to insist she was all right. Iris hurried alongside, looking lost and miserable. The PSF team members helped one another and constantly kept on guard against Fomorii.

They passed several pedestrians who gave them wide-eyed looks. "Police business," one of the officers shouted, showing a badge he had whipped out of his pocket.

"My store really isn't that far from the chief's house," Silver said, her heart clenching at the thought of the man who was murdered by the demon. "I think we're safe to go to the shop now. Even if they know where the store is, the wardings will likely help."

Hawk nodded his agreement. "The Fomorii have no magic other than taking over other life-forms, and should not be able to cross your wardings."

A bit of relief eased through Silver. "Once we're there, our witchcraft will aid us in protecting our sanctuary even further. Besides, we don't really have anywhere safer."

"Dear Ancestors, I hope you're right," Mackenzie murmured.

By the time they neared the shop, Silver had shaken off the other two witches' holds, declaring her strength had returned. Jake was walking more easily now. "I don't believe it," he said, his voice carrying on the evening breeze. "They got Hernandez. He was a damn good man."

"Let's hope they haven't infiltrated the rest of the police department," Silver said. "You're going to have to watch your back."

"No kidding."

Once they neared the shop, Jake, two PSF officers, and Hawk checked around it from the front to the alleyway to the garage in the rear, while Silver and the remaining officers watched over the other witches. When they signaled it was clear, Jake spoke with his team members. They gave short responses and nods. Two remained at the witches' insistence for healing, while the others left to retrieve the officers left at Janis's home.

The officers, witches, Jake, and Hawk slipped in through the back door and into the kitchen. Safe inside the shop, Silver made sure all three doors were securely locked.

Due to the healing magic and the gray witchcraft she'd used, Silver could hardly stand, but she put what energy she had into a repel charm to turn any attention away from her shop. It had never failed her until Hawk. She prayed it would work against the Fomorii.

And Darkwolf.

When she finished, Silver caught up with Hawk, Jake, the

officers, and the other three witches in the kitchen where Cassia was making mingled cries of joy and dismay as she saw the rescued Coven members and all of their scrapes, bruises, and blood.

"I'll brew a pain remedy and make some poultices," Silver said as she limped around the kitchen, grabbing herbs and other ingredients from the cabinets.

Cassia forced Jake and the others to sit at the kitchen table, then ran to get a bowl of warm water and a few washcloths.

Spirit darted into the room and straight into Rhiannon's lap. "Spirit!" Her short auburn hair swung forward as she hugged the huge cat. "I missed you, you little monster."

The cat mewled and it was obvious he felt the same way. He sniffed at the claw marks across her face and hissed his displeasure before rubbing himself against Rhiannon's chest.

Hawk turned to Silver, who was busy preparing poultices. "You need rest."

"I'm fine." She waved him away. "After I finish the potions, and everyone's taken care of and resting, I'll lie down. Once I cast extra warding spells. I think we're going to need all the rest we can get."

"I'll do it right now." Cassia attended all the doors yet again, then rushed back to help with the healing remedies.

When Silver had finished a few quick poultices and grabbed a few lodestones as well as creams and oils already made, she moved to the kitchen table. To one lodestone she chanted, "Heal our brother in his time of need. I pray to thee, these words to heed." She blew her warm breath onto the stone as she asked for the Ancestors' blessings, then placed it in Jake's fist. His jaw had been tense, but he relaxed a bit as he clenched the stone.

Hawk helped her peel away the makeshift bandages and then remove the man's shirt.

"The wound is clean," Hawk pronounced after doing some prodding that made Jake wince.

Silver cleansed the wound using tea tree oil for an

antiseptic, then used "herb Robert" to stop the bleeding, along with chanting words of healing magic.

Immediately the blood stopped flowing and the wound looked as if it were already mending. Jake watched as though in a dream, as if he were having a hard time focusing as he blinked hard and blinked again.

When Silver had almost finished wiping away all the blood she could see, Cassia bustled over with more jars and cloths, scents of chamomile, myrrh, and woodruff following in her wake.

Once the major wounds were attended to, the lesser were taken care of. Cassia dabbed blood from Rhiannon's face with a wet washcloth where the slashes were. She groaned as if the touch of cloth against her skin caused her pain.

Silver grabbed another lodestone. Quickly, she said the chant of healing to it. Again she blew her warm breath onto the stone as she asked for the Ancestors' blessings. She reached for Rhiannon and pushed the lodestone into her friend's palm and clasped her fingers around it.

Rhiannon sighed, apparent relief flowing through her as her body visibly relaxed against the chair. Silver knew the stone wasn't enough, but at least it would lessen the pain until her wounds could be healed with a combination of witchcraft and magical remedies.

While Cassia helped Rhiannon, Silver began tending to Mackenzie and Iris, who had scrapes, bumps, and bruises from their treatment at the hands of the Fomorii.

"When everyone is finished, put them in a couple of the guest apartments," Silver said, motioning toward the stairs where the Coven kept apartments ready for guests that came into town from other D'Anu Covens.

After Silver had done all she could to attend to everyone's injuries, Hawk wrapped an arm around her shoulders and she sagged gratefully against him. Now that she knew her friends were safe and cared for, Silver's adrenaline rush dissipated and she felt too weak to move at all.

As if reading her thoughts, Hawk scooped her into his

arms, ignoring her protests, and carried her up the stairs and into her own apartment. He took her to her bedroom and laid her gently on the bed.

"Stay," he ordered with an intense look in his amber gaze.

Silver couldn't have moved if she'd tried.

A few moments later, he brought back warm, wet cloths, a cleansing solution that smelled of chamomile, and a blanket to cover her with. While he tended to her, Hawk spoke in his deep Irish brogue, in another language that sounded like Gaelic. He talked in low soothing tones that Silver found relaxing. He slipped powdered willow bark between her lips and her mouth puckered at the bitter taste.

When he finished treating her, and after she had chased Hawk out of her apartment, wanting to be alone, she stripped out of her clothing and climbed into the shower. She ached everywhere and she stunk like the sewer. Everything that had happened over the past few days was taking its toll.

She couldn't begin to imagine how Rhiannon or the other witches must be feeling right now after their captivity. On the bright side, if there was one, at least they were witches and wouldn't take too long to heal. Hopefully her healing magic had worked well enough on Jake and the PSF officers.

Once she had taken her shower, she slid between the cool sheets, naked. Sleep refused to come to her. The events of the day played over and over in her mind.

Darkwolf . . . the pleasure she had felt in the call of the dark witchcraft . . .

Silver shook her head, her damp hair clinging to her pillow. But even as she tried to, she couldn't deny her satisfaction at striking at the demons with all the power she could muster. The almost delicious feeling that had overcome her when a darker magic had joined with hers.

She squeezed her eyes shut, but that only made the images more intense.

It was a long time before she was able to sleep. Her dreams were filled with images of a black wolf . . . and a red eye.

· · ·

Silver was so exhausted that she slept through most of the day. She couldn't believe it was early evening by the time she made her way downstairs. She was wrapped in one of her silken white robes, and she knew her hair was tousled and her eyes puffy from her disturbed sleep.

Wondrous smells filled the kitchen and her stomach growled. Baked chicken. Vegetables. And the sweet smell of lemon meringue pie. She hadn't had a decent meal in days and she was starving.

"Chicken pot pie," Cassia announced, as she clasped Silver's hand and led her to the table where everyone else was sitting and chatting.

The witches they'd rescued last night looked just as sleep-tousled as Silver, but the men looked as handsome as ever—even Jake with his bandaged arm. Both appeared to have changed clothing and they all no longer smelled of the sewer.

Silver greeted everyone with a sleepy smile and a "good afternoon," and she felt some triumph that they'd at least rescued Rhiannon, Mackenzie, and Iris. They *would* rescue the rest of the witches, and get rid of the stinking Fomorii, too.

"The surviving PSF officers have gone to work—or pretended to," Jake explained. "For now, we're making excuses for Jameson's and Sanders's absences, until we know who we can trust." He shook his head. "After Chief Hernandez, we've got to watch our step. If more demons have infiltrated the force or the city council, we'd be easy targets."

Silver lowered her head at the thought of the lost officers, but Jake was right. They had to be even more careful now—and mourning, well, that would have to wait.

Cassia brought Silver a plate of food and she dug into the delicious creamy pot pie filled with chunks of chicken, carrots, and peas. She drank deeply of the iced water and lemon that Cassia brought her and already was feeling more of her strength restored.

But when the conversation turned to the witches' captivity, Silver clenched her fork in her fist and watched each of those gathered around the table.

"Samhain," Rhiannon was saying, her green eyes sparking. "That's when they plan on bringing more of their kind."

"When the veils between worlds are at their thinnest," muttered Hawk. "We thought as much."

Mackenzie nodded. "That's why they want more witches, and want us to cooperate so badly. They killed several of the warlocks and don't have enough of them now to perform the ceremony at its full strength."

"Sow-in?" Jake asked. "Is that the same as Halloween?"

"Spelled S-a-m-h-a-i-n. Same night as Halloween." Silver put her fork down into her pot pie. "But very different."

The cop shook his head. "That only gives us five more days to exterminate these bastards."

October 27

17

It was midnight when Silver slipped through the darkness of her living room, her white satin robe swirling about her feet. She tightened her belt as she moved to where Hawk sprawled in one of her armchairs, fully dressed but sleeping. Polaris had draped himself over the back of the armchair, probably keeping an eye on him. Or just being a general nuisance.

No doubt the familiar had just returned from one of his forays, searching for food. He was often gone for hours at a time. She was certain he was clearing the attic of any rodents. She felt bad for them, but it was part of the natural circle of life.

But if Polaris tried to get a hold of Mortimer, Silver had a feeling he'd get more than he'd bargained for with that little familiar.

Before Silver could wake Hawk, Polaris hissed and flicked his tongue along the man's cheek.

Hawk acted so fast, his movements were a blur. One second he was asleep, the next he had his dagger in one hand and gripped Polaris just below the head with his other.

"Hawk!" Silver shoved his hand away, forcing him to release the python, then she moved the snake to the floor. Polaris hissed at Hawk, gave him a piercing glare, and slithered under the chair.

Hawk got to his feet. "What are you doing up, Silver?" he

demanded, one eye on the snake curled up just behind his boots.

"He's not going to hurt you." She took Hawk's dagger and sheathed it for him, then clasped her hand in his. "I need to perform the summoning ritual again. You can help me."

He didn't budge. "You're exhausted."

"I'm a witch. I'm almost at full strength." She was a little tired, but nothing that she couldn't live with. Besides, more was at stake. "Since the veils between worlds aren't thin enough for anyone to cross over from Otherworld, we have to perform this ceremony to call the D'Danann and bring more of your people here. Likely next time we won't be so lucky battling the Fomorii."

A sour taste filled her mouth at the thought of those bastards, and fire grew in her chest at what they'd done to the witches and the PSF officers. Who knew what they'd done to the other witches Silver and her friends hadn't rescued?

In the dim light, Hawk's amber eyes almost seemed to glow. "Are you certain you're well enough to perform this ritual?"

"Absolutely." She tugged his hand, trying to get him to walk to the door with her.

After a moment he finally gave a slow nod and followed her.

Silver was dressed in her white robe, and all of her ritual items were carefully packed in a wooden chest beside the door. She kept everything she needed in the chest in order to always be prepared for the times she needed to perform a ritual. Especially in cases of emergency.

She grabbed her car keys from a hook beside her apartment door. Hawk insisted on carrying the chest as they moved quietly from the apartment, downstairs, and out the back door of the cafe's kitchen. A small garage behind the store housed her yellow VW Bug that she'd named Bitty.

Silver noticed Hawk eyeing the car critically as she had him stow the box in the trunk. While he watched, Silver adjusted the seat so that it was positioned as far back as possible to fit his long legs. When she moved away she saw that he towered over the compact vehicle, and Silver was tempted to laugh when he folded his large frame into Bitty's passenger seat. He had to hunch over just to fit his head in the Bug. She showed him how to buckle the seat belt, then went to her own side of the car.

Before they started off, she turned on the car's heater to take away some of the night's chill. She backed out of the garage, used the remote to close the door, and then backed up some more and sped down the alleyway.

Even though his rapid learning and his studies of this world's ways told Hawk what everything was, he was amazed at how the machine worked. It wasn't drawn by horses or magic, but by things that were more of a mystery to him. Electronics, engine, gasoline. Hawk's people had an amazing ability to learn quickly and retain all knowledge, but it might take longer than he thought to fully grasp it all.

Even as he studied how she drove the machine, catalogued her every movement, his gut tightened as Silver drove the vehicle like a madwoman, up, up, up steep streets, and down, down, down again. He gripped the dashboard and clenched his jaw. He didn't like this feeling of being out of control and in such a confined space. Not to mention her driving was enough to make the sturdiest warrior ill.

If he wasn't close to losing his supper, he might have enjoyed the lighted bridge looping across the bay. The low-hanging fog rolling in. The towering buildings and the amazing view of thousands of lights in the city and on the other side of the bay.

She finally brought the car to an abrupt stop near a small cliff overlooking the ocean, and Hawk's stomach churned. When he managed to squeeze out of the car, he took great gulps of air to clear his head. He stretched his muscles and wished he'd stop feeling the motion of the car. On the way back to her apartment he'd fly as D'Danann, soaring above her, instead of subjecting himself to Silver's driving again.

"Come on, big guy." Silver opened the back compartment and took the chest out. "The moon is almost at its full strength for the night."

He took the chest from her and followed her down a hidden footpath, to the small cove where she'd summoned him. Waves slapped the shore and the smells of kelp and seawater were strong.

After he set it upon the sand, Silver knelt before the chest and began withdrawing items, arranging them on the beach. A small altar with a pentagram carved into it, a chalice that she filled from a bottle of water, a white candle, a small bowl of salt, and a stick of incense that smelled of sandalwood.

When she finished preparing the items, she glanced at the moon, then to Hawk. "You'll need to remove your clothing."

Hawk's jaw nearly dropped to the sand. Instead he narrowed his eyes and frowned. "Certainly not."

"To do this ceremony with only two of us, we need to be skyclad." Silver tilted her chin, determination in her gray eyes. "If you want this to work, if you want us to be able to summon a larger number of the D'Danann, it *is* necessary. Now strip."

When he saw fire in her eyes and knew he wasn't going to win this round, he began taking off his clothing. He started with his weapon belt, which he set carefully aside on the sand. By the time all his clothing was removed, he felt foolish and vulnerable, not to mention aroused by the way Silver was looking at him.

"I've never seen you naked before." She licked her lips and his cock hardened near to bursting. She smiled, a slow sensual smile that caused him to groan. "There's a very special part to this ceremony that we'll both enjoy."

Without another word, Silver let her robe slip from her shoulders to the sand at her feet, baring her exquisite body. The only things she wore were the pentagram at her throat, the snake curled around her wrist, and jewelry at her ears.

Hawk caught his breath. She was so beautiful. The glow of moonlight caressed every inch of her body that he wanted to be touching at this very moment.

She turned her back to him and bent over the altar, and treated him to a fine view of her ass—her perfectly molded cheeks, the light foam of hair between her thighs, and her firmly muscled legs. He groaned and stepped forward, ready to drive his cock into her pussy right then and there.

Silver rose and she had a crown on. It was a silver band with a crescent moon resting upside down at the front center. In her hands she held a circlet with a small pair of antlers on it.

He frowned.

She moved forward, reached up and placed the crown on his head. He didn't have time to feel foolish as her nipples brushed his chest, the heat of her body radiating to his just by her nearness.

While he watched, Silver consecrated her tools, including the dagger she used to draw a magical circle around them. Candles flickered to life where they had been placed—to the north, south, east, and west.

When she finished she stood before him. "This ritual is far more effective when two people perform it, and even more so when the entire Coven is present."

Hawk was rather relieved the Coven was *not* there at that moment, with both of them naked.

Silver took his hands in hers and she looked up at him. Her gaze filled him with emotion he couldn't define. Already he felt magic growing within her that rippled throughout him, giving him a rush of power.

"When the high priest performs the ritual with the high priestess"—Silver's voice quavered as she continued—"he kisses each of her feet, her belly, each breast, and her mouth. I'll chant the ritual words since you don't know them," she added softly.

Hawk's gut clenched and his cock grew harder at the image of his mouth all over Silver's body.

When she bade him to, he knelt before her and lowered his head. He brushed soft kisses over the top of each of her feet, the mere act making his cock throb. Silver's voice joined with the ocean breeze and the wash of waves against shore. "Bless our feet on the sacred path."

Hawk raised himself to his knees to kiss the soft skin of her belly, and felt Silver tremble beneath his lips. Silver's voice trembled, too. "Bless the womb, the goddess's gift, fertility's bath."

When Hawk stood, more than lust was raging through him. He could feel a touch, a presence, growing within himself and Silver. A magical, unearthly presence.

Slowly he kissed each of her breasts. Silver had to force her words out, hardly able to breathe, as she said, "Bless the breasts, which nurture life." Her knees almost gave out when he flicked his warm tongue over each nipple.

Hawk caught Silver's face in his hands and brought his mouth to hers. The kiss was slow and sensual, his lips gently moving over hers in a way that made her almost forget where she was and what she was supposed to be doing. When he raised his head, she whispered, "Bless our lips to praise all Ancestors alike, when honoring the Ancestors within us all."

Silver took a step back. She drew in a deep breath, trying to gain control of her body, her desires, and her emotions. She was about to attempt something she'd read about but had never done, and realized she would only do this because it would be with Hawk.

Sex magic.

She needed to touch him, taste him. Relax him.

She smiled at the thought of the addition she would make to the ritual. "Now it's your turn."

Hawk sucked in his breath as Silver gracefully knelt before him. Her silvery hair floated over her shoulders and brushed his feet as her moist lips pressed against the top of each one, and she repeated the ritual words she had spoken earlier. Only this time her voice was husky with what he was sure was desire.

She rose to her knees, her mouth level with his cock. Hawk clenched his fists at his sides as she flicked her tongue along its length, from balls to tip, then kissed the pearl of fluid at the small slit. "You need to relax to more fully join with the Ancestors," she murmured as she kissed his belly button and his cock jerked.

She softly said the chant, and then slipped her soft lips over the head of his erection.

Stunned, Hawk could only watch as the beautiful woman took his cock deep into her mouth and sucked. Hard. With one hand she cupped his balls and the other gripped his staff, moving it up and down as she swirled her tongue over the engorged head of his shaft.

Sparkles whirled around them. She was using her magic to give him pleasure beyond reason. He'd never felt anything like what Silver was doing to him now, and he didn't know if he was going to be able to continue standing as weak as his knees felt at that moment.

She sucked him deeper, brought his cock to the back of her throat, and her moan vibrated through him. He groaned and closed his eyes. He saw the same sparkles swirling in his mind, felt them caressing his body, and working their magic throughout his very being.

Closer and closer he drew to a pinnacle he'd never been to before. Nothing in his life had prepared him for what was happening to him. He slid his hands into her silky hair, nearly out of his mind.

Everything exploded, inside and out. Like a shower of stars from the sky in his mind. When he opened his eyes he saw the same waterfalls of stars flowing down around them. His orgasm seemed to last forever as Silver swallowed every last bit of his essence. He finally had to grip her hair harder and force her to stop.

He was still trying to catch his breath when she rose and kissed each of his flat nipples and murmured the ritual words. And then her mouth was on his, and he saw more stars.

When she finally tilted her head back, she murmured, "You're ready now."

At that moment, he couldn't have answered her for the world. He was so relaxed; spasms still vibrated throughout him. The sparks around them filled him, too.

Silver took Hawk by the hands and he squeezed hers within his grip. Their bodies were but a fraction apart, her nipples caressing his chest, his now moist cock brushing her belly. His member instantly grew erect at the thought of being inside her.

As she began speaking, more light sparked the air around them like hundreds of fireflies.

> *"Join us, Ancestors. Fill us with your power.*
> *We beseech for your aid in this fateful hour.*
> *Help us call the D'Danann, help us save countless*
>   *souls.*
> *Protecting witches and all humans, these are our*
>   *goals.*
> *Lend us your strength, your protection, your*
>   *grace.*
> *Bring the D'Danann for battle to face."*

The sparkles around them began swirling, becoming brighter and brighter. Silver's hair floated from her shoulders and Hawk felt light-headed and light-bodied, as if he could take to the skies without wings.

"Place your forehead to mine." Silver's voice seemed to come from nowhere, everywhere, within him, around him.

Nearly boneless, Hawk leaned down and touched his forehead to hers, and felt the press of her silver circlet against his crown of antlers. The small antlers were positioned so that they did not touch her.

"Close your eyes and see what I see." She gripped his hands tighter. "Feel what I feel."

He shut his eyes and immediately a candle flame flickered to life. "Join your strength with mine," Silver said. "Help me make the flame grow beyond these earthly bonds."

At first he didn't think he had any strength after that shattering orgasm, but then he found a greater power welling up within him. The candle flame in his mind grew until it became a roaring campfire. Sparks exploded. Wood crackled. It turned into a raging bonfire. Heat rushed through him and he felt as if he were right before it. Sweat rolled down his skin as the bonfire grew. Before he knew it, they were standing beneath a volcano—

The volcano of Otherworld.

His heart ached at the sight of it. He and his people lived

in the forest, far from the volcano, but it was a part of the soul of the D'Danann. Its every push and pull within its belly was like the heartbeat that throbbed in his chest.

A black force slammed into Silver's consciousness. Darkness that tried to shove her away from her summoning.

Her body tensed and she blocked out the force attempting to control her. Attempting to sway her from her goal.

This time the gray wasn't helping her. It was fighting her.

Her body ached and her thoughts spun. With one huge shove of her magic, she blocked out the dark witchcraft trying to overpower her and keep her from summoning the D'Danann.

How had black magic entered the protective circle? Had she brought it with her?

Sweat broke out on her skin and rolled down the sides of her face. Her head spun and she could barely stand. It took all of her concentration to return her focus to the ceremony.

"Call your warriors," Silver whispered to Hawk, forcing strength of conviction into her voice. "Summon the D'Danann."

Hawk reached deep inside and mentally gave the cry of his people. He called to them in their language, expressing the urgency in his request. Another race was in danger, and only the D'Danann could save them.

The scene in his mind switched from the volcano to his forest home and he witnessed his brethren as they emerged from the greenery. Shadowed as they were, he couldn't tell the number of D'Danann who were answering his summons, but it did not look like many.

Yet they were coming. Coming to pass judgment on his decision to join the battle against the Fomorii? Or coming to fight?

For what seemed an eternity, Silver and Hawk stood together, drawing on the power of the waxing moon and calling to his people. Finally he felt Silver's mental tug back to the present. The forest vanished and they returned to the volcano, which quickly receded. In its place was the bonfire, which was soon replaced by the campfire, and it eventually diminished to a mere candle flame. Silver's gentle breath extinguished the flame, and the thin trail of smoke vanished into the darkness of his mind.

At Silver's mental command, Hawk opened his eyes. For the longest time they stared at each other, both unable to move, to tear their gazes apart. He no longer felt weak from the orgasm, but strong and powerful, able to take on anything that might come to them—even a host of Fomorii.

Yet Silver trembled in his arms.

Sparkles swirling around them gradually faded, and Hawk's once heated skin cooled in the ocean breeze. Vaguely he heard the crash of the ocean, the sound of a foghorn.

And the cry of the D'Danann.

Still holding Silver, Hawk turned to look at the sky. His mouth curved into a smile when he saw several of his brethren circling above them. At once he recognized Sheridan, Keir, and Garrett. As the D'Danann came closer, he saw that Kirra, Aideen, Cael, Braeden, Fallon, Tiernan, and Wynne accompanied them.

The ten warriors drifted to the beach, landing gracefully in the sand just yards away, all wearing leather clothing similar to Hawk's. Sher ruffled her feathered wings and began the change at once, folding away her blue wings that matched the color of her eyes.

Garrett smiled at Hawk, his wings in shades of browns and tans. He drew in his wings. He was a tall, blond, lanky man with warm brown eyes.

Keir didn't bother to change. Hawk's fosterling brother was a rogue with a scar across one cheek, piercing black eyes, a powerful build. He gave a wicked look at Hawk and his teeth flashed white in the moonlight as he gave an irritated flap of his wings.

Silver glanced at Hawk and he caught her small smile. Concern for her flashed through his consciousness. She looked so weak and fragile.

With effort he turned his attention to the D'Danann. "Sher, Garrett, Keir," Hawk called as he looked to each warrior. He was pleased to see friends—and even his rival. Keir could be a bastard, but he fought like a maddened dragon.

Sher tossed her wheat-brown hair from her face and shook her head. "You shouldn't have come alone, Hawk."

"Rash and foolhardy as always." With a harrumph, Keir folded his arms across his chest. "I see you have sprouted horns in your absence."

Hawk nearly groaned, imagining how he must look, naked and wearing antlers. But when he saw Keir's open appreciation of Silver's naked form, Hawk was ready to smash his bastard brother's face.

Garrett shook his head and gave Hawk a crooked smile. "It's good to see you, friend."

While the D'Danann greeted one another, Silver took off her crown, said a quick chant, and removed the consecrated circle from around her and Hawk. Even the sand of the circle smoothed, and the candles extinguished with her magic.

Just as Hawk tossed aside the antler crown and started to turn to reach for his clothing, he glanced at Silver.

Her face paled and she swayed.

Hawk shouted her name, his gut twisting. Before he could catch her in his arms, Silver collapsed in a heap on the sand.

18

Jaw tense, Hawk knelt, wrapped Silver in his embrace, and held her tight to his chest. Her naked body was cold. Too cold.

He stood and said in the ancient language of the D'Danann, "I need to get Silver to her home, back to the other witches."

Sher moved to his side and pressed her hand to Silver's forehead. "She is strong. She will survive. But she needs warmth."

Hawk nodded and went to where Silver's robe lay discarded on the ground. He knelt and laid her on the sand and grabbed his tunic from his pile of clothing. With Sher's help, he eased his tunic over Silver's cold body and then added her robe, cinching it around her waist with the tie.

Hawk yanked on the rest of his clothing as fast as he could. At his instruction, Garrett and Keir collected Silver's candles, chalice, altar, and other tools of her Craft and put them into the wooden chest as quickly as they could.

"What in the gods' names happened?" Keir folded his arms across his broad chest as Hawk scooped Silver into his embrace again and stood.

Hawk returned Keir's glare, then started toward the footpath. "Apparently it is difficult for her to perform this ceremony."

Keir's lips curled into a snarl. "Then you should have been better prepared. This could have been avoided. As always, you are too rash. You do not think situations through."

Hawk clenched his fists even as he grasped Silver. He shifted her in his arms. "I don't answer to you, Keir. You had best remember that."

A muscle worked in Keir's jaw and his stare pierced Hawk. "You answer to no one but your own foolish whims."

Hawk gave a low growl. "Say that again when I am not carrying an injured woman in my arms."

Body stiff with fury at Keir and with concern for Silver, Hawk carried her to the car. He stopped and stared at it for a moment. What in the gods' names was he going to do? How was he going to get her home? Hawk could fly and carry her, but the cold would no doubt be too much on her fragile body, even with what covering he had been able to provide. The inside of the car would be much warmer.

His mind told him what he needed to do, but his gut rebelled. He ignored the feeling, opened the passenger door, and gently set Silver upon the seat. She moaned and started to slide sideways. Hawk fumbled with the seat's belt and managed to keep her upright once he figured out how to buckle the damnable thing again.

When he rose and shut the door, he turned to see the other D'Danann with expressions ranging from amusement to curiosity to doubt.

"Ah, Hawk," Garrett said, rubbing stubble that shadowed his jaw. "How do you expect to get the witch back to her home?"

Sher tossed her hair over her shoulder and reached out to run her fingers along the car's yellow hood. "A mode of transportation for this world." Her eyes met Hawk's. "Certainly you do not believe you can operate it."

"I will drive this contraption." Hawk hated the inflection of doubt in his own voice. "It's too far to her home to walk, and I certainly cannot carry her with the heights as cold as they are. It will be much warmer in the car with its heater."

Sher sighed. "He's right. Slip of a thing that she is, the air would be too cold for her."

Hawk picked up Silver's chest of items and stowed them in the still open back compartment. After he slammed the lid shut, he strode around to the driver's side door and glanced one more time at his ten comrades. "Follow."

While he folded his body into the cramped front seat of the vehicle, his comrades spread their wings and waited nearby. Hunched over, knees pressed against the steering wheel, Hawk stared at the odd gadgets and controls, and ignored the D'Danann now watching him with mirth in their eyes.

Hawk took a deep breath. Thought about what Silver had done when he'd studied how she had driven the car. He had an excellent memory.

Hopefully that memory was fully functioning.

First thing, he had to scoot the seat back so that his long legs could work the pedals. Secondly he needed to use keys. Thirdly he needed to push in the far pedal to the left with his left foot.

Hawk fumbled around beneath the seat until he finally found a lever that shot the seat back so fast it jarred his teeth. But it had moved far enough that his booted feet easily reached the pedals, even though he was still hunched over.

Next, keys. He leaned to the right and looked at the steering column, where he remembered Silver inserting them. He squinted in the dark car and found the keys dangling from the column with the wheel, glittering in the moonlight. Silver was careless with her safety, he decided. She left her apartment door unlocked, and now her keys in the car.

He turned his attention back to the car and hesitantly pressed in the pedal on the left, as he had seen Silver do. Steeling himself, he turned the key and nearly jumped out of his skin when the car came to life with a shudder, then a purr, and then a screech as he kept turning the key. He let go of the keys and the vehicle went back to a low purr and heat started to come out of the heating vents.

So far so good.

He gripped the steering wheel and stared out into the darkness. Light. He needed light. Again he fumbled in the dark interior. He turned one knob and water squirted on the glass. Clicked another and long black sticks began moving back and forth across the pane, wiping away the water.

So much for an excellent memory.

His comrades chuckled loudly enough to break his concentration and he scowled at them.

Once he managed to turn the black sticks off, he finally found the light switch and breathed a sigh of relief when the small area outside was illuminated so that he could see trees in front of him. A drop-off to the right. The road behind.

Thankfully warm air was coming from the heater, and he hoped it would take away the chill from Silver.

She moaned again and Hawk's pulse quickened. He had to get her to Cassia and Rhiannon. Silver had been through far too much in a short amount of time, and fear for her coursed his veins like liquid fire.

His fear motivated him to hurry to move the vehicle. He followed his memories, finding the stick with the knob on it. With a bit of effort he shoved it to the "R" position, then let out the pedal with his left foot and pressed the far right pedal with his right foot. The car jerked backward, hard enough to rattle Hawk's composure. The vehicle stalled, leaving only silence, then squawks of laughter from his comrades.

Their hilarity only made him angrier and more determined to master the vehicle. He paid greater attention to his memories of Silver's driving. After a few more starts and stalls he figured out how to back up the car—and came just short of tumbling over the low cliff to the shore below.

Heart pounding, Hawk put the car into the "1" position on the stick with the knob. He let out the left pedal and pressed down on the thing that accelerated the vehicle. The car lurched, bucking like an untrained horse as Hawk urged the damnable car onward.

It shot forward.

And slammed into a tree.

The sound of crunching metal echoed through the night.

Hawk's head struck the front window and sparks flashed in his head like Silver's spellfire. His chest hit the steering wheel hard enough to bruise his ribs.

The car stalled.

Laughter from the D'Danann outside nearly drove him to climb out of the vehicle and wring each of their necks.

He glanced at Silver to see her flopped forward like one of Shayla's stuffed poppets.

He gently moved Silver so that she was sitting back in the seat, her head drooping to the side. At the same time thoughts of his daughter made his throat ache. He missed her on these missions to Otherworlds, but it was his job, his responsibility to care for all beings who needed him. But godsdamn, his daughter needed him, too.

He gently cupped Silver's chin and stroked hair from her face.

And Silver needed him right now.

With renewed determination, he started the vehicle and backed the car away from the tree. He winced at the sound of metal creaking and the sight of the splintered wood of the tree and the damage to the car. Once he pulled out into the moonlight, with his keen vision, he saw the front of the car was crumpled and deep scratches lined the metal. The right light no longer functioned, obviously smashed.

Hawk managed to get the vehicle in motion. He clenched the steering wheel and clenched his teeth just as hard, while the car bucked down the tree-shaded road. The D'Danann had taken to the air and circled above, following the car and probably still laughing. Soon they could not be seen as they cloaked themselves with their magic.

A warrior of the most powerful Fae race in Otherworld, and I'm reduced to this . . .

Hawk used his own recall to find his way back to Silver's apartment. On the way he weaved the car up and down steep hills, lurched around sharp turns, and ran right through three four-way stops. He nearly smashed into two other vehicles, scraped the passenger side door against a fire hydrant, drove up on a sidewalk, barely missed a light pole, and almost slammed into Silver's garage door.

When he brought the car within a hairsbreadth of the wooden garage door, he shut off the engine. He banged his head against the steering wheel in relief and let out a low groan.

Silver groaned, too.

He forgot everything but getting her out of the car and to Cassia and Rhiannon. It took him a few frustrating moments to find the door handle, but finally he was able to unfold himself from the vehicle and hurry to Silver's side. His ribs ached and his head throbbed, but that was nothing, mere inconveniences compared to what Silver had tolerated.

Sher, Garrett, and Keir landed beside the car, then folded their wings away. Hawk ignored them as he unbuckled Silver's seat belt, and gently took her out of the battered car. He brushed past the other D'Danann as he carried her to the back door leading to the kitchen. He fumbled with the door-knob.

Locked.

Heat roared through him and he almost slammed his shoulder against the wood when it suddenly opened. Cassia stood on the other side, a black robe cinched tight around her waist.

"Up to her room," Cassia ordered Hawk. She barely spared a glance for the other warriors who followed Hawk in. "If you're hungry," she said to them, "there's food in the fridge and the pantry. Otherwise stay out of my way."

Hawk raised an eyebrow at Cassia's change in demeanor, and the fact that she had apparently been waiting for them. Her sudden take-charge attitude and intuitiveness only confirmed what he'd suspected all along. That she was something *other*.

He laid Silver on her bed for the second time in less than twenty-four hours. This time, though—this time she looked so much more wan, so much more fragile, that he was afraid he'd break her if he wasn't careful.

When her head rested on soft pillows, a comfortable covering pulled up to her chest, Hawk allowed a lump to form at the back of his throat. He'd never permitted himself to feel such genuine emotion for anyone since his wife Davina's death. The only person in his life he truly loved now was his daughter.

Yet, after knowing Silver only days, he felt her seeping into his soul, into his body like the fluid running through his veins. He didn't understand it, didn't want to at that moment. He simply needed to know she would recover.

Hawk gently stroked Silver's cool cheek with his knuckles, shivering himself at how cold she was.

He trailed the back of his hand down the curve of her neck and paused at her throat where the pentagram lay against her soft skin. The amber eye was dark.

Cassia bustled into the room, her blond hair in wild ringlets around her face, practically standing on end and making her look like a demented Medusa. And Medusa was a being he'd rather not be reminded of.

The smell of peppermint and lemon accompanying Cassia was so strong Hawk nearly reeled from its intensity. If she was *other,* what in the hells' names was she?

Cassia set aside a small pot and a couple of vials on the nightstand. She leaned over Silver. While closing her own eyes, Cassia held her hands over Silver's chest.

When she opened them she turned her gaze on Hawk. "She's nearly drained of her magical essence, her life force. What happened to her?"

Hawk explained and Cassia's frown deepened. "After all she's been through, you should have made her stay here. Should have insisted she wait at least until Rhiannon recovered. And you should have taken me."

Hawk's guilt increased as she confirmed his gut feeling. But telling Silver what to do . . . she was perhaps more stubborn than he was—if that was possible.

After opening Silver's robe, Cassia removed a cork from a vial of powder and began sprinkling it over Silver from head to toe. It smelled of apples and honeysuckle. Sparkles floated around her body, like Faerie dust. The glow grew and grew, then visibly began to seep into her body.

"What's happening?" Hawk's voice was gruff, his words sharp and dominating. "What are you doing to her?"

Cassia turned her sharp blue eyes on Hawk. "Saving her, you big dumbass."

After Cassia tended to Silver, and he was certain she would be all right, Hawk made his way downstairs to where his fellow D'Danann were feasting on whatever they had scrounged out of the refrigerator. The kitchen was so crowded with the ten D'Danann warriors that it was hard to move in the confined space. The table was littered with empty casserole dishes, salad bowls, and crumpled bags that had been filled with rolls and bread. Hawk frowned when he saw that the jar of chocolate chip cookies had been emptied.

Only three of the D'Danann would be housed in the small apartments above as the place was too small to hold all of them. The other seven would stay aboard a houseboat belonging to Rhiannon's foster parents, who were fortunately on vacation.

For now all ten of the warriors were taking up every available space in the café's kitchen.

"Is the witch all right?" Garrett asked, a smear of chocolate on his cheek.

"Silver." Hawk tried not to be irritated with his friend as he rubbed his hand over his face. "Her name is Silver."

"Well, how is she?" Sher had a cluster of purple grapes in one hand, a glass of water in the other.

"She'll be fine." Cassia came up beside Hawk. "No thanks to you."

Hawk had no response to that. He simply eyed her steadily. "Thank you for your assistance in helping Silver."

Keir sat in one of the chairs at the table, his arms folded across his chest, his legs stretched out and crossed at the ankles, and a fearsome look on his harsh features. "Hawk knows nothing of restraint."

Hawk's temper snapped. He made it to Keir in four strides. The warrior jumped to his feet in a flash. Garrett planted himself between the two men before Hawk could slam his fist into Keir's jaw.

"Enough." Garrett placed his hand on Keir's shoulder and with a firm grip encouraged Keir to take his seat. His glare would have blasted a hole through a lesser man than Hawk.

When Keir was sitting, Garrett put both hands on Hawk's shoulders. "No fighting among ourselves. Focus on the Fomorii."

Hawk took a deep breath and gave his friend a nod. With a glare of his own at Keir, he took a seat at the table beside Sher. Other warriors lounged around the table or propped themselves against the walls, their arms folded across their chests.

She tucked her wheat-brown hair behind her ear, and her blue eyes were thoughtful. "How many Fomorii are we talking about?" She leveled her gaze on Hawk. "Here, at this time."

"We are uncertain." Hawk sighed. "We now know they are holed up in a lair not too far from Silver's shop."

"Is this place protected?" Garrett asked, glancing around the kitchen. His gaze settled on Cassia who now stirred something in a black cauldron. The smells of potatoes, carrots, and corn came from the pot. "Can the Fomorii attack the witches here?"

"The witches have the premises well warded, but I am not sure it will be sufficient against demons of that magnitude," Hawk admitted. "Although the Fomorii have no magic, so it may be enough."

Garrett gave Hawk a mischievous grin and lightly punched him in the arm. "The witch—Silver—is certainly beautiful."

The fierce rush of jealousy surprised Hawk, but he tamped it down. He simply nodded his acknowledgment.

With his usual boyish enthusiasm, Garrett paced the floor, and delved into their current predicament. "Fomorii," he said. "Unbelievable that the beasts have escaped Underworld after all these centuries."

Hawk explained what he knew from Silver about the Balorite Clan of warlocks, and how the Fomorii came to be in this world. Although he had told Garrett before he left, he didn't tell the rest of the D'Danann of the Great Guardian's prediction or about her sending Hawk through the membrane between worlds. With the animosity between Fae and Elves, he didn't want to start *that* discussion.

"Why did only ten of you answer the summons?" he asked instead. "It is our responsibility to help these people just as we helped the Druids in Ireland when these monsters first attacked."

"That war is in the past." Keir gave him a fierce expression. "The Sages and Seers prayed to the gods and goddesses and deemed our ranks a sufficient number for this battle."

"We have much to consider." Garrett paused in his pacing and braced his hands on the back of a chair as he looked at his comrades. "We must prepare our battle plans and engage in reconnaissance."

"We must find a way to draw them out," Aideen said as she hitched her shoulder against a doorframe.

Hawk nearly growled. "And when we do, we shall destroy the bastards."

Needing air, needing time alone with his thoughts, Hawk left the kitchen through the back door and closed it tight behind him. He stared up toward the stars, but saw nothing through the overcast sky. He wondered how his daughter was doing. If she was looking out her window up at the stars in Otherworld.

And he wondered what Silver was doing at this moment. His attraction to her—from the moment he had met her—had been intense, fiery.

He tensed when he heard the back door open but relaxed when he heard Garrett's voice. "What do you think of the changes to this world, my friend?" Garrett asked.

Hawk turned so that he was facing Garrett and gave a slight shake of his head. "Here, in this city called San Francisco . . . it has its charm. But if I had my druthers, I would go back to our long-ago homeland, to set foot upon Ireland once again."

Garrett glanced up at the sky, as if seeking the stars, too, then looked back to Hawk. "The witch, Silver, you have feelings for her."

Hawk scowled, his automatic response coming to his lips. "Davina is the only one I will ever love."

Garrett sighed. "She would not want this, Hawk. She would want you to be happy. I am certain that where she resides in Summerland, she is at peace, and wishes the same for you."

Hawk squeezed his eyes shut and clenched his jaw. The image of her laughing and playing with Shayla came easily to his mind. How his heart had swelled with joy at the sight of the two of them!

Then Silver replaced the memory of Davina. Her fire, her spirit, her caring, her smile. His heart twinged again and he clenched his jaw tighter. From the moment he had met her, he had felt an instant attraction, something that shouldn't have been there as far as he was concerned.

He opened his eyes to see Garrett standing before him, arms across his chest. "Let her go, Hawk. Davina will not be happy in death unless you are happy in life."

Hawk shook his head. His voice came out gruffer than he intended. "These feelings I have for Silver . . . I do not understand them. Lust is all it can be."

Garrett just gave him his cocky smile. "There are forces at work greater than you and I. Perhaps Silver is your destiny."

Hawk inhaled deeply. "I no longer believe in destiny."

"You left Otherworld for her, even without the Chieftains' blessings." Garrett unfolded his arms and rested a hand on Hawk's shoulder. "You cannot tell me there was not something more than your desire to help this witch."

In his mind he saw her stealing through the night to save a child and to stop the slaying of innocents. And then in the alleyway, when they touched, it was like fire had singed them both. He had seen it in her eyes, had felt it in his heart. And so clearly Hawk could visualize Silver on the moonlit beach, her naked body caressed by moonlight. She had been so stunning, yet more than her beauty called to him.

But no, he did not understand why.

For a moment Garrett remained quiet, then his tone was uncommonly serious when he finally spoke. "The Chieftains . . ." He cleared his throat. "You are to return to Otherworld as soon as possible and face the council for your actions. For departing Otherworld without their leave."

Hawk's attention snapped to Garrett. "The Chieftains are calling me back?"

Garrett gave a heavy sigh. "If you do not return at the first opportunity, you will be banished from Otherworld. You will not see your daughter again."

Rage exploded through Hawk. With a furious growl, he whirled and slammed his fist into the garage door, driving his fist deep into the wood. The splintering sound echoed through the quiet night. When he pulled his hand away, his knuckles were numb, tiny drops of blood welling on the scrapes. His heart pounded and his blood roared.

"How much time do I have?" he asked through clenched teeth.

"Samhain," Garrett said. "You must return by Samhain."

19

Junga turned from the sight of the recent catch of humans, those with no magic, tied up in the middle of the small ballroom's floor. Many of the soon-to-be demon-food whimpered while some cursed, others prayed.

"Do it now," Junga said, facing Darkwolf in her Elizabeth form, a scowl on her face. "I don't care what you have to do, but perform a summoning. Bring the queen and the Old One."

Darkwolf glared at her, the domination in his eyes causing her pussy to ache and her nipples to throb. But she wasn't backing down. *She* was in control, and she would make sure he knew that.

"As I told you," he said through clenched teeth, "there are not enough warlocks to summon the Fomorii from the depths of Underworld. We need a few more of the D'Anu witches to cooperate to make thirteen."

Junga stretched to Elizabeth's full height, and it infuriated her that Darkwolf was still taller. Her hands shifted into her enhanced Fomorii claws, and she bared her now needle-like teeth. Her voice came out deep and guttural, a combination of Elizabeth and Junga. "You *will* obey."

The fury in the warlock high priest's eyes told her that he would seek his revenge in other ways. The thought made her shiver with lust.

Darkwolf swung away from her, past the humans, and strode to the five remaining warlocks and one witch. "Move into position."

The warlock turned and faced the witches who were in his magical prison. "Who among you will join with the Balorites?" He paced the length of the shimmering wall before the remaining witches and apprentices.

Not one of them spoke. Some didn't look at him, while others studied him almost casually as if he were nothing but a bothersome fly.

He whirled on the apprentices and focused on them. "You each have burgeoning powers not yet fully explored. Would you wait for these fools to die so that you might replace them one day?" He walked up to one female apprentice who looked scared, yet intrigued. "Would you not prefer to embrace your magic and come into your full power now? At this very moment?"

The witch licked her lips. Her eyes were wide and indecisive. Junga could see how tired the apprentice was, how badly she wanted her freedom. The warlocks were never beaten, never threatened, unlike the witches who all sported scratches, claw marks, and bruises.

Darkwolf's eyes turned starkly sensual, his words coming out soft and alluring. "You will experience power beyond your imagination."

He used a motion of his hands to push away the magical shield from the apprentice, leaving her free. It immediately closed behind her, caging in the rest of the witches. He grasped her by the shoulders, his gaze focused intently on hers. "What do you say, witch?"

She licked her lips again. Cleared her throat. "Yes," she finally said, and Junga saw the horror reflected in the other witches' eyes. "I will join you."

His smile for the witch was so carnal that the urge to claw his eyes out came sharp and sudden to Junga. At the same time she wondered why she should care.

Darkwolf helped the apprentice to her feet while the high priestess of the D'Anu Coven commanded her to stay.

"Don't, Sara," Janis Arrowsmith said. "There is no turning back. Better to suffer. Better to die in the white than give yourself over to the likes of this evil."

"You will join us one day, witch," the warlock priest snarled. "Or you will die."

Janis turned her head slowly to face him. "So be it."

Darkwolf pivoted to where the witch apprentice was standing in her dirty robe.

Junga wrinkled her nose. The witches smelled. A couple had soiled themselves before being allowed to use the restroom facilities. They reeked of their own urine, of their fear. Some refused to eat or drink and were weakening, seemingly by the minute, giving a sickly-sweet odor of death to the air. Other witches ate what was offered, perhaps sustaining their strength in hopes of escape or rescue.

She gave a slow, feline smile. As if that would ever happen. If the foolish D'Anu and their helpers came back to this lair, they'd find a few surprises in store.

"Sara, is it?" Darkwolf caught the witch by her hands and began a sensual massage of her wrists. "A beautiful name." He smiled. "You feel better already, don't you?"

Sara gave a jerky nod, seemingly entranced by Darkwolf. He wrapped one arm around her waist as she stumbled on shaky legs and walked her to where the others were standing.

Junga smiled. Surely there were enough now to bring the queen and her guards from the Underworld.

"Sex magic is strong," the high priest said as he guided Sara to stand in the circle of warlocks and the one witch he had earlier seduced to join him. "Perhaps I should fuck you in front of everyone as part of the ceremony, and as part of your initiation."

At that Junga growled aloud. The young apprentice looked terrified, and Darkwolf gave her a gentle smile. "No, not here, not on this day," he said, but his unspoken words hung on the quiet in the room. *But one day I will.*

He slipped a wand from inside his robes. "Now for the conversion ceremony."

While the witch stood quavering just behind him,

Darkwolf pointed a crystal-tipped black wand at the ballroom floor. The crystal glowed, a wicked light that fractured throughout the room as he burned the floor and a shape emerged.

An eye. He had burned Balor's eye into the flooring.

Darkwolf held one hand to the stone at this throat and began murmuring so softly that Junga could not hear what he said.

The stone eye began to glow through his fingers. Junga swallowed down a strange rush of fear and fought to keep from stepping back, farther away from the priest. A chill iced her spine as the eyeball on the floor moved. It slowly rolled side to side, up and down, as if searching for someone. When its horrid gaze rested on Sara, the witch whimpered.

"Bring one of the humans." Darkwolf released his hold on the glowing red stone at his neck to gesture to one of the Fomorii. At the same time he took Sara by her upper arm and led her to within inches of the eye.

Junga could see the witch trembling within the high priest's grasp, but as the eye continued to focus on her, Sara calmed. Her features settled into an almost serene expression as she stared at the eye. Mesmerized.

Darkwolf cast a look over his shoulder at the other uninitiated witch he had earlier convinced to join him. "Come."

The older witch moved forward, her steps hesitant. But when Darkwolf narrowed his gaze at her, she hurried to his side.

Bane dragged over a human male who must have been in his late teens. The boy shouted, kicked, and struggled, but Bane's grasp was too strong.

When they reached the eye, Darkwolf made a slicing motion with his hand. "Cut his throat."

Junga heard a collective gasp from the imprisoned witches. One of them shouted, "No, please don't!" Junga casually looked at the witch captive who had her hands pressed against the magical barrier. Junga saw all the other witches turn their heads, refusing to watch. Some had tears glistening on their cheeks.

She glanced back at Bane and the human in time to see Bane's finger extend into one of his hooked, iron-tipped claws to slice open the screaming boy's throat.

Blood flowed freely from the mortal wound and bubbled up within the human's mouth. Bane dropped the boy's body to the center of the eye as soon as he no longer struggled and his body went limp.

The boy's head lolled to the side as blood oozed out of his mouth and throat, into every crevice of the eye that had been burned into the floor.

The witch and the apprentice stared at the body, faces as white as the now dead human.

Darkwolf slowly began to circle the witches and the body as he said, "God of greatness, Balor of the Eye, we gift you with new children to bring into your fold."

The warlocks surrounding the witches and the high priest took up one another's hands and repeated Darkwolf's words.

The soon-to-be warlocks visibly trembled. If they caused this summoning to fail, Junga would offer the offending bitches to her warriors for a small meal.

Darkwolf stopped. With a simple circular motion of his wand, flames burned in a perfect circle, around himself, the warlocks, and the two witches.

Black flames sprang from the circle charred into the floor. Junga felt an unwelcome sense of awe while she watched dark fire flicker and dance around those encased within the ring of fire.

"We are Balor's warlocks." Darkwolf held his hands high. "We serve you."

A shudder rippled through the collective, and then there was a noticeable change in the appearances of the two witches. They seemed somehow larger, taller, more powerful, as did the warlocks. The presence of dark magic in the room was strong, thick. Junga couldn't help her own shudder.

From the center of the circle, Darkwolf began to swing an incense ball at the end of a black chain. The heavy odor of pine resin joined other smells swirling through the room. "Relax your minds, my new warlocks and those who are faithful to Balor," the priest said in a sensual, mesmerizing voice. "Drink deep of the dark. Fill your souls, fill your minds, fill your hearts with the wonders of the black arts.

"Pledge your allegiance to Balor." The Balorite priest swung the incense ball higher. "That you will serve him always."

Each of the witches began to speak, their voices resounding through the room, just as terrible as their appearances had become. They pledged to serve Balor, pledged to do whatever he bade them to.

The fire suddenly rose, engulfing both witches. Around them, within them so that it looked like fire bled from their eyes, their noses, their mouths, their ears. They screamed, writhed as if in pain, and dropped to their knees.

Junga stared in awe. Would the witches survive the conversion ceremony?

"Rise!" Darkwolf commanded the two at the center of the circle, near the dead body.

Slowly, both got to their feet. No longer witches—no. Now they were truly children of Balor. Warlocks.

The black fire ebbed but continued to dance in a circle around the floor. Darkwolf smiled at his two initiates. "Now join your brothers and sisters."

The new warlocks bowed and entered the circle, grasping hands of warlocks to either side of them.

Junga cleared her throat, keeping her expression blank. "Begin the summoning."

Darkwolf gave her a cold stare.

The lights dimmed. Junga blinked.

"Shift," Junga ordered the Fomorii in the room who were still in human form, and they each began the transformation to demons. She didn't intend for any one of them to be thought of as a meal by the summoned Fomorii. That was what the captured nonmagical humans at the center of the room were for.

Junga's gut clenched at her next thought. Perhaps the queen would be coming.

All would change once the bitch was here.

Junga took a deep breath and began her own transformation. Her bones expanded as her head grew, her face morphing into a demon's. She slowly dropped to all fours as her body shifted. Her claws hit the floor and her skin shifted to a thick hide instead of fragile human flesh.

The Fomorii.

Fierce. Terrible. Proud.

"Guard the warlocks," she ordered her remaining warriors, who positioned themselves around the circle so that any summoned Fomorii would not think of them as food, either.

Darkwolf focused on her. "Silence."

She narrowed her eyes. Once all the Fomorii were retrieved from Underworld on Samhain, she'd eat the warlock for dessert.

After she fucked him.

The Balorite priest held her gaze for a long moment, showing no fear. He knew her weakness. Knew how badly she wanted him.

The warlock turned back to the witches and began to chant.

> *"We call those who embrace desires burning in*
>   *our hearts.*
> *We summon those who will turn this battle for the*
>   *dark.*
> *Come to us, brothers and sisters, from far away.*
> *Join us and bring us victory this day."*

Black fire with ice-gray sparks twisted wickedly around the circle of warlocks. So high that fingers of flame scraped the low ballroom ceiling. Smells of sulfur and smoke intertwined with incense, the fog of it nearly enough to make Junga sneeze.

Heat from the black magical flames licked her body even from where she had positioned herself across the room. Desire ripped through her, sharp and sudden, and she nearly screeched her arousal. Black magic twined through the room in sensuous tendrils, caressing, stimulating, exciting. Junga imagined herself shifting into a human, taking the priest down, and fucking him in the middle of that circle of erotic black fire.

> *"Dark forces of this world, unite and come forth,*
> *Dark forces of the universe, join from east, west,*
>   *south, and north.*
> *We call the black magic that serves us all.*
> *We cherish the darkness, honor our call.*
> *We are Balor's warlocks, come to make our mark.*
> *We are Balor's warlocks, come to serve the dark."*

The warlocks swayed as they repeated his words. Their chant grew stronger with every word.

Resting on her haunches, she tried to calm the lust churning through her body. She watched the warlock priest through the fire, following his every movement. "Balor," the priest said, his voice growing deeper, louder, thunderous, "we call upon what is known and true. Aid us in this time of new beginnings for all dark forces to serve you."

Dark fog slithered around the warlocks' ankles and their black robes billowed at the hems. Heated wind fanned Junga's nose, hotter this time.

The priest began his own transformation. His presence became greater.

Larger.

Darker.

Terrible.

As if a dark entity had taken control of Darkwolf's body. His voice deepened, throbbing with power. No longer did the Balorite priest stand in the center of that circle. It was something other. Something dark.

Junga swallowed. Fomorii lived their lives pursuing what they believed to be the natural order of things. They were more intelligent, stronger, meant to be a dominant species. Humans, other beings, were intended to be food. They were meant to be conquered.

But this . . . this was evil. And the Fomorii had never considered themselves evil.

A trickle of fear coursed along Junga's spine, and she held back a whimper. She could smell fear from all other beings in the room. Fomorii, witches, and humans alike.

"The true embodiment of the dark are the Fomorii we seek," the voice thundered.

Junga wanted to shake her head no. They weren't evil. They weren't.

The entity continued.

> *"Bring forth the demons and join them to our*
> *cause.*
> *Bring forth the beasts of fangs and claws.*
> *As many of these beings loyal to the dark as we*
> *speak,*
> *That you would give us, that which we seek."*

A small shudder seemed to rock the room. Images outside the circle flickered, growing dim, then brighter, then dim again. Junga saw the queen and her guard, saw them grow almost solid enough to touch.

But then the images waned . . . until they vanished and the circle of fire died.

The summoning had failed.

Like her father, she had failed.

A sick feeling washed through Junga's belly at the thought of the evil that had been present in the room. At the thought that she served a being that was truly evil.

Did it matter?

Somehow, deep in the pit of her Fomorii heart, it did.

20

Silver snuggled into her warm protective cocoon. A sense of serenity filled her, a sense of being protected and cared for.

Gradually, slight aches and pains made themselves known, but she couldn't find a reason to mind them, she felt so good, so much at peace.

She opened her eyes. Blinked. Saw warm sunshine spilling through her bedroom window. By the position of the light streaming through, it was late morning.

Silver's body jerked at the sudden memory of the summoning of the D'Danann a few hours earlier this morning, and her eyes widened. She tried to sit up but found herself trapped. By the heady, spicy, masculine scent, and by the hard male body pressed to hers, she knew it was Hawk who held her so tight. He had one leg draped over her hip, his arm around her waist, her head tucked under his chin, and his blatantly erect cock against her backside. He gave a low murmur, and she knew he still must be sleeping, probably just beginning to wake.

Her thoughts whirled through everything that had happened with the summoning, and her body tensed even more. The last thing she remembered from the beach was the world spinning. And then everything went black.

Silver did remember slipping in and out of consciousness as Cassia cared for her, using Silver's well-stocked remedies and healing stones. One thought puzzled her, though—Cassia had seemed somehow different. Not the shy, stumbling witch she had known. Rather the apprentice had been in control, commanding even. Perhaps she was showing her true colors. That she was, as Hawk had said, *other*.

Cassia had been like Silver's younger sister. All stumbles and mishaps, but good-hearted and good-natured.

Silver closed her eyes against the pain. If only Copper were still here. How she missed her sister. What made it worse was not knowing what had happened to her, where she was, or even if she was still alive.

Lips touched Silver's hair in a soft kiss, and she tried to relax, letting sad and confused thoughts go for the present.

"Good morning, *a thaisce*." Hawk stroked hair from her face and pressed another kiss to her jawline. "How do you feel?"

She worked her way over to her other side, and he relaxed his grip long enough to allow her to face him. "Considering the last few days of hell, I'm doing all right." She trailed the back of her hand over his stubbled jaw. He looked so handsome, his dark hair mussed, his amber eyes so intent on her. She loved his scent. So utterly masculine and smelling of the wind and forest breezes. Perhaps he had been flying earlier, bringing a part of his journey back with him.

Hawk caught her hand in his and held it to his chest. "I was so afraid for you. I shouldn't have allowed you to go last night. I shouldn't have allowed you to perform the ritual."

Silver resisted rolling her eyes. Perhaps she should be angry at his arrogance, but the concern in his gaze let her know how much he had been afraid for her.

She moved her hand so that she was cupping his cheek. "As if you could have stopped me."

He gave an arrogant shrug. "Of course I could have."

This time Silver did roll her eyes. "Big oaf."

When her eyes met his again, she read something she wasn't sure how to interpret. Lust, definitely. But also caring, and perhaps a wisp of regret?

"What's wrong?" she asked, brushing a strand of his long hair from his face.

He just looked at her for a moment, his amber eyes studying her as if imprinting her upon his memory. "I must return to Otherworld."

She returned his stare, wanting to cry out at the thought of the loss of his nearness. She'd known all along that he'd have to return to his home. Why would it matter to her when he left?

Yet somehow it did.

"The Chieftains have called me to answer for coming here without their leave." Hawk twisted a lock of her hair around his finger. "If I don't return by Samhain, they will not allow me to come back at all, not even for my daughter."

Silver cupped the side of his face and forced a smile. "Then we'll just enjoy what time we have left together."

Hawk's fingers threaded through her hair. "Every minute I am with you, I enjoy, *a thaisce*."

A part of Silver wanted to cry out at the thought of him leaving. But she chose to ignore it at this moment. Right now she needed something powerful and deep, a release from everything they'd been through. She needed to feel all of him, to have him around her, inside of her. To feel his sweat-slicked flesh sliding against hers. To feel his hands on her body, his mouth everywhere.

She reached up and brushed her lips across his, and a low groan rose up from his chest. He kissed her back as if she were fragile and she might break if he pushed her too hard, too fast. His kiss was a brush against her lips. A nibble. A taste.

Silver urged him on, wanting more of this man who had captivated her so completely in just a matter of a few days. She lightly bit his lip, and this time he growled. The moment his lips parted, she slipped her tongue inside his mouth and tasted him, enjoying his flavor. And if she wasn't mistaken, he'd been into Cassia's chocolate chip cookies again.

Silver didn't want his kiss to be gentle. She wanted him hard and deep in every way. With a moan of complete desire, she moved her hand from his cheek, into his hair, and drew him tighter to her. Her own kiss became wild and wanton. Hawk lost his restraint and kissed her in an almost punishing way, just as she wanted him to. Their moans of want and need became louder, more aroused. Silver's head grew light and she felt as if she were being transported to a higher plane of existence.

She tore her mouth from his and began exploring the rough line of his jaw, enjoying the feel of his morning beard against her lips. "I want you, Hawk. Now."

His groan was louder this time and he pressed his stone-hard cock tighter to her belly. "You are too weak," he said in his deeply sexy brogue.

Silver placed her palms against his chest and he didn't resist as she pushed him onto his back. "I'll let you know when I'm too weak." She climbed on top of him, straddling him so that her bare pussy was pressed against his cloth-covered cock. He wore a black robe that he'd apparently borrowed from her shop—the tag peeked out from beneath one sleeve. He still wore the pentagram that matched hers, and she lightly ran her finger over it.

"Thank you for wearing this." She met his intense amber eyes. "It means a lot to me."

"It makes me feel more a part of you," he said, then looked surprised those words had come out of his mouth.

Silver was still wearing her white ceremonial robe, which barely remained closed with the loose tie around her waist. And then she realized she was wearing Hawk's soft leather tunic beneath it. He must have put it on her when she passed out last night.

The ties of the shirt were undone and the opening gaped, revealing her own pentagram, and surely giving him a view of her cleavage. He ran his callused hands up and down her bared thighs, nearing her aching mons, then retreating to her knees.

With a shiver of desire, Silver leaned forward and pressed her lips to his. They kissed each other again, long and deep, and she felt as if she would never get enough. His kisses, his mere presence, made her feel alive, complete, and filled with a spiritual energy that amazed her.

She gave a soft sigh and raised herself up so that she was looking down at him. She tossed aside the sheet that had been covering their legs. "I want you, Hawk."

He shook his head, but lust warred with concern in his eyes. "I don't want to hurt you."

Silver brought her hands to the tie at her waist and unraveled it. He watched, mesmerized, as she parted the robe and let it drop from her arms. She pulled the shirt over her head and flung it away, revealing herself completely to him.

The warmth of his gaze, the hunger in his eyes, made her pussy so very wet. She was certain her juices moistened his robe where her folds pressed against his cock.

He palmed her breasts almost reverently, kneading them in his large hands. Silver sighed and tipped her head back.

Hawk started in a hoarse voice, "We shouldn't—"

Silver cut him off with, "We are." She lowered her head again and this time whispered in his ear. "You are going to fuck me. Until I can't take any more."

He paused, a serious look crossing his strong features. "You could become pregnant."

Silver shook her head and smiled. "Remember, I have a magic shield within, that I use to protect myself."

Need built within Hawk. He slid his hand into Silver's hair and brought her mouth to his. He slipped his tongue deep inside her warmth, tasting her sweetness and wanting to devour all of her.

Part of his mind raged with the thought that it was too soon, that she had endured too much. But a greater part of him wanted to listen to her demands and take her *now*.

Only he intended to draw it out, make her wait, drive her crazy with need until she screamed for him to complete her.

Gods, how he wanted this woman, this witch. He had to have her. They had to have each other.

Silver's hair caressed his face, his chest, as their kiss grew stronger, more intense, nearly sending him over the edge.

Gods be damned, he wasn't waiting any longer.

She broke away, placing her hands on his chest. She rubbed herself up and down, riding him through the thin cloth of the black robe he wore. Her head was tipped back, her breasts high and firm. His gaze traveled the smooth skin of her belly to the soft seafoam curls of her mound. The flash of pink of her folds begged for his touch. He tangled his fingers in those curls and Silver moaned. She rode him harder, and he knew he had to tear away his robe, had to feel her warm, bare skin against his.

"Hold on." He caught her by the waist and flipped her over onto her back and straddled her. Silver let out a yelp of surprise and a laugh that filled his soul with a sense of rightness. Her eyes sparkled and he again saw that blue aura around her.

"Stop taking so long." She tugged at the robe's belt, which had been knotted so tight she had to fumble with it to finally free him. "That's more like it," she murmured as she pushed his robe over his shoulders.

He flung it the rest of the way off and moved between her thighs.

Silver caught her breath at the feel of Hawk's firm cock pressed against her pussy. Her nipples grew even more taut and her folds wetter than ever. Her clit ached to be stroked and her channel throbbed, needing him so very deep inside her.

Rather than driving into her core, he braced his arms to either side of her head and just looked into her eyes. "You are the most beautiful creature I have ever seen." He studied her intently, as if he couldn't get enough of her.

Silver had never had a man look at her the way Hawk did at that moment. It sent a tremendous whirl of energy and lust through her belly and her breasts. She knew she couldn't wait much longer to have him.

"Come to me." She raised her hands and linked her fingers behind his neck. "Come inside of me."

Hawk lowered his head, scraping her cheek with his stubble. He bit her earlobe, causing her to cry out and her eyes to water. "You'd better be sure you want me." He let out a growl that rippled through her. "I fuck *hard,* Silver."

His words nearly made her unravel. "I want you. Now."

He gave a low laugh, and she knew she was in trouble. He was going to draw it out, make her wait. She slid her hand between their bodies and slipped her fingers around his cock, feeling the softness of his skin against the hardness of his erection. She loved the thickness of it, the fat vein running along the underside. The way it felt like satin-covered steel. She guided his cock to her pussy and stroked her wet folds with it. Teasing him, tempting him.

Hawk groaned. "Not yet, *a thaisce,* my treasure." He moved his lips to her collarbone and nipped at the soft skin. "I'm making you wait until I've tasted every inch of you."

When his mouth latched onto one of her nipples Silver's groan had to be louder than Hawk's had been.

He chuckled and moved to her other nipple, sucking it hard. Silver buried her hands in his hair and clenched her fists in the wavy locks.

"That's it." He sucked her nipple hard enough to make her cry out again.

Silver's head swam with the sensations swirling through her and Hawk's erotic words. He moved his mouth lower, nipping at her belly, then thrusting his tongue into her navel. Again she felt that sensation of her pussy being connected to her belly button, and her clit ached impossibly more.

When he trailed his tongue through the curls of her mons, she thrust her hips up, almost without thought, her body begging for him. If he wasn't going to fuck her yet, she wanted his mouth on her.

Hawk moaned his desire as he tasted the salt of her skin, smelled the perfume of ocean breezes and moonlight on her that was as much an aphrodisiac as the sweet scent of her pussy.

He had no intention of relieving the ache he knew was building within Silver. Not yet. He was going to make her wait and wait until she was close to exploding with desire.

He traced the inside of her thigh, and Silver's grip on his hair only made him hotter. He liked the feel of her hands in his hair, the knowledge that he was driving her out of her mind.

"Please." Silver trembled as he moved lower and she had to release her hold on his hair. "I can't take this, Hawk."

He gave a soft chuckle as he licked the inside of her knee and created a damp path along her calf. "I haven't even begun," he murmured, and laughed again when she slapped the mattress to either side of her in frustration.

"Paybacks *are* a bitch, you know." Silver thrashed as he licked the arch of her foot, then began sucking each one of her toes. Slowly. One at a time.

She was tempted to kick him.

Hawk's erection was so hard that he could barely think. His blood had rushed to his cock and he had a difficult time remembering this was all about Silver's pleasure, not his own. Gods, how he wanted to drive his cock into her slick core. But it gave him supreme satisfaction to know he was affecting Silver to the point she was nearly out of control with need for him.

Silver had never in her life experienced such sensations as she was feeling with Hawk. And oh my goddess, when he sucked her toes, it was like her whole body became one shivering mass of nerves! She never realized how many erogenous zones there were on the human body, and Hawk was finding every last one of them. She writhed and she begged, but he refused to listen to her.

She gripped the sheet to anchor herself as he finally worked his way up the side of her other inner thigh and neared her mons. She held her breath and then Hawk delved into her wetness without hesitation. Silver nearly came with the intensity of his mouth on her clit. She cried out at the same time a rumbling rose up within his chest. He clenched her thighs with his massive hands, then slipped his palms beneath her ass, raising her up so that he could feast on her. His stubble scraped her thighs and her pussy lips. He thrust two fingers in and out of her channel at the same time he licked her folds.

And then he sucked on her clit.

Silver screamed.

Her body bucked against Hawk's face as her world seemed to explode with the force of her climax. Vaguely she realized she was sobbing and crying out as orgasm after orgasm wracked her body. Hawk only held her tighter, pressed his mouth harder against her pussy even when she begged him to stop.

When he finally released her, Silver continued to tremble and her vision was almost too blurred to see. The room swam and sparks literally glittered before her eyes. Hawk gave another swipe of his tongue from the soft skin between her anus and channel, all the way up to her clit, and Silver cried out again with another orgasm.

"Stop." She could barely speak, she was breathing so hard. "No more."

Hawk gave a low laugh as he moved up her sweat-slicked skin. Warmth flushed her body anew as he braced himself above her and looked down with a sexy grin that almost made her heart stop beating.

He lowered his head and his mouth met hers in a slow, sweet kiss that nearly stole what breath she had left. She tasted herself upon his tongue, a sweet taste that mingled with the masculine flavor of his mouth.

When he drew away, she pressed her hands against his muscled chest. "On your back," she demanded.

Hawk nuzzled Silver's neck, ready to plunge his cock into her sweet heat. "You can be on top next time."

"I'm not kidding." Silver's fingertips sizzled against his chest, sending streamers of fire throughout his body and straight to his erection.

He gave a low rumble, but let her take control. When he was on his back, he grabbed her hips, ready to raise her up and drive her down on his cock.

She only smiled as fingertips sparked with blue light and she ran one finger down his chest.

Sizzling warmth flooded him. Hot sensual warmth that made his blood boil and his cock so stiff it would surely snap in two if he didn't take her soon. He tried to move her, to force her down on his raging erection, but he found his hands immobile, as if tremendous weights pinned them to his sides. "Release me, witch!"

"You're mine now." Silver gave a wicked grin as she slowly brought both her hands to his chest and circled his flat nipples with her index fingers. Sparks sizzled from her fingertips and flooded his body with such desire that he had to clench his teeth to keep from shouting out loud and begging her to end the sweet torture.

She lowered her mouth to brush her lips over his Adam's apple. "I intend to have my way with you," she murmured against his chest.

"Wench," he said, but it turned into a groan as she moved down his body, her palms splayed flat against his chest, over his abs, and straight toward his cock.

He tried to move his arms again, but his palms were glued flat to the sheet. He didn't even know how his hands had moved from her hips to the bed, she had worked her magic so effectively.

Silver neared his cock and he thought he would explode. Her eyes remained focused on his as she slowly traced the base of his erection, through the coarse curls, with her fingertips. She drew a tantalizing circle around his balls, lightly scraping her fingernails over the firm skin. The entire time her hands sizzled with her magic and Hawk thought he would go insane with the need to come, the need to drive into her over and over again until she screamed loud enough for the whole of the city to hear.

She eased her beautiful naked body down, to kneel between his splayed legs. He couldn't move them, either, and he shouted out his frustration. "Release me, or you shall pay, witch!"

Silver gave a soft murmur and lowered her mouth so that her lips were barely above his cock. He tensed. His heart beat so loudly it pulsed in his ears.

She blew softly on the head of his erection and he groaned. Her eyes still focused on his, she slipped her lips over his cock, taking him deep into her warm, wet mouth. "Ah, gods," was all that he could manage to say.

Silver stroked his balls with one hand while working his cock with the other. Her magic vibrated through his erection, sending fire throughout his body and bringing him near the peak. Her mouth, so very hot. Her hands, so talented. Her magic, so intense. Black dots began to dance behind his eyes and he was certain he would pass out if he achieved orgasm.

Silver teased him more, taunted him by changing the motion of her mouth and her hands. By stopping then starting, then slipping him out of her mouth and licking the swollen purple head.

She gave a wicked little laugh as her gaze locked with his.

But then her laugh turned into a cry of surprise as he broke free of her magical hold. He gripped her hips tightly between his palms and flipped her on her back so that he forced himself between her pale thighs, his raging erection pushing at her opening.

Silver felt a thrill of excitement at the nearly insane look in Hawk's eyes. She had driven him close to the brink of madness.

He gripped her thighs tightly as he spread her open. "Do you know what I'm going to do to you now?"

Silver bit her lip and swallowed. She was afraid he was going to tease her more before he finally took possession of her.

Hawk raised her legs up so that her ankles were around his neck and his cock pushing at the swollen folds of her pussy.

"I'll tell you what I'm going to do," he said in his deep Irish brogue that throbbed through her. "I'm going to fuck you. *Hard.*"

She gasped as his cock slipped a fraction into her core. So close. So blessed close. "Take me now, Hawk," she screamed. "Now!"

With a look of supreme satisfaction and possession, Hawk drove his cock into her slick channel. He slammed against her, fucking her as hard as he'd promised. With her ankles around his neck it gave him deeper access to her, filling her in length and width like she'd never been filled before.

Silver closed her eyes and tipped her head back in ecstasy, but Hawk murmured, "Look at me."

Her eyelids flew open and her gaze met Hawk's intense amber eyes. His strokes were deep and even, his cock hitting that sensitive spot within her.

Sweat trickled down the side of his face. The sensations—the feel of his width thrusting in and out, his length pounding deep—it was all almost too much to bear.

The scent of their sweat and sex, and his masculine smell filled Silver. Her breasts bounced up and down with each thrust, adding to her already heightened senses.

She cried out with every incredible plunge of his cock and felt herself begin to spiral out of control. Her moans almost couldn't be heard above the sound of their breathing, the slap of flesh against flesh, his grunts and her cries. "I'm so close. So close."

He thrust into her three, four times more, and just when she was certain she wasn't going to be able to hold back any longer, he murmured, "Come with me, *a thaisce*. Come with me."

Silver screamed. Longer and louder than any scream she'd ever made before. Shivers racked her body with every pulse of her orgasm. The sensations were so wonderful, so sweet, she almost couldn't take it.

Hawk shouted and continued to pump in and out at a slower pace. She felt the power of his own climax, the pulse of his cock and his come spilling into her pussy. He braced his hands to either side of her, still throbbing within her channel. His breathing came harsh and uneven and a trickle of sweat from his forehead splashed onto one of her breasts.

With a groan he collapsed onto his side, drawing Silver tightly within his embrace. She shuddered with aftershocks from her orgasm that refused to stop. His cock remained inside her and was still large enough she could feel the throb of him continue within her.

He kissed her sweat-dampened hair and cuddled her close. "Gods, what did you do to me?" he murmured.

Silver gave a shuddering sigh and snuggled closer to him. "What did *you* do to *me*?"

He chuckled, a low and satisfied laugh.

The front door to the apartment slammed shut.

Hawk and Silver went still.

"Silver?" Moondust called from the living room in her ethereal tone.

Her father boomed out, "Where is that little witch?"

21

Silver groaned as her father's voice reverberated through her apartment. "Silver," he said in his most intimidating bellow, "come out here right this minute!"

"Now, Victor," came Moondust's soothing voice through the thin wall. "You can't barge in on her. This is her home, not yours."

"The spells I can't."

Hawk's erection slipped from Silver's pussy as she floundered for a rumpled sheet. She yanked it over their naked bodies a second before her father stormed into her bedroom.

"Hi, Father," she said, trying to keep a calm expression.

For precious seconds, he stood in the doorway, blustering, his face a deep crimson, his jowls vibrating. Silver almost grinned—she'd never seen her father so flustered. He was a huge, hulking man who appeared stout rather than overweight. He wore tailored suits, and his eyes were a deep, penetrating brown. He'd always reminded her of the Mafia bosses she'd seen on TV.

"What in the name of—" he started, then his gaze focused on Hawk. His jaw dropped.

For the first time Silver could remember, Victor Ashcroft was speechless.

Moondust pushed her way past him as Silver eased up in bed so that her back was to the headboard, the sheet pulled tight over her breasts. She glanced at Hawk to see him lying on his side, his head propped up on his hand, his elbow on the bed, and the sheet hanging loosely around his trim hips. His dark hair was rumpled, and he had sexy morning stubble on his cheeks. His appraising amber eyes focused on her father.

"My apologies, honey." Moondust moved close enough to the bed to clasp one of Silver's hands. "You know your father. He loves you and thinks you're still his little witch."

"Father, you've got to get over it. I'm not a child." Silver looked at her father and the heat creeping up her cheeks was like fire due to the fact that her parents were standing there while she was in bed with her lover. "Would you mind?"

Moondust studied Hawk. "Who are you, dear? You are not human, are you," she said, more as a statement than a question.

"Hawk," he said in his husky, sexy brogue, and Silver shivered from the sensual sound of it. "I am D'Danann. And you are—"

"D-D'Danann?" Victor clenched his fists at his sides, and strode toward the bed. If they could have, his eyes would have been smoking, the way he was looking at Silver. "You summoned one of the D'Danann . . . One of those from Otherworld?" He gestured toward Hawk. "And you bedded it?"

"*Him.*" Silver glared at her father and fisted the bed sheet in her hands. She couldn't believe they were having this conversation now. "Never refer to Hawk like that again." She waved one hand toward the doorway. "Out of my room. Now."

Victor's face grew darker and after another few seconds of blustering, he turned like a stiff toy soldier and marched from the room. "You had better hurry, young witch," he grumbled.

Moondust squeezed Silver's hand again, and she smiled. "Take your time, sweetheart."

"Thanks, Mother." Silver gave Moondust a quick kiss on her smooth cheek. She smelled of vanilla and brown sugar, a scent that always comforted Silver, reminding her of her childhood.

When Moondust closed the door behind her, Silver groaned again and covered her face with the sheet. All she saw was white, reminding her that she now had to confront her father about her decision to become a gray witch. Facing him would be like trying to stand up to a tornado and not get sucked up in its fury.

A shadow passed over her, then she felt the press of lips against hers as Hawk kissed her through the thin material. His lips were warm, firm. She melted from the light touch and wished they had time for another round of hot, exciting sex.

He pulled the sheet away from her face and gave her a crooked grin. "Come, *a thaisce*. We've apparently been summoned. By beings almost as fearsome as my Chieftains. Your mother—she is quite . . . interesting."

With a smile for Hawk, she stretched her muscles, which ached pleasurably from the wonderful bout of fucking. She gave him a lazy, sensual look. She moved just right, and the sheet fell from her breasts. He hissed out one long breath that made her shiver with desire, and made her pussy wetter.

He dipped his head and laved each of her nipples with his hot tongue. Silver gave a soft moan and arched her breasts. She reached for his cock beneath the sheet and wrapped her fingers around his thickness. It pleased her that he was so hard, so ready for her.

"Silver!" Victor Ashcroft shouted from the other side of the door.

Hawk captured her mouth in a quick kiss before urging her out of bed. He swatted her ass and she squealed as she hurried into the bathroom.

To Otherworld with Father, Silver thought as she took a warm shower to refresh herself. As far as she was concerned he could just wait until she was good and ready to come out of her bedroom.

When she finished, she dressed in snug black jeans, a black silk blouse, and black heeled boots. The outfit gave her a feeling of power and confidence. And she knew her father hated that she didn't wear robes or dresses all the time as he thought a good witch should.

While Hawk took his shower, Silver combed her fingers through her hair, drying the long strands with her magic in just moments. When she finished, her hair hung in long platinum ringlets to her waist. She strode out of the bedroom to meet her parents, closing the door behind her as she walked into the living room.

It smelled wonderful—of cheese, potatoes, eggs, and fresh herbs, a recipe she recognized immediately as Moondust's breakfast casserole. In the small kitchen, Moondust wore Silver's *KISS THE WITCH* apron, and was busy preparing breakfast. She was making fresh orange juice, magically squeezing the oranges with a hand juicer over a pitcher. The orange halves squeezed themselves one by one as Moondust busied herself with drawing out plates and silverware.

Silver's stomach grumbled.

She turned her gaze to her father, who sat on her couch. Her stomach pitched and she immediately lost her appetite.

Even sitting down, Victor could intimidate a warrior in full battle gear. Although she couldn't begin to imagine Hawk feeling threatened. Polaris was currently draped over her father, and Victor slowly stroked the python's head.

Traitor snake.

Silver sat in the love seat across from her father and tried to relax. She crossed her legs at her knees and met her father's eyes. She caught his scent of cherry pipe tobacco and spicy aftershave, and it brought back memories of her childhood, almost making her feel like a kid again.

"Not only did you summon creatures you had no business calling," he said, "but you *slept* with one of the Fae. A full-blooded Otherworlder. Have you any idea what kind of trouble or what kind of pain you're asking for?"

"What do you know of it?" Icy heat washed her cheeks, pushing away the earlier thoughts of her childhood. "Who I sleep with is none of your concern." She clenched the ends of her armchair. "The issues here have nothing to do with my choice of bed partner—"

"The spells they don't!" Victor pushed his bulk from his seat, letting Polaris drop to the couch. The snake hissed and gave her father what amounted to a snaky scowl, then slithered across the floor to Silver, where Victor was now towering over her.

His finger shook as he pointed it at her. "Dark magic. Summoning beings beyond your control is prohibited!"

Returning her father's glare, Silver jumped to her feet, and almost bumped into him. She wasn't about to back down, not for a second. "I told you I practice *gray* magic. I will use magic to defend my people, my loved ones, and myself. And if that means attacking evil before it attacks us, then so be it!"

Victor turned an unusual shade of purple. Before he had a chance to utter a word, Hawk shoved open the bedroom door. He was fully dressed in his leathers, along with his sheathed sword and dagger. His amber eyes almost glowed with fury directed at Victor. Hawk's presence was powerful and commanding, and Silver couldn't help the thrill that blossomed in her belly at the sight of him. Goddess, he was sexy, right from his black hair brushing his shoulders, to his sculpted jaw, on down to his broad chest, trim hips, and athletic thighs. He was delicious in every sense of the word.

"Hear your daughter before you condemn her," Hawk said in a slow, measured, and controlled voice, jolting her from her lust. "If you do not wish for all your kind to be extinguished, you would do well to understand the situation."

"I understand well enough." Victor's eyes narrowed and his fingertips sparked with his anger. He would never hurt anyone, but he'd been known to be so angry that inanimate objects in the immediate vicinity would self-combust.

"Sit." Hawk's tone was lethal this time, like a dagger plunging into ice—for a demonstration of what it might do to human flesh.

One of Silver's crystal vases crackled. The glass shattered across one of her storage chests, and dried blooms tumbled to the floor.

She sighed. Two vases in just a couple of days. Great.

"Control yourself." Moondust appeared out of nowhere, among the three of them, and she gently pushed Victor back until he sat on the couch. Springs creaked from his bulk, and he found himself with a plate of breakfast casserole in one hand, fresh squeezed orange juice in the other.

"Moon—" he started, but Moondust silenced him by narrowing her eyes and shoving a spoonful of casserole into his mouth.

"Eat," she commanded. "Then we will discuss this like rational witches."

Victor swallowed, then harrumphed. He placed his juice glass on an end table, and with a scowl dug into his breakfast.

Moondust turned on Hawk next. To Silver's surprise, he lowered his head in something like a respectful bow. Then Silver and Hawk found their hands full with breakfast plates and juice glasses, so fast that Silver was certain her mother had used a bit of magic to manipulate them all. Her mother was not a D'Anu witch, but Silver always had the feeling she was far more powerful than anyone truly knew.

Moondust kept the conversation light while the rest of them glared at one another. As they ate, she talked about the latest gossip on all of Silver's aunts, uncles, and cousins, not to mention a few of the more eccentric members of their Massachusetts D'Anu Coven.

As she spoke, Moondust's soothing presence gradually won out, and Silver found herself relaxing. A little.

Whenever she glanced at her father, she couldn't help but remember the times he had taught her beginning spells and how to make healing potions. He could be overbearing when he was upset, but he truly had a soft heart beneath that intimidating presence.

Hawk, on the other hand, looked like a true predator as he observed Silver's father. He ate at least three helpings of breakfast casserole, his gaze riveted on Victor. Her father matched Hawk plate for plate, and watched the D'Danann just as closely.

If the situation they were in with the Fomorii hadn't been so dire, Silver would have giggled at the two of them. Men!

The entire time, Polaris draped himself over Moondust's shoulders, his head raised and turning to observe each of them. The familiar had slid up the armrest the moment she sat down, apparently to find the best place to be in the center of the action.

When Moondust made the last empty plate disappear to settle in the kitchen sink, she perched like a small bird on the edge of one armchair. Polaris curled up like a beehive on the chair's cushion to the side of her.

Varying shades of amethyst clothing draped Moondust's petite figure. A peasant blouse was tucked into a loose flowing skirt that reached the tops of her sandaled feet. She wore her platinum-gray hair pinned up with a Celtic-knot, and wore only silver and amethyst jewelry, including the pentagram that glittered at her throat.

Victor leaned forward, one meaty hand braced on the couch arm, and opened his mouth to speak. Moondust held her slender hand up, silencing him with just that gesture. "Hear them out, Victor."

He scowled, but snapped his jaws shut and leaned back in his chair. His entire posture was rigid, and by the look in his eyes, Silver knew this wasn't going to be easy.

She started by explaining almost everything in detail that had occurred over the past four days, leaving out the parts about how she had been drawn to the dark.

Goddess, had it only been four days that all of this had occurred?

She started with the Pagan witch rituals and slayings; Hawk coming to warn her about the demons; the vision of the warlocks calling up the Fomorii from Underworld; the demons attacking the D'Anu and the witches being taken away; Silver summoning Hawk; their rescue of the three witches; and finishing with the summoning of the ten additional D'Danann last night.

When Silver finished, she studied her father, trying to read his expression. "I won't sit by and wait for them to attack again, Father. Next time it could be you or Mother, not to mention all of the witches here, under my protection. I will do what I have to in order to guard my own."

Victor eyed her steadily. "Even black magic?"

"No." Silver shook her head, her hair sliding over her shoulders with the movement. "Never."

"You summoned these warriors." Victor gestured toward Hawk. His eyes and voice were hard, cold. "Warriors kill, child. Warriors mean death to any they face and best in battle. That is not our way. That you would bring forth any agents of death is gray magic."

"Enough!" Hawk sprang to his feet, gripping the hilt of his sheathed sword with one hand. "You have no idea the power the Fomorii command, what they will do to your people, to your world." Silver had never seen Hawk look as furious as he did at that moment. "You are only tools or food to them. That is *their way*. They must either be eliminated or returned to exile. There are no other choices."

"Then they must be sent away, not murdered." Victor rose to his feet and clasped Moondust's hand, drawing her up beside him. "We have reservations at a hotel in Union Square. We will return tomorrow to determine how to banish the beasts back to where they came from. We will do it in the D'Anu way, with white witchcraft. We will *not* kill them."

Hawk clenched his jaw and remained where he stood, but Silver went after her parents as Victor led Moondust to the door. "Please don't leave the shop," Silver begged. "It's too dangerous out there in the streets." She placed her hand on her mother's arm. "Stay here. We—we need you here. There are so few of us—"

Her voice broke.

Moondust moved away from her husband and Silver, and stepped back to speak quietly with Hawk. Silver stared at her father, hoping for some change in his expression, some warmth.

"Father, please. I want to keep you safe from the Fomorii."

"Nonsense." Victor jerked the door open so hard the

hinges rattled. "If there is any call to, *I* will protect your mother and myself. Moondust!"

Silver stood straighter. Clenched her hands at her sides. "You don't understand. The demons are deadly. They have no regard for human or witch life."

"No, young witch. *You* don't understand." Victor's glower would have razed a skyscraper even as he took his wife's hand. "I know all of that and more, and I still choose white magic. I still choose the D'Anu way. If I die, then it's my time, and I'll damned well die principled and—and *clean.*"

That last word struck Silver like a slap. Her head actually jerked back, and she turned away from her father in helpless disgust.

Moondust stroked a strand of Silver's hair away from her cheek. "We'll be fine, sweetheart. I'm sure your father will figure out how to rid the city of these vermin." She gave Hawk a serene smile. "Blessed be, Hawk," she said, then followed Victor out the door.

Silver bit her lower lip as the door shut with a loud thump behind her parents. She suddenly felt exhausted, her body aching from the past few days. She might be a witch, but she could still feel tired and drained.

Hawk came up behind her and drew her back to his chest. "They'll be all right, *a thaisce,*" he murmured as he kissed the top of her head. "Both of your parents are powerful witches."

"My mother isn't D'Anu. Just father." Silver sank against him, allowing his strength to seep into her. "And my Coven wasn't safe."

Hawk turned her in his arms and pressed his lips to hers, silencing her. His kiss was warm, tender, and sent that now familiar thrill throughout her body, from her nipples to her pussy.

When he raised his head he smiled.

She could barely breathe, much less return his smile.

"After we brought you home, Jake, my comrades, and I discussed working out a plan." He twisted his finger in one of her silvery-blond curls. "We'll draw the Fomorii out. We *will* find a way to send them back to Underworld."

She sighed.

"No matter what, you have me," Hawk said. Silver could only sigh again and bury her face against his chest, drinking in his musky scent, enjoying the feel of his arms around her. At that moment, in his strong embrace, it was easy to imagine everything would be all right.

A sudden intense sensation in the depths of her gut, of something desperately wrong, screamed to her she was dreaming. Things were about to get far worse.

The feeling was so strong that Silver pushed Hawk away. Stumbled to her kitchen.

"Silver?" he called behind her, but she couldn't answer. Her thoughts were flying, telling her that she had to find out what was wrong, before it was too late.

When she reached her cabinet, she snatched her scrying cauldron, set it on the floor, filled it with water from the jug, and dropped to her knees. Trembling, her eyes focused on the rippling water.

Vaguely, in the background she could hear Hawk's voice, the concern in his tone. Felt his hand on her shoulder. But she was already fixed on the vision as the fog rose up to unfold before her. His voice faded until she was gone from the room and completely into the vision. As if she were there, witnessing everything that was happening.

Darkwolf held the stone eye in his hand, his eyes closed, as if communicating with the eye.

Silver's gaze lingered over him. She noticed his lashes. So long and black against the light tan of his skin. The angular cut of his jaw, the cleft in his chin. He was so handsome, so striking, and yet he cut an imposing figure that caused something strange to swirl in Silver's belly.

When Darkwolf opened his eyes, their blackness burned with fire, and Silver felt as if he were looking directly at her, as if he knew she was watching him commune with the stone eye.

He turned to a man and commanded him to arrange to have a taxi near a certain business within the hour. To station a man across the street with a phone to give the signal.

The warlock priest uttered the address, and Silver's skin chilled. It was the address to *her* shop.

Panic crawled up her throat. Was this scene happening now, or had time already passed?

The vision faded. Other figures emerged from the mist, their forms growing stronger, fuller.

Mother and Father!

Victor and Moondust Ashcroft exited through the front door of Silver's shop. He didn't even spare a glance for Eric—who was manning the front register. Victor slammed the door shut, causing the warding bells to jangle like an earthquake had just unsettled them. He cast a quick warding on the door with a flick of his fingers. He spotted a man across the street talking on a cell phone, but other than that, the street was silent.

And then everything happened so quickly, Silver's head spun from the speed of the vision.

Victor raised his head and started down the street, Moondust in tow. He practically dragged his wife along the steep hill, his face still red with fury.

Moondust jerked her hand from his and stopped on the sidewalk. Victor turned to her. When he saw her disapproving expression, he hung his head in shame. "I am sorry, my dearest. I shouldn't take my anger out on you."

She propped her hands on her slim hips, her jewelry glittering in what sunlight made it through the fog. "Silver is old enough to make her own choices. She is doing what she thinks is right. I don't believe for a moment she would turn to the dark side of magic. In your heart you know that's true. You love Silver and you should let her know it, rather than stomping around like a deranged hippopotamus."

"You're right." He heaved a heavy sigh. "I love my little witch, and I should have told her so. I will tomorrow."

"You might consider telling her the truth, too." Moondust moved closer to him and cupped his cheek. "It's time for her to know. It will explain much to her."

"That's why I'm afraid to tell her," Victor said, his

shoulders slumping slightly before turning his attention to the street.

A yellow cab crested the hill and he muttered a quick thanks to the Ancestors for the taxi appearing on this deserted street just when they needed it. "We'll discuss everything further once we reach our hotel," he said to Moondust as he signaled to the taxi and it slowed.

She held back, frowning, as though something didn't feel right to her. She visibly shivered, as if a haunt slithered along her spine.

Inside the vision, Silver tried to cry out to her parents. *"No! Something's wrong!"*

The cabbie jumped out of the car. He had a quick grin behind a dark beard, and looked like most other cabbies she'd seen. He opened the back door. A man in a tailored suit sat in the cab, and when Victor asked, "Is it all right with you?" the man replied, "I don't mind sharing the cab. Not at all."

Moondust sniffed the air, as if catching the scent of something foul. She cast one last nervous glance back to Silver's shop, then slid inside the taxi. Victor followed, hefting in his bulk, squeezing his wife between himself and the other man in the back seat.

The moment her parents were in the cab, the driver whipped a syringe out of his pants pocket and in a flash jammed the needle into Victor's neck.

Silver screamed and Moondust jerked her head up.

As Victor collapsed against Moondust, she cried out. Brought her hands together to perform a spell. Before she could do anything, the other man in the car stuck a syringe into Moondust's neck. Her eyes fluttered shut. Her body went limp.

"No!" Silver screamed. "No, no, no!"

The next thing she knew she was in Hawk's arms, but she was fighting to free herself.

"They've taken Mother and Father!" She finally pushed herself from Hawk, frantic, her heart pounding like crazy. "We've got to help them!"

Before Hawk could stop her, Silver bolted from the kitchen. He cursed beneath his breath.

Hawk shouted to alert the other D'Danann warriors they were needed. By the time Silver and Hawk had pounded down the stairs, Garrett, Keir, and Sher were already at the front door of the shop. Damn the gods, the rest must still be on Rhiannon's foster parents' houseboat.

Hawk cast a glance at Eric, who tossed his dark hair out of his face. He watched the four D'Danann and Silver exit out the door with a curious expression on his face.

"What's wrong?" Eric called after them, but no one paused even a second to respond.

"A cab! Just down this street!" Silver's terror rose as she pointed in the direction she had seen the cab travel in her vision. It wasn't there now. She started running. "You know, a yellow car with a sign—a thing on top."

Hawk's voice was a growl. "We will meet them at the demon lair before the Fomorii have a chance to take your parents inside."

He gave her a quick look, concern and anger twisting within him at the same time. "Get back into your store, where you'll be safe."

Silver clenched her fists. "I want to come with you! I need to!"

"No," Hawk said flatly. This time he was in control, he was making the decisions. Without waiting for a response, he unfurled his wings and ordered the other three D'Danann to follow him.

In seconds the four warriors pushed their bodies into the sky, pumping their wings, leaving a panic-stricken Silver behind.

"Bless it!" Silver cried as she jogged down the street, trying to follow the four. But the D'Danann were too swift, and as much as she wished to, she couldn't sprout wings like they could. And unfortunately, unlike mythical witches, she couldn't ride a broom.

Silver stopped and stared after the D'Danann. Her breathing came hard and fast from running down the steep street. A mixture of emotions raged through her. Fear for her parents. Fear for Hawk. Fear for all the D'Danann. Anger at not being able to help.

And a deep sense of foreboding . . . something more than her parents' abduction.

When she reached the shop, she felt as if a lava rock weighted her belly, hot and heavy. Warding bells tinkled when she pushed open Moon Song's door, and she wanted to zap them for sounding so damn cheerful.

A customer stood at the counter, and Silver barely noticed that Eric was absent from his post at the register. He had probably darted into the storeroom to get something for the customer.

Her boot steps were heavy as she made her way through the shop toward the kitchen. She was thankful there were only a couple of customers in the shop. She ignored their curious looks and pushed her way behind the café counter and through the kitchen door.

The scent of patchouli incense rose above the smells of fresh baked cornbread and homemade chili. No doubt Cassia had chosen that scent for protection.

Cassia's back was to the door and she started when the door slammed behind Silver. The apprentice jumped and black stones tumbled out of her hands and onto the kitchen floor. She quickly scrambled to gather the stones. "I can get them," she said when Silver stooped beside her.

"What in the goddess's name?" Silver's hand trembled as she picked up a smooth black hematite stone and held it in her palm. A gold rune was cut into its surface. "What are you doing with these?" she asked as her gaze rose to meet Cassia's. "Who made them?"

The witch paused for a heartbeat. Licked her lips. Raised her chin. "I was reading my rune stones. I created them."

Silver blinked. Cassia was supposed to be a young apprentice. She shouldn't know how to read rune stones yet, much less have the power to make a set of her own until she had served at least her twenty years and one day as an apprentice. Only then would she be an Adept. "You what?"

The witch's words tumbled over one another like leaves over grass as Silver stared at her. "I know I have much to explain, but now is not the time."

"You're an Adept?" The fiery rock in Silver's belly grew heavier and hotter as she tried to absorb Cassia's words. "How can I trust you—you're not who I thought you were, are you?"

Cassia straightened and visibly changed. Her features looked more confident, her shoulders back, her hands relaxed. "Trust me. I'm here to help."

At this moment, Silver didn't even trust her senses. Those same senses had failed to know the witch was an Adept. Or was Cassia even a witch? But why then had her parents allowed her to come from the Massachusetts Coven to work with Silver? Why had Janis allowed it? Why had they all brushed off Silver's concerns?

Demons . . . my parents being taken . . . my father talking about telling me the truth . . . Cassia being an Adept . . . what in the name of the goddess is going on here?

Too many mysteries. Too many threads to unwind.

Silver ground her teeth and clenched her fist around the rune stone she held. "Tell me who you are. *What* you are."

Cassia sighed and let the rest of the rune stones tumble onto the countertop. "I can't."

"Yes you can!" Silver shouted, all her anger, her fury, her fear for her parents combining into one ball of energy that caused her hair to rise from her scalp and her fingertips to crackle.

Cassia shook her head, almost sadly. "It is up to your parents to tell you."

Silver almost screamed. "Then leave!" She slammed the rune stone she held onto the countertop next to the others scattered across its surface.

Cassia brought her attention to the rune stones and her features grew tense as she studied them. "Things are not going as planned." She turned totally away from Silver and ran one finger lightly over the stones. "I told them not to leave the shop."

It took everything Silver had not to shake the witch, or whatever she was. "What in the goddess's name are you talking about?"

Tucking unruly blond curls behind one ear, Cassia turned back to Silver. Suddenly she could see wisdom beyond wisdom in Cassia's blue eyes. Eyes that almost seemed to glow. "You have many choices to make, Silver Ashcroft. One of them is to choose whether or not I am to leave, or to remain at your side. If I were not here to help, I could have hurt you long ago."

For a long moment, Silver studied those incredible, almost familiar eyes. "My family or Janis would never have let you near me if they didn't trust you," she finally said. "You've done me no harm that I know of. I'll give you the benefit of the doubt." She paused before adding, "For now."

Hawk's wings sliced through chill, wet San Francisco air as he led the other D'Danann toward the Fomorii's lair at the hotel. Using mind-speak, Hawk briefed the others on what had happened and their current mission. With their magic, they were cloaked from human sight, but could still see one another.

"Foolish," Keir growled through their mind-link as they soared up and over a tall brown building. *"These are but two of many lives to save. We need to make plans. We need the others."*

Before Hawk could respond, Sher said, *"Keir is right. You know that, Hawk."*

Garrett just gave Hawk a look of support.

"We must save them." Hawk practically yelled in mind-speak as they dodged a church spire. *"They are two of the most powerful of their kind. More importantly, they are Silver's parents. I know she has lost her sister as well, and her Coven. Another unbearable pain might kill her spirit."*

There was no time left to argue as they arrived at the hotel. A yellow vehicle was pulled up to the curb. Only a short red carpet beneath a striped awning separated the car from the hotel doors.

No doubt it was two Fomorii posing as men who wrestled with the large, bulky, and unconscious Victor Ashcroft, trying to drag his body from the vehicle. The male witch was half in, half out of the cab.

When he glanced through the back window of the car, Hawk saw Moondust wasn't there. Fury rocked him. The Fomorii already had Silver's mother in their lair.

The D'Danann attacked, their hands turning into deadly claws which they used to rip away the awning. Unfortunately the D'Danann could not remain cloaked when in battle, so the Fomorii could easily see who their attackers were.

It took a single rake of Hawk's nails to tear the throat of one of the Fomorii in his human form, beheading him at the same time. As the man dropped, his body shifted into a Fomorii demon. Blood spurted across the red carpet and onto the sidewalk as the body pitched forward. The head was flung against the window of the hotel, leaving a splatter and a blood slick as it slid down the glass pane and dropped to the ground, before crumbling away.

Screams rent the air. Hawk spared a glance to see two human women across the street, and heard more screams coming from inside the hotel.

He didn't have another second to think about onlookers, or how to retrieve Victor Ashcroft from the car. Two more demons bounded from the hotel and attacked the D'Danann.

"Command our retreat," Keir demanded of Hawk as they battled. *"We cannot fight them now."*

"Destroy these bastards. Save Silver's father." Hawk dove, sword drawn, avoiding claws. Tried to slice his weapon across a beast's neck, but missed.

From somewhere came a woman's sharp, eager laughter. The sound chilled Hawk even in the heat of the fight. He spun to slay the demon attacking him, but missed again. When the beast's claws swiped at him, he saw sunlight gleam off the tips. A foul magical aura surrounded those tips.

"What in the name of—" Hawk wheeled in the air to find Garrett.

Garrett was battling with his usual skill and finesse, his sword flashing a brilliant hue as he lunged for one of the demons.

The Fomorii swiped at Garrett in a movement so fast it caught the D'Danann off guard. The demon snatched Hawk's friend from the air by one leg, sinking those shiny, magic-infested claws into Garrett's leg and yanking him down.

"Gods!" Garrett shouted as he tried to push himself back into the air. "Their claws. Watch out for their claws!"

Garrett gave a fierce warrior cry. He sliced his sword across the Fomorii's throat, where its skin was thinnest. The demon was not beheaded. Its throat instantly healed.

Hawk had the disturbing sense that Garrett was fighting the demon who had laughed that hideous-bitch laughter. He folded his wings and plunged toward Garrett.

Garrett shouted as he tried to fly up. Tried to push himself away from the Fomorii and the melee. He should have been able to escape. But just as he rose, another enormous demon gave a loud roar. The beast pounced on Garrett, burying him beneath its bulk and digging claws into Garrett's chest. Claws that once more flashed a magical metallic glint.

Iron, Hawk knew instantly, pulling up hard. *Bonded to the tips with magic. Iron. Gods!*

Garrett cried out and was pinned beneath the massive beast.

A roar echoed down the street.

Iron-tipped claws drove into Garrett's chest, plunging deep. With a sickening pop, the demon ripped out his heart. It pulsed in the sunlight, and for a moment Garrett stared at it in horror as the demon crammed the heart into its hideous mouth.

Then Garrett's body went slack. His eyes closed and his body was encased in a silver glow. He shimmered. Silver sparkles swirled from where his body had been, sending his soul on to Summerland.

Horror, shock, then fury burned Hawk's belly. Intent on revenge, he dove for the demon that had slaughtered Garrett.

By all the gods, he was going to kill the bitch that had murdered his friend.

Sher and Keir swooped in Hawk's way. Forced him back with their powerful arms and wings.

"Listen to me!" Keir mind-shouted. *"There are too many. We are too few."*

"It is too late for Garrett," Sher said.

Hawk's vision was crimson. Keir's words barely penetrated his rage and the blood pounding in his ears. The other two D'Danann shoved him back, farther from the carnage. From his side vision he watched the Fomorii take out the spectators, slitting their throats with quick swipes of their claws and dragging them into the hotel. The bastards would feast well tonight, no doubt.

There would be no witnesses.

He'd failed Silver; her parents had been captured.

And Garrett was dead.

22

With a purr of satisfaction, Junga strolled across the ballroom floor in her human form. She paced to and fro before the still unconscious Moondust and Victor Ashcroft, relishing her victory.

In this, she had not failed.

Well, the victory was both hers and Darkwolf's. The warlock had had the vision that had led them to the parents of Silver Ashcroft. But it was Junga's warriors who had made the capture.

Now that she had Silver's parents, Junga would find a way to blackmail them into turning to black magic to summon more Fomorii. She intended to exploit the Ashcrofts' powers, and would use them to lure Silver to her. The Ashcrofts certainly wouldn't want to see their precious little bitch die.

Darkwolf was equally certain Silver was so close to the dark, teetering on the brink, that with another push or two, he would be able to turn her. After what he had witnessed in his visions and in person, he believed that she alone had the power of a host of witches. Her strength would give them what they needed to summon the balance of the Fomorii come Samhain.

While her warrior captains watched Junga's stride, her movements were deliberately sexual. She was excited, and what humans would call "horny." She knew she could have her pick of any male in the host and fuck him unconscious.

But today she wanted something . . . more.

She paused and studied her human fingernails. Just moments before she had been in her demon form and had raked her own powerful claws through the D'Danann warrior. The magically bonded iron—perfection. The bastard hadn't known what hit him.

His heart had been delicious. There was nothing like the taste of D'Danann blood to fill her with satisfaction.

Slowly she faced the Balorite warlock who had so effectively used his Seer's powers to let them know about the arrival of Silver's parents and had helped plan their capture.

Darkwolf was considered handsome for a human, and Junga shuddered with lust at the thought of what it was like to be taken by him again and again. She reached up to touch his face and scraped one sharp nail down the warlock's cheek. Desire flared in his eyes and she knew he wanted to take her again. To dominate her completely.

"I am very pleased," she said, and moved her lips closer to his. "You have done exceedingly well."

She brought her other hand to his jean-covered cock and squeezed. She was gratified at his body's immediate response, and delighted she had such power over him. He was even larger than Bane, his erection thick and fulfilling. His expression grew tight and his balls drew up as she cupped him.

Perhaps three men would assuage her need for human sex. One thrusting into her ass, one her pussy, and one her mouth. The thought nearly made her eyes cross and she had to fight to maintain her cool demeanor.

Three cocks. Every sensual opening engaged. Now there was an idea worth merit.

Darkwolf leaned forward and murmured in her ear. "You will be punished. I'm going to whip your ass and fuck you until you pass out . . . again."

Junga shivered. Licked her lips. Tried to regain her control. Maybe she shouldn't do this. She needed to be in complete control of herself at all times.

But this human sex—by the god Balor, she had to do it at least one more time.

Junga released Darkwolf's cock and glanced at the remaining witches in the ballroom, most of whom had yet to give in to her demands to aid them in the summoning. "Convince these witches their lives will be short if they do not aid me," she said to Hur, one of her head warriors.

Hur gave a stiff nod and attended to her orders.

She turned to Bane and Darkwolf. "I have matters to discuss with you both."

The corner of the Balorite priest's mouth curved into a knowing smile and Bane folded his arms across his chest and gave a deep nod.

Junga tossed her gaze to Za, another warrior in human form who would have made Elizabeth's panties wet. He certainly made Junga's body ache. "Join us," she commanded.

She led the way from the well-guarded ballroom, through the lobby, and into the elevator.

The moment the four were alone, the elevator doors closed behind them, Darkwolf and Bane began rubbing their hands over Junga's body, even though she hadn't given them permission. But she couldn't think as the warlock ripped the front of her suit jacket open. Buttons popped and flew across the elevator floor. Bane yanked down her bra and began suckling her nipples.

Darkwolf jerked up her skirt and pushed her panties down to her thighs.

Junga's eyes nearly rolled back in her head at the feel of male hands all over her body. By Balor, these humans had such sensitive skin. She felt every touch, every lick of their tongues, every stroke of their callused hands over her soft flesh.

Za looked on with a confused expression, but the rigidness in his slacks showed he was most definitely aroused.

Bane raised his head from Junga's wet nipples. "Touch her," he told Za. "She likes it."

He licked a line from between her breasts and up her throat. "She'll beg for it."

Darkwolf slipped his fingers into her wet folds and she cried out, her legs already trembling. "Smell her," he said. "She wants to be fucked."

Junga couldn't stop moaning and squirming. She wanted to control the moment, but she could do nothing but feel, and groan, and wriggle. Her pussy gushed with wetness and her nipples were rigid and swollen. Her breasts ached and her entire body felt wild with desire.

The bell dinged, indicating they were at the penthouse floor. Darkwolf grabbed her to him. He kissed her so hard he bruised her lips. He carried her into the penthouse suite, his hands everywhere as he bit her bottom lip. Hard enough to make her cry out.

Once inside the suite, Darkwolf slid her down so that she was on her knees looking up at him. He held her by her shoulders, gripping her so tight she couldn't move. By the power in his expression, she knew these men owned her at this moment. There was nothing she could do but let them think this was how she wanted it.

The frightening thing was she *did* desire this mastery from them.

Darkwolf ordered Za to stand so that his groin was in front of Junga's face.

"Unfasten his pants," the warlock demanded with a rough, aroused edge to his voice. "Suck Za's cock."

With a shiver of excitement, Junga obeyed. It felt so erotic with her breasts bared, her skirt up at her waist, and her panties around her thighs.

She didn't even fumble with Za's belt or his zipper—she had them both undone in a flash. Elizabeth's mind imprints made it easy for Junga. The woman had loved to be fucked, loved to be dominated. No matter that she had been a ball-buster outside the bedroom, inside she wanted the man in control.

Junga grasped Za's warm cock in her hands and slipped his long, hard length into her mouth. He groaned. "By Balor, that feels incredible," he said in a hoarse voice, and Junga sucked him harder.

"Grab her hair." Darkwolf pushed down on Junga's head. "Hard."

Junga looked up at Za as he buried his fists in her hair and started pumping his hips against her mouth.

Bane and Darkwolf got to their knees. They fondled her body, driving her out of her mind with their mouths, their tongues, their hands, their teeth. They sucked and bit her nipples, stroked her pussy, nipped her soft skin. One of them stuck three fingers up her ass and she gasped.

"Stop," the warlock ordered when Junga came close to orgasm. "Lie flat on the floor, Za."

He reluctantly withdrew his cock from Junga's mouth and she nearly whimpered because no one was touching her at that moment, and she *needed it*.

She cried out as Darkwolf dragged her by her hair until she was half over Za. "Fuck him."

Junga shook back her long black hair and purred her pleasure. This was what she wanted. This would fulfill the need she'd had since Bane and Darkwolf had taken her the first time.

She climbed on top of Za, but couldn't straddle his hips with her underwear still around her thighs. Bane's claws elongated from his human fingers, and in the next second he shredded the underwear, allowing her to fully straddle Za.

Junga grasped Za's cock in her hand, still wet from her mouth. Darkwolf held her hips for a long moment, not allowing her to sink onto Za's erection, until she whimpered. Finally he shoved her down, and she let out a trembling cry of pleasure as Za's cock thrust into her channel. He sucked in his breath and she could tell he was close to coming. So was she.

"Do not climax until I give you permission," Darkwolf said from behind her, as if reading her mind. She almost spoke her dissatisfaction.

The next thing she felt was a strap across her ass. Junga cried out at the burning pain of it. She paused and started to turn, but the Balorite priest whipped her ass again. This time she screamed.

"Don't stop fucking Za," Darkwolf ordered. "You've been a very bad warrioress, Junga. You must be punished."

"You can't—" She started to struggle, but Bane was suddenly in front of her.

"Shut up, bitch." Bane grabbed her by her hair, forced his cock between her lips and began fucking her mouth. "You are like your father Kae. You are not a leader. You want to be dominated. To be taken again and again."

Heat rushed through her, heat of anger, heat of embarrassment, heat of lust. With his cock in her mouth, and the force with which he was taking her, she could do nothing, say nothing.

It wasn't true. She *wasn't* weak.

Darkwolf whipped her, and she would have shouted if her mouth weren't full.

Strangely, the pain of the whipping turned into sweet agony, a sort of pleasure that made her arousal grow unbelievably stronger. She started to anticipate it. Want it.

Pain . . . pleasure . . . pain . . . pleasure. The males thrust in and out of her pussy and her mouth, and swatted her across the ass. She couldn't get enough.

When the warlock plunged his cock into her tight anus she screamed against the thickness of the cock in her mouth. "That's it, bitch." Darkwolf pumped in and out of her at the same time Za drove into her pussy, and Bane rammed his erection nearly down her throat. "You want more, don't you?"

"Yes," she cried out when Bane pulled his cock out of her mouth long enough for her to reply. Then he forced his erection back through her lips.

Oh, Balor. She couldn't take much more. She squirmed. Fought off the orgasm. Three men fucking her at once was almost more than she could bear. Za massaged her breasts with his hands, his cock bucking in and out of her pussy. Darkwolf bit the back of her neck, his erection ramming her tight ass. Bane clenched his fists in her hair so hard she felt more pain and pleasure from it, while he continued to drive his cock into her mouth.

"Come, now!" Darkwolf shouted.

Junga screamed around her mouthful of Bane's cock. Her body rocked with such incredible force she thought she was being transported through space and time again, by the warlocks' summoning. Small explosions burst behind her eyelids. Fire licked her body. Burning. Burning. Burning.

Male shouts filled the air. Cocks throbbed within her. Everywhere. The salty-sweet taste of come filled her mouth. Wet heat filled her pussy, her ass. The smell of sweat and sex filled her senses. Her mind whirled and spun. She felt herself starting to pitch into that black abyss, that place she'd vanished into the time before.

Fear rocked her.

"You liked that, didn't you, bitch?" Darkwolf said as he slapped her ass, jerking her attention back to him and causing another tremor to rip through her.

Junga couldn't even answer.

Their breathing was so heavy the room seemed to breathe with them. Their skin was slick with sweat and the smell of sex, and a hot masculine odor mixed with her own musk.

The men withdrew from her, their cocks now flaccid, but quickly growing erect again. Za eased Junga to the floor and she tried to keep from swaying and collapsing to the carpet.

She pushed her dark hair from her face as she rested on her hands and knees, and looked up at Darkwolf. A dominant expression crossed the warlock's features and he folded his arms across his chest. He glanced at the other males, then back to Junga.

Darkwolf's cruel smile horrified her—and excited her in new, dangerous ways.

"Fuck her again," he commanded. "Now."

23

Fury seared Silver's veins and fear pumped through her heart. The Fomorii had captured her parents! She could no longer focus on the fact that Cassia was not who Silver thought she was, about how all the pieces fit together. To hell with the puzzle. To hell with everything.

She needed to go help the D'Danann get her parents back.

Silver snatched her car keys off the key hook and started to head through the back door, when Jake Macgregor walked in. The second he saw her expression, the way she clutched her keys in her hand and the tightness of her jaw, he grabbed her by the shoulders.

"Whoa. What's going on here?" he asked in his cop voice, which pissed her off. She tried to jerk away from his hold. But he was too strong. She considered a little spellfire, but went for explaining what had happened instead, in as few words as possible.

"The Fomorii have my parents." She ground her teeth and her hands started to shake. "Hawk and three other D'Danann went after Mother and Father. I'm going to help."

"There are more of those winged guys now?" Jake shook the question off. "No way I'm going to let you go by yourself. You might be magically strong, Silver, but I can't let you tear off after them like this."

Through gritted teeth, Silver said, "Let. Me. Go."

Her rage was pushing her to use her magic, almost as if some voice in her head were daring her to cast a harmful spell in anger. Just a little damage. Just a little step across that oh-so-thin little line.

"I'm not turning you loose." His voice was cold, his expression fierce. "You know as well as I do that you can't go off half-cocked. You need to figure out a plan."

Would it be black magic to knee him in the groin? Silver thought not. Only her affection for the man kept her leg from moving. "We're talking about my mother and father! There's no time!"

The back door to the kitchen opened again, forcing Jake and Silver to stumble away from it. Keir and Sher strode through, their wings tucked away beneath their leather shirts. They both smelled of sweat, blood and battle, and the rotten fish stench of the Fomorii. Silver saw Jake's hand move to rest on his gun.

"Did you get Mother and Father?" she asked, her voice trembling. This time Jake let her go as she pushed herself away and went to the two D'Danann. "Are they all right?"

Keir's expression was so fierce the powerful warrior could have slain a host of demons with one glance.

Sher moved in front of Keir. "The demons took your family into their lair," she said.

"Oh, dear goddess." Blood drained from Silver's face. She could feel it sliding from her head to her toes. "Were they alive?"

The D'Danann woman laid her hand upon Silver's forearm and squeezed. "I believe so."

Silver swallowed and for the first time realized the other two warriors were not in the room. "Where are Hawk and Garrett?"

Sher glanced at Keir, whose expression went impossibly harsher, and then she said, "Garrett is dead."

Silver grew so light-headed that she stumbled back and was vaguely aware of Jake helping her to a seat at the kitchen table. "And Hawk?" she whispered.

The scarred warrior growled and Sher elbowed him—hard by the look of it. "Hawk is none the worse for the battle. But he blames himself for Garrett's death." She paused and moistened her lips. "Hawk did not return with us—I believe he needs time alone. Garrett was his closest friend."

For a long moment everything was quiet in the kitchen, save for the harsh breathing of the warriors and the tick of the ancient clock hanging over the sink.

Everything was too, too much. Silver did the only thing she could at that moment. She buried her face in her hands and cried.

Hours later, Silver stared out the window of her apartment, waiting for Rhiannon to come in. Silver's eyes still ached, her head ached, and her heart ached.

With her parents taken hostage along with all the other witches and Hawk still not back, she was crazy with worry, crazy with the need to take action. She hadn't been able to sit still.

If not for all the hotel guests and the witches, she would search for some spell to bring down that damned hotel on the demons' heads.

Stop thinking like that. It's dangerous. That would be black magic—even if my intentions are pure. The corruption would be immediate, and I'd be lost.

She began pacing the room as if to distance herself from the steadily rising temptation to draw on more power, to seek a source of magic that would guarantee her success. First Copper. Then her Coven. Two PSF officers' deaths. Now her parents were taken and Hawk's friend dead—how much more devastation would they be forced to endure?

Maybe just a few spells. Just across the line. A little stronger. A little more forceful.

No. No. No. I won't. But . . .

She nearly tripped over Polaris. She picked up the python, who curled around her arm like the snake bracelet on her opposite wrist. Her familiar gave her a reproachful gaze, making her realize she'd been hopping around like a half-crazed rabbit.

"Where is Hawk?" she asked Polaris as she stroked his head. He stuck his tongue out at her and she frowned. "You're such a jealous male."

She clenched her fist in a lock of her hair and yanked it as she tried to hold back more tears. She wanted to cry because another life had been taken. Her heart ached for Hawk, who had lost his best friend.

Silver wanted to cry and scream for her parents. Run out and find them herself right this minute. She would try if it weren't for the D'Danann, Jake, and the other witches standing guard over the shop to make sure she didn't leave.

Silver let Polaris slink back onto the floor. Blessed goddess, why couldn't witches fly? Appear and disappear at will?

A knock at the door, then the knob turned and Rhiannon poked her head around the door before walking in and shutting it behind her. Her loose, flowing skirts swirled around her legs. She wore her usual bright-colored clothing, her dress in layers of lemon yellow and turquoise. In her arms she carried Spirit.

Polaris flicked his tongue out at Spirit. The cat hissed.

"Sorry I'm late." A concerned expression was on Rhiannon's pretty face, and her chin-length amber hair swung forward with every movement she made. The scars on her cheek were healing, but Silver was still uncertain if they would ever fully be gone. "Iris is such a basket case."

Silver hugged Rhiannon and Spirit gave an annoyed cry between them before squeezing out of Rhiannon's arms and jumping to the floor, bounding past Polaris.

Rhiannon's embrace and light citrus scent comforted Silver in a time when she needed comfort. How it pained her that she would have to send Rhiannon away, when she needed her friend. But she would be safer this way, anyway.

"What is it?" Rhiannon cocked her head as they drew apart. Sunlight from the window highlighted the sprinkling of freckles across her nose and glinted on the small gold and onyx pentagram at her throat.

"I need you to go to the other D'Anu Covens." Silver caught Rhiannon's fingers with her own. "You can convince them to send help."

Rhiannon blinked, then an adamant expression crossed her face and she raised her tone. "I'm not leaving you to fight the Fomorii alone."

"I'm not alone." Silver gave a deep sigh. "But I feel—I am certain that we need more D'Anu to aid us."

This time Rhiannon shook her head, her amber hair swinging about her cheeks. "Send Eric or Mackenzie. Iris even." She paused and gave an almost-smile. "Er, not Iris. The woman is such a wuss."

Silver resisted a laugh at Rhiannon's accurate description of the D'Anu witch who had been mumbling about dark magic ever since she arrived and refused to go anywhere near the D'Danann.

"You have the strength of spirit we need to convince the D'Anu." Silver squeezed Rhiannon's fingers before releasing them. "You have experienced the horrors of being captured by the demons. You know what we're going through and how much we need aid."

Rhiannon shook her head again and took a step back from Silver. "I'm in for the fight."

Silver closed her eyes and pinched the bridge of her nose with her thumb and forefinger before releasing it and dropping her hand to look at her friend again. "Believe me. I can't think of anyone I'd like better fighting at my side. But this is more important, and I think you're the only one capable of the task."

Rhiannon hugged herself and rubbed her arms as if a sudden chill had come over her. "It isn't right."

"It is." Silver brushed her sweating palms on her jeans. "Do this for me. For all of us. Please?"

For a long moment Rhiannon simply studied her. Silver practically held her breath, waiting for her friend's answer.

Silver felt a small presence, and looked down to see Spirit wrapping himself around Rhiannon's ankles, just below her flowing broomstick skirt.

Rhiannon looked down at her familiar and frowned. "Not you, too?"

Spirit gave a loud mewl and planted himself on his haunches in front of Rhiannon. He mewled again and Rhiannon slowly nodded.

Polaris rose up from beside Silver and gazed intently at Rhiannon.

She raised her head and looked at Silver. "Just know that this is under duress. I can't fight all of you."

"I'll give you the Coven's credit card." Silver hid her relief from her friend. "You'll need it for airfare and food."

"Janis will likely kill us both."

Silver snorted. "As long as you're getting other D'Anu, and keeping to the white, what can she say?" Her eyes lost focus for a moment as she looked away. "Me, I've already been judged and condemned for the gray magic I've used right in front of her pointy nose."

"Surely she isn't that stupid." Rhiannon said. "She's got to know that everything you've done has been for the good."

Silver gave a little smile. "That's the problem with gray magic. The more you use it, the more you feel the call of the dark. The more you think you can use it for the good. I feel like I'm in a constant battle for my soul."

Rhiannon planted her hands on her hips. "I don't believe for a minute you'd ever, ever cross."

Spirit yowled. Polaris hissed. Whether it was in agreement with Silver or Rhiannon, Silver couldn't tell.

When Rhiannon left to pack, Silver realized she needed to center herself. She walked to the middle of her living room, straightened her stance, closed her eyes, and took a deep breath. She raised her hands high overhead and imagined herself a great white oak. Her roots delved through the apartment floor, down through the floor of the shop until they hit dirt.

They spread deep, deep, into the center of the Earth, seeking cool soil, crystal water.

Her arms, spread wide, became branches in her mind. Her branches extended up through the ceiling of her apartment, through the roof and into the sky. They soared through the fog until reaching healing sunshine.

It was unusually difficult this time, but then, she'd never had such horrors in her life before. When she felt reasonably grounded, she said, "Ancestors, please aid me in recovering those lost. In sending back to exile the demons who are murdering witches and humans alike." Her words turned into a desperate plea. "What must I do? Please send me a sign."

Nothing happened.

Silver quavered with the force of her need for guidance. The image of her oak leaves trembling filled her mind's eye.

"Please, my Ancestors," she whispered.

Doubt in herself and her abilities twisted like a cold ritual sword through her belly. She imagined soft rain falling on oak leaves and tears pricked the corners of her eyes. The Ancestors weren't answering her call. What was she supposed to do now?

Outside her apartment door, boot steps thumped in the hallway. She was jolted out of her trance and in her mind withdrew her branches and roots until she was fully within herself again.

With no doubt that it was Hawk on the other side of her door, Silver practically flew to it and wrenched it open to see him standing there, so real, so masculine.

Perhaps *he* was the Ancestors' answer to her pleas.

"Hawk!" She threw herself against his chest, wrapping her arms around his waist and hugging him tight. He smelled of wind and fog—and of Fomorii and blood, a smell that caused her to shiver at the thought of what he'd tolerated.

Slowly he lowered his arms and wrapped her in his embrace, but seemed reluctant. They stood in the doorway for a moment before he pushed her away, setting her apart from him. Wounded, Silver studied Hawk's impassive features, trying to see some emotion in his expression, trying to sense what he was feeling.

She got absolutely nothing.

He was completely blocked off to her, distant and frozen. Like a stranger.

Silver's heart twisted harder than ever. Her friends, her parents, now Hawk . . . she felt as if a part of herself were being stolen and locked away, leaving her lonely inside. Would she be completely empty or dead before this battle ended?

Hawk wanted to take Silver right back into his arms and hold her forever. But he could no longer allow himself to become too close to anyone. It was his fault Garrett had been murdered. Davina had died because he hadn't been there to protect her. He wouldn't take those same risks with Silver.

By the gods, who would have thought the Fomorii would find a way to battle them with iron? They could wield no swords. But with their enhanced claws—they would be far more formidable opponents.

Silver remained silent as he walked into the apartment and away from her. Away from her warmth, her sweet scent of lilies and woman. Away from the way she made his heart ache with an undefined need every time he was close to her.

He came up short when he saw Polaris curled up on the armchair. The snake hissed at him, its wicked black eyes glinting. Hawk growled, wanting to take his sword and dice the creature into tiny pieces.

From behind him, Silver said softly, "I'm sorry about Garrett."

He bowed his head and rubbed his temples where blood pounded with anger again. Anger at the demons for murdering Garrett.

But mostly he was furious at himself. Keir was right. If it wasn't for Hawk's foolishness, his recklessness, Garrett would be alive.

"Hawk." Silver came up beside him where he could see her lovely face, feel her warmth again, feel that ache again.

She laid her fingers on his arm and the silver snake on her hand and wrist glittered in the low lighting. How ironic that the one creature he feared was the totem of this beautiful woman. She had simply bewitched him. Her beauty, her passion, her courage, her strength, her determination, her compassion. Everything about her called to him in ways he had never imagined possible.

In an instant his thoughts turned back to his first and only meeting with Moondust mere hours ago. Recognition had flashed through him the moment he saw her eyes and her Elvin features. He had been certain she was more than a witch—that she, too, was *other*. When she had spoken to him, he agreed to hold his peace for now.

But what did that mean about Silver?

Was she *other*, too?

"I've come up with a plan." He held emotion from his tone and kept his expression flat. "We need a large, open space to draw out the Fomorii on Samhain. We can't fight them indoors or in confined locations. It makes the D'Danann too vulnerable if we don't have room to fly."

Silver took her hand from his arm and pushed her heavy fall of silvery-blond hair from her face. "Golden Gate Park. It's south of us, not too far away."

He slowly nodded. It took all his strength to resist touching her, holding her.

Choking back a sigh of need, Silver went toward him, needing his embrace, his comfort.

Hawk shook his head and stepped back. "I cannot," he said, then turned and strode out the door.

For a long moment, Silver stood and looked at the door, her heart in her throat. Why did she crave his embrace so much? Need to have his shoulder to lean on?

No, he was right. The focus had to be on battle plans. Not lust. Not physical need.

She swallowed. No emotional need of any kind.

October 28

24

Silver twirled her fork in her noodles while she sat in the shop's kitchen and waited for Hawk to meet her, then let the noodles fall away from the tines.

Rhiannon had already packed and left on a flight to San Diego last night, the first stop on her way to visit each of the twelve other Covens. Spirit had accompanied her, none too pleased at being forced to travel in the cat carrier. Eric and Cassia were working in the shop and the café, and she was alone.

Silver stabbed at a piece of zucchini-cranberry bread over and over again, turning it into nothing but a pile of crumbles as she thought about getting rid of the demons. How they were going to send the Fomorii back to Underworld would present a very large problem.

She stopped attacking the bread as she mentally went over their plan. From what Rhiannon and the others had said, the Fomorii planned on summoning a great number of demons on Samhain. Now if the witches and the D'Danann were to turn the tables on the Fomorii, call them out on Samhain and defeat them in battle . . . then *they* could send the Fomorii back to Underworld.

Silver's thoughts returned to the present and she fought the desire to grab her car keys, head out to Bitty, drive over to where the demons had her parents, and blast the hell out of all of them with her magic. But that would be stupid and reckless and she would probably be captured, too. Then where would she be? Completely unable to help her own people.

Silver dropped the fork to her plate and pushed away from the table, the chair's legs squeaking on the old tiled floor. The kitchen smelled of warm spices and the special lunch Cassia had prepared earlier—noodles in faerie butter, asparagus salad, zucchini-cranberry bread, and honor cake for dessert. Silver had mostly scooted her food around the plate, although the food had been delicious. Since her parents' abduction, she'd hardly been able to eat, and last night she barely got any sleep.

And Hawk hadn't been there to hold her. To comfort her.

That's not his job, she reminded herself forcefully as she tapped one sandal on the floor. *He's not my keeper.*

She mentally shook off the thought of missing him last night. This was a war, not a lovefest. It was time she started acting more like a warrior herself.

Silver had to smile. Some warrior she was today. This morning she had dressed in her favorite strappy sandals, a form-fitting blue skirt that went to her upper thighs and a matching blue silk blouse. Her hair hung loosely over her shoulders and straight down to the middle of her back. It had given her some feeling of normalcy dressing the way she usually did—that is, when not tracking down deviant warlocks and demons. But she could fight just as well in sandals as in her boots.

Hell, she had to admit it. She dressed this way for Hawk. She wanted him to notice her again.

"Ready, Silver?" Hawk walked in through the kitchen's back door and closed it behind him, and she wanted to melt just from the sight of him, so handsome, so masculine. His gaze dropped to her short skirt and lingered on her bare legs before allowing his eyes to meet hers again. "I . . ." He visibly swallowed. "I need to scout this Golden Gate Park."

Silver held back a grin. "Sure."

But when she turned to head for the door, he said, "There's, ah, something I need to tell you."

Silver looked away from him and jerked open the back door. "You can tell me on the way—"

She came to an abrupt stop. Closed her eyes. Opened them again.

"Bitty!" Shock vibrated her body at the sight of the vehicle's battered form. From where she was standing, she saw the fender was mangled. At least one headlight smashed. The hood crumpled. The right side mirror gone. The passenger side bludgeoned. Bright yellow paint scraped away, leaving cold gray metal beneath.

Jaw slack, she whirled to face Hawk. "My car!"

He looked like a teenager who'd been caught taking his parents' sedan for a joy ride and had ended up wrecking it. "I, well . . . I had to get you home the night we summoned my comrades. Had to keep you warm. I had, ah, some difficulty driving your vehicle."

"*Some* difficulty?" Silver almost whimpered when she looked again at her once beautiful VW Bug. When she turned to Hawk, she sighed. "Does it still run?"

He shifted, still looking guilty. "I believe so."

With an inward groan, Silver strode out the door toward her wreck of a car. "Come on, then."

Silver walked around the Bug. Bitty's driver's side was little better than the passenger's. Metal creaked when she opened it, and Hawk had to yank the other door open. Grateful the handle didn't come off in his hand with the power of his jerk, she slid into the driver's seat, which was as far back as it was possible to go—obviously to accommodate Hawk's much larger size. She positioned it where it belonged, jammed the key into the ignition, pushed in the clutch and turned the key. The car started immediately, with only a small shudder, but she could swear Bitty groaned from all its bumps and bruises.

Her poor car!

When Hawk slid into Bitty, his intoxicating scent surrounded her. She couldn't help the immediate ache in her breasts, the tightness of her nipples beneath her silk blouse, or the wetness of her pussy beneath her short skirt. The desire to be with him.

For one long moment they looked at each other. Silver almost reached out to Hawk, needing to feel his lips against hers, needing to taste him again.

Instead she glanced away and cleared her throat. "I hope my little Bug makes it," she said as she backed out of the driveway.

Sitting so close to Silver, Hawk found he could barely breathe. Just being near her brought back all the longing, all the need for her. She smelled of lilies, soap, and pure woman. Her breasts peaked beneath her shirt, and her eyes darkened with such desire that his cock stiffened painfully against his breeches.

He turned his head and focused on the city as Silver's car chugged up and down steep hills, into neighborhoods of homes stacked against one another, through rows of small businesses, near huge buildings that scraped the sky, and passed a trolley that clanged cheerfully in the foggy afternoon. With such heavy concerns on his mind, it was almost too much to process.

"Tell me about Otherworld," Silver said as she drove, interrupting his thoughts.

Hawk looked at her profile. Such an adorable nose she had. Such perfect skin.

He cleared his throat. "Like your world, Otherworld varies depending on where you go. It is a magical place, no matter where one resides. The sidhe where I live is particularly beautiful."

She kept her eye on the road. "What's it like?"

With a shrug he looked out the window. "My daughter and I live in the forest with other D'Danann, as well as Fae of all kind."

When he glanced back at Silver, she looked intrigued. "I have seen a bit of Otherworld in my visions, but truly not much. I would love to see more."

He smiled. He could easily imagine her in his world. Could imagine showing her the places that were special to him. "It is a thing of beauty. Our homes are in the trees themselves."

She spared him a quick look before turning her attention back to the road. "Homes in the trees. Fascinating."

"The D'Danann made a trade with the Dryads. The use of their trees for protection against the Pixies, Brownies, and Gnomes. Their quarrel goes far beyond my memory. We have no quarrel ourselves with any of the beings. We simply keep the peace among the Fae." He sighed. "Although at times that in itself is challenging. The Brownies are particularly mischievous and malevolent."

"I know many of the Elementals who reside on Earth," Silver said. "As far as I know they live in harmony."

Hawk shifted in his seat thinking of the rivalry between Fae and Elves. "If it were so easy in Otherworld."

"I bet you miss your daughter."

"Aye." For a moment there was silence as he thought of his beautiful child. He slipped his hand into his pocket and withdrew the tiny poppet she had sent with him when he left. His fingers ran over the graceful if slightly crumpled wings.

"Is that your daughter's?" He glanced up and his eyes met Silver's gray ones for a quick moment before she turned her attention back to her driving.

"I gave it to her as a gift after I first met you." He stroked the poppet's black hair. "She insisted I bring it with me on this mission. A good luck token of sorts."

Silver gave him a smile and he returned it to his pocket.

When she asked him about his childhood, he shared with her his youth, growing up near Ireland of centuries ago. When she pushed him further, he spoke of his family, his unbending father and his strict mother. And his friends. He even found the words to talk about his childhood adventures with Garrett, and his battles with Keir.

"That's why you're at each other's throats most of the time," she said as they crested a hill.

He shrugged. There was more to it than simple childhood rivalries, but he didn't want to discuss those aspects of his childhood and adult life.

When Hawk asked Silver about her own childhood, her mind turned back the pages in time—time so much shorter than Hawk's centuries of living. How young she was compared to him.

As they approached the park, she quickly ran through her childhood, of growing up with magic that she had to learn to control. About the time she burned several locks of her sister's hair with spellfire and was grounded from using magic for an entire week. She wrinkled her nose. "Singed hair smells really bad," she said, and he laughed.

She told him about her extended family back in Massachusetts. Aunts, uncles, cousins, some she missed, some she didn't care if she saw again. Her mother was orphaned, so all of her relatives were on her father's side. She shared with him how she and Copper were chosen to serve as D'Anu apprentices because of their magic and because they came from a long line of D'Anu. She had begun her apprenticeship in the Massachusetts Coven, but when she came of age, she moved to San Francisco to complete her training. Her father was simply too overbearing as far as she was concerned, and it had been time for her to spread her wings and fly.

Silver drove as far into the park as she could before they had to walk. Bitty's doors squeaked as they climbed out, and she flinched at the rusty injured sound of them opening and closing.

Both she and Hawk were silent as they walked down a tree-shaded path. Fortunately the park was big enough that at times you could walk along the paths and pass few people. They got a few looks from an occasional jogger or cyclist when they saw Hawk decked out in his leathers, sheathed dagger, and sword.

Bless it. She should have made him leave the sword back home.

Silver had always loved coming to the park. To her it was alluring, a place filled with positive magic. She only hoped the D'Dananns' strength and the witches' powers, combined with that positive magic, would be enough come Samhain.

Today was unusually clear for San Francisco. Late afternoon sunlight dappled through fall-flowering eucalyptus leaves and cypress, and danced on the walkway. Sparrows flitted from tree to tree as a crisp breeze ruffled the sleeves of her blouse and pressed silk against her breasts. Her hair lifted from her shoulders and her pentagram earrings swung against her neck.

Despite the coolness of the October wind, she felt Hawk's warmth as he shortened his strides to keep pace with her.

The park was so huge they had to walk for a while to reach the spot she thought would be a good location to fight the Fomorii. When she was sure no one would see them, she broke away from the public paths, and took him through the trees toward her own hideaway. Her sandals only sank slightly in the moist earth as they walked. They didn't talk along the way, and it was a comfortable silence. Instead of conversing, Silver tried to center herself, breathing in the scents of Monterey pine and cypress, and the salty breeze blowing off the ocean.

When Silver and Hawk reached their destination, they stood just outside the meadow that had a small pond on one side of it. Wind rippled the clear surface and a pair of ring-necked ducks waddled from the grass into the water.

The meadow was far away from the public paths, through a thick grove of trees, away from the usual haunts of park visitors. This was her place, she liked to think. Secluded, safe, special. She had often stood right in the center of this meadow on a moonlit night, and performed various rituals. The Elementals and spirits—Faeries, Dragons, Gnomes, and Undines that had chosen not to go to Otherworld—tended the meadow and pond, adding to its strong magic.

Her heart ached. She would ask the spirits and Elementals that lived here for permission before she allowed the D'Danann to bring the beasts here. After the Fomorii were lured to this spot, it most likely would no longer be a place of solitude and joy. But in her heart she knew it was the right location to send the evil back where it came from.

Hawk took in the meadow, and he nodded his approval. "Now we just need a way to draw out the bastards."

Silver took a deep breath as her gaze rested on a yellow warbler perching on a cypress branch, before she turned back to Hawk. "Rhiannon said they need more D'Anu witches to help summon a great number of Fomorii."

"What about other Balorites in other cities?" Hawk asked.

"From what I understand, the Balorite Clans don't answer to one another," she said. "There's too much of a power struggle between the Clans. I don't think we have to worry about them."

"Thank the gods," Hawk muttered.

"Since other Balorites probably aren't an option, and our Covens are so far apart, Rhiannon, Mackenzie, Iris, and I are the only D'Anu they could come after," Silver said, and paused before adding, "Unless more D'Anu arrive from the other Covens before Samhain.

"Rhiannon said Darkwolf wants me because I have strong gray magic. He thinks he can turn me." Silver blew out her breath, stirring a lock of her hair. "On Samhain I can be the bait. I can draw them out."

"No." The angles of Hawk's face were harsh as he looked down at her. "I won't risk you."

She planted her hands on her slim hips. "It's not all about you, or even me. This is about something much bigger."

Hawk's features shifted from anger to torture to something she couldn't read. He brought his hands to her upper arms and stroked her skin through the silk of her shirt, causing her to shiver. "Please, Silver. Don't ask me to let you do this."

She reached up to cup his stubbled cheeks. "I need to. For the good of all witches. For the good of every human in this city. Maybe beyond San Francisco." She smiled. "Besides. I don't intend to be caught by the bastards."

He leaned his cheek into one of her hands and closed his eyes. He looked so tired, and for the first time she was sure she saw fear in his expression. Not for himself. Fear for her.

She rose up on her tiptoes and brushed her mouth over his. An instant sizzling sensation traveled from the touch of his lips, throughout her body. His eyes opened and his hands tightened on her arms.

"Hey," she said against his lips. "It's okay." She felt him stiffen, felt his restraint as she slipped her hands from his cheeks and wrapped her arms around his neck. "I'm a pretty tough witch, if I do say so myself."

Before he could say a word, she moved her mouth against his, kissing him slowly, seductively. She nipped his lower lip, licked the spot, then bit him again. Hawk groaned and crushed his mouth against hers. His kiss was hard, fierce, wild. And she wanted more, had to have all of him.

He slipped his hands from her arms to her waist and pulled her against his hips. His cock pressed hard against her belly, and her sex grew damp with her juices.

Their moans met and became one as their bodies melted into each other. Silver lost herself in the kiss, his lips hot and wet against hers, his tongue deep inside her mouth. He tasted of all that was male and she breathed deeply of his masculine scent that heightened her arousal, made her want him so much that she whimpered her desire.

Hawk groaned again and pulled away from her, his amber eyes smoldering. "We shouldn't—"

Silver moved a finger to his lips to shush him. "Let's enjoy each other. We won't have a lot of time, but we can take pleasure in what we have."

His amber eyes nearly glowed with arousal. And perhaps something more. "Are you certain?"

"I couldn't be more sure of myself than I am right now." She slipped both hands into his hair and brought him down to her again. "I need you inside me."

His hands clenched her skirt even as he said, "Here?"

"Yes." She smiled and wriggled against him. "Now."

25

Silver clasped one of Hawk's hands and led him deeper into the trees, to a tiny patch of grass and leaves hidden from the meadow. A secluded place where they would be alone to enjoy these precious moments together.

Hawk took Silver gently down to the ground, his gaze never leaving hers. A part of him still tried to tell himself he shouldn't be doing this, but a much larger part needed her, and knew she needed him. Just touching her gave him such a feeling of completion he couldn't find the words to describe it.

He knelt beside her and ran his fingertips down the side of her face and along the curve of her neck to her pentagram, where he paused. "Are you sure?" he asked again, tracing a circle around her pendant.

"I never do anything I'm not sure about." She smiled and lifted her head to brush her lips against his.

Hawk's heart twisted. He moved his fingers from the pentagram to the vee of her blouse, and goose bumps rose on her soft skin as she shivered. "You are the loveliest creature I have ever known," he murmured as he moved his fingers to circle one taut nipple rising beneath the silk of her blouse. "I can't get enough of you."

"Then take me." She clasped her hand over his and pressed it hard to her breast. "Take me to places no one else can."

Hawk lowered his head and his lips met hers in a soft kiss. He could never get enough of Silver's sweet taste, her scent, the warmth of her body next to his.

He moved his lips to her throat and flicked out his tongue, enjoying the salt of her skin as he trailed his lips down the curve of her neck. He traveled farther until his mouth was moving along the curve of one breast. Silver's soft moans joined with the sound of birds chirping in the trees, the chatter of squirrels, and the gentle sound of wind through leaves and pine needles.

She slipped her fingers into his hair. "Make love to me, Hawk."

"I am, my sweet little witch," he replied with a gentle nip at her breast through her silk blouse.

Silver moaned again and clenched her hands tighter in his hair. "Faster, Hawk. I need to feel you against me. Inside me."

"Uh-uh." He sucked her nipple, wetting the silk and making it transparent enough to see the rosy bud. "I'm going to take it slow with you. You're too special."

"I guess a little magic is needed." Silver writhed beneath him. "If I'm going to have my way with you."

He rose up and the corner of his mouth quirked. "And what magic would that be, witch?"

Silver slipped her hand from his hair and ran one finger down his throat to his taut belly, and straight to his cock. As she traced the path he felt a burst of warmth and sizzling sensations throughout his body, much like the first time they'd experienced sexual pleasure. But this was different. By the time she reached his erection, his whole body was on fire, and all he could think of was plunging his cock into her pussy and taking her hard and fast.

She traced the line of his erection, teasing him with her touch. She circled her free hand in the air three times. A blue glow and silver sparkles immediately surrounded them. Filled him with such arousal that he fought to restrain himself. He thought he'd reach orgasm just from her magic.

"Like it?" She drew him to her, guiding him between her thighs. By the almost pained pleasure on her face and the hoarseness of her voice, he could tell her own magic affected her as much as it affected him.

"Gods, yes." He braced his hands to either side of her chest. "I'm ready to fuck you until you beg for mercy."

"Do it." She waved her hand again and the buttons of her blouse simply slipped out of their holes and the silk parted, revealing her perfect breasts.

Her nipples were high and ripe for his mouth. He took one hungrily. Licked and sucked at the taut pebble. His arousal elevated dangerously high and he didn't know how he could control himself much longer. The blue glow and silver sparkles continued to swirl around them, between them, through him.

"Don't hold back, Hawk." She arched her back as he took possession of her other nipple. "Please."

He shoved her tiny skirt up around her waist where she was completely bare. At the same time she simply ran her finger up the front of his pants. The ties magically came undone and his cock and balls sprang out.

Hawk groaned as her small, cool fingers wrapped around his erection and guided him toward her wet channel. The magic glow and sparkles never stopped, and he thought he'd go mad with the blood rushing through him, the pounding of his heart, the stiffness of his cock.

"Do it," she begged again. "Fuck me."

With a near roar, he drove himself deep within her and Silver gave a purr of delight. He closed his eyes and just held still, afraid that if he moved he might come. Her warmth wrapped him like a velvet night and he could see her magical sparkles behind his eyelids. Her witchcraft radiated through him, inside her core, sensations that made his cock feel harder, thicker, longer.

Hawk felt so good inside her that Silver shuddered with pleasure. Even as he held himself still, she began pumping her hips, forcing him to join her in the rhythm. His eyes opened and his gaze fixed on hers. Those beautiful golden-amber eyes that sent another thrill straight to her belly and her pussy.

"Hard," she demanded, raking her fingernails along his back. "I want it hard and deep. I want to feel all of you."

Sweat rolled down Hawk's face and landed on Silver's bare breast. She felt him tremble with the force of his need. "I want to take it slow with you. I want to give you pleasure like you've never felt before," he said in his deep Irish brogue that caused her to shiver all the more.

"Unleash yourself," she urged him. "Let go."

Hawk focused on Silver as he began thrusting in and out of her. Hard. Deep. Just like she wanted it. She cried out at the feel of him inside her, expanding her, filling her. Her breasts bounced as he pounded into her. The feel of his leather pants scraping her bare thighs, his leather shirt against her belly, felt so erotic she moaned in ecstasy.

She smelled her own juices, the scent of their desire. In the blue sparkling glow of her magic, his amber eyes burned hot, warming her naked breasts with just one rake of his penetrating gaze.

As he thrust he caught one of her nipples with his teeth and flicked his tongue over it. Silver squirmed beneath him, lightly scraping her nails from his shoulder blades to his muscled ass and back. She wrapped her thighs around his waist.

He pumped his hips so hard the sound of flesh against flesh echoed in their hidden spot. "*Mine,*" he said against her breasts.

Silver's orgasm hit so hard and so fast, she never saw it coming. Sparks exploded in her mind and throughout her body. She screamed and barely recognized the sounds of birds scattering and calling out as if joining in the primal cry spilling from her lips.

Hawk continued to fuck her hard, and she came again and again. Her own magic enhanced her orgasm so much that she almost called it back because it was too much to bear. But she wanted to give him as much pleasure as he'd given her.

He pounded harder and harder, and then came with a shout. He pumped in and out a few more times as his warm come spilled into her and his cock throbbed in her channel.

"Silver." He rolled onto his side, dead leaves crunching beneath his weight. Keeping her tight within his embrace, his eyes met hers. "I can't get enough of you. Have you cast some kind of spell on me?"

She smiled as she stroked the side of his face, his stubble tickling her palm. "If I have, then you have cast one on me, as well."

"My witch." He kissed her softly. "My sweet little witch."

Silver stood skyclad in the center of the park's hidden meadow, cool air caressing her naked body, her heart still beating with the power of her lovemaking with Hawk. Her nipples and breasts were tender and her body had the sweet ache of their sexual pleasure.

He stood at the edge of the meadow, watching her intently. He looked so incredibly handsome, from the proud tilt of his head to his dark hair stirring around his shoulders to his finely muscled body and powerful legs. She felt safe and secure when he was near, as if nothing could happen when they were together.

An illusion, at best, with danger threatening them at every moment. But her heart couldn't hold back the joy she felt just being with him.

They were in nature, always a sacred place, so she didn't need to cast a circle before she called to the Elementals. The muffled evening noises of ducks and birds were music to her ears, as well as the sound of wind teasing leaves and branches of the surrounding trees. It smelled of pine and cypress, water, rich earth, and the remnants of sunshine as the afternoon headed toward evening.

"In this enchanted and bewitching place, I respectfully summon the Faeries, Gnomes, Undines, and Dragons," she said in a loud, clear voice. "This is your home. You tend the grass, flowers, and the pond. You speak to the trees and to all of nature." Her voice carried through the evening air as she spoke to those who rightfully owned the meadow.

"Respectfully I ask of you the use of your home to cleanse what is evil and send it back to where it came from." Her throat ached and she felt the sudden need to cry. "This evil threatens the lives of all witches, all humans, and all that is good and pure."

She swallowed and continued, "To fight this evil we need the use of your home. Blood may be shed. The unpure may destroy what is serene and at peace. I ask this of you to save us all from the Fomorii."

Silver's voice trailed away, and for a moment the meadow was completely silent.

Fog began to rise from the ground. A light, gentle fog that caressed her ankles, swirled around them. A glitter appeared before her and then a shape, no bigger than the length of her hand. A tiny being fluttered her wings as she flew high enough to meet Silver's gaze.

The Faerie was so beautiful that tears ran freely down Silver's cheeks. The creature wore nothing on her perfect tiny figure, and her long dark hair spilled to her buttocks. Silver realized the glitter came from the Faerie's wings, every time she opened and shut them.

With a knowing but sad smile, the Faerie stretched out her small hand. Automatically, Silver raised hers, and cupped her palm in front of the Faerie. Upon it appeared a perfect feather. "From the blackbird," the Faerie said, in a voice like the most beautiful song on a clear night. "For defending your territory. Our territory," she continued. "Black for the banishment of evil. You have our blessing, Silver of the D'Anu."

"Thank you," Silver said to the Air Elemental, the word coming out a mere tremble on her lips.

The Faerie darted away, into the forest, leaving a trail of glitter behind. Silver watched until every sparkle had vanished into the evening air.

"Ah-hem," a voice said at her feet, jerking Silver's attention from the darkness to the fog swirling around her ankles. An old man stood there, no taller than her knee. He had gnarled features, like the bark of an oak tree, wore gray and brown clothing, and held a staff as gnarled as his face. "Would you ignore those of the Earth?" he asked, but with a glint of humor in his eye.

Silver smiled. "Never."

He held up his hand and Silver lowered hers. Beside the blackbird feather he placed a large, sparkling green diamond-cut stone. "Emerald for strength and bravery. Green for healing."

With a respectful nod, she said, "Thank you for your gift, one with the Earth."

"Use it well." The Gnome returned her nod, then hobbled away, through the swirling fog.

The moment the Gnome vanished from sight, Silver heard a splash in the pond. An Undine rose from the shallow water. The beautiful woman stepped out to stand on its grassy bank. Silver walked toward the naked being whose long blond hair did nothing to cover her breasts, her nipples hard and a luscious deep red. The hair on her mound was thick with blond curls. Her green eyes glowed with sensuality in the evening light. The Undine was as tall as Silver, yet she had risen from what was a small pond.

A sad and wistful expression crossed the spirit's beautiful features. "The Water Elementals know we will likely suffer much loss, but what must be done, must be done." She dropped into Silver's hand a water-smoothed stone with a hole in the center, in a light shade of turquoise blue. "A hag stone for protection. Blue for hope and peace."

Before Silver could say a word, the Undine stepped away and vanished into the pond. The splash of water sounded like a sob, and more tears trickled down Silver's cheeks. "Thank you," she whispered.

Fire swirled up out of the fog, rising and rising until it was over Silver's head. Her heart beat faster as a Dragon's head appeared in the flames. The Dragon was a deep crimson, its face all ridges and scales, its yellow eyes and features somewhat cranky looking.

"You call me, the most powerful Elemental, last?" The Dragon's roar caused Silver to step back and her body to tremble. "You have been calling upon the Element of Fire much of late. We deserve far more respect."

Silver fought back a small rush of fear. Fire Elementals were temperamental and demanding, and it was usually best not to call upon them too often. She lowered her eyes, before looking to him again. "You have assisted us in more ways than we can thank you for. We must call upon you again. Will you help us?"

The Dragon gave another growl and he flapped his wings in the fire. "Your requests are noble and shall be answered."

Silver gave a tiny sigh of relief, but almost jumped when the Dragon breathed fire onto her outstretched palm. For a moment she feared the other three gifts would be charred, along with her hand, but the fire melted away and felt like no more than a warm breath upon her skin.

Except for a tiny flame that danced in her hand next to the other gifts. The small fire flickered in varying shades of red, but didn't burn her palm.

"Close your hand," the Dragon said, and she obeyed.

The flame snuffed out, but the moment she opened her hand again, the little fire sprang up. She smiled in delight.

"Flame for power and strength," the Dragon said. "Red for protection."

Silver bowed to the Fire Elemental. "Our thanks for this gift and for your assistance. For all you have done for witches and humans alike."

The Dragon gave an arrogant toss of his massive head. "Now kick their scaly asses."

After Silver dressed, he watched as she stuffed the Elementals' gifts into her skirt pocket. His heart warmed as he took her hand and they walked away from the meadow, through the trees, and back toward the path. When they reached the concrete, Silver's sandals clicked on the hard surface. Her silk shirt was pulled taut over her bare breasts and her short skirt was a bit on the rumpled side.

Silver's small hand felt good in Hawk's, and he found himself squeezing her fingers tighter, not wanting to let her go. When he looked down at Silver, her smile was sunshine warming his soul, chasing away the graying evening. Guilt stabbed at him, that he should have any feelings at all for another woman when his heart had belonged to Davina.

Silver's smile vanished and she went completely still, drawing him to a stop.

"They're here," she said, a heartbeat before rumbles rose out of the evening gloom.

Hawk released her hand. Grabbed the hilt of his sword and began to unfurl his wings. He had to protect Silver.

"I can take care of myself," Silver said, as two Fomorii bounded out of the forest.

Hawk gave the D'Danann cry as his wings spread wide and he lifted himself into the air. With one powerful sweep, his blade met yellow scales, but bounced off the tough hide when he struck the demon's collarbone. Hawk flapped his wings, grabbed his sword in both hands, and dove again for the snarling demon.

From behind him he heard Silver engaged in her own battle against the bastards. Her blue spellfire lit up the dusky evening, and her cries of anger met his ears. Heat raged through him that she was in danger. Godsdamn, he should have been more prepared.

He tasted anger, the lust of battle, and revenge on his tongue. He whirled in the air, dove again for the beast, and his sword clanged against the demon's iron-tipped claws.

The Fomorii thrust itself upward in a powerful lunge. Its hot breath and rotten-fish stench blasted over Hawk. He flapped his great wings and dodged to the side, feeling the rush of air where the Fomorii had swiped with one of its claws.

Hawk swung his weapon at the demon's neck again. The Fomorii raised one arm, blocking the lethal blow.

Hawk's sword sliced through the demon's arm. It flew onto the concrete where it crumbled into dust. Iron tips made a clattering sound as they came to a rest, all that remained of the demon's claws.

The beast gave a bellow that echoed through the park. Black blood spurted from its stump.

In his fury and his desire to wipe out the miserable demon he was battling, Hawk made a miscalculation and dove too close to the beast.

Fomorii claws lashed out at Hawk. The iron-tipped claws caught his sword arm. Pain nearly blinded him, the iron immediately weakening him. Bone snapped and his agony doubled. His sword flew from his grip.

The yellow demon spun Hawk to the ground. He landed flat on his back. His head struck the hard ground and stars sparked behind his eyes.

As Silver launched another spellfire ball at the green multilegged demon she was battling, she saw Hawk driven to the ground.

"Hawk," she screamed as the yellow Fomorii pinned Hawk's wing beneath one massive paw.

Its other arm was a bloody stump. The demon lowered its head toward Hawk's throat.

Hawk tried to flap his free wing and push the demon away with his good arm. "Run!" he said in a strangled shout. He managed to wedge one booted foot between his and the Fomorii's bodies, keeping the demon from closing in on him. The claws of the beast's remaining paw clenched into his sword arm and caused such searing pain, pain like he'd never felt before.

Silver dodged the green demon she'd been fighting and gathered a large ball of spellfire between her palms. Anger made her teeth clench. Rage made her blood boil. The magical fire surged hotter and hotter in her grip. Dark power flowed through her, into her hands, into the spell she commanded.

Her hair lifted off her neck.

Sparks traveled across her skin.

Still running, she flung the now-purple ball at the yellow Fomorii on top of Hawk.

Spellfire spread across the beast's thick yellow hide in a

wicked blue and purple glow. It snapped the beast's head to the side but didn't move it from atop Hawk.

Silver roared. Her entire world seemed to turn red and darken. That thing was trying to kill him—would kill him! Damn the demon to the depths of the world!

More fire blazed in her hands, deep purple, so dark it looked nearly black.

Her vision narrowed to nothing but the beast. She would destroy it. She would turn it to absolute ashes.

With a banshee's screech, she hurled her ball of spellfire just as instinct made her dodge left. The green Fomorii charging her thundered by and collapsed in a tangle of its own legs and scales.

Her spellfire almost hit Hawk, but sizzled against the yellow Fomorii's skin, brighter purple yet.

The power of the spellfire flung the beast back just enough that Hawk was able to draw his dagger. But then the Fomorii pounced on Hawk again, grinding his broken arm into the hard ground.

Silver's sandals sank into the grass as she dodged the green demon again, and readied more spellfire as she faced Hawk's tormentor.

With a roar the other demon planted his front claws on Silver's back. Slammed her facefirst to the ground. Grass and dirt filled her mouth and pebbles scraped her cheek.

Silver spat dirt from her mouth. Screamed and struggled as she waited for the beast's teeth to sink into her neck.

Pain ripped through Hawk as his arm lay mangled beneath one giant demon paw. The Fomorii stared down at him, grinning in a way that told Hawk the beast intended to taunt him rather than deliver a quick death.

Hawk clenched his dagger in his free hand.

At the same time he thrust his knee into the demon's gut, he jammed the blade into the Fomorii's throat and twisted.

The demon-beast shrieked. Jerked its head up and away from the knife before Hawk had the chance to completely slice its throat.

The massive body slumped on top of Hawk, pinning him

to the grass. Blood poured from the Fomorii's throat, onto Hawk's face and soaking his shirt. The rotten-fish stench was nearly overpowering.

The demon wasn't dead, though, didn't turn to silt. The yellow beast gurgled, clinging to life, its wound trying to heal around the dagger that Hawk kept twisting in its throat.

Trying to shove the demon off with his good arm, he looked back to Silver, fear clenching his heart.

The Fomorii who tackled her had shifted into a man. He now had Silver before him, her hands tied behind her back. She thrashed. Stomped her heel onto the man's foot and caused him to shout out and slap her face.

Anger seared him at the sight and the fact she was being taken by the Fomorii. He couldn't even move to save her.

He struggled beneath the bulk on top of him. Pain screamed through his useless arm. Burning, burning, burning pain. Fomorii claws were still clenched in his flesh and he could feel the iron begin to seep into his body. He ground his teeth as he shoved at the groaning Fomorii with his legs and one hand. The body shifted. Slightly. The claws relaxed. A little. If only he could get his hand in position again to finish the job. Then the demon would be dirt.

Hawk's gaze tore from the Fomorii, back to where Silver had been.

She was gone.

In the distance he heard her scream echo through the late evening air.

Cursing, Silver fought the Fomorii-man every step of the way as he shoved her through the gloom across the street. She couldn't spell him with her hands tied behind her back. Couldn't do anything but make taking her as hard on him as possible.

Dark energy still rippled through her, flowing up and down her skin, feeding off her anger and fear. It spoke to her, urged her to damage the bastard, kill him if she could. A rock would do. A knife to the gut. Anything, if she just got the chance.

She dropped to her knees, trying to stall him. Asphalt and pebbles ground into her knees.

"Move, witch-bitch." The monster-in-a-human wrapped his hand in her long hair and yanked her forward.

Silver shouted out her pain as he dragged her over the asphalt, scraping her skin, tearing at her blouse. Fire licked her tender scalp, but she bit her lip to keep more cries from escaping. Damned if she would let this—this thing know she was afraid and hurting.

Then new fear blazed through her at the thought of Hawk. The last thing she had seen was the demon slowly lowering his jaws to Hawk's throat.

What if he was already dead? She didn't sense it. Could he be dying slowly, his life force draining even as she was taken away from him?

More sparks coursed up and down her body from her magic. She caught the smell of something burning. Her hair? Her clothes? The cloth binding her wrists?

The man dragged her to where a car was parked. She fought him. Jerked away and stumbled. She tripped and landed flat on her back, knocking the breath from her. Her head smacked against brutal asphalt.

Silver cried out at the pain. Tiny bolts of gray magic were loosed from her prone form, firing into nothing as they went. The demon-man grabbed one of her legs, yelped, let her go, then grabbed her again.

Burn, she thought viciously. *If I could free my hands, I'd toast you myself.* Power seemed to hover closer and closer to her. If only she could make a hand-spell. If only she could call it, *use* it!

She twisted onto her belly and tried to crawl out from beneath her captor. Felt her blouse shred and the asphalt abrade her flesh. Smells of oil and tar filled her nose.

The Fomorii's fingers elongated into claws, and the nails dug into the flesh of Silver's calves, sending fresh bouts of pain through her. Oh, goddess! The pain from those claws was nearly blinding.

As she thrashed, concrete scraped her arms and legs, and her cheeks stung. He yanked her harder by the leg, then brought her to an abrupt stop next to her car. All she could see of it was a tire and part of the fender. The entire time she fought against the cloth binding her wrists. The madder she got, the more pain she felt, the more she saw the sparks and smelled that odd burning scent.

Were her bindings starting to loosen?

"Junga and Darkwolf are going to be very pleased." The man released her hair long enough to grab her by her shoulders and force her to her feet. "You've been a hard little bitch to capture," he said as he jerked the back door of the car open.

"Bastard." She kicked his shin as hard as she could with the narrow toe of her shoe, then jammed the heel onto his foot. Sparks actually crackled at the point of impact.

He screamed and shoved her backward. With a cry she tumbled into the car, her head striking the unforgiving worn springs poking through the seat and scraping her back and arms.

Before she could push herself up, the man flung himself on top of her and shoved apart her thighs, forcing her skirt up and baring her nakedness below.

"Yeah, that's what I'll do, bitch." He ground his groin against her belly. "I'll fuck you before Darkwolf has the chance to get a taste."

A new, hatefully dark rage mingled with terror and drove Silver into a frenzy. Dark sparks lifted off her skin to hover in the air above her attacker. He didn't seem to notice.

The springs beneath her back and arms scraped her skin as she struggled beneath his weight. The large Fomorii-man was trying to hold her still with one hand holding down her shoulder while attempting to unfasten his pants with his other. His foul breath brushed her cheek and she fought all the harder. She felt hot all over, and cold at the same time, and oddly, more and more full of a power matching the depth of her fury.

The springs scraped her harder.

Use them, some animal part of her brain demanded.

Snarling, she jerked her arms behind her back and caught the cloth of her bonds on one of the springs.

At the same time the demon grew frustrated with his attempts to unfasten his pants. His fingers elongated into claws and he ripped apart the fastenings, freeing a large penis that caused Silver to try to shred her torn bonds against the spring with all her might.

She need not have bothered.

The bonds were on fire, burning to ash, just like the inside of the car was burning. Only the purple-black flames didn't touch her at all.

The beast-man stopped moving, obviously shocked.

Roaring with the full force of her anger, Silver slammed her fist into his ugly face.

He shouted as his head snapped up, encountering the dark flames racing through the car's interior.

His human hair started to burn.

Silver shoved him off her, giving it everything she had. She jammed her sandal against his knee at the same time. He shouted, then wailed as he slid out of the car, on fire, his bare penis scraping over a coil sticking up in the seat.

Silver seethed at the sight of him trying to grab his crotch and his burning hair at the same time.

He fell back, and she slammed her foot against his face. His nose gave a sickening crunch beneath her shoe.

She scrambled up in the seat. By the time her sandals hit the pavement and she was standing, the car was a roaring inferno and the man had shifted back into a green demon. It snarled, saliva dripping from its hideous mouth. Purplish flames danced around its scales.

Silver watched the fire grow. Her fingers twitched. She was only vaguely aware of controlling the flames.

All her anger, all her fury, all her pain went into the cold smile she gave that demon. In those mere instants she felt everything. The loss of her Coven and her parents, Hawk possibly dead beneath another Fomorii's attack.

The power within her magnified.

The flames were really burning the demon. Eyes wide, it smacked at itself, trying to put them out.

Silver's hatred burned, too. She relished the sight of those flames, growing, growing, and growing. Vaguely she felt a call, a presence, something pushing at her mind, pushing her to raise her hands and bring the flames to a crescendo.

In the fraction of time it took her to lift her fingers, to feel the dark emotions raging through her, the demon lunged.

Silver spread her fingers and threw the whole force of her magic into the flames.

Deep purple spellfire swallowed the demon's head. It screamed as it fell away, overpowered by her magic.

Silver kept her hands up, kept the flames hot, then paused as skin began to slough off the Fomorii's head, revealing its skull beneath.

This time when she saw the vision of the wolf and the eye, she didn't shrink from it. She ignored it.

The fire burned and burned just as her anger did. A feeling of satisfaction filled her as the beast shrieked and held its head as it burned away.

Its head toppled off and rolled into the empty street.

The demon's body teetered, and then it slammed onto the asphalt.

Everything faded into black dust. A breeze swept up some of the silt and caused it to swirl in the air and vanish.

Behind Silver, the car, coated in magical fire, dissolved into nothing with the briefest of metallic clatters.

Bit by bit, the dark fire burned itself out, too. Little purplish sparks skittered over Silver's skin, then winked away. With them went that terrible tide of emotion.

Silver's feeling of satisfaction began to flow into horror.

She couldn't breathe. Bile rose in her throat. A sick feeling weighted her belly like a cauldron full of hot coals.

She had called on a magic deeper and darker than she'd ever known, magic so powerful it responded to her will, not just her spells.

She'd just killed another being. Burned it to death as it screamed in agony.

And goddess help her, she had *enjoyed* it.

26

Silver forced herself to run from the death scene, to leave it behind her as she sought Hawk. She couldn't think about what she'd just done. Not now. If Hawk wasn't dead, he needed her. Somehow she knew he had to be alive. Wouldn't she have felt it if he'd died? They had a connection. Something special.

Tears flowed down her face as she ran across the street. She stumbled. Fell. Cried out in frustration and pain. With the quivering feeling in her scraped-up and bruised body, she had a hard time keeping her balance.

When she finally reached the place where they'd been attacked, her heart nearly stopped. Hawk was in human form, his wings tucked away, but pinned beneath the huge body of a Fomorii.

Then she saw Hawk was moving. Thrashing against the demon. Trying to force the enormous Fomorii off his body. He took his dagger and twisted it in the Fomorii's throat again and again.

She gathered more magic, but inside she still felt the mingled exultation and horror of her kill.

Drawing deeply from her power, her own power and only hers this time, her fingertips sizzled. Blue light shot from her hands and struck one side of the Fomorii.

She pushed with her power, so hard she grew dizzy from it. The demon's body moved a tiny bit. She clenched her jaws and pushed harder. The Fomorii moved a few inches. She stumbled forward.

Fresh fury rippled through her. A cry tore from her as she shoved at her magic. The Fomorii tumbled off Hawk, its body thumping in the cold, still evening. The dagger still in its throat, blood pouring onto the grass. It thrashed and tried to get up.

Pain exploded in her head and she stumbled toward Hawk. She dropped to her knees. A sob escaped her at the sight of him.

His sword, he needed his sword. She crawled to it, wrapped her fingers around the cold hilt. The weapon was so heavy she could barely wield it as she got to her feet and brought it to him.

With the movements of an old man, Hawk had pushed himself to a sitting position. He was covered in blood and his right arm hung uselessly at his side. He took the sword from her and pushed himself to his feet. Just as the demon yanked the dagger from its healing neck, Hawk raised the sword up with his left hand and sliced down, severing the demon's head.

Silver shivered at the sight of the Fomorii crumbling into dirt before her eyes. Satisfaction and horror sent her head reeling.

"There are more of the demons." Hawk's voice came out in a wheeze as he dropped to one knee. "Somewhere in the park."

"I know." Silver dropped to her own knees and flung her arms around him. Blood smeared her cheek from his, and more blood soaked her silk blouse. "I can sense them."

But she couldn't move. She cried, shudders wracking her body as he held her with his good arm. They rocked back and forth, clinging to each other, both unable to let go.

Silver wasn't sure how she and Hawk made it back to Moon Song after their fight with the Fomorii. Did Hawk drive the

VW or did she? Who carried who in the back door of the shop?

Ridiculous. She couldn't have carried Hawk. But she thought maybe they'd supported each other.

It didn't matter. The moment they stumbled inside, someone screamed. Cassia? Mackenzie? The next thing Silver knew she was torn away from Hawk, surrounded by her two friends. Her vision blurred so badly she could barely see.

"No," she mumbled, not wanting to be separated from Hawk. She needed him.

What was it that was making her so sick? So unable to function?

You killed, Silver. You killed.

Horror rocked her and her knees wouldn't hold her anymore. Only Cassia and Mackenzie kept her from falling to the floor.

Keir's and Sher's voices sounded far-off and distant. "What in the name of the Underworld have you done?" Keir was saying, and Sher said, "Shut up, you godsforsaken nakherder," then Hawk's, "I'll kill the bastard now and be done with it."

"Get Hawk upstairs," Cassia ordered in a needle-sharp tone. "Mackenzie and I will help Silver."

Silver blinked, tried to focus, but gave up as she was led upstairs, stumbling, dragging. Behind her she heard curses, boot steps, and Hawk's harsh breathing.

Reaching the hallway, then making it through her apartment door, was a monumental effort for Silver, even supported to either side by her friends. All along, Mackenzie murmured soothing words, like "You'll be all right, honey," and Cassia muttered about "Going off on foolhardy errands alone."

Silver almost cried when they finally made it to her bed. Blessed softness.

Blood caked her clothing, had dried on her face, in her hair. The rotten-fish odor of the Fomorii clung to her, clogged her nose. Where the Fomorii claws had dug into her leg it burned like fire.

The weight on the bed shifted, then she heard Hawk's groan and Sher's and Keir's voices. Relief tugged at her to know that they'd put her and Hawk together in her bed. Having him beside her made her feel safer, somehow, and like she could protect him, too. They could be there for each other.

"Not Silver's blood." Mackenzie produced a warm washcloth and wiped it across Silver's eyes, her face. "It's black. And it smells foul."

Cassia leaned over Silver, her eyes focused on the other side of the bed, away from Silver. "Not Hawk's, either."

"Fomorii," came Sher's voice from somewhere in the distance. "It's their stench you smell."

Mackenzie wiped Silver's cheeks and hair. The warm cloth soothed her. When Mackenzie finished, she began smoothing something cool and pleasant over Silver's face and the burns began to ease. Marigold and comfrey, by the scent of it.

At the same time, someone worked on stripping off her ruined clothing. Silver was so dizzy, everything seemed so surreal, that she felt like it all was happening to someone else.

Silver felt herself slipping, barely holding on to consciousness by a fine thread. She turned her head toward Hawk and saw him receiving the same treatment from Keir and Sher.

His gaze met hers. His face was scratched and bloody, his hair matted, and his right arm lay broken across his chest. She reached out to him and he extended his good arm.

He clasped hers in his warm grip.

Silver managed a smile for him. Her lids fluttered. She no longer had the strength to keep them open.

She slipped away into the darkness.

Hawk watched Silver's body relax, felt her grip loosen in his as she passed out. Her lips parted and she was obviously deep under in just moments.

Hawk tried to ignore the screaming pain in his broken arm. His godsdamn sword arm. He couldn't fight with a sword as well with his left hand, although he handled a dagger fairly well. That didn't stop his anger or the feeling of uselessness that clenched his gut.

The Fomorii claws . . . gods, but the iron had burned like nothing he had ever felt before. Those same claws had snapped his arm, the iron working its way into his bones. No doubt it would hinder the mending of his limb.

Sher came into focus as she cut his shirt away. "Damned fool," she grumbled. "You should have taken us with you. What were you thinking when you slipped out without telling us where you were going?"

Of course she was right. Memories of the Fomorii's capture of Silver made the ache in his gut feel like boulders slamming against one another.

She'd had to save herself.

The thought tasted bitter on his tongue. He should have been the one to save her.

Keir and Sher stripped him of his clothing while Mackenzie and Cassia cared for Silver. Hawk refused to allow himself sleep. He deserved to feel every stabbing ache, every screaming pain, after what he'd allowed Silver to go through.

Sher gasped as she wiped blood from his arm and saw the deep black gouges. "These wounds. No common Fomorii claw made them." She glanced at Keir. "The iron that tipped the beast's claws, it is burning into his bloodstream."

Cassia shoved her way between Keir and Sher, holding a bottle with blue potion swirling within it. "This will stop the iron, draw it back to his arm so that we can leach it out."

"How?" Sher set aside the bloodied cloth she'd been using. "Even the D'Danann do not know how to stop iron poisoning."

Cassia did not bother to respond. She uncorked the round bottle, tilted it, and the oily blue fluid spilled onto the claw marks.

Immediately pain doubled on pain, and Hawk clenched both fists and ground his teeth. The next sensation he felt was a magnetic pull, as if the potion were drawing the pain that had been spreading through his body, and instead bringing it back to rest solely in his wounds. He looked to his arm and saw the cuts were bubbling, the blue potion battling with the iron.

Keir grunted. "The wounds are closing."

Hawk felt the pain lessen some, and he relaxed a little.

"Remnants of iron will still hinder his healing." Cassia re-corked the bottle, and Hawk studied her intense turquoise eyes. "But he *will* heal." She turned and slipped between the two D'Danann and vanished from Hawk's line of vision.

He no longer had any doubts. Cassia was definitely not of this world.

"You should rest now," Mackenzie said as she moved a chair close to the bedside.

"I am fine," Hawk said through gritted teeth. "Just set the damnable thing."

"Stubborn ass," Sher was saying as she sponge-bathed him, cleaning away more of the Fomorii stench. "Get some sleep."

Keir kept grumbling, saying things like "Fool," "Arrogant bastard," and "Our ruin."

Before today Hawk would have slugged Keir, but at that moment he had to agree. He'd failed. He'd put Silver and the mission in danger. And now, what good was he with his mangled arm?

He set his jaw. He'd damn well get the job done with or without his right arm.

Hawk barely retained consciousness as he and Silver were bathed, their wounds tended.

When the bedding was changed, Hawk insisted on standing without assistance. He gritted his teeth at the sight of Keir lifting a naked Silver from the bed while the bedding was changed.

Ridding the room of the filthy clothes, blankets, and sheets helped to alleviate the stench of the Fomorii. He braced his broken arm against his chest. It was numb now, the lack of feeling extending up into his shoulder. But at least the burn from the iron was lessened by far.

After Hawk and Silver were settled back into the bed, Cassia propped her hands on her hips. "We'll have to set that arm now."

Hawk winced.

Sher came into view, and ruffled her hair in distraction. "If we had some spirits, that would lessen the pain."

"We don't." Mackenzie pulled the chair closer to the bed and massaged oil into Hawk's neck and shoulders with a firm, experienced touch. Lavender by the scent of it. "To relax you," she said.

Great. Now he'd smell like a woman.

"No pain relievers," he forced out through clenched teeth.

"Stubborn ass," Sher said again.

Despite his declaration, Cassia and Keir thrust tablets into Hawk's mouth, along with a good dose of tea that tasted of chamomile and peppermint. "The tablets are arnica and willow bark," Cassia said. "You need it for the shock and pain."

Hawk protested and Mackenzie shoved a smooth stick crosswise between his teeth. It was about five inches long and an inch thick. "Bite down on this. It's willow for healing," she said, but looked concerned.

Before he'd had a chance to process what they were about to do, Cassia and Keir moved his arm in a rotating, wrenching motion. Bone crunched and gave sickening pops as it set into place.

Hawk shouted from behind the stick in his mouth—from surprise and the incredible, shrieking pain tearing through his body.

Darkness hit him hard and fast.

Silver woke to the smells of witch hazel and tea tree oil, and her body lightly burning from the remnants of scrapes and scratches, especially where the Fomorii claws had raked her leg. She vaguely remembered Cassia pouring oily blue fluid on it, and it had smelled of citrus.

She felt clean, despite what they'd been through. Before she opened her eyes she realized she'd been given a sponge bath, the bedding had been changed, a soft robe and softer blanket wrapped around her.

Even her eyes ached as she opened them and her neck hurt. But when she turned onto her side to face Hawk, Silver's body felt surprisingly good, considering the punishment she had taken.

Hawk didn't say anything when their gazes met, just looked at her with something like frustration and longing in his eyes.

She managed a smile, but he didn't return it.

"I am sorry," he said, his voice low and gruff.

She frowned. "For what?"

"It is my fault you were injured." Anger darkened his eyes. "I shouldn't have exposed you at all."

"What's this macho bullshit? It's not all about you, you know." Silver's frown deepened. "We all make our own choices. I wanted to be with you. As a matter of fact, *I* should have been smart enough to realize that I was exposing us to danger."

This time he managed a half-smile. "It's not all about you."

She couldn't help her own little smile. Her gaze dropped to his chest. The black sling around his arm and the homemade cast peeking through reminded her of how she'd almost lost him. Her heart clenched. "I'm so sorry," she said. He shrugged one shoulder, then flinched.

A sharp burst of pain in her head came on suddenly. She winced and closed her eyes.

Hawk took her hand, his warmth enveloping her. "Silver? Are you all right?"

Before she could answer, Cassia bustled into the room. "About time you woke up."

Silver didn't bother to respond to Hawk as Cassia gave

her willow bark tablets for the headache. The witch massaged Silver's temples, neck, and shoulders with lavender oil, giving almost instant relief to the pain.

Hawk kept a grip on her hand, never letting her go, but saying nothing more.

27

With a hiss of displeasure, Junga clenched her human hands into fists until the nails dug into flesh, and she felt blood dripping down her palms. "They failed." She repeated what the messenger had just told her. "Za and Hur failed to retrieve the witch."

The messenger bowed, and in her fury, Junga had the urge to rip out his throat with one swipe of her Fomorii claws.

"Don't kill the messenger," came Elizabeth's voice in her mind. Junga had the insane desire to laugh. These humans had the damnedest aphorisms.

"Change to Fomorii." Her lips thinned and her eyes narrowed. "Guard the witches." Being in their natural forms would protect them from any of the Fomorii who might need a good meal once summoned. The demons had also captured more stray humans for that—anyone they found alone and vulnerable.

The messenger bowed again, shifted into his gangling orange form, and left, a definite hurry to his lope as he crossed the ballroom and joined the guard standing before the witches.

Junga held her stance for a moment, trying to ignore the sick feeling at the pit of her belly that hit her at the realization that Za was dead.

No. He was simply another Fomorii. His death meant nothing to her.

But the ache in her chest was so great she almost stumbled. For the first time in her life she felt an incredible sadness weigh her down at the loss of one of her mates.

With her fingertips, she wiped wetness that had formed at one eye. What was wrong with her?

It had to be this damnable human body.

Straightening her shoulders and raising her chin, she forced her attention back to the preparations for the summoning. They now had twelve, counting the new converts and the Balorite priest. The Fomorii had not been able to convince one more to participate, despite threats and beatings, and Darkwolf's seductive skills.

Junga intended to find Silver Ashcroft and hold her as hostage to force the equally powerful Victor and Moondust Ashcroft to join the summoning. She had tried threatening to kill one of them if the other did not aid her, but both said they would rather die.

She growled low in her throat. She was certain things would be different if she captured Silver. By threatening to kill either of her parents, she would ensure the aid of at least Silver. Yes, by threatening her parents, no doubt Silver would turn.

Darkwolf had informed her that the witch had started down the path already.

One little shove.

Good. Very good.

Raising her head, Junga moved closer to the circle with the now black-robed witches, who would soon become warlocks as they gave themselves to the dark. Off to the side, the Ashcrofts were propped against each other behind the magical shield, both bruised from their beatings, but both refusing to participate.

Junga's lips curled, baring her teeth.

She swallowed and clenched her human hands again, until she almost cried out from the pain. Her gaze turned toward the twenty or so humans the Fomorii had quietly hunted down and brought back to the hotel. The humans huddled at the center of the ballroom where they were guarded by several demons. Some of the people were quiet, fear glazing their eyes. Others cried, and there were those who even shouted to be freed.

The pathetic humans would be food for the summoned Fomorii, to avoid the deaths of any of the warlocks.

She gathered herself and brought her attention to the warlock priest. With the membrane between Underworld and this world so thick, it would be difficult to bring anything but a small number of Fomorii to this world with a summoning. But the Balorite priest was certain it was possible, if the number of cooperating witches and warlocks was enough.

Darkwolf started the summoning at a new location in the ballroom. Again he took his crystal-tipped black wand and burned an eye into the floor. Again he called for a human sacrifice that covered the floor with blood. Again he drew a circle around the witches. Black fire shot up from the ring being burned into the floor and the dancing flames almost mesmerized Junga. The ritual fascinated her as much this time as it had the last.

Fascinated yet horrified her.

The initiation and summoning ceremonies were nearly identical to the others, and Junga sent a prayer to Balor that this one would work.

Yet at the same time she flinched from the thought of serving a god that was truly evil. The Fomorii—they did as they were meant to. Conquer and spread their numbers. This—this *evil* caused her skin to crawl.

No doubts. No fears. They were who they were.

The Fomorii. Mighty. Strong. And *not* evil.

Darkwolf chanted to the dark forces of the world, and of the universe. They were Balor's warlocks, his children, calling upon the great one-eyed god for his aid in this most important moment.

Impossibly, this ceremony seemed more impressive than the last. Stronger, harsher. The power in the air was like electricity, searing through one being after another. Junga felt it in her body and her heart.

The low-hanging fog that grew around the warlocks' feet carried the odor of burned wood. Then the stench of something much worse filled the room. Like death and decay. The more the warlocks chanted, the stronger it became. The sense of evil filling the room was much more palpable this time, so much more so that Junga's heart stuttered.

Suddenly the room shook and shuddered so hard that Junga heard Elizabeth's voice shouting in her mind, *Earthquake. Like the enormous one in 1989.* There was real terror in that voice, which frightened Junga as much as the rocking of the room, the sway of the chandeliers. Mirrors cracked. Shattered. Witches, as well as the humans huddled at the center of the room, screamed.

Despite the fact she stumbled in her human form, Junga maintained a sense of pride that her warriors didn't move. Junga braced one arm against a wall as her warriors dug their mighty claws into the floor to keep from sliding or falling in the bucking room. By the twitch of their eyes she could see their terror was as great as her own, but they maintained their posts.

Strange thoughts flickered through her mind as the bucking seemed to continue forever. Was this lone room rocking within a still hotel? Or was the hotel trembling within a silent city? Or was the entire city being shaken to its core?

A giant chunk of ceiling plaster landed on Junga's head and for a moment her sight blurred from the pain of it. She shook her head and saw more plaster raining from the ceiling. Dust joined other smells in the room.

The black fire had grown so large Junga could barely see the now twelve warlocks within its heated core. Her eyes watered from the smoke, dust, and incense. The swaying figures continued chanting, the sound merging with the splinter of wood, the crack of mirrors, the thudding of plaster. Then their voices rose higher and higher, until Junga could hear their words.

"Bring forth the Fomorii, let it be done. Harbingers of the dark rule to come."

Air stirred. The room's rocking began to slow.

Junga straightened. Blood pounded so hard in her veins that it vibrated through her.

Black light flickered throughout the room like lightning in a boiling thunderstorm. Shapes began to appear around the circle of warlocks. Wavering at first. Becoming solid, then transparent again.

"Bring forth the Fomorii, let it be done. Harbingers of the dark rule to come," the chanting continued, so loud Junga's ears rang with it.

The shapes surrounding the warlocks solidified. Enormous demon shapes. Fomorii. Greater than the number that had made the crossing with Junga.

The rocking of the room stopped. Sounds of crying and screams of the humans faded to moans and sobs. Only an occasional thud of ceiling plaster broke the silence. Flames around the circle slowly died as Junga looked from Fomorii to Fomorii to Fomorii. All great warriors she recognized.

Including Queen Kanji. Who looked at Junga, obviously recognizing her even though she was in her human form.

But the Old One—she was not with the others. A shiver erupted beneath Junga's skin.

Furious at herself for allowing any fear to enter her mind, Junga stiffened and growled at Bane to guard the witches and set the disposable human prey free.

Fomorii always enjoyed a good chase.

October 29

28

Silver's body still ached as she sat at the computer desk in her apartment. She stared blankly at a sheet of paper beneath the pen she held poised in her hand. Polaris was curled around her feet, as if to offer his support.

She didn't truly see the paper. Instead, upon its virginal white surface she saw the scenes from yesterday unfold before her eyes.

One day later, the battle at the park was still fresh in her mind. The horror of it. The sheer pleasure she had felt from killing that fucking beast.

Tears blurred her eyes and she used her free hand to scrub away the moisture. Goddess, what had she done?

What you needed to do, Silver. What had to be done to save yourself and Hawk.

She clenched the pen tighter with her fingers until they ached.

The path she was taking . . . was there any turning back?

The next thought stunned her.

Did she want to turn back?

Silver bit the inside of her cheek, hard. She blinked to clear her vision and the paper came into focus again.

Slowly she lowered her pen to the paper and began to scratch words across its surface that would hopefully draw the Fomorii out on Samhain, to where she and her team would have the advantage. She wanted to do it *now,* but Samhain was only the day after tomorrow. Just two more days.

Her pen made a scratching noise across the paper as she wrote:

> *Junga, leader of the Fomorii,*
> *I wish to make an exchange with you. My life, my magic,*
> *for my parents. They must be whole, must be safe, must*
> *be freed to ensure my assistance. You will have my*
> *cooperation, so long as you meet me at the location on*
> *the enclosed map of Golden Gate Park. You must arrive*
> *exactly at midnight on Samhain.*
> > *My life, my magic, for my parents.*
> > > *Silver Ashcroft*

She read the letter over and over, wondering if there was anything else she should say. Anything else she could do to make sure the demons would be there.

Intuitively she knew they were overconfident, sure of their greater numbers. Earlier she had scried in her cauldron and witnessed the fact that Darkwolf had managed to bring more Fomorii to this world. Not many, but enough to outnumber the free witches and the D'Danann.

Slowly, carefully, she folded the letter into thirds, creasing each fold sharply before tucking it into a plain white envelope. Her mind and body ached with every movement she made, as if she were handling the most difficult of tasks.

Just as slowly, she slipped the park map inside the envelope. When she finished, she taped the flap closed, unwilling to lick the seal of something that would soon be handled by evil. She could barely bring herself to touch the thing that she knew would be in the hands of the demons.

On the front of the envelope she wrote in block letters:

ATTENTION: ELIZABETH BLACK
RE: JUNGA

Silver dropped the pen to the table with a light clatter.
That should get her attention.

Thanks to the escaped witches, Silver and the others
knew the name of the leader, and the name of her host body,
the woman who had owned the hotel before being possessed
by the damned demons.

Releasing a sigh filled with all the pain and trials of the
past few days, Silver pushed herself from her chair at the
desk, the envelope clutched in her hand. With heavy steps,
she left her apartment and headed downstairs to give one of
the D'Danann the envelope to deliver to the hotel, and to
hopefully be passed on to the legion leader's hands.

Now all she could do was pray to the goddess and the Ancestors. And prepare.

29

Junga's human lips turned into a smile reflecting her humor at the irony of the situation. She was in Elizabeth's elegant penthouse with Darkwolf, planning to pen a note to Silver Ashcroft, when a hotel employee delivered this letter to her.

Ah, yes. The witch had saved her the trouble. Junga had no intention of releasing the elder Ashcrofts, she simply planned to use them as bait.

Darkwolf moved closer to her and she felt the heat of his body, smelled his spicy human male scent. He took the letter from her grasp, leaving her momentarily annoyed at his arrogance.

He studied the note, then clenched the paper so tightly in his fist that it crumpled within his grip. He brought his other hand to his throat and to the stone eye.

Junga stared in fascination as red light bled through his fingers, the stone glowing in his grasp. Darkwolf began breathing heavily, his eyes moving beneath his closed lids as if he were watching a movie.

A wicked smile creased his face, and he opened his eyes so that his dark gaze met Junga's.

"We will not have to wait until Samhain to get Silver Ashcroft." Darkwolf released the stone eye, which continued to glow even as his hand dropped away. A sick sense of horror roiled through Junga's belly as the eye darted back and forth, and then focused on her.

She cleared her throat. Tore her gaze from the glowing stone to meet Darkwolf's gaze again. "If you know of a way to claim Silver and the other witches, then speak."

"Tomorrow night they will all be in an ideal location that will be to the benefit of the Fomorii. They will be unprepared for attack."

The letter drifted from his hand to settle on the living room's carpet. The look in his eyes became suddenly erotic, as if he were thinking of something that pleased him sexually. "And then I will have Silver Ashcroft."

Irrational anger flashed through Junga at his obvious desire for another woman. Followed by sick dread when she heard the queen calling her name from another part of the penthouse.

A beautiful blonde carrying a handbag and dressed in a revealing blue evening gown sauntered into the room. Kanji. The former human had been Barbara Wentworth, a wealthy woman and senator's wife. Barbara had been staying at the hotel when Kanji murdered her and took over her shell.

Kanji fastened her gaze on Darkwolf and it turned seductive as her eyes raked him from head to toe. "Such a fine specimen. For a human," she murmured.

A sensual smile eased across the warlock's expression.

Horror crawled up Junga's throat like Fomorii claws. If Kanji forced sex on her with Darkwolf, the queen could learn Junga's secret.

"I will . . ." Junga's gaze darted to the elevator doors leading from the suite. "I will check on the witches."

"You will stay." Kanji's cold voice brought Junga's gaze snapping back to the queen. "It will please me to see the warlock fuck you in this human form."

No, no, no!

The look in the queen's blue eyes held fire and a promise that if she wasn't obeyed, she could very likely slay Junga where she stood.

Kanji folded her human arms and tapped the toe of her heel. "Remove your clothing."

Junga clenched and unclenched her jaw, trying hard not to let the queen see her defiance or her fear. She lowered her head in a submissive bow, gritting her teeth before saying, "Yes, my queen."

When she looked up at Kanji, she had the blond woman's haughty look upon her features. "Do it."

Junga caught the amusement and desire in Darkwolf's gaze as she slowly unbuttoned her tailored suit to reveal the black lace bra that did little to cover her breasts. She let the jacket slide down her arms and to the carpeting. Her nipples betrayed her, growing hard beneath their gazes and pressing against the lace. Even her pussy grew damp and her musk rose in the coolness of the suite.

Kanji gave a throaty laugh. "Hurry, bitch."

Startled by the use of the word that Darkwolf called her during their frequent matings, Junga's hands trembled at the back fastening of her skirt. Had the damnable warlock told the queen about Junga's submissiveness during sex? As she fumbled with the zipper, Kanji gave a sound of impatience. Junga quickly unzipped the skirt and let it drop around her ankles, then stepped out of it. She remained in only her bra, thigh-high stockings and garters. Her pussy was bare as she had taken to not wearing panties. She had enjoyed the sensual feel of being partially naked beneath Elizabeth's business suits.

Junga struggled to keep herself from trembling beneath the queen's gaze. Kanji began to walk around Junga, studying her. "I can see it," Kanji murmured, and in that instant she knew the bastard had betrayed her. "She wants you to fuck her. To beat her into submission."

Darkwolf's eyes held both amusement and a promise.

Junga trembled with anger, fear, and horribly intense arousal.

It was then that Kanji unsnapped the evening bag that matched her elegant gown. From within the purse she drew out a large hook.

Junga's blood went cold.

"Bind her wrists," Kanji ordered the warlock as she moved to one wall, hook in hand.

Darkwolf 's smile widened as he approached Junga, and she filled her gaze with hate. That only seemed to amuse the bastard more. He reached up and grasped her bra where the front clasp connected beneath her breasts. Damn him to Underworld, how she hated the way his touch automatically made her want him.

He ripped open the bra, completely baring her breasts, then jerked the shoulder straps down her arms until it was free. He quickly grabbed her by her wrists and wrapped the bra around them both, effectively binding her. "Admit it, bitch," he said. "You're enjoying this, aren't you." A statement, not a question.

She tilted her chin, refusing to let this warlock see any fear or intimidation in her expression. And especially not arousal. No, not that.

Oh, god Balor, why did her body continually betray her? she thought as a twinge of excitement mixed with the fear and anger.

The queen laughed. At the same time she raised the hook far above her head, her fingers elongated and her hand turned into the powerful claws of the Fomorii. She slammed the hook into the wall, then tugged on it, ensuring it was lodged in a beam. Small chips of paint and plaster floated down and onto the white carpet.

Junga's eyes widened and her belly flipped. Darkwolf took her by one arm and led her around a couch to where Kanji stood beside the wall. Junga flashed a look of hatred at Darkwolf, promising with her eyes that she would seek retribution, one way or another.

He guided her to where the hook jutted out, away from the wall. Without ceremony, he forced her arms up until they were almost within reach of the hook. He yanked on the bindings on her wrists, causing her to nearly rise from the floor as he looped it over the hook.

She bit back a cry of vulnerability. She was completely at their mercy, unable to protect herself, unable to do anything but let Darkwolf and Kanji observe her nearly naked body. Her breasts were completely bared, as was her pussy. All she wore were black stockings and garters, and her black heels, on which she was forced to stand on the tips of her toes.

"Show me." Kanji gave Darkwolf a burning look as she tossed her evening bag aside and began to strip out of her evening gown.

"My pleasure, Your Majesty." The warlock let his black robe drop, revealing his magnificent form.

Junga's body immediately responded, filling with awareness and excitement. How could she feel this way when they were forcing such humiliation upon her?

Yet it didn't feel like humiliation as Darkwolf pressed his body against hers, grabbed her hair in his hand, and took her mouth with his own at the same time he slipped the fingers of his other hand in her drenched folds. Before she had the chance to catch her breath, his tongue was in her mouth, taking her, mastering her.

Balor bedamned, she should fight, should not feel this aware. Should not have this *desire* to be taken by him over and over, in front of the queen. Like this. What was wrong with her? Was she not fit to rule?

That thought alone caused her to struggle against Darkwolf's mouth and hand. But her nipples brushed his powerful chest, and his cock pressed against her belly.

She was lost.

He suddenly tore himself from her, leaving her feeling bereft. That was until she saw the flogger in the queen's hands. Not a belt, but a flogger. One with many braided leather straps sprouting from the handle.

Junga's breathing hitched and true fear poured through her body. She should change to her Fomorii form, rip her hands from the wall and destroy the pair of them!

Only Darkwolf grabbed her by the thighs and forced himself between them. "Wrap your legs around my waist, bitch."

Junga didn't know why she obeyed so quickly, but she

did. She crossed her ankles behind his back. She now hung from the hook, her side to the wall, Darkwolf's hands at her hips, her legs wrapped around him.

"Remember the rules, bitch." He held his cock at the entrance to her pussy. "You'd better not come without permission. Do you understand?"

She knew what was expected of her, but she didn't want to say it in front of Kanji. He raised one hand and twisted her nipple so hard that a cry of pain and pleasure ripped from her throat. "Yes. Yes, Master."

The queen laughed from behind Junga and a shiver crept up her spine.

She didn't have time to think, though. Without ceremony, Darkwolf plunged his cock into her pussy. At the same time, Kanji whipped the flogger across her ass.

Junga screamed. From the pleasure of Darkwolf's cock inside her core. From the pain of the strap across her bare flesh. Yet that pain turned into a wicked sort of pleasure.

"You enjoyed that, didn't you?" he asked.

The warlock fucked Junga harder and harder, while Kanji laughed and flogged her. Junga's head spun. Her body slipped into another plane of existence, where pleasure and pain became one. The promise of a powerful climax bore down on her so fiercely that all she could think of was coming.

"Hold back," Darkwolf ordered.

But Junga was too far gone. Her release came so fast, so hard, so sudden. She screamed louder than she had ever screamed before. She was sobbing, tears pouring down her face.

Darkwolf dropped her legs so that she was again swinging from the hook. She didn't care. Couldn't care. She was barely aware of Darkwolf saying something to Kanji when they traded places.

Suddenly the queen was facing her, their bare breasts rubbing against one another. "My, have you been bad, Junga." The queen slipped her fingers into Junga's wetness and pinched her clit, causing her to cry out again. "I think you need to be further punished," the queen said, just before she bit Junga's nipple and Darkwolf spanked her with the flat of his hand.

Junga screamed, entirely lost. Too far gone to ever go back.

October 30

30

Two days after the attack at the park, Silver snuggled deeper into her black bomber jacket while she climbed onto the houseboat. The majority of the D'Danann were housed there until the battle because they were too numerous to stay in the apartments above the shop. Icy bay wind tugged long tendrils from the Celtic serpent knot clipping her hair back. Her black pants clung snugly to her thighs, her boots comfortably warming her feet and calves.

Silver walked with the witches and PSF team below the deck to the room where the D'Danann were gathered and where tables were laden with food. For the strategy meeting tonight, there was plenty to eat. Roasted chickens, spiraled hams, cornbread muffins, potato chips and dip, and anything else Silver and Hawk had been able to find precooked at the grocery store.

In addition, the witches had made plenty more—vegetarian pizzas, homemade pastas, rice, and other dishes along with lots of sweets such as cinnamon rolls, cakes, and sugar cookies. The D'Danann were insatiable. Jake and his PSF team were there for the meeting as well, and their appetites seemed almost as strong as those of the D'Danann.

Silver had begun to wonder if they'd have to buy a grocery store.

Hawk had hoarded all the chocolate chip cookies, and

Silver had to smile. Her warrior, the chocolate chip cookie monster.

While she watched the famished warriors eat, Silver leaned back against the doorway in front of another door with steps that led to a lower level of the boat. Her appetite wasn't even piqued by the delicious smells.

Hawk, Keir, and Sher had joined their comrades and were also eating their fill. Sounds of laughter and conversation, not to mention a good deal of belching, came from the bunch.

Silver cast a look to Eric, Mackenzie, and Cassia and she couldn't help a grin. "Guess that means they approve."

Mackenzie pushed her hair behind her ear. "Jeez, can these guys eat."

After everyone had eaten their fill, the D'Danann gathered around the table in the houseboat. Some stood, some sat, all were focused intently on the subject at hand.

For a moment Silver stood and watched them. It was amazing having so many fierce, proud warriors on the houseboat all at once. One could almost taste their lust for battle, yet their sense of fairness and justice. And damn, the men were powerful, muscular, and gorgeous, and the women beautiful with well-defined muscles and curves.

Her gaze turned to Keir. Did that man ever need an attitude adjustment. He was dark and powerful, but talk about a real bad boy.

The warrior named Tiernan fascinated her, too, a blond god of a man. She'd learned from Sher that he was a lord of the higher echelon of D'Danann society, used to having his orders followed and not questioned. Silver had noticed that he appeared to be fierce, and proud, methodical, and never impulsive. Yeah, the man really needed a woman who could bring him down to earth and shake him up a little.

Jake stood just inside a doorway, his arms crossed over his finely sculpted chest, his intense eyes following the conversation, his gaze moving from warrior to warrior. He was just as fierce and deadly looking, not to mention as good-looking, as every other male in the room. That included the PSF team.

A couple of D'Danann glanced at her, then focused their attention back on the conversation. Silver saw Mortimer watching the D'Danann intently from Cassia's pocket, his gaze traveling from one warrior to the next, his whiskers twitching.

Hawk hitched one shoulder against the wall of the house-boat while he watched and listened to the arguing warriors. At one time he would have been in the middle of the fray, his voice raised louder than anyone's.

But after being responsible for Garrett's death, after his failure to protect Silver at the park, and after almost dying and leaving his daughter parentless, Hawk questioned his own judgment. Not that long ago he had wanted to rush into tomorrow night, certain in his arrogance that the D'Danann would win with no casualties.

With the recent skirmishes and loss of life, he just wasn't so certain any longer. The Fomorii were the most ruthless of foes, the most difficult to fight. The most dangerous. Now with their claws of iron, they were even more so.

And Silver . . . Ah, gods. If anything happened to her . . .

The thought ripped at his heart more than he would have imagined.

After they sent the beasts back to Underworld tomorrow night, he would be returning to Otherworld, to face the council for his actions or be forever banished.

Shayla. Gods, he could never bear it if he was forced to be separated from her.

Why did the thought of leaving Silver tear at him, too?

Keir's loud voice, and Hawk's name being spoken, brought him back to the argument at hand.

"Hawk is right to choose Samhain as the night to face the demons and return them to Underworld," Keir was saying. To hear his nemesis supporting him nearly shocked Hawk out of his boots. "I've scouted the area Hawk and Silver chose for the reckoning with the bastards," Keir continued. "It is ideal."

The other D'Danann in the room went quiet, as if just as

surprised Keir had taken Hawk's side. It was no secret the
two never saw eye to eye. A few D'Danann scowled, some
nodded, others simply listened and observed.

Sher propped her hands on her slim hips and came up to
Hawk. "Keir is correct. This is the logical choice. We must
move tomorrow tonight."

As she crossed her arms across her chest, Aideen's posture relayed her obvious displeasure. "We haven't had time
to train. No time to adapt to this world."

"You are correct," Hawk said, and the room went silent
again.

Tiernan cocked an eyebrow. "Are you vacillating now,
Hawk? What happened to rushing headlong into every fight?"

Hawk clenched and unclenched the hand of his broken
arm, the pain shooting through him a reminder of what was
at stake. If he didn't stand behind his original decision, and
if he didn't back Keir and Sher, he would bring doubt to the
group and the plans they made. He would cause more dis-
sension among the D'Danann.

Even though doubt clouded his mind at his own ability to
make a sound judgment, he knew in his heart what was right.
This was no impulsive decision, but a well-thought-out plan.

Hawk took a deep breath, his gaze moving again to each
member of the group. "This one night, what the witches call
Samhain, is when all the worlds are most accessible." He
pushed away from the wall and raked his fingers through his
hair. "I have little doubt we will be able to return the Fomorii
to Underworld."

With a wave of her hand, Aideen brushed off Hawk's
words. "The note the witch sent takes away any opportunity
for the element of surprise."

"We're counting on that." Keir's voice was gruff as he
scowled at Aideen. "The Fomorii will believe they have us
trapped, but we will turn the tables on them."

Aideen perched on the edge of a vacant chair at the table,
braced her forearms and her palms flat on the wood surface.
"How?"

"Elementals," came Silver's voice from the doorway, and Hawk cut his gaze to meet hers. "They've given us their blessings. They'll do what they can to assist us. I know they will."

Cael rolled his eyes. "Faeries and Gnomes. What good are these creatures against such powerful beings as the Fomorii?"

"Don't discount them." Mackenzie moved beside Silver, an irritated glint in her eyes. "Elementals are very powerful beings when they choose to be."

"Did they promise assistance?" Aideen asked, her eyes focused on Silver.

Silver slipped one hand into the front pocket of her black pants. Hawk imagined her fingering the charm bag filled with gifts from the Elementals, as she often did since that day at the park.

"No," Silver finally said. "No promises, but we received their blessings, and their gifts."

Cael tipped back in his chair so that it rested on two legs. "What gifts?"

Silver bit her lower lip as she pulled her hand from her pocket. In it she held the white charm bag. While the D'Danann, Cassia, Eric, and Mackenzie watched, Silver withdrew the black feather, the water-smoothed hag stone, and the emerald, setting each on the table. Lastly she brought out the bright red flame, and kept it on her outstretched palm where it danced and flickered.

A few looked on in amazement at the flame. Tiernan snorted, and another D'Danann outright laughed.

Cael chuckled and gestured to the gifts of the Elementals. "These bits of nothing will aid us in our battle? I think not."

Silver's jaw tightened as she carefully slipped the flame into the bag, followed by each item. When she raised her head, fire glowed in her eyes. "You're right," she said. "We can't rely on these gifts alone. We have to help ourselves and do what we can. But we have aid—we only have to ask."

"And you have us." Mackenzie stepped forward, a determined look in her green gaze.

"Mere witches? With spells and potions, no doubt." Tiernan gave a condescending look. "And humans. What good can they do?"

Hawk ground his teeth. "Do not speak against what you know nothing of. It is with the witches' aid we will return the Fomorii to Underworld. The humans . . . they will help in their own way."

Jake stared down Tiernan while the other PSF officers glared at the D'Danann warrior. "Now that we know what we're up against," Jake said, "we'll be better prepared. We have firepower that can blow their fucking heads off."

No one spoke for a moment, then Kirra, the redheaded green-eyed captain, pushed herself up from her seat beside the table. She looked around the room as she studied each person—witch, D'Danann, and human.

"It is time for us to make a decision as a group," Kirra said in a calm tone. "We either go into the night with all our hearts and souls, or we vote to put our attack off until what we believe is a better time."

The D'Danann, PSF team, and the witches studied one another for a long moment. Keir stepped forward, his dark brows narrowed, a fierce expression upon his features. "I say we take on the bastards tomorrow night."

Sher moved beside Keir. Raised her chin high. "My vote is the same. If we wait much longer, it could be too late. The Fomorii could possibly summon thousands of their kind on Samhain, and then there would be far too many to battle. We need to take them now, while there are fewer of them."

Hawk's gaze moved to his comrades who sat at the table, and those who stood around the room. Braeden with his expression of deep contemplation. Fallon with her head cocked, her intelligent eyes assessing the situation. Each of the D'Danann would make their decision according to what they felt was right . . . as it should be.

Kirra cleared her throat. "I am with Sher, Keir, and Hawk. We should take advantage of this Samhain and clear out the demons now."

The knot in Hawk's gut lessened as Braeden, Cael, Fallon, and Aideen nodded and each murmured their assent. The rest of the D'Danann followed their lead and all PSF officers nodded.

Tiernan was last. He studied Hawk and said nothing while silence reigned.

"Yes," Tiernan finally said. "Come this witching hour, we will fight."

After plans had been formally made, Hawk turned from the conversation and watched Silver slip away, down the stairs to the bottom level of the boat. His tough little warrior woman looked uncommonly pale and fragile, and he hoped she had sufficiently recovered from the ordeal at the park. She had been through so much in the week since she had first summoned him that he wondered how she continued seemingly as strong and vibrant as before.

Right now she didn't look strong at all.

While he strode across the crowded room to follow Silver, Hawk crammed the rest of his chocolate chip cookie into his mouth and swallowed, then wiped crumbs from his fingers onto his breeches. He'd been trying to keep an emotional distance from her the past couple of days, and it was tearing him apart. Gods, how he needed her.

His boot steps rang against the metal stairs as he walked down until he reached the lower deck with a solid thump. The room was shadowed, most of the light coming from the doorway he had just come through.

Silver stood with her back to him, staring out a porthole. Emotion tugged at his heart, pulling him closer to her. He could no more have stopped himself than he could have taken to the skies with a broken wing.

When he reached her, the tension in her shoulders was obvious. He reached up with his good hand and massaged her neck with his fingers. She leaned back against him. Her skin was soft beneath his touch, but her shoulders knotted.

"That feels soooo good." She tipped her head back and loose strands of her hair tickled his hand.

He pressed a kiss to the top of her head as he continued massaging her neck and shoulders, first one side, then the other. She smelled of ocean breezes and her own sweet womanly scent that always hardened his cock in a rush. How could just the smell of her make him desire her so much he could hardly bear it?

She sighed and leaned back fully, molding her body to his. He let out a low groan as his body reacted, his cock stiffening and pushing against the top of her ass.

"Why have you been so distant the past couple of days?" she asked softly, surprising him again with her direct question. "I thought we resolved this at the park. Our time together is short, but . . ."

She deserved nothing but honesty. He glanced at the glass of the porthole and her eyes met his in the reflection. He rested his palm on her shoulder. "It's hard enough knowing I'll have to return to Otherworld and leave you behind."

Silver remained still beneath his hand, her gaze focused on him in the reflection. "What if I want to spend every moment I can with you?" She raised her hand to her shoulder and interlocked her fingers with his. "What if I choose to be with you even though I know you can't stay?" She squeezed his fingers, then released his hand and turned to him. "I'm not going to take no for an answer."

Hawk couldn't take his eyes from her, and still didn't think he could breathe. Before he had a chance to try, Silver wrapped her arms around his neck and brought his head down so that their mouths nearly touched and her warm breath teased his lips.

"I'm not kidding." She kissed him in a hard, hot rush. Her mouth demanded more of him, took from him, gave to him.

Lust raged through Hawk, equally hard and fast. He pressed her up against the wall by the porthole and took possession of her mouth, her body.

She slipped her hands into his hair, her moans vibrating through him, straight to his erection. He rubbed himself against her belly, wanting to be inside her now more than anything. He couldn't think past Silver.

He didn't let anything hold him back as he tasted her. His broken arm was pressed between them, but he could feel her softness, her warmth, through the thick membrane of the cast.

His free hand roamed her body, from her shoulders to her waist, down her back and over her ass and up again. He couldn't stop touching her, tasting her, being with her.

"Gods, your taste, your scent . . . you're driving me out of my mind." He slipped his hand into her hair and pressed her tighter to him, drinking as much of her in as he possibly could. What he shared with her these remaining two days would have to last him a lifetime.

When they finally broke the kiss, both breathed hard. In the light coming in through the porthole, her eyes glittered with passion, her face was flushed, her nipples high and rising against her dark sweater. Her lips were moist and she licked them, as if savoring his taste.

"Now," she said in a tone so demanding that it was as if she'd cast a spell that wouldn't allow him to refuse her. "Take me *now*."

Not that he could have refused her anything at that moment.

Vaguely he was aware of the sound of voices upstairs where the D'Danann were eating and talking.

"We don't have much time." She let go of his hair and moved her hand in the air between them. His pants came undone with her magic, and his cock and balls thrust out the opening. She grasped his erection, wrapping her small fingers around its thickness. "Fuck me."

A primal growl rose within Hawk's chest. She released her hold on him as he spun her around to face the wall. "Brace your hands," he demanded, and she shivered as she complied.

With his one good hand, he unbuttoned and unzipped her pants, and pushed them down over her knees. "Widen your thighs."

She spread her legs as best she could with her pants around her knees and moaned as he slipped his fingers into her drenched folds. He couldn't help himself when he brought his hand to his nose to drink in her scent, slipped his fingers into his mouth to taste her.

Silver gave an impatient sound. Hands still on the wall, she moved farther back so that she was bent over just right, ready for him.

"Damn, Silver." He grasped his erection and placed it at the opening of her channel, causing her to give a delighted gasp. "I can't think when I'm around you."

"Don't think." She pushed herself back so that he slid a fraction into her, an incredible feeling that she needed more of. "Just fuck."

"You're a delicious little witch." He grasped her slim hip in his hand and drove his cock deep inside her wet core.

Silver cried out and he felt mini-spasms in her pussy, clenching his erection. His thighs tensed. He held himself still, and kept her from moving by his tight grip on her.

"Someone's going to find us here." She squirmed. "Come on."

Though it pained him to keep her waiting, he kept motionless inside her. He leaned over her back and murmured close to her ear, "Would you like that, Silver? Would you like to be watched as I fuck you?"

Tingling sensations skittered through her at just the idea of someone seeing them. Her nipples tightened as the forbidden thought both intrigued and horrified her, that she might be a closet exhibitionist. She bit her lower lip and ground her hips against him. "Come on, Hawk. I need you."

He gave a soft laugh, and she was sure he knew how it had turned her on just thinking about the idea.

"You feel so good." He began thrusting in and out of her, and she almost cried at the sweet sensations. "Perfect. Perfect for me."

More spasms erupted in her channel, like they had when he'd first entered her. She was so close to exploding.

He moved inside her core in long, slow strokes. "Someone's coming down," he murmured as he bent over her. His warm breath stirred hair at her nape. "Maybe more than one."

All the sensations in her body heightened as he spoke. "Stop teasing me," she said, and pushed back against him.

"Who's teasing?" He began to pound harder into her.

"They're on the stairs now. Watching. Wanting to fuck like I'm fucking you."

Silver couldn't help her scream as she came hard. It echoed throughout the room and surely reached everyone upstairs, as well. His words had thrown her so far that there was no returning. While Hawk continued to move in and out of her pussy, lights glittered in her mind like the city's reflection on the bay. Orgasm after orgasm washed through her, in time with ripples on the water from a passing boat . . . wave after wave after wave.

"They just saw you come, Silver. Heard you, too," he said, and she cried out with another climax.

Silver truly didn't know if Hawk was teasing or serious, and right now she didn't care. He felt so good inside her, made her feel so complete.

Hawk couldn't hold back from coming much longer. In the dim light he watched his slick cock move in and out of Silver, below her perfect ass. His balls slapped her pussy and the smack of flesh against flesh sounded loud and satisfying. Her scent was strong and fulfilling, and he only wished he had time to lick her clit and taste her juices thoroughly.

Her channel continued to throb and contract around his cock. No one had actually come into the room, but it had been a fine ride teasing her about it.

She moaned and wiggled, and shuddered with another orgasm. "Too much," she said between gasps. "It's too much."

"Not enough," he said, but then hit his own climax with a shout and an explosion of sensation that rocked him from the top of his head to his booted toes.

His cock throbbed in her hot core and he spurted come inside her with every pulse. He slowly stopped with a shuddering sigh of completion.

"We've got to," Silver said between panting breaths, "get dressed."

Hawk reached his hand around her, stroked her clit, and was rewarded with her cry and a jerk of her hips as she came again.

He chuckled and kissed the back of her neck. He withdrew his cock, which glistened with her juices in the moonlight pouring through the small window.

Silver groaned and straightened. She visibly trembled as she leaned down and drew up her pants. Just the sight of her bending over, and then wiggling her ass as she eased up the material, was enough to make his cock hard again.

She turned as she fastened the button of her pants and shook her head. "You are so naughty. But I love it."

He glanced down at his cock as he tried to tug his pants closed with one hand, since his other was in a cast. "I, ah, need your help."

"Oh, really?" She planted her hands on her hips and when he looked into her gray eyes she had a mischievous expression. "I think I'll just leave you like that. After all, you don't mind being watched."

He grasped her by her arm and jerked her close. "Watch it, woman, or you'll be on your knees, sucking my cock."

Silver ran her tongue along her lower lip. "Promise?" She laughed and slowly fastened his pants, brushing her fingers against his cock and causing him to groan. She finished just as she heard footsteps on the stairs.

"Silver? Hawk?" came Mackenzie's voice, and then a pause. They both looked up toward the stairs to see the witch. Silver had no doubt her friend had a good idea what she and Hawk had been up to. "Ooops," Mackenzie said. "Just wanted to let you know we're ready to head back to the store." Her eyes held a knowing glint and she laughed before she turned and jogged back up the stairs.

Silver smiled at Mackenzie's retreating backside, then returned her attention to Hawk. She reached up, linked her hands behind Hawk's neck, and brought his face close to hers. Her senses filled with his smell of leather and musk, his scent of fresh air and mountain breezes. Goddess, could she ever get enough of him?

There was something between them. Something sure and strong—but nothing that could last. She sighed and tipped her forehead against his so that their gazes were locked, their breathing as one.

Hawk's chest tightened, and for one long moment he could only look at her, his beautiful witch.

Something stirred in his heart, something soul-deep. As if his attraction were more than lust, more than the need to have her. More than the need to be with her every waking moment.

His heart pounded against his ribs at his next thought . . . Could he have fallen in love with Silver in mere days?

No. He would never love another.

Could never love another.

Silver drew away and pressed her finger to his lips. "Nothing you could say could possibly mean more than the way you're looking at me now." Her smile brightened the dim room. "Like I am the most cherished woman in this world."

Hawk captured her chin with one hand and her fingertip slipped from his lips and trailed across his cheek. He brought his mouth to hers in a fierce, possessive kiss. By all the gods, she was his. Maybe for only a short time, but she was *his*.

He raised his head and smiled a second before his skin started to crawl.

A shot rang out.

A scream split the air.

31

"The Fomorii!" Silver shouted, even as Hawk tore away from her and bolted for the stairs.

He took them two at a time, damning the fates for his broken arm. Silver's boot steps echoed after his, a rapid-fire sound as she hurried behind him.

Jake's and the PSF team's gunshots, the sound of wings whumping in the air, and the D'Danann battle cry met Hawk's ears, mixing with Fomorii roars and shrieks. Fury burned Hawk's blood while he ran through the now empty dining area, up the next set of stairs, and onto the deck.

What madness was this?

Hideous Fomorii slithered into the docked houseboat. More demons crawled from the water, oozing slime as they slopped across wood and metal.

How had they missed this attack? They had posted guards. They had been cautious!

The water. The bastard-demons had to have been hiding in the water to mask their stench. No other explanation.

His broken arm bedamned. Hawk snarled as he used his left hand to rip his sword from its sheath. Wound or no wound, he would, by gods, do some damage.

Lights from the boat and from the pier illuminated the battle scene.

Swords thudded against leathery hides. Several D'Danann

went sword to skin with the nasty beasts. Battle cries rang in the air as more D'Danann struck from the sky.

Eyes wide, screaming like a schoolchild, the witch Iris ducked into the room where the food had been.

Hawk whirled.

Jake thundered across the deck, a dagger in one hand and a gun in the other. The human threw himself between a demon and Cassia and Mackenzie.

"Move, you idiot!" Cassia's screech was almost lost in a blast of grunts, curses, and battle shouts. She and Mackenzie shoved Jake, tried to move him out of their way and join the fight, but the human held his ground.

Eric stood on top of the houseboat's cabin, lobbing spellfire from his vantage point, and stunning them with his white magic.

Hawk's eyes watered. His nostrils flared against the stink of demon and blood and fear. Hot blood rumbled in his ears. He lunged at the first Fomorii that crossed his path. The boat rocked beneath his feet and his sword slammed against the beast's thick purple hide.

The demon whirled and slashed with iron-tipped claws. Hawk dodged right, barely avoiding that fatal swipe.

"Too slow!" he bellowed. He swung his weapon and shaved off one of the huge demon's purple ears. The beast roared as Hawk fought to regain his balance from his off-hand strike.

Silver created a ball of purplish-blue fire between her palms. Her features tense with fury, she reared back, then flung the fireball at the demon's face.

A direct hit. The Fomorii shrieked. Flung back its head. Its face burst into flames!

Hawk gave his own D'Danann cry and sliced the Fomorii's head off with one smooth stroke. The beast went down as Hawk staggered, the demon's fiery head still screaming as Hawk managed to keep on his feet and regain his grip on his bloodied weapon.

The demon had barely turned to black dirt when Hawk spun around to assess the situation.

Jake fired his pistol. More shots rang into the night—Jake's team, doing what fighting they could. D'Danann wings beat the air. Battle cries warred with bellows and more curses. Spellfire flashed. Hawk choked on the rotten-fish stench, trying to ignore the distinct coppery smell of human blood. No time for worries. No time for mourning.

Hawk's blood pounded harder in his head. Battle lust filled his soul while he and Silver squared off with the next growling, snarling demon. A green beast with three arms. Good. All the better to hack it to bits. His other hand felt more comfortable now, more easy in the grip and swing. The power of his people hammered through him, giving him strength.

He would kill them all.

Silver stung the monster with a burst of flame.

From the corner of his eye, Hawk saw Cassia and Mackenzie burst past Jake, both flinging spellfire balls. Stunned Fomorii staggered and fell. Jake pumped bullets into the beasts' necks, yelling at the witches to get back. They ignored him.

Gods. If only the PSF had the full firepower they planned to use on Samhain.

But no matter. The D'Danann would slay each of the filthy beasts and—a human cry sliced into Hawk's fiery certainty. He hacked an arm off the demon in front of him, then glanced toward the sound.

A PSF officer flailed on the bloody, dirty deck. Before anyone could save the human, a hulking red demon ripped out her throat.

Silver's rage swelled so fast she felt it like a hard ache between her eyes. McNulty. Down. Mangled. Dead.

By the goddess, that red demon would *pay*.

Dark magic rose up within her so fast, so strong, that her hair crackled with its ferocity.

As if sensing her bloodlust, Hawk hacked the head off the monster they had been fighting. It turned to foul black dirt.

The rush of death only strengthened Silver's resolve. Her skin tingled. Her senses expanded.

"Make them pay," a voice sang in her mind, and she wasn't sure if it was hers or another's.

She didn't even care.

All that mattered was sending the demon who'd killed McNulty straight to Underworld.

Her spellfire grew as her rage fed it, hot, hotter, so purple and fiery it almost singed her own hands. Rearing back, she flung the ball straight at the demon feasting on its prize.

Dark flames engulfed the Fomorii. It stumbled away from the woman's body. The demon hit the railing as it clawed at the fire searing its skin.

The Fomorii turned and dove into the bay. Water hissed and steam rose. Hair prickled on Silver's scalp as the demon crawled back onto the boat, the fire doused, its skin burned in-patches and its flesh and bone showing, yet it began to heal.

Anger. Rage. Hate.

Anger. Rage. Hate.

"Kill the bastard," the voice said in her mind, and this time she recognized it as not her own.

Darkwolf. *"It killed your friend,"* he continued. *"Burn it. Burn it to dirt and ashes."*

Silver trembled.

Yes. Kill the horrid, murdering abomination. Fire for the good. Fire for cleansing. She would use her witchcraft, her goddess-given strength, and she would burn the monster to protect.

To avenge!

The red beast bounded toward her.

At the same time she felt a push at her mind. A nudge, really.

Silver ignored the mind-touch.

Her eyes fixed on the damaged red demon.

"Come on," she growled.

Spellfire leaped between her palms, such a deep purple it could almost have been black.

"Bastard!" she screamed. "This time when I kill you, die!"

Her spellfire struck the Fomorii—and the demon exploded. Exploded.

Into nothing.

Instantly, Silver felt that same nothing, way down inside. Total quiet. Absolute emptiness.

"Come to me," Darkwolf said in her mind. Only this time she could feel his presence. He was close. Chills rippled across her skin.

"I am here, Silver Ashcroft." That voice. So seductive. So sensual. *"Come to me."*

As chaos reigned around her, D'Danann and PSF battling Fomorii, Silver turned her head to the dock, as if in slow motion.

Darkwolf stood on the pier. As before, he was even more devastatingly handsome in person. His black hair curled just above his collar; his dark eyes looked directly at her. This time he wore a black turtleneck, faded blue jeans, and a pair of black running shoes. Around his neck hung the heavy chain with the stone eye.

It seemed as if he had stolen her very breath. She felt nothing but that magnetic pull that had bound the two of them before. From his eyes she could tell that he felt it, too.

Slowly she walked through the battle. Nothing came near her, nothing touched her. Purple shimmered around her and she knew Darkwolf was protecting her from everything.

Everything but himself.

Her steps were heavy, but she was powerless to stop herself. Did she want to stop? Or did she want to go to the man who commanded her in ways no one had ever done before?

Her feet found the gangplank. Her boots echoed as she strode across it to the pier.

A demon drove itself toward Hawk, eyes glowing red. Hawk dodged the Fomorii just in time and it slammed its head into the houseboat's cabin. Metal creaked and wood splintered. The beast shook its massive body. Stumbled back. Hawk thrust his sword and connected with thick hide and his weapon strike reverberated through his arm. With the D'Danann battle cry, Hawk raised his sword again, and this time hit home, slicing off the demon's head and bringing the Fomorii down.

And then the creature was gone.

Roars, shrieks, and shouts rent the air. Through the haze and near darkness, Hawk's fellow warriors dove from the sky while others fought from the deck.

Piles of black silt littered the deck, giving him some sense of satisfaction.

Slowly, slowly, the D'Danann were able to drive some of the Fomorii to the edges of the boat. Backing them up until one, two, then three tumbled over the sides, only to have the water demons climb back onto the boat.

Hawk's gut sickened when he saw one of his D'Danann warriors ripped from the air. The demon took Wynne down to the deck and tore out his heart with its iron-tipped claws, leaving nothing but silvery dust where the warrior had been.

With a battle roar, sword held high, Hawk charged the demon that had taken his comrade down.

His weapon connected with thick hide and he stumbled. Nearly lost his footing.

The green Fomorii slid, then bounded toward Hawk. Bloody saliva dripped from its massive jaws.

Hawk whirled. Dodged the snap of the demon's teeth.

He twisted in a movement too fast for the Fomorii to react. Hawk sliced his weapon down on the back of the beast's neck, aiming for the thinnest part of the skin.

He missed, his blade glancing off the tough hide. The demon growled, lunged, and took Hawk down to the deck.

Pain slammed into Hawk as his head hit unforgiving wood. Gut clenching, he blocked the demon's jaws with his sword. At the same time he thrust his booted feet at the beast's chest and shoved.

The demon slipped on the bloody deck and slid toward the railing. Its force was so great, it flipped into the bay.

Hawk bounded to his feet, ready to take on the next foe.

But everything and everyone had gone still.

His blood went cold as his gaze cut to the ramp.

Silver stood face-to-face with Darkwolf and a Fomorii warrior—and that warrior was no mere foot soldier.

Heart pounding, Silver faced Darkwolf. Perhaps ten feet separated them, and it was all she could do to remain rooted to where she stood on the wooden pier. She clenched her hands and her teeth.

Somehow she knew she had to fight him, no matter how much she was drawn to him.

Yet . . . why shouldn't she want him? His power, the things he could teach her—*he* took her powers seriously. He understood about gray magic. She took a single step forward and stopped. She blinked. There was someone else. Someone else who mattered to her.

Right?

Colorless fog seemed to swirl through her mind, hiding truths and lies alike.

Darkwolf gave her such a carnal smile that her knees almost buckled. Vivid images of him stripping her of her clothing and sliding between her thighs filled her mind.

"You want me," he murmured in her thoughts. *"I want you."*

Silver shook her head. Or tried to. It felt as if a huge weight had been tied around her neck and she couldn't move.

Yes, there was something she should remember. Something she should be doing. Someone she cared about. Many that she cared for. That damned fog—what was it hiding?

But Darkwolf . . . he was everywhere in her mind. Invading, taking, persuading.

Silver wanted to take another step, and another, and throw herself into his arms. Somehow she knew his touch would be beyond electric.

A blue demon loped up beside Darkwolf and the warlock's attention snapped to it. He scowled at the beast.

The fog in Silver's brain thinned. Just enough for her to shake her head and realize she had been seeing images, feeling emotions projected by Darkwolf.

An enchantment? Some kind of mesmerizing spell?

Vaguely, she understood she had to try to force Darkwolf from her mind. She had to get rid of the fog!

But he was so powerful. So seductive. And she wanted him. Didn't she?

Silver shook her head again. She ground her teeth. With all her might she tore at the fog around her thoughts. Almost gone. She could . . . almost see . . . What did she need to see?

Darkwolf shoved the blue demon away from him and returned his attention to Silver. His eyes narrowed.

Silver felt the fog surge back, battling her will, turning darker by the second. There was no way she could stop it. Did she even want to stop it? The gorgeous man was drifting closer to her, almost floating like the fog. She wouldn't have been surprised if he sprouted wings and—

Wings!

With one mighty burst of consciousness, Silver burned the fog off her mind.

Darkwolf actually stumbled backward. His lips drew back in a furious, pained snarl.

Silver felt a rush of strength, followed by a wave of awareness. She could feel Darkwolf's essence lurking at the fringes of her essence, but she did her best to keep it at bay.

Goddess. Hawk! My friends! What's been happening? He's kept me blind!

So much hatred shot through her that sparks crackled at the end of her hair. *The bastard. He summoned the Fomorii! He is responsible for all this death and destruction!*

Silver formed a purple ball of spellfire between her palms. She fed everything into it. All the fury she could muster. She would burn the warlock alive and the blue beast with him.

The large blue demon slowly paced toward her, its wicked eyes almost laughing.

Darkwolf glared at the creature, ignoring Silver's spellfire. "This one is mine, bitch. Back away."

The demon paid him no heed and took another step closer to Silver.

Silver's stomach pitched, but she was prepared to make the demon explode. Yes, yes. She would kill this worthless beast.

She was vaguely aware that on the pier, behind the beast, behind Darkwolf, stood several men and women, presumably Fomorii in human form.

They held guns. All trained on Silver.

Silver could have thrown up a spellshield, but she wanted to wipe this demon and warlock off the pier. She had to keep her shield down in order to use her spellfire.

Before Silver had a chance to make a move, the demon before her began to shift. As it rose up on its hind feet, it slowly morphed. Its features smoothed. Its blue flesh turned to a creamy ivory. Black hair tumbled down the back of a beautiful woman with a finely curved body.

The woman's smirk made Silver want to slap her.

"Do it, Silver." Darkwolf edged into Silver's mind again when her concentration faltered. *"You and I . . . we will control these beasts together. Use your hate and destroy the bitch."*

Yes, it was no more than the demon deserved.

Silver raised her hand to lob her spellfire at the Fomorii, when the woman spoke. "Would you like to see your parents again?"

Darkwolf cut his gaze to Junga.

Shock stilled Silver. She barely pulled back her blast in time. Her hand trembled and the sparks within it sizzled and then faded away. "Where are they?"

The woman gave a slight tilt of her head toward a group of cars waiting on the abandoned pier. "In one of the cars. I'll let them live if you join us."

Vaguely Silver heard almost complete silence behind her. No more roars. No more D'Danann shouts. Not even Darkwolf's voice in her mind. Just the lap of water against the pier and a foghorn in the distance.

A pair of boot steps approached. Hawk, she knew instinctively.

Darkwolf's eyes grew darker and his handsome face twisted into a scowl as her lover came to her side.

"I am Junga, legion leader." The Fomorii woman barely spared Hawk a glance as he reached Silver. "You, your mother, and your father die now if you and the other witches do not come with me."

"She's mine," Darkwolf growled, and the stone eye around his neck began to glow.

"No," Hawk said, his voice harsh with fury. "You will not have Silver."

Silver held up her hand, indicating she wanted him to be quiet. He audibly sucked in his breath.

Raising her chin, she spoke only to Junga, "Let my parents go and I'll come with you."

"No!" Hawk shouted this time and grasped Silver's upper arm, jerking her against him.

She shot her elbow into his gut and shook off his hold. She never took her gaze from Junga.

Darkwolf smiled. His gaze was solely for her. As if she were the only being in this world at this moment. That magnetism—she felt it was stronger than ever. Goddess, why did she feel such an attraction to this—this monster? Yes, that's what he was. A monster.

Her resolve strengthened and she used her will to block his pull on her.

"I want all three of you." Junga gave a sound like a low purr. "I always get what I want."

Silver did her best to ignore Darkwolf. She stared at the Fomorii woman head-on, even though her knees threatened to give out from fear for her parents. "You won't kill them. You won't kill me. You need me too badly."

"Come now. I demand it. Aid me in bringing all of my people to this city." Junga scowled, fierce, predatory. "Do not think to defy me. I assure you, I will not hesitate to kill anyone who stands against me." The demon-woman smirked again. "You choose."

Chills rolled over Silver and this time her gut pitched as panic for her parents engulfed her. "Take me," she said. "But first prove you really have my parents here."

Junga nodded to the men and women behind her, who

held the guns trained on her and Hawk. *Why haven't the Fomorii shot the PSF or D'Danann?* Silver wondered. *Perhaps they haven't mastered the unfamiliar weapons, or don't know what to do with them . . . Unless they had taken over the bodies of cops or criminals, and then they* would *know.*

At that thought her heart beat even faster.

From her side vision she saw Hawk clench the hilt of his bloodied sword in his good hand. He looked prepared to take off Junga's and Darkwolf's heads with one swift blow. Yet Silver knew he was holding back, holding back to protect her.

"My parents will never help you. If you kill them, you'll never get me," Silver hurried to say. "Turn them over and take me, or no deal."

"Oh, I will have you," Darkwolf said in her mind in a tone so full of conviction that Silver could almost believe him. *"Now or later, you will be mine."*

Silver shivered with a strange awareness as he projected the thoughts. Her . . . Darkwolf. Her and Darkwolf. The two of them. What they could do together . . .

"Fight him, a thaisce." Hawk's deep Irish brogue flooded her mind. *"I cannot hear what he says, but I can see it on his face, I can sense it. He is in your head. Fight him!"*

Hawk's words, the endearment he used whenever they made love, sent a flood of warmth through her chest.

She took a step closer to her true lover. He was the only man she wanted. Not this—this *scum.*

"Get out," Silver snarled in her mind. *"You'll never touch me."*

Darkwolf scowled.

"Me in exchange for my parents." Silver forced the words out, turning her focus on Junga and keeping her gaze from straying to Darkwolf.

Junga pursed her lips in consideration. The Ashcrofts had been exceedingly difficult. The pair had been willing to sacrifice their own lives rather than participate in the summoning. *The idiots.*

Of course, Junga had lied. The Ashcrofts were not with her.

Perhaps she would arrange to take Silver and the other witches to the hotel, and release one parent. Not both. She required something to ensure Silver's cooperation.

Junga opened her mouth to give Silver her terms, but she never had a chance to speak. A D'Danann shout split the salty air. The man at Silver's side swung his blade at Junga, and she barely dodged his blow in time.

A purple fireball snapped and crackled in Silver's hands, and that look of rage flooded her features again. She flung it at Darkwolf, but he had thrown up a force field. The purple shimmer surrounding him simply absorbed her power.

With a furious roar, Junga shifted into her demon form. The D'Danann lunged for her and she swiped her claws at him, nearly raking him with the iron tips.

At that second, the other D'Danann attacked from above. From the boat. From the pier.

The air filled with the sound of powerful wings. The cries of humans. The snarling of Fomorii.

Gunshots rang in the night as Junga's warriors tried to use the weapons they carried. PSF marksmen easily picked off a few of her warriors in human form. They had the same vulnerabilities as humans and dropped to the pier. Dead.

A couple of Junga's own shooters hit their marks and two D'Danann plunged from the sky. Not dead, no. Only injured, as there were no silver sparkles indicating their deaths.

One by one, Junga's legion began to fall.

Again!

Fury surging in her blood, Junga growled the order to retreat. She could ill afford more casualties. If the queen would even let her live after this defeat. After the loss of so many Fomorii lives, and the loss of the witches.

Darkwolf casually strode to his own car, his purple shield shimmering around him. Bullets bounced off the force field as he climbed into his black Jaguar. Even as bullets continued to ring out, his car was protected with his magic. A mighty roar, and then the car sped into the night.

The remaining Fomorii—those who could move unassisted—piled into the waiting cars at Junga's sharp command. She shifted into human form and slipped into a vehicle just as a D'Danann's talons raked the back of her neck, ripping clothing and flesh from her body.

Pain seared Junga. Tears of agony nearly blinded her human eyes. She slammed the door of the car, blocking another attack.

"Drive!" she ordered, ignoring the rush of blood down her shoulders.

Junga felt faint, even dizzy, which doubled her fury. Asserting her will over the pitiful strength of her host, she raised her chin and glared out the windows into the darkness.

This wasn't over. Come tomorrow night Darkwolf would have his thirteen. One more was all he needed, and Silver Ashcroft would be the one.

When Hawk raised his head to take on the next Fomorii, he saw only the blond-haired and yellow-winged Aideen battling the remaining beast. She fought from the air. Took the demon down with a slice of her sword across its throat, beheading it.

Junga and the bastard Darkwolf had vanished into waiting vehicles. The cars' wheels screeched across the pier's asphalt as they shot into the night. Two more vehicles tore after those.

"Hold," Hawk ordered the D'Danann before they could follow. When everyone landed on the pier he said, "We will fight the bastards when the time is right."

The Fomorii that died had turned to dirt. The murdered D'Danann's soul had returned to Summerland, a silver sparkle that rode between worlds. The only body was that of the PSF officer, and her furious team members cared for the body.

The witches, Jake, the PSF team, and the D'Danann spent the next hour cleansing the ship of all blood and silt and trying to repair what damage they could.

Exhaustion was a physical weight on Silver's body when the dark magic fled her. A headache pierced her skull and she could barely hold her head up while she helped with the cleanup effort.

When Mackenzie cleansed a bloodied railing beside Silver, she paused in her movements and said, "The magic you used—you—it was . . ." Mackenzie obviously struggled for words to express herself. She bit her lower lip, then continued, "It was too much, Silver. It was full of rage."

Silver's head shot up and she clenched her teeth as she glared at Mackenzie. "You don't know what you're talking about."

She whirled, turning her back on her friend, and went to another part of the boat where she could work alone. But not much later, Cassia approached and watched Silver, for a moment saying nothing. When she spoke, her words weren't welcome.

"What you did, Silver. It was not gray magic. You stepped over the line, and I fear you won't be able to step back. Don't allow black magic to consume you."

Silver shoved herself away from the deck she'd been scrubbing. "Leave me alone," was all she said before stalking away to get as far from everyone as possible. She shoved her way past Eric, stomped onto the ramp, hugging herself, trying not to let tears fall. It was too much. All too much.

Goddess, she had *killed*.

Again.

Did they think she didn't care?

Did they think she didn't *know*?

Damn it, she was standing on the edge of a very steep cliff. Nobody knew that better than she.

Whatever the opinions of the witches or the D'Danann, they all stayed well clear of her for a few hours.

By the time the cleanup effort was finished, the sky had grown lighter with the false dawn, the time between the depths of night and true dawn. Fog rolled in thick across the bay, and Silver shivered at the eerier-than-normal quality of the heavy mist.

It made her think of the mist Darkwolf had forced into her thoughts when she was so open to the dark.

So far over the edge, just as Mackenzie and Cassia had said.

Her gut began to grow heavy, and she fought back the bile rising in her throat. Goddess, her head hurt. Her body ached. Her mind—the scenes played over and over and over in her head until she was almost crazy from them.

Oh, goddess. What had she done? Was it too late?

Shivers racked her, and she sat down on the far end of the scrubbed decks and hugged herself again.

Maybe it was too late for her, but the killing had been necessary. It was necessary, damn it!

But . . . would she do it all again if she had to?

Silver shivered again. Her teeth clenched and her eyes narrowed.

Yes.

The answer was yes.

32

The moment they returned to the shop and entered the kitchen, Silver bolted for the sink and retched. She couldn't stop the dry heaves that racked her body when she had nothing left to throw up.

Dear Ancestors. She'd helped to murder those bastards and she had taken *pleasure* in seeing them pass from this world. Again. Again. Again.

And she would do it all over if she had to.

Darkwolf . . . the power he'd had over her made her even more ill. How could he have such a seductive pull on her when he was nothing short of evil? How could she have been drawn to him so?

Oh, goddess. What if that demon—Junga—spent her anger on Silver's parents now, no matter how much the bitch needed them?

"I'm sorry, *a thaisce*." Hawk wrapped his arm around her as she bent over the sink, and kissed the side of her head. He didn't seem to mind the horrible acidic smell in the sink, or the mess she'd made.

He'd no doubt seen far worse.

The thought made Silver retch again, and she felt faint enough to drop to the floor. Hawk's arm steadied her.

After a couple of minutes she raised her head, stood, and turned on the water. She cupped her hands and washed out her mouth with the cool fluid. With a shaking hand she cleansed the sink with the spray nozzle.

Vaguely she was aware of Sher, Keir, and Jake now crowding the shop's kitchen. Cassia was bustling about with healing herbs, creams, and oils, tending to those who needed it. Mackenzie and Eric helped her while Iris sat at the table, sheet-white, and seemed intimidated by everything.

Hawk kept his hold on Silver as she grabbed a clean towel from a hook on the wall to dry her face. She welcomed his support, needed it. When she finished, she leaned into him. No matter that his clothes carried the Fomorii stench, the smell of battle and sweat, she could still catch his masculine scent beneath it all.

He kissed the top of her head. "Let's clean up. Then I am going to get you to bed."

"You, too." She felt grimy. Covered with dirt and blood. "You need your rest."

"Mmmm," he murmured, a noncommittal sound.

"Is Silver all right?" came Mackenzie's voice from behind.

"I'll take care of her," Hawk said.

Mackenzie went back to assist the others with the healing. She began helping Jake, washing the blood and gore from him. Silver saw Mortimer peeking out of Cassia's jacket pocket and his tiny black eyes stared directly at her. As if judging her. Convicting her.

Silver tried to ignore the familiar's stare and leaned against Hawk as they made their way upstairs to her own apartment. Goddess, what a week. What a night.

She shuddered as she thought of the battle, the dead Fomorii, the D'Danann, and the PSF officer. She almost threw up again.

Hawk took her straight to the bathroom.

"How about a bath instead of a shower?" he asked as he reached for the faucet.

Silver gave him a tired nod. "Sounds wonderful."

After turning on the tap to fill the claw-footed tub with warm water, Hawk helped Silver strip out of her filthy outfit. When she was naked, she reached up and kissed him. It was

a feather-soft kiss, and when she drew back he had a smile
that turned her inside out. For that moment she could forget
about everything that had happened, and just *be* with him.

A gift from the goddess, the distraction. Otherwise, she
might have lost her mind.

He felt so good under her hands as she helped him remove his sling and clothing, taking care not to hurt his broken arm. When they were both naked, they slipped into the
narrow tub, and Silver turned off the water.

Steam rose from the surface. The water felt so warm and
welcome that she sighed and melted against Hawk as he
sat behind her. He wrapped his good arm around her waist
and braced his cast on the side of the porcelain tub. When
she leaned into his chest, his hard cock pressed up against
her backside.

"I want to stay like this forever," she murmured. If only
she could forget everything that had happened. But even as
she tried to relax in Hawk's embrace, his naked skin next to
hers, she couldn't put all the horrors out of her mind.
Couldn't quite force Darkwolf's image from her mind.

"Just be easy." Hawk nuzzled her hair before taking the
clip out and letting the mass tumble down his chest. He set
aside the clip and picked up the blue cup that perched on the
vanity table beside the bathtub. As she rested against him, he
poured water from the tub onto her hair, letting the warmth
seep through the wet strands to her scalp.

"That feels so good," she murmured, her lids heavy. If
she closed her eyes for only a moment, she was sure to fall
asleep.

When he reached for the shampoo, she reached with him
and squirted some of the lily-scented liquid onto his palm.
With one hand he managed to soap her hair from her scalp
all the way down to the ends.

"Such beautiful hair." His fingertips massaged her nape.
"Like starlight and the moon's glow on the clearest of
nights."

His voice made her heart tug in a way she couldn't define.

"Turn on the water, *a thaisce*." He leaned forward and she

moved with him as he placed the cup under the tap. He poured water over her hair as it ran from the spout, carefully rinsing out her hair until all the shampoo was gone.

When he began to wash her body with a sponge and lily-scented soap, he said, "Do you want to talk about what happened tonight?"

"My mother and father, in the hands of those beasts." Silver blinked back tears. "What if that Junga demon has already killed them?"

Hawk continued soaping her as he spoke. "I don't believe she would be that rash, bitch that she is."

"I pray to all the Ancestors you're right." Silver gave a long, shuddering sigh. "I'm not sure I know how to deal with killing any kind of being, Hawk. I don't know if I ever will be able to accept that I have. Witches believe that whatever we do will come back to us threefold."

She swallowed hard before continuing. "I'm afraid, Hawk. I'm afraid for my family. I'm afraid for my Coven. What if my killings bring death to those around me? Or ill fortune to our endeavor? The universe can be so cruel. When it balances—well, mercy and pity aren't much in the equation."

He stopped washing her, slipped his arm around her slick body, and held her tight. "It was your only choice. Many could have died if not for you. *You* could have died. Perhaps the grief and guilt growing in your spirit is the balance."

Silver bit her lower lip and couldn't talk for one long moment. So many emotions whirled through her that she could hardly think straight. Anger at the Fomorii, fear for what was yet to come, concern for her friends and the D'Danann. And her parents. Her mother and father, still trapped by the demons.

And that fact again, that she would kill more of the demons if she had a chance. What had made her most sick afterward was how it almost thrilled her to see them go down.

What price would be extracted from her when this was all

over? *Whatever you send out into the universe, Silver, will come back to you threefold.*

When would the payment be called due? Now? Next week? A year?

But it would come due. And it wouldn't be as simple as guilt and grief, as much as she would like to believe that.

Silver buried her face in her wet hands. Tears came hot and fast and her body shook with the force of her sobs. Hawk held her tight, his cheek against her wet hair, his body enveloping hers. She cried until she couldn't cry anymore.

33

Junga trembled with both fury and fear as she knelt before Queen Kanji in Elizabeth's penthouse suite. Both were in their Fomorii form, as the queen had ordered. Junga kept her head and eyes lowered, her body still. Not only for protocol, but to avoid the queen observing Junga's churning emotions in her expression.

"Daughter of Kae, like your father you are nothing but a disappointment," the queen rumbled in the Fomorii tongue, her tone filled with disgust as she spoke to Junga. "Such a simple task. Wipe out the miserable D'Danann and capture the witches you lost and Silver Ashcroft. Our warriors doubled the D'Danann ranks, yet we lost more than they. What do you have to say?"

It took great effort for Junga to keep her head bowed and her claws still. "You are right, of course, my queen."

"Not only did you fail this night, but you have continuously done so since your arrival." The queen snorted. "You failed to bring the Old One and we now have no one to speak directly with Balor. Not even Darkwolf has the powers she wields."

Junga clenched her jaw and her fists. If only she dared challenge the queen and rip her throat out. Junga would be more than legion leader then, and *no one* would dare challenge her. But the queen's thick, thick hide protected her too well. Perhaps in her weaker human form, when the queen was at her most vulnerable . . .

If only Junga dared.

"Rise," the queen ordered.

Junga eased to stand firmly on all four limbs. She clenched her massive jaw tighter and fought to keep her eyes from showing her hate.

"Take your inferior human form," the queen said. "Return to the ballroom and speak to the witch parents of Silver Ashcroft. Convince them to help—whatever it takes."

Junga slowly shifted into human form until she towered over the queen. She was tempted to rub the back of her neck where D'Danann talons had torn the flesh, but it was already healed. Once she had shifted into a demon, the wounds vanished.

Apparently the queen didn't like having to look up at Junga. Kanji growled and transformed into her human form. Features shifted. Claws retracted. She rose to stand on two feet.

The beautiful blond woman again stared at Junga eye to eye. The knowledge in Kanji's expression made Junga's belly twist. How Darkwolf and the queen had whipped and fucked her and how she had enjoyed it . . .

Balor, please help me.

Junga lowered her eyes again to keep her emotions hidden.

"Perhaps you need another lesson in obedience," Kanji said, and pinched Junga's nipple so hard that she cried out and her gaze shot up to meet the queen's. Kanji's eyes casually glanced at where the hook was still jutting from the wall before looking back to Junga.

Heat flushed Junga's human cheeks.

Kanji's voice lowered to a growl. "You're nothing but a little slave-bitch. I should replace you immediately with one of those who do *not* enjoy submission."

Junga kept her fists from clenching and gave a bow from her shoulders. "I will see to the witches now."

With a wave of her elegant hand, Kanji urged Junga to leave her. "Go. Now."

The queen casually reclined on one of the sumptuous couches and watched Junga with almost mirth in her eyes.

Junga left the queen in the large suite that had once been Elizabeth's. The suite where she had been erotically punished by Kanji and Darkwolf. The suite where she had fucked and been fucked countless times by Bane, Darkwolf, and Za.

At the thought of Za, murdered by the D'Danann and Silver, her human heart twisted.

She shook off the feeling, raised her chin, took the elevator to the lobby, and strode to the ballroom where all the witches were still kept captive.

When she walked through the double doors of the ballroom, she stormed past the guards to where Victor and Moondust Ashcroft were propped against the wall behind the force field. Moondust rested her head on Victor's shoulder, her eyes closed, her face drawn and pinched.

Junga took a deep breath and composed her features so that she appeared cool and confident when she reached the Ashcrofts. Both looked exhausted and filthy from their days of captivity. All the captives had been well fed with human foods, and allowed to use the restroom facilities one at a time with their hands bound behind their backs. A pleasant discovery had been that they could not perform magic while bound.

"You are running out of time," Junga said to the Ashcrofts.

Moondust opened her eyes, lifted her head, and met Junga's gaze head-on. In that moment, she no longer looked tired. She appeared as vibrant as the day she had been captured.

Junga gnashed her teeth.

"You will receive no help from Victor or myself," Moondust said in a soothing voice that made Junga want to claw her eyes out.

Victor's face reddened, and Junga could tell his control was tenuous. "We will die before performing black witchcraft for you or anyone else."

Irritation clenched Junga's belly, but she held it in check. Instead she tapped her chin with one long fingernail, as if the witches' lives meant nothing to her. It irked her to no end that she needed these powerful beings to bring the tremendous number of demons remaining in Underworld to this world. If only Fomorii had the power to summon through host bodies. Then they could kill the witches, take over their bodies and minds, and be done with it.

"You have no choice," Junga said with her best haughty smile. "Your daughter will die if you do not."

Victor's face paled for a fraction of a second before he recovered himself. He snorted, an arrogant tilt to his head. "You need her badly. You won't kill her."

Narrowing her eyes, Junga stepped forward. Her needle-sharp teeth elongated and nearly punctured her lower lip. Her claws slipped from her human fingers and dug into her palms, deep enough that warm blood trickled down the soft flesh, but she was too furious to feel the pain. "Trust me. If I do not get cooperation from either of you, or Silver, I have no problem feeding the lot of you to my warriors."

Victor's face turned a deeper shade of purple. Despite his bravado, she had seen the fear for his daughter. "Do what you will," he finally said, but she heard the slightest waver in his voice. "Do what you will."

Junga straightened and gave them Elizabeth's smirk. "Come tomorrow night, be prepared."

Bloodlust and hunger burned in Junga's chest. She turned, cast a look back over her shoulder, and gave a wicked smile as an appealing thought came to her. She focused on the Ashcrofts again. "For every time you refuse me, I will eat one apprentice or lesser witch."

Moondust sucked in her breath, her eyes widening as Victor's color deepened.

But the male witch only said, "We never, ever, compromise with evil."

"*Fine,*" Junga snarled and straightened her black suit— one of many from Elizabeth's closet. "In the meantime, simply to show you my sincerity, I will dine on one of your apprentice witches now."

"No!" Moondust cried, horror twisting her pale features.

If Victor turned any more purple than he already was, he was sure to have heart failure.

Junga simply smiled and gave a soft laugh before she shifted into her demon form and dropped to all fours. She slowly padded across the ballroom to one of the apprentice witches, one with little power according to the warlock priest. Junga was hungry and ready for a good meal. This plump witch on the end would be perfect.

With a bat of her tremendous paw, Junga knocked the witch facedown. The female screamed. So did several other witches.

"No! Please don't hurt Sandy!" another witch cried as Junga sank her incisors into the redheaded witch's nape.

The instant rush of blood flowing over her tongue was an aphrodisiac like no other. She dragged the screaming witch, *Sandy*, from the room, intent on enjoying a good meal.

October 31

34

Late on the afternoon following the battle, on the day they would again face the Fomorii on Samhain, Silver woke in Hawk's arms. Despite what they'd experienced the previous night, right this minute she felt safe and secure in his embrace. She was facing him, her head tucked under his chin.

No matter that she was bone weary, she needed him in ways she couldn't begin to understand. She needed to heal. To feel complete. To hang on to whatever comfort she could have.

She needed to feel him inside, outside, and every way she could have him.

The curtains were drawn, and only a slight yellow cast of sunlight peeked through the shades. Hawk and Silver were naked beneath the covers, their legs and arms intertwined, his cock pressed against her belly. Her sex ached and moistened. Renewed energy poured into her body. A magical lift radiated through her in wondrous sensations. Sensations she wanted to share with Hawk.

Silver kissed the curve of his neck. He smelled clean and masculine, of the lily-scented soap and his intoxicating musk that she'd become addicted to in such a short time. Barely a week ago he'd come into her world. How could she have come to need him so much in such a short amount of time?

She brushed her mouth over his Adam's apple, the stubble rough beneath her lips. He stirred, shifted.

"You need rest," he murmured in a sleep-roughened voice.

"I need *you.*" Silver flicked her tongue along his throat to his strong jaw, tasting the salt of his skin.

A rumbling groan of desire rose up within his chest. She pushed gently at his shoulder, guiding him onto his back. With his good hand at her waist, he took her with him and the sheet slipped from her shoulders, down to her buttocks, baring her, baring him.

She straddled his waist, his cock firmly nestled against the folds of her pussy. Rocking slowly on top of Hawk, she enjoyed the feel of his lean hips between her thighs. Her wetness slicked his length, and her moans mingled with his.

With a sigh of pleasure, she leaned forward. Her long, silken-clean hair drifted over her shoulders and across his chest.

She placed her forehead to his. "Love me, Hawk. Love me like we have forever."

Silver took his mouth, claiming him as her own. While she continued to rock, she gently nipped at his lower lip and he responded with a low groan. He slipped his tongue into her mouth and she took it within her, lightly sucking, tasting. His flavor was as intoxicating as his scent, and her head spun.

With a sigh of complete surrender to the emotions filling her, Silver tangled her tongue with his. Their lips met, their teeth nipped, and their tongues danced.

When Silver couldn't take any more, she rose up, prepared to bring his cock to her core and take him deep. But he caught her with his palm against her back and brought her down so that one of her breasts was even with his mouth. He sucked her nipple and she hissed her pleasure at the sensations rippling from her breast to her mons.

Hawk couldn't get enough of Silver's taste as he pulled at the puckered nipple in his mouth. He kept his hand at her back and Silver moaned even louder as he caught her other nipple between his teeth.

"Hawk." Her hair tumbled over her shoulder and caressed

him as if it had a life of its own. "Please come inside me. I want you there."

Reluctantly he let her nipple go, or maybe not so reluctantly when her small hand wrapped around his erection. She rose up on her knees just enough to place the head of his cock at the entrance to her pussy.

A fraction at a time, she eased down on him. Dear gods, she was sweet. He watched her in the dim light as she took his length deep inside her and she moaned. She bit her kiss-swollen lower lip while she began to rock against him in slow, even strokes. A small gasp escaped her with every thrust. He traced the curve of one breast with his fingers and she shivered beneath his touch.

She arched her back, her breasts thrusting high, her chin tilted up and her eyes closed. Her hair floated over her shoulders, all the way down her back, to whisper across his thighs.

Hawk felt so heavenly inside her that tears gathered at the corners of Silver's closed eyes. His possession was complete and total.

She opened her eyes and her gaze met his. She rocked a little faster, the sound of flesh meeting flesh mixing with their breathing and the pounding of her heart.

Her juices coated him, her scent warm, welcome. She loved the smell of her and Hawk together. Of man and woman, and everything that should be.

Her pace increased and she rocked harder against him. It felt as if his cock reached her belly button, he was so very deep.

That twisting, spiraling sensation in her abdomen grew stronger and she felt it begin to swell throughout her body. She held back, waiting, waiting for Hawk. He thrust into her as she moved against him, their joining becoming harder, more needy.

Their eyes never wavered from each other. Silver moaned and sparks began to glitter around her. She couldn't help the magic slipping from her.

"Come with me, *a thaisce*." Hawk plunged harder. "I want you to come with me."

Silver gasped as her orgasm burst through her. A rainbow glittered behind her eyes and then shimmered out of her, filling the room with her magic, reaching every corner, every space. The orgasm swelled within and without, and left her feeling so perfect, so complete.

Hawk released a shout and his cock pulsed within her channel. She continued to shudder as she rode him, rode him until he gripped her hip and rolled her onto her side.

Her mind spun with the suddenness of the move and the glitters around them spun, too. Gradually the sparkles faded as her orgasm slowed to small clenches in her channel. Her nipples brushed his chest with every breath she took. He moved so that his cast rested on her hip, their legs intertwined, much like they had been when she'd woken.

Still struggling to find the breath to speak, Silver caressed Hawk's stubbled jaw with her fingertips. A sensation swept over her from head to toe and she knew it was going to be so hard to let this man go.

Hawk tucked Silver tighter to his chest, and she breathed deeply of him, imprinting his scent and the feel of him into her memory.

A deep shuddering sigh racked Silver's body. Why did it feel as if her heart were being ripped into tiny pieces?

35

All the way to Golden Gate Park with Hawk, Silver's throat was so dry she could barely swallow.

Her sweaty palms slipped on the steering wheel as she maneuvered the battered car through the dark San Francisco night. Neon lights illuminated one street where several nightclubs competed to drown out one another with music so loud it pounded in Silver's head. She caught glimpses of adults in Halloween costumes—demons, vampires, werewolves, and of course witches. In the past she had often wondered what humans would do if they knew what *really* came out at night.

Tonight she was too worried to care.

While Silver drove the VW up and down city hills, through neighborhoods and past young trick-or-treaters, Hawk sat quietly beside her, his gaze fixed somewhere in the distance. No doubt his mind churned over their plans for tonight.

Despite Silver's protests, he had removed his sling, but at least his black cast remained, holding his broken bones together. Of course he'd sheathed his sword and dagger.

Silver tried to swallow again, but her dry throat refused her. *It's really happening. We're going out to meet the Fomorii head-on.*

Her stomach cramped again. What if she was responsible for more deaths?

But so what if she was? Wasn't killing preferable to what the beasts would do?

The cramp in her stomach nearly brought tears to her eyes. *What's wrong with me? How could I have come to this point, to feel nothing at the thought of the demons' deaths?*

And Darkwolf . . . what if he was there, and she couldn't fight the mental hold he seemed to have over her when she was near him?

The thought of his sensual pull, those dark eyes, that magnetism, caused her to bite the inside of her cheek, hard.

I will not let him get to me!

She forced herself to focus on the plan. It had to work.

What if her witchcraft failed her?

High above, cloaked with their magic, she was certain the D'Danann kept pace with the beat-up yellow VW. Behind Silver's vehicle, Mackenzie followed in her little car, Cassia riding with her, Mortimer in Cassia's pocket. Silver had left Polaris at home, not wanting the familiar to be in the middle of the battle. Jake and his team might already be at the park. But Eric—he'd been nowhere to be found. A knot of concern for him rose up within her. It wasn't like him to not show up on time.

Goddess, please, Silver prayed as she turned her thoughts to what they must do. *Please let this work.*

She stopped at a traffic light and clenched and un-clenched her hands as a ghost, a Faerie, and a superhero made their way along the crosswalk. The rising harvest moon illuminated the trick-or-treaters in an eerie glow.

This will work. It must work.

Hawk remained silent the entire trip to the park. Once they arrived and climbed out of the car, he met her at the back of the vehicle. He grasped Silver's hand and drew her into his embrace with his good arm, and her head rested against his chest. His warm length pressed flush against hers, and as always, her body reacted to him. Wanted him.

Needed him. A need so great it pushed all thoughts from her mind for that moment.

She closed her eyes and breathed in his masculine scent that somehow gave her strength and calmed the bat wings darting around her belly. Somehow this man made her feel like everything was going to be all right.

An ache enveloped her heart and she suddenly felt a burst of something for Hawk that she couldn't clearly define until the word came to her.

Love.

Was there such a thing as love at first sight? Love so soon? They'd only known each other for just over a week.

Definitely lust at first sight, but love?

Yet it had been magical between them from the moment they met.

She shivered and bit her lip to hold back any words that threatened to spill through her lips. Now wasn't the time. Hawk was leaving and she would likely never see him again.

When he pulled away, she opened her eyes and tilted her face up to look at him. In the light of the harvest moon, his features were dark and proud.

Silver reached up to meet his lips and he kissed her in such a long, sensual kiss that it melted away the last of her nervousness, giving her a sense of calmness. A sense of rightness.

An ache squeezed Hawk's heart as he drew away to look down at his beautiful Silver. Her gray eyes glittered and the glow of the full moon highlighted her features. She smelled of lilies and starlight, and a cool breeze off the bay. She'd been so warm, so very warm in his embrace. So perfect.

"You are my hero, Hawk." She looked up at him, and he could see the sorrow in her eyes. Sorrow that he was leaving? "You always will be, no matter what."

He tweaked a strand of her hair. "And you are mine."

Together they walked hand in hand to join the others. It was over an hour yet to midnight, and they needed to be ready. They hoped the Fomorii hadn't arrived already.

After Sher and Aideen scouted the meadow and the surrounding trees for signs of the Fomorii and found none, Keir led the rest of the winged D'Danann to the meadow. They were to settle in the trees surrounding the clearing and await the arrival of the demons.

When he, Silver, Cassia, and Mackenzie entered the woods, Hawk paused.

Silence. Complete and total silence.

Not the sound of a breath. Not the crack of a twig. Not the twitter of a bird. Not the trickle of water. Not the hum of insects.

Nothing.

It was the nothing he didn't like.

They slipped into the trees, Silver leading since she knew the path. She used her illumination spell, the soft blue glow lighting their way down the invisible path. The air smelled of rich earth and pine, yet something sinister, too. A smell that caused hair to rise at his nape.

Behind him Cassia stepped on a branch. A loud crack echoed through the trees.

Mortimer gave a squeak from her pocket that sounded like a reprimand.

Hawk winced and cast a disapproving look over his shoulder at Cassia, and she gave an apologetic grimace.

The blue glow that had been surrounding them dimmed and in that fraction of time all went dark.

Hawk turned back to follow Silver—

She was gone.

There was no sign of her blue glow.

He cut his gaze back toward Cassia.

Only Mackenzie stood behind him. Open-mouthed. Eyes wide.

Cassia had vanished.

Silver heard the crack of a branch behind her, but didn't stop to look. She crept through the near darkness, focused on finding the meadow until she finally reached the treeline. Moonlight bled across the open space before her.

She glanced up at the full moon. A red cloud passed over the yellow-orange globe.

Red cloud. Blood will be shed tonight.

The thought made her shudder.

The meadow appeared eerie beneath the unearthly moonlight. Not a ripple on the pond's surface. Not a ruffle of grass. Not a movement in the trees. Not a breeze over her skin. Yet there was a strange shimmer to the air . . .

Hair prickled on her scalp. Nothing felt right. She turned her worried expression toward Hawk.

No one was there.

Silver's heart pounded in her dry throat. She raised her hands and magnified the glow from her fingers to see better.

Nothing. No Hawk. No Cassia. No Mackenzie.

Sensations like worms crawling over her skin caused Silver to shudder again.

She heard a soft hiss . . . then another . . . and another . . . All around her. Everywhere. She saw the eyes. Black glittering eyes.

Snakes!

They began to slither from the trees, from the ground, coming straight toward her.

Silver stumbled backward, out of the trees and to the middle of the meadow, near the pond. A branch cracked beneath her feet, the sound like a shot through her heart. She slapped her hand over her mouth to hold back a scream as the snakes slithered closer.

She tripped over her feet, almost falling. She whirled to run.

And nearly slammed into Eric.

Silver came up short and held her hand to her chest. "Eric. Thank the goddess it's you. Where have you been?" Her gaze whipped back to the snakes that now were still. Some rose up, nearly standing on their tails, as if watching Silver and Eric. She blinked in surprise.

She cut her eyes back to Eric.

He smiled. An evil, chilling smile that turned Silver's blood to ice.

Her name came out of his mouth in a long hiss, "Sssssil-ver."

Silver's jaw dropped. "Eric? What's wrong with you?"

His smile was broad and two long, sharp fangs appeared, like a rattler's. "Eric is dead."

Stunned at the sight of the fangs and his words, Silver shook her head. Nothing made sense. *Eric dead?*

Taking a step back, she let a spellfire ball grow between her palms. "What the hell is going on here?"

Eric—or not Eric—advanced on her. "Just a nice little surprise for you, Ssssilver."

Eric was really dead? Silver swallowed and her stomach pitched. *Is that why we couldn't find him tonight?*

The spellfire ball grew bigger in her hands. Darker.

His eyes slowly shuttered from the sides. A long, forked tongue flicked through his lips. "And now you have sssssssserved your purposssssse. You have led the other witchesssss here and I will ensssssssure your asssssssisssss-tance."

Silver's eyes widened and she shook her head in disbelief. She took another step back. Tripped near the pond. Her booted foot slipped in the slick mud. She fell so hard on her ass that pain shot up her spine.

His features melted away.

Melted.

His arms vanished.

His legs molded together.

His head flattened. Elongated. Shifted.

A beast rose up so that it towered above her, its body nearly twice as wide as hers. It had thick red scales and a yellow underbelly, a yellow and red fan of cartilage and skin behind its head.

It was no longer in Eric's form. The creature was a Basilisk.

Without hesitating, Silver flung the dark ball of purple fire at the Basilisk. The fire enveloped the creature—but instead of stunning it, or burning it, the creature seemed to grow in width and height.

Oh, goddess, help me!

Powerful fog flew from her fingertips to wrap around the creature's length. *"Sleep, damn it!"* she commanded in her thoughts. *"Sleep!"*

"Sssssssilver," the Basilisk hissed as its head slowly moved from side to side in a methodic, mesmerizing motion. "*You* ssssleeeep, Ssssssilver. It ississssssss time. Firssssst you help ussssss, then you join sssissssster."

Silver blinked. Swayed. Fought the hypnotic hold of those black eyes.

Her magic faltered.

It happened so fast.

Silver screamed. Tried to turn and run.

In a flash, the Basilisk coiled itself around her body.

Pain wrenched her. She heard and felt the sickening pop of bones in her chest. Felt air whoosh from her lungs. Black spots appeared before her eyes, and her grip on consciousness faded.

The Basilisk clenched harder.

Squeezing the life out of her.

The next thing she heard was Cassia's shout. Saw a flash of blinding white light searing everything in its path.

Silver's world went black.

"Cassia just vanished. Gone." Mackenzie's gaze cut to the leaf-strewn ground, then back to Hawk, anger etched on her features. "She was there, and then she wasn't."

"It had to be a transport spell," Hawk nearly growled. "But only one of the Fae can cast a spell like that."

Mackenzie bit her lower lip. "Or a very powerful warlock."

"Godsdamn." Hawk drew his sword. Metal scraped against leather. He turned and bolted through the near darkness, in the direction he thought the meadow was. "Stay with me!"

Behind him Mackenzie's boot steps crunched sticks and leaves. Branches slapped Hawk's face and snagged his clothing like hag claws.

Adrenaline pumped through his body and fury burned him like the fires of the volcano of Otherworld.

Hawk crashed through more underbrush. "We should have been there by now."

"Where's the meadow?" Mackenzie's breathing was heavy as her footsteps crunched leaves and sticks behind him. "I have no idea where we are."

Hawk roared as he ran.

Not one of his brethren answered him.

Something dropped from a tree. Slithered on Hawk's neck. A hiss filled his ear.

"Shit!" Hawk shouted. He passed his sword to the hand of his broken arm, reached up and grabbed the scaly creature. He flung it against a tree while he ran. And then he saw them. Dozens of glittering black eyes. Dozens of snakes draped over branches, hanging from trees. Squirming on the ground.

His heart pounded and his chest seized. That old feeling clenched his body as the memories bombarded him. Of being trapped in a pit of snakes. Of his wife dying by a Basilisk bite.

Snakes. Gods, the snakes!

He would not let them keep him from Silver.

Wouldn't allow them to harm her.

Mackenzie cried out behind him. He saw a golden glow as she zapped some while she ran. "They're everywhere!"

Hawk gripped his sword in his good hand. Hacked his way through the dangling snakes.

Somewhere close by, Silver screamed. A flash of blinding white light followed.

Hawk stopped and shaded his eyes. Mackenzie smacked into his back and caught his shirt in her fists to stabilize herself.

Silver's cry and the light had come from his left. They'd been going the wrong way.

A snake dropped on his neck, but again he flung it away. He wheeled and charged in the direction of Silver's scream, tearing himself from Mackenzie's grip. Her footfalls pounded leaves and earth behind him.

Silver. He had to find her. Where? How? He gripped his weapon so hard his fingers ached. Snakes roiled about his feet as he ran. He trampled them without mercy. Silver!

Hawk doubled his speed. Branches scraped his face. He hacked at the snakes. Flung more away that dropped on his shoulders. Sliced branches. Fear for Silver pushed him faster. His breathing came in sharp gusts.

Strong moonlight up ahead. Beyond the treeline, a grassy meadow.

Hawk tore out of the trees and came up short. A stabbing pain shot through his chest.

Silver lay crumpled on the ground. Unmoving.

Cassia stood beside Silver's body, facing a creature rising up to tower well over Hawk's height. A gigantic snake. No— a Basilisk.

A horrified shout tore from Mackenzie's lips.

Cassia raised her arms and a flash of white light brightened the meadow, so bright it nearly blinded Hawk. Snakes fell from trees, others wiggled, and all crumbled to ash upon the grass.

But her power did nothing to the Basilisk.

"Sssssssooooo ssssssorrry," the creature hissed in a laughing tone as it turned to Hawk. "You are ssssso very late."

Hawk's vision sharpened. His fury and his pain at the thought that Silver could be dead was gut wrenching. He gave the D'Danann cry and charged.

The Basilisk's eyes narrowed. It unhinged its jaws. Coiled. Ready to spring.

Still yelling, Hawk raised his sword. Cut his weapon in a wide arc. Made contact just below the beast's head.

Hawk's sword bounced off the Basilisk's armorlike scales. The force of the rebound threw him back and vibrated through his arm.

He landed on his broken arm. Felt bone shatter again.

Pain nearly blinded him, but he lurched to his feet. Staggered. Sword still in his good hand.

The Basilisk was nearly on him. Fangs glistening in moonlight, dripping with green poison only a Basilisk would possess. Jaws as wide as a cavern. Ready to swallow Hawk whole.

Fury chased away every bit of pain. Every bit of fear.

Hawk charged the beast again. The moment he reached the Basilisk, he drove his sword straight into its mouth. Up into the creature's brain.

A hissing scream shattered the meadow's near tranquility. The scream was both human and inhuman.

Blood spurted from the snake in a fountain of gore. Hawk stumbled back, his sword coming free. Before he had the chance to avoid them, the beast's fangs gnashed and pierced the flesh of his good arm.

Pain—incredible blazing pain—burned his body like a firestorm. *Heat. Gods, the heat!* It was like being branded, molten metal against pliant flesh.

The Basilisk yanked up its head. Blood continued spurting from its mouth. Green poison flowed from fangs covered with Hawk's blood.

With a screeching death cry, the Basilisk crumpled to the meadow floor and faded away.

Hawk's vision began to darken. He stumbled sideways. His sword fell from the hand of what had been his good arm.

And then there was nothing.

Silver stirred. Her chest ached and one of her ribs gave a sickening pop, followed by excruciating pain. Cassia was running her hands over Silver, an eerie yellow glow passing between their bodies.

"Silver! Hawk!" came Mackenzie's anguished cry as she broke through the trees into the meadow, and then she was beside Silver, pushing Cassia away.

"You were in league with that creature who killed Eric, weren't you?" Silver said to Cassia as she forced herself to sit up. Her palms pressed against grass and earth. Her sight went dim again. The pain was almost too much.

Mortimer poked his head from Cassia's pocket and gave an angry chitter, as if chiding Silver.

"Never." Cassia shook her head, her features pale.

Mackenzie knelt before Silver, face tight with fear, eyes beyond worried. "Thank the Ancestors you're alive."

As Mackenzie helped her up, the agony was so intense Silver found it difficult to breathe. Difficult to speak.

Through her haze of pain, Silver's eyes rested on Mackenzie. "Hawk. Where is he?"

"I—" Mackenzie glanced away from Silver. "I don't know if he—he's all right."

Silver turned in the direction Mackenzie was looking and saw Hawk.

Bloody. His body twisted, green pus rolling from two deep punctures in his arm.

Silver blocked thoughts of her own pain from her mind. She lurched to her feet. Stumbled and fell to her hands and knees. Crawled to Hawk. Tears rolled down Silver's face. "No. Please, no."

Mackenzie knelt and touched her hand to Hawk's neck and her eyes were wide. "No pulse."

Cassia murmured, "A Basilisk bite—one of the only things that can kill one of the Fae."

"He's not dead." Silver ripped her gaze to Mackenzie, unreasonably angry with her friend. "He's in there. I know it. He hasn't turned to dust. He's not dead!

"Where are the damned D'Danann?" Silver raised her head and cried out, "Elementals, I know you're here. Help me. Please!"

Silence answered her call. Nothing moved. Nothing made a sound in or outside the meadow.

The gifts of the Elements. The thought sang in Silver's mind like the whisper of wind through trees.

She pushed herself to her haunches. Pain clenched her chest. A few broken ribs, she had no doubt. She bit the inside of her cheek, shoved her hand into her pocket and dug into the charm bag.

Through the warmth of the small flame, she felt the roughness of the emerald against her fingertips.

"For healing," came the Gnome's voice in her mind.

She yanked out the large emerald. Nearly without thought, she pressed it to one of the puncture wounds on

Hawk's arm. The malodor of the green pus, like the scent of death, made her eyes water. She quickly began to chant, "By the power of the Ancestors and the gift of the Earth Elementals, please heal this man. So mote it be."

At once blood stopped flowing from the quarter-sized puncture. Green pus vanished, as if sucked into the emerald. Skin covered the hole, leaving nothing but a thick pink scar. Silver paused from the shock of it. The stone had worked!

"I can hardly believe it." Mackenzie leaned closer. "I've never seen such a deadly wound completely healed like this before."

"Thank the goddess," Cassia whispered.

Hawk stirred. Groaned. Silver hurried to heal the other wound. She chanted as she pressed the emerald against the second fang mark. Again blood stopped flowing, green ooze vanished into the emerald, along with the stench of the poison. Skin healed, leaving another pink scar.

Silver almost cried in relief. She sat back on her haunches and the emerald crumbled in her fist, turning into rich dark dirt that trickled through her fingers. It had served its purpose and returned to the earth.

Hawk opened his eyes as if waking from a long nap. He blinked. Looked from Silver to Mackenzie. Then complete awareness returned to his amber eyes as he narrowed his brows, focusing on Cassia who stood a few feet away.

Hawk pushed himself to a sitting position and he leaned into Silver, his eyes still on Cassia. No matter how welcome Hawk's touch was, she couldn't help the cry that tore from her lips from the agony ripping through her chest.

Hawk moved away from her at once, fury in his expression. "What did the thing do to you?"

"A couple of my ribs. Broken." Silver could hardly get the words out it hurt so much to breathe, much less talk.

His eyes cut from her to Cassia as he pushed himself to his feet, good hand clenched around his sword. "What have you to do with all of this? You had better speak quickly."

Cassia stood her ground and raised her chin. When she spoke, her voice was different, Otherworldly. Even her features changed . . . to Elvin. Beautiful beyond mere mortals. "Moondust sent me to watch over Silver once Copper vanished. She suspected foul play and worried for her remaining daughter."

Silver gave a soft gasp, a sense of the surreal flowing over her skin in small prickles. "Mother? She knew about all of this? I don't believe it."

"That is why I was sent to be your apprentice before serving any other Coven member." Cassia turned to look at what remained of the Basilisk which was now like soot scattered upon the grass. "I was warned of the Basilisk and Fomorii after Copper vanished."

"How?" Hawk demanded.

"The Great Guardian warned me." Cassia turned back to both of them, her expression thoughtful, as if contemplating how much to say.

Hawk's voice was harsh as he said, "How could you have spoken with her?"

Cassia's features became resolute, as if reaching a decision. "I can move between worlds as I wish. I am half Elvin and half human, as your mother is, Silver."

Silver felt as if her head were going to explode. Her mother—half human, half Elvin?

She had no time to contemplate it.

Her attention snapped to the surrounding trees. "They're here."

36

"The Fomorii." Silver forced her words through the pain clenching her chest so badly she thought she was going to collapse. "We're trapped."

Dark shapes shifted from shadows, creeping into the moonlit meadow like black fog. They formed a large circle around Silver, Hawk, Mackenzie, Cassia, and the small pond beside them. The once sweet, clean air grew foul with Fomorii stench.

Silver's heart pounded so hard she thought her chest would split. With her broken ribs, she had to fight for each breath. Each throb, every breath she took, was agony. She had no healing remedies with her, no way to alleviate the pain except to ignore it. She might be a witch, but her bones still needed to be set.

Hawk gripped his sword firmly, his jaw tense as he cut his gaze around the circle of trees while demons crept forward, from out of the underbrush.

Where were the D'Danann? Where was Jake and his team?

Silver swallowed hard as Fomorii in human form walked through the circle of giant demons. They each forced a D'Anu witch to walk in front of them. Witches with hands bound behind their backs. Without the use of their hands they could do nothing. Could perform no magic.

Some witches stumbled, fell to their knees—were dragged by their hair.

The witches looked beyond exhausted. Even beneath the eerie moonlight, Silver could see black shadows darkening their eyes, their matted and frizzled hair, their soiled robes. Many had expressions of having seen terrors beyond imagination.

No doubt they had.

Silver's heart ached for the witches. She sensed several were ready to break at any moment. To give in to the Fomorii demands and become warlocks to summon more of the demons.

Mortimer bounded out of Cassia's pocket and straight toward a gray-haired witch—Janis.

Mackenzie held her hands in front of her, palms facing the advancing Fomorii, a furious look on her features. "Right now would be a real good time for your friends to show up, Hawk."

He searched the treetops with his eyes. "Where in the gods' names are they?"

Silver, Cassia, Mackenzie, and Hawk eased around so that they stood in a minicircle, back to back, while the Fomorii slowly approached, prodding the witches to walk in front of them.

Silver's gut twisted when she saw her parents.

"Mother. Father." She started to step forward, but Hawk held his bloodied sword in front of her like a barrier.

Despite their worn expressions, their battered faces, their neglected appearances, hands tied behind their backs, both Moondust and Victor held their heads high and proud. Mingled with their exhaustion, Silver saw concern, love, and pride for her in their eyes.

Silver wanted to run to her parents, throw her arms around them. Take them away from this horrid mess.

But she could do nothing. *Not yet. But I will. Somehow, some way, I will.*

Soon Hawk, Mackenzie, Cassia, and Silver were surrounded by the captive witches, all backed by Fomorii.

Black-robed warlocks stepped from the shadows.

Goose bumps pricked Silver's skin as she recognized witches and apprentices from her own Coven who had succumbed to the dark side of magic. Not only did Silver's senses tell her they were now Balorite warlocks, but it was in their eyes—something that told her they were now owned by Darkness.

There was no hope for these former witches. They had given in. They had sacrificed their souls, their hearts, and all that was pure and good . . . either for ultimate power, or simply to live.

But what kind of life would it be?

"They've sold their souls to black magic," Silver said aloud, still unable to believe what was right before her eyes.

"And so will you." The Fomorii leader called Junga strolled in human form through the ring of demons, then the circle of witches, then through the warlocks, to stand just feet from the quartet at the center. She wore clothing much like Silver's jeans and top, only she appeared impeccably tailored.

Junga turned her haughty gaze on Hawk. "No doubt you wish to cut me down." She gestured to his sword. "But if you attempt to, you and your precious Silver will die." Junga glanced to Fomorii in human form who stood behind the bound witches. Their firearms were fixed on the four of them standing back to back at the center of the meadow.

"They may not be well trained with these weapons," Junga said with a smirk. "But at least one of them is certain to hit their mark at such close range."

Hawk growled.

Silver swallowed down her panic, and even that hurt her broken ribs. They were completely surrounded. Injured. Her friends and family were held captive. Guns were aimed at her, Hawk, Cassia, and Mackenzie.

Dear Ancestors, please guide me in this time of need, Silver thought. She took a deep breath and winced as her ribs creaked and pain clenched her again.

"Where are the D'Danann?" Silver asked, trying to find some way to give them more time.

Junga cocked an eyebrow. "Interesting, isn't it? Your friends have abandoned you."

"Never." Hawk's golden-amber eyes nearly blazed in the moonlight.

"That shimmer." Mackenzie jerked her head up to look above them. "They have a protective glamour around the meadow."

"A spell," Silver said, "to allow the Fomorii and witches through, but to keep D'Danann out."

Silver's heart nearly stopped as she sensed a push at her mind, a slow burning sensation throughout her body, and an undeniable draw toward the man approaching her.

Darkwolf strolled through the Fomorii, warlocks, and witches to stand just feet from Silver. He was wearing black jeans this time and a black T-shirt, the black stone eye hanging from the chain around his neck. How could someone so evil look so handsome?

"Are you ready to join me?" He gave her that slow seductive smile that pulled at her like the strongest of magnets. "You have touched the dark many times. You enjoy the power. I know you want more."

Silver slowly shook her head. "I will never cross that line."

"You already have." The warlock high priest's deep voice rang through the meadow. "You have killed, Silver Ashcroft. You have taken life in rage, you have taken life for vengeance—and you enjoyed it. That alone makes you one of us."

Tears burned at the back of Silver's eyes and she heard Janis's gasp and Mortimer's chitter of disapproval when Silver didn't argue the point. Before she could stop herself, Silver shouted, "Those Fomorii deserved to die!" Her body shook with the force of her words. "They are nothing but servants of evil!"

The wickedly handsome man smiled and beckoned to her again. "Come to your destiny, Silver."

She gritted her teeth. *"No!"*

The connection between them shivered, then cracked with an almost audible sound.

Darkwolf's eyes grew decidedly less merry. "Do you wish to see your parents remain alive?" His lips pulled back in that much less attractive snarl. "Do you wish to see Copper again?"

She straightened, her heart hammering at the mention of her parents and her sister. "What did you do to Copper? Is she alive?"

The corner of his mouth twitched, whether in mirth or anger, she couldn't tell. "She's someplace . . . safe."

Was he telling the truth? Did he really know where Copper was?

"You have feelings for this one, do you not?" Darkwolf turned to look almost casually at Hawk. "Unacceptable. It will only be you and me, Silver, my love."

Darkwolf raised his hand and clenched his fist tight.

Hawk made a choking sound. Silver's horrified gaze darted to him and saw his face turning purple, his eyes bulging. His grip on his sword loosened.

Anger so intense, so fiery, burned through Silver. Nearly without thought she flung a powerful ball of spellfire at Darkwolf that should have singed his entire body.

It flowed over him like water over stone.

"That's it, Silver," came Darkwolf's alluring voice in her mind. *"Feed your witchcraft with your anger."*

Hawk made a strangled sound and dropped to his knees.

Goddess damn. Spellfire wouldn't work. She reached down and yanked one stiletto dagger from her boot so fast that she barely saw Darkwolf's startled expression. She flung it at his thigh and he roared as the blade pierced his flesh. His eyes blazed with black fire.

Despite the dagger still lodged in his thigh and blood pouring down his leg, he used his black magic to tighten his grip on Hawk's throat.

Silver felt a sudden stirring in her pocket. As if something were trying to get out. She jammed her hand into her pocket as fast as she could.

The feather shot to Silver's hand as if the Faerie who had given it were guiding it straight to her grasp.

Silver brought her hand from her pocket and opened it. The feather rested on her palm. It was a perfect feather, sleek and blue-black in the moonlight.

"Are you going to tickle me to death?" Darkwolf gave a soft laugh as he clenched his fist tighter.

Hawk's face had turned a dark shade of red.

Silver moved her lips in a quick chant.

> *"Feather of Air, feather so light,*
> *Please release the sky this night."*

The feather rose, as if caught in a strong breeze, gliding higher and higher.

Everyone in the circle tipped their heads back to watch the quick spiraling movement of the feather, which zoomed to the sky as if pulled by an invisible thread. All stood transfixed, mesmerized, as if held tight in some magical binding.

Even Darkwolf was caught in the Fae magic and his hold on Hawk lessened.

Hawk wheezed, drawing in breath.

Before anyone had time to react, the feather brushed the overhead shimmer. An explosion of sparks spattered the black sky.

The meadow that had once been eerily devoid of normal sound filled with the sleepy, muffled chirps of birds, frenetic cricket song, and the distant blare of traffic.

D'Danann shouts cut through the air. The night erupted with the whump of powerful wings. Dark forms appeared overhead.

Silver saw moonlight glint on the muzzles of PSF officers' guns peeking through the trees, surrounding them.

Demons snarled. Witches screamed as the Fomorii in human form forced the D'Anu to their knees, guns to their heads.

Hawk took a gasping breath, roared, then dove for Darkwolf. His good hand grabbed the stiletto buried in the warlock's thigh and yanked down on it.

With a blast of black fire, Darkwolf slammed his power into Hawk's chest, knocking him and the dagger back several feet.

Darkwolf looked casually at Silver, as if nothing that had happened mattered. As if his flesh weren't torn, as if blood weren't pouring down his thigh.

"Hold!" Hawk ordered his comrades and the PSF, raising his hand from where he had landed. The D'Danann circled the meadow with angry cries, then settled in the trees surrounding the clearing. Watching. Waiting.

A bit of relief eased some of the fear within Silver. The D'Danann and the PSF were here! But they were in no way out of the mess. Not by a very long shot.

Junga scowled as her gaze narrowed on Silver. "If you wish for the witches to live, then you will cooperate."

"She will," Darkwolf said in a soft, mesmerizing tone.

Silver shuddered and fought off the warlock's hold. "Fuck you."

"Exactly my plan," he said and smiled. "Here, now, for everyone to see."

Hawk pushed himself to his feet with a roar of fury and started to lunge at Darkwolf again. The warlock simply held up his hand and Hawk slammed into a shimmering purple shield.

Hawk stumbled back, barely keeping to his feet.

"Ask Mommy and Daddy what I will do with the rest of the witches without your cooperation." Junga ignored Hawk and Darkwolf. She tossed a look over her shoulder at Victor and Moondust, then looked back to Silver and smiled wickedly. "They have already seen how much I enjoy a delicious meal of D'Anu."

Ice crept over Silver's skin when her eyes met her parents'.

She read the truth in their gazes.

"You see," Junga said with a little tilt of her head. "Many of your witches are not worth a fraction of what you and your parents are, especially with you so willing to embrace the gray." She tossed a look over her shoulder before turning back to Silver. "And *Mother* no doubt can tell you just how close she walks the line between black and white with you."

Silver fought to think clearly. The comment that Cassia had made earlier about her mother being part Elvin—one of the neutrally aligned races—could that be true? If it was, then it would explain how Silver could wield gray magic so easily. In her studies with the old witch Mrs. Illes, Silver had learned about various Elvin clans and their ability to wield gray magic with little consequence. Their very nature was gray.

"The weaklings," Junga was saying, breaking into Silver's thoughts, "who have little power—we will simply eat them one at a time until you agree."

Silver shook so hard her ribs creaked again, but she welcomed the pain, held on to it tight to remind her what was at stake. Lives of witches she cared for. Had known for years.

"You wouldn't." Silver looked around the circle of witches, then back to Junga. "You need them, too."

Junga smiled. "No longer. We have twelve warlocks here now, thanks to those D'Anu who turned to black witchcraft. You will be thirteen."

A witch screamed. Silver's heart pounded as the tall brown-haired witch named Mary stumbled to her knees, then fell, her face shoved into earth and grass. An enormous white Fomorii planted claws on the witch's shoulders and legs, and stared at Silver, thick hide shivering with obvious delight.

"The queen is apparently hungry," Junga said in a droll tone with a glance at the white demon.

"No." Silver shook her head, terror clawing its way up her throat. "Don't!"

The demon roared and sank its teeth into the witch's neck.

Mary screamed. Blood flowed. The Fomorii jerked its head up, a mouthful of flesh hanging from its jaws.

Bile rose in Silver's throat. "No. No. *No!*"

The witch screamed again and thrashed. The queen flipped Mary over and ripped out her throat. The witch gurgled as blood poured from the wound. Her sightless eyes rolled back and stared at Silver.

Mackenzie cried out as if in pain.

Silver's gut heaved. She threw up, spewing her dinner all over Junga.

The Fomorii woman growled as vomit rolled down her blouse. She slapped Silver with such power she sent her sprawling onto the grass beside the pond. Silver hit the ground so hard one of her ribs popped. Pain screeched through her.

Silver's head spun as she held her hand to her chest and tried to stand. She couldn't. She was in so much pain her legs and arms refused to work.

Hawk gave a cry and raised his sword to strike at Junga. At once he was surrounded by Fomorii, who blocked him from the demon.

Love for Hawk helped Silver push through the pain.

The song of the Undines threaded through Silver's mind, banishing all other thoughts. She slipped her hand into her pocket and yanked out the water-smoothed hag stone. She quickly chanted,

> *"Stone from Water, stop those who wish ill.*
> *Set all witches free, hold all evil still."*

She flung the stone into the pond.

Water exploded.

Like a meteor smashing into the ocean and shooting tidal waves in all directions.

More water than should have been in that small pond.

Water slammed into the Fomorii and the warlocks. Knocked them backward and toward the trees.

Magically it missed all of the witches and Hawk. As if protective air-filled bubbles surrounded each of them.

It missed Darkwolf and Junga, too. A purple shimmer surrounded the pair.

When the water subsided, the air filled with D'Danann

shouts. Hawk and Mackenzie helped Silver to her feet. Fomorii scattered across the meadow struggled to get up.

The D'Danann swooped and sliced the bonds of the witches with their talons as the Fomorii staggered and fought to regain themselves. When they finished unbinding the witches, the D'Danann began rounding up the stunned demons.

"Surround the Fomorii and join hands!" Silver ordered the witches. She knew they were likely weak, maybe numb from being bound so long. But they had no choices now.

Silver glanced to the sky. By the position of the moon it was almost the mid of night, the witching hour, the time when the veil between worlds would thin to nearly nothing.

Silver's gaze cut to the Fomorii queen.

The queen pushed herself to her feet, all four paws showing she was ready to spring at Silver.

But with a quick whirl of her massive body, she shrieked and slammed into Moondust instead.

Silver screamed. "No!"

The queen cast a glance at Silver, wicked eyes narrowed. She lowered her head. Jaws wide. Dripping with saliva.

Everything else ceased to exist. Silver saw red. The largest spellfire ball she'd ever made hissed and sparked between her hands. So dark this time it *was* black.

She reared back to fling it at the bitch, feeling nothing but cold, dank hatred.

The hatred was all-encompassing. Power beyond power filled her.

"Yes," came Darkwolf's sensuous voice in her mind, and she could see the brilliant red eye glowing around his neck in her mind. *"Use your anger. Kill the bitch."*

Silver felt the darkness swirl within her. Felt the call. The power. The ability to make right what was wrong. Yes, that's what she would do.

She raised her arm to fling the ball of death at the Fomorii.

Moondust shouted, bracing her hands against the demon's chest. "Don't cross the line!"

Silver aimed. Moondust's cry barely registered in her ears. She would kill the Fomorii bitch and send her to oblivion.

She could picture it. Could see herself eliminating the demon with one blow of the spellfire. She'd done it before. She could do it now.

This time, though, the magic that coursed her body was black. So very black. She knew without question that if she used the power, she'd never be able to give it up.

"Don't cross the line," flooded through Silver's mind as she struggled with herself. *"There's no turning back once you surrender to black magic."*

She gazed into her mother's eyes.

Tears began streaming down Silver's face.

No. She wouldn't—couldn't—turn to black magic.

The power of the ball faded in her hands to that of spellfire that could merely send the Fomorii flying.

Relief filled Moondust's gaze and her body relaxed beneath the demon.

Instead of the death Silver had almost delivered to the queen, she flung a brutal spellfire, just enough to knock the demon off her mother. Not a killing fire, no. But one filled with power.

It slammed into the demon, flowed around the Fomorii, encasing it in purplish-blue fire.

Instead of sending the queen flying it only caused the huge beast to shudder, to stumble back.

Shouting out her fury, Silver readied another ball, greater this time. One that had to knock the queen across the meadow.

The beast shook her great hide. She growled. At the same moment Silver flung the spellfire, the queen pounced again on Moondust and dug her iron-tipped claws into Moondust's chest. The spellfire slammed into the queen. Her claws shredded flesh from Moondust's chest as the Fomorii's body was knocked across the clearing, plowing down other demons like bowling pins.

But she had left a gaping hole in Moondust's chest. A hole that was burning a deep black trench as if from contact with the iron.

"No!" Silver screamed.

Blood spurted. Victor cried out and Silver screamed again.

Tears flooded Silver's eyes as she flung another ball of spellfire at the queen. The fireball knocked her from her feet again and slammed her great body into a massive tree trunk.

Hawk charged toward the demon, sword drawn in his weaker hand. Before the queen had time to rise, Hawk drove his sword into her neck.

She roared and jerked away from the blade. Hawk gritted his teeth, putting all his power into his next swing.

He was flung back with the force of the impact against her tough hide.

Hawk scrambled to his feet, but before he or the queen could move, a huge blue Fomorii rammed into the queen, driving her to the ground.

The pair rolled and fought. Fangs gnashed. Claws ripped flesh. Growls roared through the night.

Hawk clenched his sword at the same time he glanced around the meadow to see everyone else guarded and still as stone.

Only Darkwolf looked unconcerned, as if certain all was not lost.

Junga fought the queen with everything she had. The fucking bitch! She'd had it with all the queen had done to her. She'd show the rest of the Fomorii who should rule.

Kanji sank her large teeth into Junga's shoulder and she screeched her rage and pain. She flipped the queen off her, felt flesh tear.

Junga threw the queen onto her back and planted her paws on Kanji's chest. Without pause, Junga jammed her powerful claws into Kanji's rib cage, through the thick hide, through flesh, bone, sinew, and wrapped her claws around the queen's heart.

Kanji clawed at Junga's face, but with a feeling of triumph, Junga yanked the queen's heart out and held it high for all to see.

The queen stared in horror at her still-beating heart, and her body began to thrash as Junga lowered the heart to her mouth and chewed it between her powerful jaws.

Stunned silence reigned in the clearing as the queen's body crumbled into black dirt.

"I am queen!" Junga roared in the language of her people.

Before anyone could react, she bolted into the woods. Gunfire followed in her wake. She felt bullets riddle her hide, but they fell out as her body quickly healed. Triumph filled her at the taste of the queen's heart in her mouth. The bitch was dead! Junga was queen!

She heard pounding footsteps in the brush behind her. The heat of something loud and powerful grazed her head. She leaped into the air and bounded through the trees, her great strength allowing her to outdistance her pursuers.

And then she was free.

37

Silver and Victor had both gone to Moondust, and were holding her. Both sobbed and Victor was doing his best to heal his wife, but the wound was too serious. Nothing could be done for her, no matter what magic they attempted. The iron was eating her heart.

Around them Silver heard the sounds of battle, but she didn't care about anything except her mother.

Moondust's words rose in a bubbling gasp as she spoke. "Victor, Silver's right. Gray magic was needed—*is* needed—to save our people."

"No." Silver shook her head. "*He* was right. I should never have used it."

Moondust gave a weak smile. "Victor, you will explain."

He nodded. "Yes, my love."

Silver crumpled against her father as he rocked Moondust tight to his chest. "Please don't die," Silver cried. "I love you. Please don't die."

"I love you, too, my sweet one." Moondust reached out a cold hand and squeezed Silver's arm.

Her gaze turned to Victor. "You have always been the witch of my dreams," she said in halting words.

Tears rolled down his face. A droplet trickled onto her forehead as he bent to press his lips to her temple. "Travel well, my heart. I will meet you in Summerland."

Moondust gave a weak nod and her expression was serene. "In Summerland, my love."

Her eyelids drifted closed. In moments Silver sensed her mother's spirit leaving, slipping away to wait for her family on another plane.

And then she was gone. Like the D'Danann, her body sparkled, but more of a crystal white.

Moondust's body disappeared.

Silver stared in complete shock for a moment. Her mother's body had *vanished*. It was all true. By the goddess, her mother was part Elvin.

With a sob Silver embraced her father. For what seemed moments on end, Silver and Victor clung to each other, unable to let go.

Before Silver had the chance to truly grieve for her mother, a strong hand gripped her shoulder and she was yanked to her feet.

The motion sent her spinning around to face Darkwolf.

The warlock's grip was hot and the fire of lust raged in his eyes. She'd never been this close to him, just inches away, and the power he exuded was almost more than she could fight. His scent was of sandalwood, and from the stone on the chain around his neck she caught the smell of aged rock and earth. And evil . . . powerful and dark.

Silver gritted her teeth and jerked her arm hard, trying to escape his grasp. His fingers dug into her skin and she flinched from the pain of it. A shimmering spellshield surrounded them, blocking her and Darkwolf from all that was happening in the meadow.

PSF officers blew holes the size of cannonballs through Fomorii with the incredible fire power they had brought with them, but the demons couldn't be killed unless their hearts were hit dead-on, or their heads exploded or were severed from their necks.

D'Danann fought demons with daggers, swords, and other weapons. Many of the Fomorii fled with D'Danann and PSF officers chasing them through the wooded area.

Hawk moved up to Silver and Darkwolf. Fury creased his

features and his amber eyes glowed with such anger as Silver had never seen in him before. "Release Silver," Hawk growled as he dropped his sword and drew his dagger. "Now."

Darkwolf simply smiled. "Attack if you will, D'Danann bastard. But know that Silver Ashcroft is mine."

Hawk roared and drove his dagger straight at the heart of the warlock. His weapon came in contact with the spellshield. When his dagger bounced off the force field, the strength of his own attack drove him backward to land on his ass.

"This is my fight, Hawk." Silver turned her glare on the warlock who had her in his grasp. Her heart pounded and her eyes still ached with tears for Moondust, but more than anything she felt fury at this man who had ultimately caused the death of her mother.

Pain shot through her broken ribs as she brought her knee up to jam him in the groin. But what she was really doing was going for the second dagger from her boot sheath. Darkwolf blocked her knee, but his eyes narrowed as the point of the stiletto whipped up and met his belly.

"I should gut you." Silver pressed the point of the dagger harder into his taut stomach. Her gaze never flinched from his, and the sight of his smile made her push harder. "You fucking bastard."

"But you won't," he said so softly that it startled her. "You would never hurt me."

"The hell I wouldn't—" she started just as his eyes grew darker, his gaze mesmerizing her. And then she was melting, softening like clay.

With one hand he wrapped his palm around the hilt of the dagger pressed to his stomach and flung it to the grass at their feet. He reached up and pushed his other hand into her silken hair and let the strands slip through his fingers. *"I have dreamed of touching you since the first vision I had of you,"* he whispered in her mind. *"I will slide between your beautiful thighs and fuck you until you scream my name."*

The shiver that ran through Silver at his touch both aroused her and infuriated her.

He's using magic to make me feel this way. Fight, Silver. Fight!

Trying to shake herself from his mental grasp, she imagined steel doors slamming down, one after another in her mind. Her body trembled and sweat beaded on her upper lip from the force of her effort. He was so strong. So strong!

When his expression of lust shifted to anger, Silver felt a break in his hold on her. He grabbed a handful of her hair and jerked her up against him, the pain in her chest bringing more tears to her eyes. But she had power now. She could feel her witchcraft blossoming again within her.

Keeping her mind shielded from his, she clenched one hand. With all her anger at everything this warlock had caused, she slammed her fist into Darkwolf's eye.

Her knuckles connected with bone and flesh, and pain shot through her hand. But it was nothing compared to the pleasure she felt as he cried out in obvious surprise and pain.

He stumbled back a step, releasing her just that fraction of a moment she needed to move away. Her body hit the spellshield behind her, but her hands were up and already a crackling ball of energy grew between her palms.

Darkwolf dropped his hand from his eye, and no emotion could be read on his features. "You can't hurt me, Silver. You won't."

"Wanna bet?" she said the moment she released the spellfire.

The power in her magic slammed Darkwolf up against the wall of his own force field.

The spellshield's shimmer wavered.

Silver never paused. The second she released the first spellfire she prepared another. This one she flung above her, slamming it into the force field.

The shield dropped.

Hawk raised his dagger and charged.

For just that moment, when everything seemed to happen in slow motion, Silver saw Darkwolf smile at her.

He broke through her mental barriers. *"I'm not finished with you."*

And then he was gone.

Vanished.

Hawk stumbled forward with the momentum of his attack. When his dagger struck nothing but air, he whirled, prepared to fight, but nothing was there.

Slowly Silver and Hawk looked at the carnage around them. Piles of dirt were scattered across the meadow. Two PSF officers lay sprawled upon the grass, blood pouring from their bodies.

Silver had no idea how many Fomorii had escaped, but the few that remained were guarded well, and stood within a ring of witches. The Fomorii growled and threatened to advance, but the presence of the D'Danann and the PSF officers with cannon guns held them back.

Mortimer was perched on Janis's shoulder, and they both looked at Silver with unfathomable expressions. Silver knew that despite the outcome, because of the force she'd used with her gray magic, she was in deep shit. Just how deep, she didn't know.

Mackenzie and Cassia approached Silver and Hawk and took them each by the hand.

"It's time." Mackenzie brushed tears from Silver's cheeks with her fingers. "Time to send the remaining beasts back to where they came from."

Silver swallowed hard at the realization that both Junga and Darkwolf had escaped.

And the Balorite warlocks—what had happened to them? Had they escaped the water? Or had they the power to vanish as Darkwolf had?

"Such a tantalizing power that would be," purred Darkwolf's voice in her mind. Goddess, he was near, but there was nothing she could do about him now.

Silver didn't have time to ponder it any longer. They had to send back the remaining Fomorii to Underworld. She glanced at her father. Victor nodded and Silver took a deep breath.

Victor entered the circle of witches surrounding the beasts, and joined hands with Mackenzie. Janis Arrowsmith with Mortimer on her shoulder was gripping John Steed's and another witch's hands as she joined the circle. Her eyes were cold. Hard. Condemning. Within moments the witches made a complete circle around the remaining demons.

Barely able to think through her anger and her grief, Silver clenched Cassia's and Mackenzie's hands as the D'Danann and PSF officers waited behind them. She felt the power of the witches joining, building. The very air vibrated with it. Electricity crackled through the air and Silver's hair rose on her scalp. Power built within her, a different power from any she'd felt before.

Silver struggled to concentrate. Felt warmth in her pocket. She released Cassia's hand long enough to fish out the tiny red flame from the dragon and slowly set it on the grass in front of her and Cassia.

The flame grew brighter and brighter, taller and fiercer. Yet Silver felt no real heat, just gentle warmth. The flame spread around the circle of witches, surrounding the Fomorii.

Silver began the chant.

> *"Blessed Ancestors, send these beasts away.*
> *Please help us save all that is good this day.*
> *Help us banish this evil times three.*
> *Please help us now. So mote it be."*

The fire engulfed the Fomorii. Electricity snapped and zipped along their skin, the red glow encasing each one of them. It went no further than the demons. Did not touch the witches.

Silver repeated the chant, her voice growing louder and louder. The fire growing higher and higher. The intensity becoming almost too much to bear.

It was if the Samhain moon reached out to them. Its light poured down from the sky. Blended with the fire. Touched each of the Fomorii.

The bodies of the demon-beasts shimmered.

Became faint.
Then stronger again.
Angry snarls echoed through the night.
Quieted.
The beasts vanished.

38

Silver could hardly face the truth as Hawk moved through the circle of witches and stopped to take her hands in his.

He didn't smile. Only looked at her with those intense amber eyes.

It was time.

The other D'Danann were staying to search for the rest of the Fomorii, but Hawk was leaving to face the Chieftains and to be with his daughter.

Her heart couldn't believe he was leaving. She felt something so intense for him that her chest ached with it.

Could it be love? So soon? So strong?

The fire settled at the center of the witches, dancing and flickering. Silver felt a throb to the air, a pulsing as if the fire were waiting.

Hawk squeezed both her hands within his as he braced his forehead against hers. "Please come with me."

"What?" Silver drew away and could only stare at him in complete shock. "You're asking me to go to Otherworld with you?"

He stroked her cheekbone with his knuckles. "I care for you. I need you."

The fact that he had asked her was incredible. Crazy. And at this moment when her life was completely in tatters. It would be so easy to escape with him. To leave all this behind.

Magic of a different kind had truly invaded her heart. At that moment she knew she *did* love him in a very special way. There was no doubt in her mind. But leave with him?

"Do you love me?" The question came out before she could stop herself. "Could you love me?"

Hawk's look hardened. "I loved my wife. I cannot love another."

Tears burned at the back of Silver's eyes, but she refused to cry. How could she have expected him to feel the same way?

"You have your answer then." She released him and moved away from his hold, stepping far beyond his reach. "I can't live with a man who could never give me his heart as well as his body and soul. I can't and I won't."

Pain flashed across Hawk's face, then his features turned to stone once more. He gave a stiff nod.

Silver trembled but she glanced to the moon and saw its light pouring down upon the meadow. The harvest moon focused on Hawk like a gentle spotlight.

"Come with me." He drew her attention back to him. "I can't imagine life without you."

One tear escaped and Silver ignored it, allowing it to trickle down her face and to her jaw. She backed farther away and took Cassia's and Mackenzie's hands in hers again. Witches all joined hands. They circled Hawk and the magical fire moved to surround his feet, then flicker up higher and higher so that she could only see his face in flashes.

Silver's voice rang clear as she spoke,

> *"Ancestors, send Hawk this eve,*
> *To be with his daughter, his love and joy,*
> *To be judged as brave and true,*
> *It is your help, dear Ancestors, we wish to employ,*
> *To send Hawk to Otherworld. This we ask of you."*

Silver's heart beat like crazy and tears flowed freely down her cheeks. Surprise coursed through her as the amber at the center of her pentagram glowed. A matching glow answered from Hawk's pentagram, connecting them with a steady stream of amber light through the fire.

His gaze held hers as the fire around him grew thicker, danced higher. She felt as if the fire rising between them were cutting her in two.

His form wavered.

Flickered.

He was gone.

November 8

39

A week after Samhain, Silver stood at the center of the remaining D'Anu witches and apprentices, in the once sacred chamber. The hole in the earth had been refilled, and almost all signs of the Fomorii attack were gone from the room. Yet it would never be the same.

Her father had returned home, too heartbroken over Moondust's loss to stay. Cassia had left for Otherworld. The D'Danann had remained in the city to seek out Junga, Darkwolf, and the rest of the Fomorii.

With every labored breath she took, pain lanced Silver's bandaged chest. She was healing faster than a nonwitch would, but broken bones took longer to mend.

She wore her white ceremonial robe, and held her head high. Her amber and silver pendant felt warm against her throat, and her snake bracelet almost seemed to move in the wavering candlelight, flicking its tongue at the high priestess.

The surviving D'Anu witches ringed her. Witches with judgment in their eyes and her future in their hands.

Silver felt Mackenzie's presence directly behind her, supporting her. Mackenzie's anger was a palpable thing. It had been all Silver could do to convince Mackenzie, along with her other friends, to not intervene, no matter the outcome of this meeting.

The air was stifling as Janis Arrowsmith's icy gaze pinned

Silver. "You broke Coven law after Coven law. You disobeyed a direct commandment and summoned beings from Otherworld." She leaned forward on her dais, her eyes becoming even colder. Her next words were punctuated like a hammer driving a nail into Silver's chest. "You crossed the line, Silver Ashcroft. You used the worst of gray magic. You murdered other beings."

Silver's emotions were so raw at that moment, she wanted to scream at the high priestess. If not for her and her friends, they would all be dead. The city overrun by Fomorii. What was wrong with the Coven?

Yet Janis was right. Silver had killed Fomorii and felt no remorse.

What did that make her?

Janis leaned back in her chair. "What do you have to say, Silver?"

Silver's throat was so dry she didn't think she could speak. Her voice creaked as she finally spoke. "I did what I thought was right."

Janis's voice remained at a steady condemning tone. "The use of such horrible gray magic upsets the balance of all that is good, all that is right. The D'Anu would rather perish than become so weak as to use gray magic. Than to kill, demon or no."

Except for the few who chose the dark over the light to save themselves. But that thought remained unspoken. The witches' names would never be uttered in this chamber again.

"I tried to save you." Silver hated the plea in her voice as she looked from one witch to another. Confusion flickered in the eyes of some. John's, Iris's, and others' remained stolid. "And those beasts—the city would be overrun with them."

When she looked back to Janis she saw the unwavering condemnation in the high priestess's eyes.

Silver could not utter another word. Her lips trembled but her throat refused to work.

"It is my judgment," Janis began in a slow, measured tone. Calm even. "That you, Silver Ashcroft, be stripped of your status as D'Anu and banished forevermore. You will no longer be responsible for the Coven's store, and you will no longer live in the apartment above."

The words slammed Silver like a blow to her already aching ribs. She felt Mackenzie behind her, sensed that her friend wanted to shout at the high priestess, but Silver held up a hand meant to halt all of her friends. What few she had. She had already explained they were needed in the Coven, that the fight with the Fomorii wasn't over yet. If they were banished, too, the Coven would be that much weaker for it.

"You may leave our presence now." Janis waved her fingers toward the ancient stone staircase. "Find what peace you may."

Tears were already blinding Silver as she moved through the crowd of witches that parted for her like a small sea. Each step she took away from the Coven was like an arrow piercing her heart.

She was no longer D'Anu. She had lost almost everything. Her Coven, her mother, her sister. Her store. Her home.

Hawk.

The pain in her chest was now almost too much to bear.

When she reached the exit from the Coven meeting hall, Silver grabbed her backpack and keys from the desk beside the stairwell, and walked away from everything that had ever mattered to her.

November 14

40

Salem, Massachusetts

With a heavy sigh, Victor picked up a photograph of their family that had once been four, and clenched it in his large hand.

Tears formed in the corners of Silver's eyes. It was two weeks after Samhain and the loss of Moondust. Goddess, how she missed her mother. And her sister . . . what had Darkwolf meant when he had said she was someplace secure? Did he truly know where Copper was?

Polaris curled around Silver's feet as she shifted on the leather chair in Victor's library. The room smelled of cherry pipe tobacco and the thousands of books the enormous room held. The scent of leather made her think of Hawk and that familiar ache stabbed her again.

At one time the library had been a room she and her sister had never been allowed into when they were children, unless they were in trouble. Like the time Silver had accidentally spelled their pet hamster. The poor thing hadn't looked at his cage in quite the same way after that incident.

Silver had spent the week with her father at their home in Salem, Massachusetts, since her mother had died, since Silver had lost everything. Every time she looked into her father's eyes his pain doubled her own. Often she wondered if her mother's death had been the result of Silver's tampering with gray magic. Had this been what the universe had wrought on her, threefold?

How could the universe be so cruel?

But the goddess and the Ancestors. Even the Elementals. They answered my pleas. How could what she'd done been wrong? Perhaps the D'Anu had grown away from the original teachings of the Ancient Druids. Perhaps she hadn't been wrong. She sighed. *Someday, the D'Anu are going to have to reexamine all of these ancient beliefs. Just because they're old and traditional doesn't make them right. The world is a grayer place now.*

But would her mother still be alive if Silver hadn't tapped such powerful magic?

Polaris slunk onto the seat beside her as she bit her lower lip and stared at the family picture her father held. Her chest ached and squeezed so much it almost felt as if her ribs hadn't healed.

It was a picture taken only a couple of years ago, when they had spent three weeks together in Ireland. They stood before one of the ancient castles, a happy if not unusual family. Copper with her laughing cinnamon eyes, mischievous smile, and shoulder-length hair the same color as her name. Silver with her head tilted to the side, her hand to the pendant at her throat and her serpent bracelet shining in what sunlight there had been. Victor standing behind his three women, his head high and a fierce and proud look to his eyes. And then there was Moondust with her ethereal glow . . . which Silver could now see was from Elvin blood.

Victor cleared his throat as he set the photograph back on the bookcase. "There's much I've been putting off telling you, Silver."

She started and looked from the photograph to her father's face. "We had a good time on that trip."

"The last trip before . . ." Victor cleared his throat again. "Before your sister disappeared, and your mother . . ."

Silver stood and went to her father and wrapped her arms around his neck. His familiar scent of cherry pipe tobacco clung to his woolen suit, and she could smell his spicy aftershave, bringing back more childhood memories.

"I'm so sorry about Mother." Silver's tears ran freely now. "If I hadn't—"

Victor took her by the shoulders so abruptly that he caught her by surprise. "None of this was your fault. You did what you thought was best, and damn the Coven's blind eyes, but you saved a lot of witches, a lot of people." He gently rubbed her shoulders. "I'm proud of you, Silver, and nothing will change that."

She swallowed, not knowing what to say, but the tears wouldn't stop.

"Now for what I've been putting off." From the massive mahogany desk in the library, Victor grabbed a box of tissue. He handed it to Silver and she clutched the box to her chest with one hand while using the other to dab at her eyes with a tissue. "Sit down, my sweet."

Silver dropped into her chair, her stomach clenching as she set the box beside her. She sniffed, trying to hold back more tears.

Victor put his hands behind his back and began pacing the deep burgundy carpet from one side of the library to the next. "It was my fault. I should have told you sooner." Silver started to say something, but her father stopped her with a raised hand. "Perhaps it is clichéd, but I fell for her the moment I saw her."

No, not clichéd at all. Silver's heart stuttered. She had fallen for Hawk in such a short time, as well.

He paused and cleared his throat yet again, but didn't stop pacing. "When I discovered she was half Elvin, I was so concerned that it would affect you and your sister in being accepted by the D'Anu that I deemed it best to keep it secret." He sighed. "Your mother, gracious as always, agreed.

"When I learned you were practicing gray magic—" At this his face darkened and Silver clenched the tissue in her lap. "I was upset because of my beliefs, but also because I realized that by your being part Elvin, a more neutral alignment is literally in your blood—so you were at more risk."

He stopped and slammed his fist on the mahogany desk so hard that Silver jumped in her seat. "The Ancestors wouldn't have stood for this." His face turned a darker shade. "Your being banished from the Coven, stripped of your status—unforgivable. I ought to wring Janis Arrow-smith's neck myself."

Polaris hissed as if in agreement.

Silver almost slid right out of her seat. In the week she'd been staying with him, he'd never said anything like that.

Victor turned his glare on his robe hanging from a coat rack in one corner of the library. The robe that signified his status as high priest of his Coven. "I'm considering leaving the D'Anu."

She shot straight up to her feet, knocking the tissue box to the carpeted floor with a thud. "You can't do that. With the San Francisco Coven torn and broken, they need you more than ever to keep the natural balance."

He fixed his gaze on her and Silver's cheeks heated. She felt like a little girl all over again, but it didn't stop her from saying, "The San Francisco Coven will be rebuilt with the Adept apprentices being sent from around the country. They will be fine. But your Coven needs you more than anything."

"Sit," her father ordered.

Silver gulped and dropped to the burgundy leather chair again.

"Your power has grown. I can sense it emanating from you." He put his hands behind his back and looked up at the library ceiling. Silver almost stared at it, too, but kept her eyes on her father. She was too stunned at what he was saying to really know how to respond.

"This could be the Ancestors blessing your intentions, in-dicating that you're right," he continued. "Or perhaps it's be-cause you're part Elvin."

Silver still couldn't get used to knowing that she was part of a race so old and powerful that she could barely compre-hend it. "How old was Mother?" she asked.

Victor rubbed the bridge of his nose with his thumb and forefinger. "So hard to keep track . . . I believe she was over eight hundred years old when she passed on to Summerland."

Silver's eyes widened. "So she was—"

He waved his hand and nodded. "Many years older than myself. D'Anu witches, as you know, do not have as long of a life span. But we live far longer than humans do. I was a mere child in comparison." A smile managed to touch his lips. "She kept me grounded."

Silver didn't know what to say so she just waited for her father to continue.

Victor hitched up the pant legs of his suit as he placed his bulk in the seat next to Silver, then took her hands. "Copper is out there somewhere. I scried and saw only that she is lost and needs to find her way home."

"She's alive?" Silver clenched her father's hands tighter. "I need to find her, at once!"

Polaris raised up, his eyes focused on Victor.

Her father shook his head. "As I said, Copper needs to find her own way home." His dark eyes fixed intently on Silver's. "As you need to find yours."

November 21

41

San Francisco

Silver had made her way back to the City by the Bay. She had planned to spend more time with her father, but she'd felt the call so fiercely to come to the city to aid the D'Danann that she had driven across the country in her beat-up little VW in just a matter of days.

The first thing she did was go to the beach where she'd practiced rituals so many times before. She hadn't stopped to see any of her friends. No one. She wasn't ready, not yet. She wasn't even sure whether she'd be welcome. Numb from more than mere cold, Silver sat with her arms around her knees in the small cove where she had first called upon the D'Danann—and Hawk had come. Just the thought of him made her ache all over again.

She'd left Polaris snuggled in a big blanket in the car, not even wanting her familiar for company. No, she needed to be alone.

The waning moon was rising, and what light could filter through the foggy night caressed Silver, as if to offer her some comfort. The briny smell of the ocean, the feel of sand beneath her booted feet, and the sound of waves slapping the shore was reassuring. At least some things remained the same.

These past few weeks, she'd replayed over and over in her mind all that had happened, and couldn't come to the conclusion that she would have done anything differently. She had set out to do what she believed to be right, and had helped to stop an invasion of demons that would have overrun the city. Now, as far as she knew, relatively few remained.

And those demons needed to be sought out and sent back to Underworld.

Silver's jaw tightened in determination. She had lost everything, everything but her magic, her sense of justice, and her ability to make at least some things right.

She was back, and she would help with the battle, with or without the force of the D'Anu behind her. She'd found her way home. She was now a solo practitioner, but she was home.

A chill rolled through her. *But Darkwolf is here, too. What if he seeks me out again? What if this time I can't fight him?*

Her jacket fluttered in the breeze and sand shifted beneath her feet as she hugged her knees tighter. She pushed away those thoughts and at least some of the melancholy gripping her as best she could, but she couldn't help the ache in her heart for all she had lost.

Her mother. Her sister. Her Coven. Her store.

The man she had fallen in love with.

A cold, cold tear rolled down her cheek, but it dried from the even colder breeze. She was a witch, able to withstand varying temperatures, but right now she wouldn't be surprised if that failed her, too, no matter that her father believed her magic was stronger than ever.

Whump. Whump. The sound jolted her from her thoughts. *Whump.*

Wings. Big wings.

She couldn't move, but didn't dare to hope.

A break in the fog revealed a being flying toward her. Could it be one of the D'Danann who had stayed to help find the rest of the Fomorii?

Could it be Hawk?

Silver's heart raced as the being came closer. When she recognized the brilliant blue wings of Sher, that heart dropped right into the pit of her stomach.

Sher landed easily on the sand, her booted feet barely making an indentation. Her wheat-blond hair swung at her shoulders and her smile met her blue eyes. "Mackenzie's tarot cards told me I'd find you here."

Silver tried to smile back, but faltered. "How is everyone?"

The D'Danann warrior folded away her wings and settled on the sand beside Silver. She smelled of clear night sky and jasmine. Her blue eyes looked dark and thoughtful. "Much has happened since you have been gone. More of the San Francisco D'Anu Coven fractured."

Silver's eyes widened. "But who? Why? What about the balance between Covens?"

With a slight shrug, Sher said, "There were enough apprentices in the other twelve Covens ready to step forward. The Coven will be fine." She started to create a design in the sand with her fingertip. "Mackenzie, Hannah, Sydney, Alyssa, Cassia, and Rhiannon all left the Coven. They believed too strongly that you were right and the rest of the D'Anu were wrong. They think that gray magic is needed to rid this city of the Fomorii. They have started a new Coven. With you it will be seven."

Seven. A good number.

Silver just shook her head. "What—how—where—"

Sher laughed. She had a beautiful laugh that rang through the cool night, above the roar of the ocean. "Jake owns an apartment complex in the Haight-Ashbury district by your Golden Gate Park. The area and the locals are a little odd, but all the D'Danann and the witches are using it as a base."

"How is Jake?"

"Well." Pink tinged Sher's cheeks. "He and the PSF are determined to aid us in the fight against the Fomorii."

Silver almost didn't dare to ask, but she had to. "And Hawk?"

Sher's shoulders lifted and settled with a sigh. "Since he returned to Otherworld, none have heard from him. But then, he cannot cross over unless it is one of the nights when the membranes between worlds are thin enough."

The D'Danann woman stared into the dark sky as she softly said, "Unless he is aided by one of Elvin blood," she added.

Silver's heart pounded a little more rapidly again. "But he hasn't come back."

Their gazes met again. "No," Sher said, and continued to trace the design into the sand. "We have not seen him. I have not sensed him."

That part of Silver holding on to her love for Hawk weakened. "He can't leave his daughter, and I wouldn't expect him to. And the Chieftains—they may have locked him in the cells."

That thought made her so ill, she shuddered.

Sher just traced the design in the sand with her finger, and when she finished, Silver saw that the design was a Celtic love knot. Sher looked back up at Silver. "Where there is love, the heart will find a way."

Silver could only shake her head again. "It's not meant to be."

With the grace of her species, Sher moved to her feet and unfurled her wings. She spread the beautiful blue feathers and lifted into the air. "When you are ready, we are waiting for you."

Before Silver could say anything more, Sher darted into the night sky, pumped her wings, waved, and flew back toward the city.

For a long time Silver just sat and stared at the ocean, and listened to the waves slap the shore. She had a home and friends to return to. Others willing to fight the Fomorii—probably already seeking them out. Perhaps over the past weeks they had already located them and were ridding the city of the demons.

Silver's thoughts turned back to the time with her father. They had come to an understanding, and she had hope again for her sister. That Copper would one day come back.

Another *whump* of wings startled Silver. This time the sound was stronger, more powerful. A dark shape was closing in on her, moving faster and faster.

As the winged figure drew closer, Silver's heart started to pound so hard she almost couldn't breathe. When he finally touched down on the sand she put a hand to her mouth, certain she was seeing things.

Hawk.

42

Hawk strode across the sand toward Silver, his ebony wings stretched wide. Before he reached her, he folded the wings away until they vanished.

He never paused in his stride. He was tall, powerful, each well-defined muscle rippling with strength, and his long ebony hair whipping in the wind around the strong curve of his jaw. He no longer had a cast on his arm, but he still wore the pentagram at his throat. The one that matched her own.

When Hawk reached Silver, he scooped her up in his embrace, causing her to cry out in surprise and to wrap her arms around his neck as if he might drop her. He cradled her to his chest. *"A thaisce,"* he murmured and kissed the top of her head.

Ah, goddess, the feel of his arms around her, his clean scent of forest breezes and man . . . it was almost too much. It didn't even seem real. She'd missed the feel of him, the power in his embrace, the scent of him, his touch.

No. *No.*

"Let me down," she said quietly as his lips hovered over hers.

Hawk's warm breath fanned her face as he shook his head. "I will not," he murmured a moment before his lips touched hers.

His kiss was achingly slow and Silver couldn't help but close her eyes and melt into it. How she'd missed this. How she'd missed *him*.

He gently moved his mouth over hers and his tongue darted out to taste her lips. When he nipped at her lower lip, she gave something between a sigh and a little cry, and he slipped his tongue into her mouth.

Hawk's gut clenched at the incredible feel of Silver in his arms again. Gods, how he had missed her. How he had regretted their parting. And how it had nearly driven him out of his mind not to be able to return to her sooner. The Chieftains—they had taken long to consider, but had finally ruled that he remain a D'Danann Enforcer and could pass between worlds if he so had the aid.

Silver's scent of lilies and moonlight flowed over him, filled his senses. And her taste, how he had missed everything about her.

Silver couldn't help herself. She relaxed against him, within his arms. As their tongues mated, he tasted so wonderful—of pure male . . . and she could almost swear he tasted of chocolate chip cookies, too.

She wanted to deepen the kiss, but Hawk pulled away from her and she found herself looking into his incredible amber eyes.

"What are you doing here?" She brought one hand from his neck to cup his stubbled cheek. "You're supposed to be in Otherworld with your daughter."

"The Great Guardian led me through." He hugged her tighter to him. "I have come to bring you home with me."

Silver bit her lower lip and turned her face away. "Let me down."

This time he released her, letting her slide down his length. She felt every inch of him through her jacket and jeans, from his powerful chest to the rigid cock between his thighs. Even though he set her on her booted feet, he held her close, and she knew he wouldn't completely let her go. Not yet.

She couldn't help the immediate awareness of him, and how much her body desired him. But her heart wanted more. Needed more.

Hawk took in his beautiful woman, from her shining silvery-blond hair floating in the ocean breeze to her Elvin features and gray eyes. Her supple body was clothed, hiding it from his view. How he wanted to strip her bare and take her now, to be inside her and claim her completely. To let her know she belonged to him.

The way she was looking at him tugged at his heart. He had hurt her. It was in her eyes, in the slight tremble of her well-kissed lips. And he had ached just as much. Had known the minute he left her that he'd been wrong in not telling her of his love. He had had to return to his daughter and to face the Chieftains, yes. But he hadn't admitted the truth, even to himself.

Silver pressed her palms against his chest and his gaze held hers. "I can't go back with you," she said.

Hawk's heart twisted, but he shook his head. "I'm not taking no for an answer, *a thaisce*."

With amazement in her eyes, she stared up at his determined features. "There's no way I'm going with you."

"Why?" He didn't allow his determined expression to waver.

"Because—because you don't love me, for one. And you said you never will." The words spilled out faster than Silver could think to hold them back. "And I have to help the D'Danann and the other gray witches rid San Francisco of the remaining Fomorii." *And I have to see if I can help my sister, no matter that Father says she must find her own way.*

"You're wrong." Hawk took a handful of her long hair and pulled their faces closer together as his words spilled out in that Irish brogue of his that made her melt. "I do love you, Silver. I didn't realize it until I lost you. I thought I could never love again. Until you."

Silver's blood heated, warming her from head to toe. She could barely speak. "Honestly?"

"I would have come sooner if I could have." His grip

tightened in her hair and she welcomed the feeling that grounded her in the moment. "I can't imagine life without you. Please come home with me and be my forever-mate."

Her head reeled and she hardly knew what to think. What to do.

But he had told her he couldn't love her because of his love for his dead wife.

Did he really and truly love her?

Time. I need time. Right?

Silver clutched his shirt tight with her fingers as her heart somersaulted at his words. "I—I can't leave the Fomorii to take over my city and the ones I love. Like I said, I've already been gone too long."

Hawk smiled and more heat flushed over her. "You are part Elvin through your mother, and you may pass between worlds at your will, as she could have. The Great Guardian will teach you how, and then you will be able to take me across with you. Others in your Coven with Elvin blood will be taught to cross over. Rhiannon and I think perhaps Mackenzie is part Elvin, as well."

"I knew Cassia was, but Rhiannon and Mackenzie, too?" she said in surprise.

The idea of crossing back with him seemed too simple, but so right. The ache in Silver's chest lessened, but still she shook her head. "No."

"I love you, Silver. I cannot live without you." He brought up his hands to cup her face within them. "By all the gods, I swear I would never return to Otherworld, if only to live a life here with you. But I have Shayla, and I can't take her from her home, from all that she's known."

"What would your daughter think of me?" Silver asked.

"It may take time," he said, and she appreciated his honesty. "But I believe she will come to love you as much as I do. I have already told her of you and she is anxious to meet you."

For a long moment Silver looked up at him. She had memorized the line of his jaw, his firm lips, his intense amber eyes, the way his dark hair brushed his shoulders. But seeing him now—it was as if she were falling in love with him all over again. "You truly do love me?"

He gave a slow nod. "With all my heart."

I love him. He loves me.

Silver took a deep breath. Images of her life flashed by. The good times. The sad times. The horror.

And her love for Hawk. How badly she had missed him, needed him.

Silver relaxed her hold on his shirt. "If what you say is true . . ."

His mouth curved into that sexy grin that made her heart melt all over again. "Trust me."

With a smile she said, "How could I not?" She rose up on her toes and brushed her lips against his. "I love you."

Hawk moaned and gripped her shoulders as he pressed his mouth to hers, fiercely. Possessive. Dominating. A warrior staking his claim.

She responded with as much fervor, just as much intensity. Staking her own claim. Her fingers made their way up his chest to his hair and she tangled them in the silky strands. He felt so good, so right.

He broke away from their kiss, his amber eyes glittering in the moonlight. "I need you, Silver. I need you now."

"Goddess, yes."

In the next moment he was shrugging out of his shirt and spreading it out on the sand. He was so big that the shirt would easily cradle her from neck to thighs.

He sighed with pleasure as Silver began exploring his chest with her mouth, her hands. She kissed every scar she found on him, every well-defined muscle. He let her take control, let her relearn every curve and dip of his body. She felt so good, so right, within his arms.

Hawk's skin was salty, yet had a softly musky taste that caused Silver to shiver with desire. Her pussy was wet, her breasts aching with need to touch him more, and to be touched.

He helped her to remove his boots, then to ease off his

black leather pants and toss them aside on the sandy beach. When she had revealed his cock her eyelids lowered with arousal and she knelt before him and sand shifted beneath her knees. She wrapped her hand around his erection, her fingers so small against his girth. Slowly she stroked him, enjoying the hiss of his breath as she moved her hand from his balls to where the drop of semen glistened at the tiny slit.

"Silver, *a thaisce,* you're killing me," he groaned, not sure if he would be able to take more of her sensual attack.

With a wicked little smile, she slipped his erection into her mouth and he clenched his hands in her hair as she went down on him. Her mouth felt so warm and he slowly pumped in and out of her wetness. She stroked his cock with one hand moving in time with her mouth, while her other hand fondled his balls. His body trembled with the force it took to hold back his climax.

When the sac began to draw up tight, and he could not take her erotic torture any longer, he forced her to stop. "My turn," he said in a low rumble.

Hawk picked her up and flipped her gently onto her back so that she was lying on his shirt. She stared up at him as he slowly stripped her of her clothing, revealing her body inch by precious inch. Her pale skin glowed beneath the moonlight and her nipples were taut peaks that begged for his mouth. He couldn't wait to taste her, to be inside her.

When she was completely naked he sucked in his breath at the beautiful sight. "I have missed you more than I can say."

Hawk knelt on the sand before Silver, and she couldn't help her smile. Her great naked warrior. He grasped one foot and slowly stroked his index finger along her instep. "You have lovely feet," he murmured as he caressed the arch of her foot.

Silver shivered at the sensual touch. "Bless it, Hawk. You're driving me crazy."

He simply chuckled and pushed her legs wide so that he

was kneeling between her thighs. He kissed her and she gave a soft moan and slipped her fingers into his wild dark hair. He was hers. All hers.

She clenched her hands tighter in his hair and cried out as he latched on to one of her nipples. "Your mouth." Silver caught the scent of her arousal mounting, adding to his intoxicating male musk. "I love the way you bite me, suck me."

In response, he bit down on her nipple and she gasped with pleasure. He licked and sucked and she felt answering spasms in her core.

The air felt cool on her bare skin, yet heated from Hawk's aroused gaze, his every touch.

Still on his knees, he slowly made a trail down her stomach to kiss her belly button. He flicked his tongue inside and she had to clench her hands in his hair to keep her grounded from the quivering sensations that made her entire body weak.

Without mercy, he continued trailing his lips down, following the path of his fingers to her curls. He audibly drew in his breath. "Your woman's perfume. I can never get enough."

"I love the scent of us together," she managed to say, even as moisture flowed from her pussy. His mouth latched on to her clit and she nearly shouted. He licked and sucked at her, and she could no longer speak.

Hawk reveled in Silver's taste, the sweetness of her flesh against his tongue. How he had missed this, missed her. Everything about her called to him. Her strength, her courage, her sense of rightness, her compassion. She meant the world to him, and he wanted to give it to her.

When he brought her so close to climax that she started to whimper and her thighs began to tremble, he eased back up and braced himself above her, their eyes locked. Neither seemed able to move. "I cannot believe you are truly with me again, *a thaisce*."

"I can." She brought her hands to his face and cupped his cheeks. "Wherever you are, that's where I belong."

Hawk slid his cock into Silver and she gasped at the depth he took her. She'd missed his touch so much. Had missed the way he felt inside her.

They never stopped looking at each other as they made love. He rocked back and forth, the rhythm of his thrusts matching the push and pull of the waves. The slap of water against the shore was like the slap of their flesh against flesh. The roar of the ocean nearly matched the one in her ears as she climbed higher and higher with each plunge of his cock inside her pussy.

Slowly, so slowly he took her, letting her know that she was his and that he possessed her in every way. He would never let Silver go. She was his heart. His soul.

Silver gave a little wave of her fingers and blue light sparkled around them, and her more powerful magic moved through them both.

Hawk groaned at the incredible sensations rippling through his body, and his thrusts became stronger and harder as they made love. Their eyes remained fixed on each other as their bodies moved in a sweet rhythm.

Silver wanted to cry from the sheer beauty of it. They were made for each other. A perfect match in every way. Tears formed in her eyes from the joy filling her heart and soul.

When it became too much to bear, when she couldn't hold back her orgasm any longer, she scraped her hands along Hawk's back. "I'm going to come."

"Do it, *a thaisce*," he urged her. "Come with me."

Silver cried out with the beauty and the incredible fulfillment of her orgasm. The blue sparks of her magic became flames, surrounding, warming their bodies. Her power continued to weave around them, trapping them in that moment.

Hawk shouted at the same time she came. His fluid pumped into her body, and she felt the strength of his climax. She saw the love in his eyes and the need she knew was mirrored in her own.

The incredible bond of love they shared, love that transcended worlds and time.

When his body stopped pulsing within hers, and the blue flames of her magic slowly faded to sparkles, Hawk kissed her slowly.

"My sweet little witch," he murmured against her lips, "I love you."

Silver smiled, such joy and happiness filling her that she felt as if fireworks sparked throughout her. "My warrior, my heart."